Quintessentially

BY

PEPPER WINTERS

Published: Pepper Winters 2013: **pepperwinters@gmail.com**
Publishing assisted by Black Firefly: **http://www.blackfirefly.com/**
(Shedding light on your self-publishing journey)

Editing: Stephanie Parent
French Translation: Louise Pion
Cover Design: by Ari at Cover it! Designs:
http://salon.io/#coveritdesigns
Proofreading by: TJ Loveless and Robin Alexander @ Black Firefly
Formatting by: **http://www.blackfirefly.com/**
Images in Manuscript from Canstock Photos:
http://www.canstockphoto.com

This is a story of eroticism, horror, and sweet tragedy. It contains graphic scenes, but there's always light in the darkness.

For all the esclaves *of Q and lovers of twisted romance.*

Prologue
Quincy

I ache to see your flesh bleed, scream for me, give me what I need,
let the rivers run, the monster inside has won…

I thought I would be her nightmare—her terror and darkness. I wanted to be. I needed her more than food or sunlight. Only when she came into my life did I start to live—intoxicated by her taste, screams, and joy.

But our fucked-up-fairy-tale didn't exactly have a happy ending.

Tess.

My Tess.

My *esclave*—so strong and fierce and sexually feral—wasn't strong enough for what happened.

Her cage wasn't me anymore.

It was them.

One
Quincy

Naked and restrained, this darkness cannot be contained,
you, my esclave, have been claimed...

All I could think was—she's dead. She had to be. All that blood, so bright with a coppery tang, almost sweet.

Her snowy skin was extra frosty, grey-blue eyes closed to me.

Rage and terror strangled me as I fell to my knees in the warm puddle of crimson. The whip in my hands grew slippery with sweat, and I hurled it away in disgust. I did this. I let myself go and showed my true self. The monster inside ruined the only brightness in my life.

"Tess?" I pulled her into my arms, dragging her cold, lifeless form closer. Blood smeared over us. Her red-welted body oozed with damnation.

"Wake up, *esclave*," I growled, hoping an order would force those dove-blue eyes open.

No response.

I bent, pressing my cheek against her mouth, waiting endlessly for a small puff of breath, a signal I hadn't gone too far.

Nothing.

Fear stopped my heart, and all I wanted to do was reverse time. Rewind to a simpler place where I lived with needs and urges, but never let myself believe I could be free. Rewind to the day when Tess arrived and I promptly sent her back to her stupid boyfriend Brax. At least if I did she would be safe, and my life wouldn't have ended.

At least then, Tess would be alive.

My demons killed her.

I killed her.

I threw my head back and howled.

"Q. Q!"

Something sharp bit my shoulder, and I flinched. Rolling away, I tried to ignore the call. I deserved to stay in this nightmarish hell. The hell I created for killing the one woman who stole my life and showed me an emotion I never dared dream of. A dream I never knew I wanted until Tess came into my life.

My cheek smarted as if someone slapped me, blazing through the darkness with a bite of pain.

I wrenched my eyes open to find a wild-eyed, blonde goddess on top of me. The debilitating terror wouldn't leave, even though she was alive and glaring with passion I grew to know so well.

"What the hell, Q? That's the third time this week. You going to tell me what you're dreaming about to warrant howling like a werewolf?" Tess pinned my shoulders to the mattress, and I couldn't stop muscles from tensing. I liked her on top, but I didn't like her holding me as if she was in control. It wasn't how I worked.

"None of your business." I rolled, grabbing her hips to pin her beneath me. I risked a small smile. With her under me, my world righted again. I ran hands over her waist, up her throat, to her lips. Her breath fluttered, coming faster; the rest of my panic receded.

She was still breathing.

I hadn't killed her.

Yet.

Tess ran her hand softly over my cheek, tickling. "You should tell me what you're afraid of. Brax used to—"

I froze, grinding my teeth. "If you know what's good for you, you won't finish that sentence." Goddammit, why did she have to bring the ghost of her idiot boyfriend who treated her like a fragile princess into our bed?

Tess squeezed her eyes. "Sorry. I didn't mean to…it's just—I'm concerned. If you're having bad dreams because of me, give me the opportunity to make them go away."

It was too early in the morning to suffer an inquisition.

Four days had passed since Tess appeared on my doorstep and gave me no choice but to accept her. Accept her fire, spirit, and sharp tenacity. I may be a controlling bastard, but the moment Tess stalked into my life I lost my balls to her.

I hoped she didn't know just how much she affected me, because I was shit terrified of what the future meant for us.

The promises she made of being strong enough for me; the blood oath that linked us together for as long as that blood pumped in our veins.

Four days since my life changed forever and I'd been in constant, excruciating pain ever since.

"Leave it alone," I grumbled. This woman was an icy glacier to my unmovable mountain of a vow. My solemn vow that I'd never accept the fucking darkness or be a sadistic asshole like my father. The same vow that stopped me from stringing up helpless women like he did. But the glacier was winning—millimetre by millimetre, centimetre by centimetre. Her ice slithered between the hairline fractures of my will, making them larger, making the cracks harder to ignore.

For four days, I'd successfully ignored her advances for sex. Memories of taking her over the bar in the gaming room were still too raw. Tess couldn't sit without wincing. I knew she hurt—not that she ever complained. I watched her every movement like a vulture studying the weakness of his prey. She thought she'd convinced me that she was fine, that the bruises didn't affect her. *Me.* A man who smelled pain and fear as if it were a heady perfume— I knew the truth.

She said I hadn't hurt her with my belt. She lied. I drew blood, for fuck's sake. And I lived in a constant battleground, fighting the delicious satisfaction at her pain against my morality and horror at hurting her.

I never knew where the black urges came from. They were as much a part of me as my genetic code.

Tess didn't deserve to be hurt—no woman did. But she was willing to sacrifice her screams for me. For the promise of something I wasn't sure I could give.

I fucking shouldn't want to beat the ever-living daylights out of her, but I did. Oh, shit how I did.

"Q. You can't keep all your thoughts locked up now you've let me into your life. I see the torment in your eyes. You promised you'd talk and let me in." Her voice bled pain while her tiny fists clutched the sheets in annoyance.

We'd both made promises, and so far, neither of us had lived up to them. Not that it mattered—I had every intention of breaking my end of the bargain. She wasn't strong enough. *I* wasn't strong enough.

Ce sont les premiers jours, idiot. Détends toi. Early days, idiot. Just relax.

But I couldn't relax. I wasn't strong enough to fight the urge to be such a manic bastard if I didn't keep a tight rein at all times. Look what I did when Tess first arrived as my slave. I had no choice but to hunt her, hurt her, *devour* her.

If I had been a better man, I would've walked back up the stairs and ordered Franco to remove her immediately. Now I stood on the precipice of a dream come true—a woman who saw the real me, accepted me, and wanted a future with me—and all I could do was drown in nightmares of killing her.

"I'm exhausted," I murmured. Did she hear the ulterior confession? That it hadn't even been a week of accepting this relationship, and I was already fucking frayed. I needn't have asked—of course Tess saw the truth. She saw too damn much.

"Stop fighting then. You haven't touched me since I came back to you. We may share a bed, but you hardly look at me apart from when I flinch if I sit on a sore spot on my ass. You're more remote than when I was sold to you."

I growled deep in my chest at the sold remark. I hated the cunts who'd stolen and sold her. Every time I thought about what might've happened to Tess if she'd been given to another, I wanted to turn feral—to strip the falseness of businessman and paint my walls with their blood. Screw having civilized business meetings with criminals. I was done with that shit.

Images of Tess bound and beaten, raped and ruined, constantly assaulted me. The ironic thing was—now I was the bastard responsible. But by letting me use her, I found myself wanting to offer everything I had in return for her gasps of fear and whimpers of pain. I didn't feel worthy and didn't think I'd ever repay the debt of her gift.

My hands curled, and I trembled with pent-up rage. Anger directed at myself.

I'm fucking insane.

I sighed deeply, sucking in courage to give Tess a little of what she needed—a tiny insight into my rotten core of a mind.

"I can't be tender with you. And I hate that I got carried away with hitting you." There? Was she fucking satisfied? I opened up to her about things I wished I could vomit out of me. Hurl this darkness from deep inside; purge my heart so I could be sweet and kind and the perfect man for her. Not the savage, sex-hungry beast.

Her breath caught, and a soft finger trailed along my forearm. "Thank you. You don't know what a relief it is for you to talk to me. Can you tell me about your nightmare now?"

I glared at her and sat upright. Pushy woman. She'd successfully freaked me out and pissed me off with her questions.

Rolling to the side of the huge bed, I perched on the edge with my head in my hands. I didn't want to be a coward and run, but this was all too new. My tower room with its massive fireplace and ocean-sized white carpet still looked the same, nothing outward had changed, but Tess wreaked havoc on my soul. I didn't know if I'd survive allowing her to dig deeper into my world.

The nightmare roared back to full colour. *All that blood, so bright with a coppery tang, almost sweet.*

No. I couldn't do this. I wasn't strong enough. Somehow the evilness of my father would make me do the one thing I'd run from my entire life. I lived my life with rules, shackles. I wasn't prepared to let a delicate, fragile little bird taunt me to untwine myself and chase her.

I'd win.

And I'd lose when I killed her.

On dirait une fille, putain, mercer! You sound like a fucking girl, Mercer.

I flinched as Tess scampered across the bedspread and draped herself over my naked back. Her soft fingertips traced my tattoo of fluttering sparrows and barbwire. I clenched my jaw as her touch whispered lower and lower, down my abs, heading to my cock.

I meant to stop her. I really did, but she grasped me hard through my boxer-briefs; I groaned. One touch was all I needed to make me achingly hard and drowning in dark desire.

Tess coaxed me to rigidness, all the while nibbling on my ear. "If you're frightened of hurting me, Q…you won't. I trust you not to go too far."

I bit out, "I don't trust you yet. I don't want to break you." *I don't trust myself to stop.*

She stopped stroking and pulled back. Her warmth left me

with a shiver. "I gave you my word to fight you. I've slept in your bed for four nights, and the most you've done is peck my cheek good night. You haven't used your belt or chains or any of those toys I glimpsed in that mirrored chest of yours."

Her eyes flittered to the end of the bed where the chest lay. Locked. No way did I want her going in there.

I groaned, gripping my head with stabbing fingers. What monster wanted to capture the blood of the woman he'd given his life to? What animal wanted to ensnare her screams to repeat over and over again like a perfect chorus?

I was right to keep myself so aloof, so obsessed with work. By staying overworked, I had no time for other needs.

I hadn't been to work in four days. A new emotion kept me at home, never far from Tess's side. The terror that she'd wake up one morning and realize she made a huge mistake kept me anxious and snappy. The thought of coming home from work to find her gone—well, both the man and the beast hated the very idea. But it was a mistake to think I could give up my way of life and not suffer consequences.

I had to find a way to cure myself. I had to stop this before Tess successfully goaded me into doing something I regretted.

Tess grumbled something and swung her legs off the bed. Her ass bore purple shadows from my belt. How many lashes did I give her that night? I counted thirty, but that was after the ones I'd already struck. My heart squeezed at the thought of how easy it was to lose myself around her, but a millisecond later it was overshadowed by the overwhelming urge to create more raw, angry bruises on her perfect skin. I wanted her over my knee. I wanted to have those perfect crystal tears splashing my thigh as I hit her.

Goddammit, she said I scarred her soul…would she let me scar her skin?

Tess stood before me. Her toned legs splayed, hands on her hips. So proud and regal in her own body. I couldn't tear my eyes away. The beast inside prowled and hurled itself against the cage, trying so hard to get at her. To rip her. Ravage her.

I chained the monster back up, pulling myself together.

Tess folded to her knees between my legs and pressed her lips against my boxer-clad cock.

I jolted, gasping. The heat of her breath, the delicateness of her lips, drove me insane.

"If you won't tell me your concerns, I'll just taunt you until you can't help it. You have me. I'm your slave while we're in the bedroom, and I want to be used. I crave it. Why don't you get that yet?"

She wanted to taunt me? Fine. I lashed out and grabbed a thick handful of messy blonde curls. Leaning down to her eye level, I stared right into the depths of her being, allowing her to see the turmoil in mine. The need, the anguish, the fine line of hatred and love for her for forcing me to accept this part of myself.

Tess sucked in a breath, shrinking beneath the weight of my stare. I shook her, loving the small blaze of pain in her eyes. Shit, would I ever become repulsed by hurting her rather than turned on?

"I understand you want me to show you what my fantasies are, but you have to give me time, *esclave*." My heart raced at the word. For four days, I'd refused to call her anything but Tess. She wasn't my slave. She wasn't my possession. Never had been and never would be. I hated how even though I knew she was there on her own accord, I still wanted ultimate ownership. I wanted her chained and completely dependent on me. I wanted to feed her and bathe her. I wanted to be the very reason she stayed alive.

Fuck, I should get a pet.

Tess isn't a pet, you bastard. She's your equal. She's Tess. Elle est à toi. *She's yours.*

Her eyelids slammed closed and she swayed into me, her lips parting. "Say it again, *maître*. Remind me of my place."

Shit, this fucking woman. She wasn't curing me, she made

it worse. How could I expect to avoid my nightmares when she forced me down this path?

Something unlocked inside, some darkness billowed, blocking out the light I'd been fighting so hard to keep bright.

Tess noticed. Her body tensed, her fingers digging into my thighs.

I bent closer, glowering. My heart beat thickly as black excitement unfurled. "You're disobeying me, *esclave*. I think I may have to punish you." The word *punish* set my muscles on edge and I gripped her harder.

She shuddered under my touch, eyes flaring wide with a sexy glint. The same glint that told me she was about to rebel and cause me to snap. Shit, I didn't have the strength to stop myself again. My energy was depleted. The gates unlocked, and the monster was in full control.

Tess stroked my thigh once. "You aren't allowed to punish me. I'll run. I'll leave you."

My hands clenched into fists, digging into her flesh. Her threat was too close to my true fears, and I shuddered with rage. Even though I knew she did it deliberately it still riled me up. "You wouldn't fucking dare. You returned to me. This isn't a vacation, *esclave*. You don't get to come and go as you please. You belong to me and I can do what I want to you."

Her mouth parted, and she sucked in a shaky breath, but her eyes blazed with grey fire. "Don't you dare touch me; I'll ruin you."

Ah shit, I was a goner. I was completely and mind-bendingly falling for this woman.

I swallowed back the thick taste of lust and murmured, "Too fucking late, *esclave*. I'm ruined beyond redemption." In the last moment of gentleness, I pressed my forehead against hers and breathed deep. "I'm lost." Then the gentleness left, abandoning me to the hard-edged need to hurt.

In one swoop, I hauled her upright. Her hands flew to mine clutched in her silky curls. Her gaze smouldered to smoke, and her perfect pink lips trembled.

"You really shouldn't push me. I asked for time." I shook her hard, furious for making me lose control. Control was my one weakness—take that away from me and the consequences were disastrous. "I'm done fighting. You happy now?"

Her chest rose sharply as she sucked in another unsteady breath. A flicker of indecision filled her eyes before being swallowed by heavy, heated lust. "Yes. Extremely. There's the man I returned to. The one I want to fuck me."

My cock lurched forward in the prison of boxer-briefs, aching with the need to plunge deep inside her. I pulled her forward, licking my lips. I'd take her hard. I didn't want docile; I wanted savage.

Her eyes fluttered closed as I crushed my mouth against hers.

She sighed as I licked her lower lip with an angry tongue. Her body yielded into my touch, surrendering her false fight, showing me just how much she needed this—this violence.

I pulled away, releasing her hair to capture her wrist. The same tattooed wrist with barcode bars and fluttering sparrow. A mockery of her slave status and a talisman of her freedom. "You should know by now I don't do things you want me to do, *esclave*. Your permission isn't what gets me off."

She frowned as I dragged her across the thick white carpet and forced her to kneel in front of the mirrored chest. Breathing hard, I stalked to where I left my trousers on the floor last night and withdrew the key.

"Open it." I passed the key to her, my hand steady, but heart beating wildly.

She glared, hesitating for a moment. Her body language stiffened at the command. I thought she'd disobey again, but she nodded and slipped the key obediently into the lock.

My back turned rigid, every muscle throbbing on high alert. Tess thought I had a soul, a heart. What I stored in the chest would prove all her stupid sweet fantasies were false.

There was no doubt I wanted Tess. There was no question she made me feel something I'd never felt before…but there was also no doubt that it wasn't enough. I was too damaged from too young an age to be able to change.

Tess took a deep breath, cracking open the lid. I expected a squeal, a gasp…something to indicate awareness of what she tempted, but deathly silence filled the room.

I gritted my teeth, looking over her shoulder. The first lot of apparatus was tame. Any sex shop or adventurous couple would have a few sneaky purchases.

Three whips; four floggers of different thickness; two paddles; three sets of nipples clamps; butt plugs and cuffs of every description. In fact, they were so tame, they turned me off at the thought of using them on Tess.

Tess ran delicate fingers along the items, a slight frown on her face. Why the hell was she frowning?

"Speak. Are you disappointed? Expect to find a rape kit in there? A shovel to get rid of your body, perhaps?"

She flinched at the word rape and I cursed myself to hell for using it. Once again my rage and hatred toward Lefebvre rose; I wanted to hack his corpse into worm food. Fucking bastard for hurting what was mine to protect.

Tess looked up, craning her swan-white neck. "It's just… I expected—" She swallowed and didn't continue. Instead, she shook her head slightly and returned to the chest.

Picking up a black rubber dildo, she murmured, "I don't want dildos when I can have your cock. I knew you had the whips and floggers, but I don't know…" Her voice dwindled off, and damn it to hell, she made me feel like I lacked. That I wasn't hard-core enough for her.

I would only be completely satisfied when she was red with blood and whimpering in my arms. That's the sort of sick fuck I was. For Tess to think I was tame. Shit, it made me want to prove just how dark I wanted. Just what sort of depraved thoughts lived in my skull.

I ran a hand over my head, cursing her silently. *You're competing with yourself. Do you see how fucked up this is?*

Merde. "It's a shelf. Look harder." My voice didn't sound

right. Too dark, too coarse.

Her eyes flashed to mine, and something sparked between us. The chemistry and need that always simmered roared into an out-of-control fire. My heart raced, and my already rock-hard cock throbbed with need. All I could think about was the taste of Tess on my tongue and the memory of whipping her in my mind.

Inching higher on her knees, Tess found the small latch on the shelf and pulled it away.

"Oh," she whispered.

Yes, oh. The sickness and blackness was there for her to see. I hadn't used any of the toys—not that they could be called toys. More like torture equipment. I didn't know why I owned them. I never planned to use them. Until now.

Tess lifted out the Japanese silk rope. It was said to tie into a knot so strong, not even blade or teeth could get it undone. It burned the skin when the captive wiggled, and the glowing crimson of the threads looked so like blood my mouth watered.

Tess stroked the rope once, before draping it over her naked thighs and reaching for the next item. I didn't want to tear my eyes away from the rope on her skin, but my stomach twisted at the next item.

A harness.

The same type my sick, perverted father used to string women up with their heads between their legs hanging from the ceiling. Arms bound, legs bound, head bound…there would be nowhere Tess could run. No place I wouldn't be able to touch.

I shuddered as a band of need squeezed my balls. The thought of Tess strung up so helpless filled me with restless urges. I stepped forward, compelled to pounce and truss her up. To make her scream, needing my cock.

Her eyes flashed to mine as I took another step, nudging her knee with my foot. She gazed from beneath her thick lashes, eyes swirling with complexities that I couldn't figure out. Her chest rose as courage, sharp and brittle, etched her face.

"Do you like the thought of having nowhere to run? Nowhere to hide, *esclave?*"

Slowly, ever so slowly, she put the harness to the side. Her nipples sprung to a peak beneath my white T-shirt she wore to bed. "I know I can't run from you, Q. And I wouldn't want to. Not truly."

Her voice was breathy but tense, and instead of amping my lust, it dampened it. I froze as she reached for another item. Why exactly was I letting her see this? My hands itched to slam the lid and barricade her from ever looking again.

Tess pulled out a bright red ball gag, a vinyl bodysuit with only a mouth slit and an opening between the legs, and a bar with cuffs for wrists and ankles.

Each item Tess placed on the floor filled me with more and more repulsion. Laid by my feet was evidence of my true sickness. My needs transcended middle-class kink and verged on life-threatening. I didn't want fake fear or tears. No. I wanted the whole damn truth. I wanted to possess and obsess and consume. I wanted to be the air that Tess breathed. I wanted to be the water she drank. Keeping her alive all while wanting to kill her.

I never spoke truer words to Tess before. I was totally and utterly *exhausted.*

Tess made a noise, dragging me from my thoughts. I flinched at the item in her grasp: a red leather bag. I lunged for it, just as Tess pulled the zipper.

She moved too fast, swiping it out of my reach. "Let me see." Her tone bordered on angry and a plea. Such a sweet cocktail of sounds.

I nodded, backing away from the items in the bag. Items I really, really wanted to use at that moment.

Tess lifted out a pair of silver scissors, a small knife, and three crystal vials. She didn't bother pulling out the suction syringe I knew was in there to collect blood.

She rocked on her heels, pinning me with her grey stare. "I always wondered why you ruined so many of my clothes. You could've demanded I strip, but you always preferred to cut them, or burn, or tear. Is it because you secretly want to do that to my body? Tear me apart? Flay me? See my blood running like a river?"

I shut my eyes. I couldn't handle the image she painted. The image I wanted. So. Fucking. Much.

Tess grabbed my ankle, pulling herself up my mostly naked form until she stood before me. Her warmth seeped into mine, and I wondered what would happen if I reached for her to give her something as simple as a hug: a show of tenderness, of sweet emotion. Could I survive it or would I crush her, squeeze her—go too far like I did every time?

Tess answered for me. She pressed a flogger into my grip. "You're wrong to think your box of horrors scares me. It doesn't."

My eyes, heavy with regret and self-loathing, opened to drown in hers. She was so close, the swirls of blue and grey in her irises looked like angry seas. I tried to decipher the fear, stubbornness, and lust in her soul.

Her voice dropped to a whisper. "You need to talk to me. You can't keep secrets, *maître*. Not anymore. I won't let you." Stepping back, she ripped my T-shirt over her head, standing before me naked. With the courage of a warrioress, she pinched the white flesh of her lower abdomen. "Here. I want you to scar me here. Mark me if it will make you feel better. I want you to accept what I'm giving you. I want you to embrace it."

I threw the flogger down. She didn't offer me her body. She offered insanity. I wasn't man enough for her, but I sure as hell had enough beast inside. But the man was a coward. I refused to drop the walls and let myself be fully free—no matter what promises Tess made me say. Scar her? Didn't she know I wouldn't—couldn't—stop at one?

I touched her taut belly with a fingertip. So smooth, so silky, so feminine. Tess panted softly, and her breasts rose and fell, teasing me, making me lose all inhibitions. Only she could spin this sort of web around me. Only she could make me so fucked up and confused.

Cupping her breast, I pinched her nipple, hard. No gentle foreplay, just a possessive clinch. Her head fell forward, resting on my chest. Her scent of orchids and frost was the last of my undoing.

I gave up.

I gave in.

I wanted, and I wouldn't stop.

I'd been going around in circles, letting my thoughts tangle and trip. Now, I was clearheaded and eager. Eager to embrace the role of hurtful, insatiable master.

My hand trailed from her breast up her neck and captured her throat. Wrenching her head back, I met her turbulent eyes with mine. Anger blazed through me. "You couldn't just give me time, could you, *esclave*? Now I'm pissed and angry, and I don't know the limits of my control. I've given in and nothing else matters but fucking you." I shook her, tightening my fingers around her neck.

She didn't move, her arms stayed by her sides, and she let me throttle her. I tested her, noosing my fingers until the yielding, fragile muscles in her neck made my head swim with delirium.

Tess did nothing.

Forcing my fingers to loosen, I frowned. "Do you trust me not to go too far? Are you really that stupid?"

One hand flew to cover mine, but she didn't tug or try to get me to release her. Her other palm rested on my unshaven cheek, jolting me with a dose of unconditional acceptance, need, want, and everything else that lived between us.

Shit, I'm lucky. And so unworthy.

"I promised you I would fight. I'm not stupid enough to relinquish myself into your control completely, Q. But I do trust that I know your limits even more than you do. I trust you...here."

She dropped her hand to rest above my heart. It raced and pumped like a demon thing, bucking beneath her touch. "Let yourself feel. Let yourself accept. You're more human than you want to believe."

The softness in her tone enraged me. I didn't let myself consider the truth; I kissed her instead.

I captured her mouth like she was the last woman on earth. The only woman for me. My tongue speared through her soft, sweet lips, and I took and took and took. I stole her taste, her breath. I forced her to accept every inch of need from my tongue to hers.

She moaned, pressing hard against me, dragging more from me until I couldn't tell where her lips began and mine ended.

My fingers tightened on their own accord, searching for the sweet surrender, the ultimate control. I kissed her while choking her until her legs wobbled, and I caught her as she buckled completely.

The knowledge she let me bring her to the point of such weakness made my heart swell until it no longer fit in my ribcage. I didn't think I'd find anything as satisfying as causing pain, but the complete submission and trust was the ultimate aphrodisiac.

Releasing her, I scooped up her limp body and carried her across the room. Past the fireplace, away from the chains in the ceiling where I'd strung her up the first time, heading toward the back of the tower.

Tess blinked, foggy from lack of oxygen. "Where are we going?"

Gulping a deep breath, completely at the mercy of my throbbing cock and thick desire, I repositioned Tess in my arms to pull at the thick velvet curtain to the left of the massive turret window.

The dark green material slithered off, landing in a puddle like a melted forest.

Tess gasped and snuggled closer, gaping at the human-sized cross. Its well-oiled dark wood and bright red leather restraints appeared medieval and terrifying. Apparatus such as these had been used to flay a man alive or strip him limb from limb. It was barbaric. It was horrific. It was delicious.

Tess would be completely restrained. Completely at my mercy. Completely mine.

She moaned and shivered, sending shockwaves of need through my limbs. My voice dripped with blackness.

"It's time you began your initiation into my world, *esclave*."

TWO
Tess

I relish the snap, welcome the burn, don't stop yet it's still my turn.
Tighten your grip, make me bleed, this is a hunger I need to feed...

Two emotions battled within me: uncertainty and excitement. I won the battle I'd been fighting for four days: I made Q give in. But at what cost? I could no longer read his body—he was wound too tightly, bristling with lust. His pale jade eyes unreadable, shuttered against anything but the burn of dominance.

Staring at the cross, everything slowed to a standstill. Life paused, and I stood in a little bubble of reflection. My initiation into his mysterious world had started, and I teetered on the threshold, wondering if I'd ever see light again.

My throat ached from where he'd held me. His large hand had crushed my windpipe and the urge to scratch him, fight until he let go had been unbearable. But somehow, I knew Q needed to be taught the most important factor of any relationship. He had to learn that for any sort of love to grow between us, it needed a firm foundation to last. A foundation based on unshakable trust and faith in each other.

I said I trusted Q. I didn't. Not yet. And I was damn sure he didn't trust me. We both fumbled in the dark, trying to figure out the rules of our connection, and until we learned to read and believe in each other, we were doomed.

My fingertips touched my bruised neck; I winced as I swallowed. The ache was a justified experiment to see just how far Q would go. I'd been one heartbeat from unconsciousness, but he hadn't pushed me over the edge.

I allowed my faith in him to evolve just a little.

Q shifted beside me, watching my fingers stroking my throat. His eyes flashed with shame and remorse before being swallowed by blazing heat and darkness. "I won't apologise for hurting you. You provoked me. *Je ne peux pas me priver si longtemps.*" I can only deny myself for so long.

My body reacted; melting, loosening, preparing to accept his body into mine. Q's eyes acted as an accelerant to the slow burn in my belly and it spread like a holocaust, turning my insides to ash. "I don't expect an apology," I whispered.

"Good." He cupped my cheek. It would've been a tender move, but with Q it still seethed with silent rage.

I held my ground as Q looped his finger behind my ear, securing a lock of escaped hair. Shivering, I looked into his gaze. Stared deep into the heart of the monster I'd chosen over a sweet boy like Brax.

Where Brax was the sun, Q was the endless sucking void of space. A black-hole full of mystery and hidden worlds. My eyes skittered to the cross. *Am I in for a world of pain?* Had Q finally snapped beyond all control?

The inception into his world meant I had a lot to learn. How brave could I be and how strong was my pain threshold?

"I've been stupid, *maître.*" My eyes dropped to his lips. They were wet from his tongue, making my mouth water at the thought of kissing him again.

His hand dropped from my ear, grazing my nipple on the way down. I flinched, and my pussy clenched at the innocuous touch.

"You have been stupid. Courageously stupid, *esclave*."

I nodded, my breathing shallow as Q dropped his head and kissed my lips whisper-softly. I swooned into him, desperate to sling my arms around his neck and press my breasts against his strength. Some basic part of me, the unthinking but all-sensing part, knew I had to break Q completely before he could embrace the softer side of what we could have.

He was afraid.

But afraid of what? Maybe because he'd never had a bond like this before. Maybe he truly believed he was the devil and incapable of true love. But I wouldn't give up on him.

Q deepened the kiss, and I moaned. Throwing my arms around his neck, I jerked him closer. He grunted, steadying us on the wooden cross behind me. Then his hands captured my wrists and removed them forcibly from around his neck.

"You know you're stupid, and yet you continue to push me. Would you try to stroke a panther when it's hunting? *Non, parce que la mort te trouverait rapidement.*" No, because death would find you swiftly. His words were clipped as bullets.

Images of predators and killing and blood saturated my mind.

Q was born into darkness, created by circumstances he wouldn't share with me, but if any one of us was damaged, it was him. I wanted him to no longer fear himself. He no longer had to be alone.

With my wrists cuffed in his fingers, I said, "Do you want to know what I thought when I returned to you. The promise I made to myself?"

Q froze, nostrils flaring.

I took his silence as approval and continued, "I said I'd fight for you. That you deserved to be fought for. I didn't know then, and I still don't know what I need to finally get through to you—" I leaned forward, trying to get close enough to kiss him. He stiffened and his hold gave no room for movement.

"—but I'll never stop. I was right. You're worth every fight. Every argument and bump in the road. I'll fight because I'm falling for you, Q."

How could I not fall for this man? This complex, emotionally tangled man. The saver of slaves and property tycoon. Q was all my nightmares, fantasies, and needs rolled into one bestial package. He was my drug of choice and I'd been craving him for four long days.

"Don't fall for me." He grabbed my shoulders. His touch was hot and his fingertips branded me with force. "I can't be responsible for that."

My heart beat too fast as I breathed in his scent of sandalwood and citrus. His body was so close, it befuddled me with lust and toe-curling need.

"Be responsible for what?" I took a risk, ducking my head to kiss him on his forearm. The corded muscle leapt beneath my lips, and he let go as if I'd bitten him.

"I'm sure to break other parts of you, but I don't want the curse of breaking your heart."

"You can't break something that is freely given." A small part of me wanted him to say he'd treasure it, guard it, and nurture it forever, but that softness wasn't there yet.

He struggled every day with my demands and expectations. I knew he did. I saw it in his eyes, the way he watched me with a mixture of awe and annoyance, even a touch of fear. One moment he'd answer my seemingly harmless question, the next he'd shut me out as easily as a storm cloud swallows the moon.

Every day I kept prying, kept prodding. Being a pest and a nuisance, waiting for the day when his self-control snapped and tore me into pieces.

"Enough," Q roared. His chest strained as he pushed me hard against the cross. My back crashed against the eerily warm wood. I flinched as Q pressed his long frame against mine, sandwiching me completely. "Now is not the time to talk about hearts and falling, *esclave*. Now is the time for pain and fucking.

See how the two don't mix?"

He pushed off, swiping his face with an angry palm. "I'm tired. Too tired to keep fighting. I want you. I've wanted to make you scream for four fucking long days. I tried to behave. I tried to stop the darkness, but you just wouldn't let it go. And now it's my turn. You're going to give me what I want. Take this obsessive sick need from me and help grant me a reprieve."

Something black gleamed over the pale green of Q's eyes. Something I'd only seen flickers of. Something that terrified as much as enthralled me.

"Not another word, or I'll use the ball gag. I only want moans and my name on your lips when I come deep inside you. Understand?" He breathed hard, and the tip of his cock nudged at the waistband of his boxer-briefs, excessively hard and calling to me like an addiction.

I'd never felt more alive or more frightened.

"I understand, *maître*," I whispered.

My voice was the starting gun. Q gritted his teeth, visibly shuddering. All along he'd been searching for my permission—whether he knew it or not. He shed the angry tension and relaxed, transforming into a composed master.

I waited for him to buckle the myriad of straps around me, but he paused.

Waited and watched.

Breathed and deliberated.

Then he lurched forward; his mouth crushed mine. My neck protested from where he'd strangled me and I couldn't breathe as his tongue darted past the seam of my lips and took. My God, he fucking took. He demanded and cajoled with every twist of his tongue. Every lick and sweep.

The kiss held fury and promises. His lips spoke how much he already cared for me, all the while trying to eat me alive.

With unrestrained hands, I let myself do what I'd wanted for so long. I allowed myself to touch him. My arms flew up and my fingers swept through his thick, short hair.

He moaned as I dug nails deep, remembering his migraine

and how he let me massage him back to health. How, by letting me tend to him, my emotions blossomed and grew. I'd been a slave—a possession—then. Now, I belonged. I was truly his, but only because I chose it.

I'd found where I belonged. I was done fighting my desires. Q was everything I wanted and more.

Running my hands down his scalp, I captured the back of his neck, pulling him closer. His taut body landed on mine with a heavy lurch, pressing me hard against the cross. His mouth bruised mine as our lips melded and clashed against each other.

Spearing my tongue with his, I battled his taste until we were both heaving and clawing at each other. I lost sense of how hard I scratched his neck and shoulders. I lost sensation of how hard his fingers dug into my hips. Nothing existed but our kiss.

Sharp, sweet pain made me gasp. My eyes watered as Q pulled back, licking his lips free from a small trace of accusing red.

"You bit me," I panted.

I opened my mouth and ran a fingertip over my already swelling tongue. Metallic blood pooled just a little; I swallowed.

He stared at me unrepentant, eyes glassy with lust. "I couldn't stop it. I had to taste you." His throat rippled as he swallowed, taking some part of me deep into him.

My thoughts raced. Even though Q was so hard to read, I began to see his true depth of need. His need for scars and blood and primal connection. He wasn't faking it. It wasn't about the kink or whipping. It was purely about opening me up, cracking open my very existence, and possessing me.

I'd be lying if I didn't admit it scared me. I liked pain. I loved the taboo line of pleasure in accepting a whip's kiss or a flogger's smack—subservient entirely to my master's whim. But I wasn't ready to die.

Will Q ever be satisfied? My heart sank, plummeted right to my toes.

Panic rose in my throat, forming into an uncomfortable

knot. "Will I ever be enough? Will I ever be able to give you what you crave?"

Q jolted upright, his entire body jerking to a rigid halt. It wasn't until he took a fumbling step back I realized I'd spoken aloud.

Oh, shit.

My eyes flew to Q's blazing jade ones, and my heart died a little more. *Tess, you idiot.* Rushing forward, I grabbed his arm and squeezed hard muscle. "I didn't mean that. I know this is all so new. It's strange...for both of us."

Q looked at me as if I were an alien species. His eyes went blank, face contorted with confusion and regret.

I cupped his cheek, desperate to have him come back to me. I could almost follow his thoughts. See the blood splatter, the hatred for himself.

When he didn't react to my soft touch, I tried hard instead. I slapped him.

The noise of flesh against flesh snapped him out of his zombified state. He blinked, rubbing his cheek absentmindedly. A few seconds passed while he gathered himself together.

Finally, he scowled. All the fire and lust from before blazed in his gaze.

"I told you not to speak unless it was screaming my name."

His body rippled as he allowed his demons to come fully into the light. "And banish those thoughts from your head, *esclave*. No matter what I say, you are enough. Too much. *Trop pure et parfaite pour un homme comme moi.*" Too pure and perfect for a man like me.

He rolled his shoulders, growling, "But it won't stop me from trying to ruin you."

My legs trembled, and in that moment I wanted nothing more than a simple hug. I wanted him to be soft and sweet, touch me and comfort me. He said I was enough, but I wasn't so sure, and the insecurity made me desolate.

Q didn't give me time to wallow. He slammed against me, pushing backward with the strength of a brick wall. My back connected with the cross and oxygen fled my lungs.

Q dropped his head and his lips latched onto my neck.

"Q—" My voice was breathy, a plea for something. Something I doubted I would ever receive.

His mouth sucked hard on my skin, bruising the delicate flesh. I shivered in his arms as he licked along my collarbone. His hands roamed over my hips, up my ribcage to find my breasts. With an angry hold, he took the weight, pinching my nipples hard as his teeth whispered across my neck.

"Ah!" I jolted as a sharp slice burned my throat.

My mouth hung open as he lapped and groaned. "You taste so good. Not your skin, or sweat, or perfume. The very depth of you. Your life-force. Your blood." He licked again before soothing my nipples with his thumbs. "Does that disgust you? Does it horrify you that I need this to feel connected? That this is a part of being loved by me?"

His tone hinted that he expected me to say yes. Even now, even though I gave him promises and slept beside him while he suffered nightmares of doing untold things to me, he still expected me to leave. I just hoped to God I was strong enough to keep my promises.

"No. I understand who you are and what you need. I didn't—"

Q bit me particularly hard, drawing more blood. His throat contracted as he swallowed and when he went to pull away, I hugged his head to me, forcing his lips against the bite.

Goosebumps sprang over my skin as his hot breath charred me into cinders. "Drink me if that's what you need. Fuck me if it will help you believe. *Je suis à toi.*" I'm yours.

He groaned, thrusting his hips against mine; the hardness of his cock, trapped in his boxer-briefs, speared against my belly button.

My heart twisted as my core melted. My mind spiralled into the darkness Q was so good at conjuring. I didn't care it was socially wrong to share blood. I didn't care that societies protecting women would be horrified with what I let Q do to me.

The world didn't matter. This was us. This was our fuckedupness learning how to live without guilt and shame.

Q nibbled his way up my neck, along my jaw, to my lips. When he kissed me, he didn't hold back. His tongue swept deep, bringing with it the metallic taste of rust and a need so basic it threatened to steal my thoughts, unlearn everything I knew, and embrace a life of existing purely to be with Q.

His hands dropped to caress my body. Squeezing my hips once, he captured my right wrist and fanned my arm out, all the while fucking my mouth with his sinful tongue. He pulled away when the back of my hand touched wood. His eyes were bright and pupils dilated. "Everything about you is mine. Do you deny it?"

Breathing hard, battling the urge to rub my pussy against his leg between my thighs, I shook my head. "I don't deny it."

With a sharp nod, Q reached over me to wrap a soft leather cuff around my wrist. With a fierce expression, he tightened it until I felt a faint heartbeat in my fingertips. A sharp burst of panic rose from nowhere, gripping my heart, making it flurry.

Q froze, staring at me unguarded. The lust sheening his face caused more wetness to trickle. I couldn't run and the knowledge turned my body on beyond compare.

"You're frightened." His voice was so gruff, I barely understood him.

I opened my mouth to deny it, but why would I hide the truth? Q lived for the truth, he fought for authentic fear.

"You tied it so tight. I'm afraid I'll never be free."

He chuckled. "And you think you're free when you're not restrained? You don't know me at all, *esclave*." Capturing my left arm, he repeated the process until miniature beating hearts thrummed in my fingers. "You'll never be free of me. I'll never be free of you. It's fate who decides, and fate gave us each

35

other."

Memories of our blood oath sprung to mind. *"Nous sommes les uns des autres."* We are each other's.

He sucked in a breath; his face danced with shadows caused by early morning clouds. The sun dappled the room in spotlights of warmth, but not this corner. In this corner only shade was permitted.

"Oui." He bent to kiss me, but I kept my eyes wide open. Focusing on his sculptured cheekbones and how achingly lonely his gaze appeared. We never looked away as his lips worked mine, soft but dangerous at the same time. His tongue skirted the fine line of unbreakable discipline and uncontrollable passion.

His large hands cupped my face, holding me still as he bent his head to angle the kiss deeper. The back of my head hit the wooden cross, and I moaned as he pressed his entire muscular body against mine. His naked skin heated my own, feverish, hot as the devil.

Pulling away, Q breathed hard, sending his sparrow tattoo fluttering like crazy. The rolling black clouds and barbwire seemed to be particularly violent, devouring more birds, erupting more feathers, spiralling in their bid for freedom. Q expected me to fly away. I needed to find a way to prove I wasn't going to.

A flash of inspiration hit, and I murmured, "You're my wings. You made me fly."

He froze, hands unmoving on my cheeks. His pale eyes seared into my soul.

Q wasn't just my master in the bedroom. He was the master of my heart.

Finally, he whispered in his deep, accented voice, "You stole my loneliness. I may have given you wings, but you've become my gravity. I'll never be free of your force."

I melted. If my arms hadn't been imprisoned by the cross, I would've thrown them around Q and climbed his body. I would've freed his straining erection from his boxer-briefs and pushed myself on top of him. I needed connection. I needed to bind us. Entwine us. Imprint and devour us.

Q seemed to feel the same way. His eyes morphed from deep and smouldering to bright and glittering. His composure tightened from tense to coiled. A predator, a wolf, a killer about to indulge in his prey. "No more talking, Tess."

I shivered with the way he said my name. It held every inch of emotion that he couldn't verbalize.

Q dropped to his knees, thudding against the thick white carpet. He tugged my left leg to line up with the cross and its buckle in one sharp move. I stumbled, relying on the cuffs around my wrists to grant me balance.

As his fingers worked around my ankle, sending spasms of intense awareness up my inner thigh, Q murmured, "One day, I'll break you completely. One day, I'll be strong enough."

The thrill of his confession shot like an arrow through my heart. I wanted with all my soul to tell him I hoped to God he did, but I didn't think he meant it like that. He didn't want to break me until I was ruined—he wanted to own me completely. The difference was I didn't think Q knew what he meant.

Or, maybe he did, and I was a stupid little girl. Nevertheless, I fell back into unwilling slave—the role that turned my master and me crazy. The role that guaranteed explosive sex, battle of wills, and deep satisfaction.

Gathering a deep breath, I hissed, "No. You'll never break me."

Q snapped.

The barrier dropped once and for all. With brutal fingers, he spread my other leg and secured me tightly against the warm wood. Gone were the soft caresses. This was pure animalistic control. He stood in one quick move, grabbing the two pieces of leather hanging on either side of my hips.

Jerking across my belly, he tightened them. He didn't say a word, but we glared and dared and warred with our eyes. The room crackled with pent-up frustration, unkept promises, and a slight undercurrent of fear. Whose fear I didn't know, but it added to the thick cloud of emotion engulfing us.

Q leaned forward, reaching behind my neck. Securing the last remaining strap, he looked deep into my eyes. "You're going to be the death of both of us."

True undiluted fear raced through my blood. The tightness of the strap across my throat signified complete submission. Something I never really gave, even though I let Q dominate me.

I may be a masochist, but I wasn't a submissive, and that's why Q needed me.

Once the strap was tight across my throat, and I was truly immobile, Q dragged his finger from the tip of my nose, down my lips, over my throat and breasts, dipping past my ribs and belly right to my pussy. He stroked my clit, once, twice, before moving lower.

I trembled with every millimetre he touched. The need to have him took over every thought.

His eyes tightened as his finger dipped inside me ever so slowly.

My jaw went slack and I moaned at the leisurely possession. His finger felt like pure ecstasy. I shuddered around his touch, sucking him deeper, my body begging for more.

Q growled, pressing harder until his knuckles connected against my core. "Fuck, you're wet. Every time, *esclave*. Every time, you're ready for me." His voice held awed pleasure.

My hips tried to work, to entice him further, but the straps became the perfect prison.

He pressed deeper; I groaned as he curved his finger to stroke my g-spot. "You lied. You said I couldn't break you. And yet, here I am breaking you, bit by bit. And you fucking love it. Your body screams the truth. When will you admit it?"

I bared my teeth, my body was a molten volcano, every blood cell erupting. "Never."

He chuckled. The dark sound echoed in my ears, down my neck and spine. "Never is a long time." Easing out of me, he quickly inserted two fingers, stretching me wide, coaxing my body to accept him, regardless of the sudden intrusion.

My head fell forward, and all I wanted to do was surrender. To let Q do whatever he wanted to me; to bask in the onslaught of sensations. But for Q to let go, I had to pretend. Pretend he scared, hurt, and horrified me. I didn't want to think how that troubled me—how I didn't understand why Q needed it that way.

For once, I didn't like the role play. I wanted him to know how much I needed this part of him, to let him know it was okay with me. More than okay—I lived for it. I wanted to scream for him to hit me, fuck me, debase me, but I couldn't because permission wasn't what he sought. It was the hunt, the chase, the crime of causing agony.

Q took a step back. My thoughts screeched to a halt as he paced away, heading toward the mirrored chest.

He took his sweet time choosing from the scattered remains on the carpet. I craned my neck, trying to see, but the strap around my waist and throat pinned me in place.

Finally, he stalked back, looking chiseled and determined in his black boxer-briefs. His hands stayed behind his back, obstructing whatever torture equipment he planned to use.

"As much as I want to scar you, etch my name into your belly so you'll always know who you belong to, I'm not ready. When I break your virgin skin, I won't stop, and I don't want to live with yet another addiction." His eyes flared as if he hadn't meant to confide those thoughts. His face darkened as he cleared his throat. "I'm giving you a choice. Sharp pain or radiating pain."

I blinked, trying to figure out the riddle of what toys Q had behind his back.

When I didn't answer, he growled, "An answer, *esclave*, or I'll use both. Believe me, I want to use everything on you all at once, but I'm not a murderer." He lowered his voice. "Well, not a murderer of women at least."

The image of Q shooting a man in cold blood slammed into my head—the night he found me, being raped and defiled by Driver and Brute. I hung my head, voluntarily choking myself on the strap, trying to forget.

"Was that a beg, treasure? You want me?"

"I think she's asking you to fuck her. Better give her what she wants."

My body went numb at the memory of being taken by force. The pain, the sounds of him rutting like a fucking beast inside me.

Make it stop. Make it stop!

"Fuck." Q closed the distance between us in a split second, and captured my chin. "I'd kill him a thousand times over for what he did, but I refuse to let you think about him." Q kissed both of my eyelids, murmuring, "You promised you'd only think of our night together. Purge that fucking bastard from your mind. Or I'll whip it out of you."

Q's odd mixture of sweet and harsh halted the memory and shoved the rape out of my mind, but I couldn't rid myself of the metallic taste of Driver's fingers in my mouth.

I needed Q to whip me; to force me to obey and burn the memories to dust.

"Hurt me, *maître*. Make it disappear. I want sharp pain. I want you to slice the evil free." My breath caught, and my body shook with the beginnings of real fear. I offered myself to Q to help free me once and for all, but I also permitted him to truly hurt me. He wouldn't hold back—not now.

The wetness between my legs increased and my teeth chattered as Q sucked in a breath, dropping one of the items in his hands. It slithered against the carpet, lying like a dormant snake; any moment it would raise its head and strike with deadly fangs.

Q held up his other arm, showing me what he intended to use. My heart rate exploded.

In his palm lay a cat-o'-nine-tails. The intricate whip handle exploded from one thick cylinder into nine pieces of lethal leather. Each strand was woven with tiny silver beads along the length.

Adrenaline washed over me. My skin flushed, and I wiggled in the bindings. It looked painful. It looked cruel. It looked like it would pulverize my thoughts and turn my body into a crisscrossed canvas of agony.

I tried to stay calm, tried to keep my heart from galloping out of control, but shit, I couldn't. The whip was too dangerous.

My eyes flew to his. "No. I can't. It's too much."

Fear swarmed thick and fast as Q smiled thinly, shaking his head. "If this is what it takes to eliminate that cocksucker from your brain, so be it." He stepped away a little, letting the whip dangle.

"Q—please. I'm not ready."

"You'll never be ready for this, *esclave*. I know that, and I hate myself for what I'm about to do, but I'm not going to stop." He hung his head, watching me from shadowed eyes. "So help me, I want to whip you. Cry for me, Tess."

He struck.

The multiple-beaded whip whistled through the air and licked my naked belly. Each silver bead dug deep into my flesh, singeing me with pain.

I cried out, jolting in the straps with the heat of the first lash.

Q groaned, his entire body vibrating, eyes locked on the blush of red already blooming on my stomach. His lips parted as his nostrils flared, almost as if he could truly taste my pain and fear.

"Don't hate me for what I need," he implored, just before he struck again. The bunch of muscles as he swung set his tattoo fluttering with shadows.

The whip kissed me brutally while the little beads bit with tiny fangs. The first tang of tears burned.

Through my glassy eyes, Q danced and quivered; my vision turned wonky from adrenaline. I panicked and hated I couldn't move. This wasn't fun or sexy or erotic.

I was a prisoner with a monster who was my master. A

man who didn't trust his own self-control.

A single tear cascaded down my cheek, and Q's chest rose with intensity. "I want more than one, Tess." He came forward and kissed below each eye, whispering, *"J'aime te marquer."* I love marking you.

I shook my head, past being able to talk. Too fucked up with too many emotions. Somehow he turned this against me. I wanted this. I knew that, but Q had blocked me out, embraced his wickedness, leaving me behind.

I was a stupid girl for thinking I could take Q on. To try and love this man who had so many issues. What made me strong enough to be what he needed?

Q took a step backward, and I squeezed my eyes. I didn't want to watch him bristle with lust when he hit me. I didn't want to witness the way his perfect body flexed as he swung. I didn't want any part of this.

Waiting in the dark was an eternity of torture, but Q didn't strike. I waited and waited, but no whip's kiss or bead's bite touched me.

I hesitated opening my eyes, then my mouth popped wide as a soul-wrenching moan erupted from my lips.

Q had knelt between my spread and bound legs. His mouth latched onto my swollen pussy, and he licked as if he'd die if he didn't drink all of me.

Oh, *God.*

His teeth found my clit, and he bit gently. No part of my body existed except that tiny, sensitive nub.

Q gripped my ass, pulling my pussy harder against his mouth. His tongue speared inside me and I screamed. "Q. Fuck. Please. Yes."

He groaned as my body wept. Moisture trickled down my thigh, mixing with Q's saliva. Holding me captive with one hand, he pushed three fingers deep inside.

I screamed in bliss as he rocked his hand. His mouth centred on my clit as his fingers drove me into a frenzy.

My knees trembled, and I wished I could fall—fall onto

his mouth, impale myself onto his cock. His fingers were heaven but his cock would be delirium.

A sharp band of an orgasm built in my lower spine, radiating through my belly to grip around Q's fingers.

Instantly, he stopped and stood in one sharp move. I gawked and panted and cursed. My body quaked with the need to come; the need to come apart and surrender.

Q raised his arm, and the whip licked my lower belly. The nine pieces of leather coaxed red to shadow and pain to flourish.

I tried to bend over, to protect my innocent stomach, but the cross held me inert.

Q hit me again, this one higher, just below my breasts. My ribcage bellowed as the tiny beads bruised my flesh.

Again he swung. And again.

The cat-o'-nine-tails rained. It felt like Q delivered a thunderstorm: the thunder of his pleasure, my swirling feelings a blistering squall, and nine sparks of lightning all delivered at once.

I transcended. My body entered a realm of insane sensitivity and I welcomed the whip. The pain morphed into unbearable pleasure until I reverberated with all-encompassing want.

My thoughts swirled with bright lights and my body wailed for release.

By the tenth strike, I arched my back, pushing my breasts out, welcoming the gluttony of punishment.

Q's breathing rasped, and our eyes never left each other's. He looked wild and untamed and completely diabolical.

Half of me hated him for dragging me over the point of pain and turning me into a monster like him, but the other adored and worshipped him. No sex between us would ever be easy and completely consenting.

With our gazes locked, Q struck wide. My thigh howled as the strips of leather flayed me.

"What do you want from me? Why do you let me break

you?" he panted, his chest straining with exertion.

My heart flurried; I wondered if I dare speak the truth. Tell him what I hoped he'd become. The future I dared envision.

He struck me across my belly, just above the lattice of red from a previous strike. I winced and suffered a wave of pleasure that almost made me come from no other stimulation.

"Speak, *esclave*. For every second you fail, I'll hit you."

I gaped, scrambling for the right words.

I cried out as, true to his word, he hit me again on my left thigh. Branding me with nine matching red stripes and blemishes from the beads.

"I want you to hurt me, but I also want you to care for me," I exploded, vibrating with the need to come. It echoed in my teeth, it danced in the pain of the marks. Every inch of me was strung out and on edge.

He paused, relaxing his stance to run the cat-o'-nine-tails through his hands like one would with a pet. "I do care for you. Too damn much. You've turned me inside out and changed my entire world."

Everything crunched to a halt. I never expected him to be so honest. Maybe he dropped his walls when he cast away the barriers to his demons.

We didn't move as if terrified we'd break the moment. Our souls were stripped bare and free for the briefest of moments.

Q's pale eyes darkened, hiding his vulnerability. He ran the whip through his strong fingers once again.

I trembled in the bindings waiting for the next strike, dreading it, wanting it, *craving* it.

"Jusqu'où tu me laisserais aller?" How far would you let me go? He murmured so low, I barely heard him.

My heart stopped beating, and I came up blank. I couldn't answer his question. I didn't know my boundaries; I didn't want to put limits on learning how to coexist, and I definitely didn't want to show the depth of fear I had that Q would eventually go too far and kill me.

Q's eyes met mine. He let the hand holding the whip fall to his side. He rolled his shoulders, and my skin sprinkled with goose-bumps. The air crackled with sudden energy.

Q bowed his head, staring at me from under his darkened brow. "I understand why you won't respond, *esclave*. I don't have an answer either."

I gulped as he took one step closer, obliterating the small distance between us, bringing his heat and proximity to scald my skin.

His free hand cupped my throat over the strap while his hips pressed against mine hard and quick. "You didn't struggle when I cut off your oxygen before. Why?"

I shook my head, trying to pry free, but his fingers stiffened, holding me just as firmly as the leather across my limbs. Q breathed hard, never looking away from my eyes. The pale green faded as his pupils dilated in pleasure. "You let me decide how far to go," he whispered, amazement in his tone.

His fingers tightened around my neck, hurting the already bruised column of muscle. My heart raced and bucked as more adrenaline exploded fast and swift, arcing in my blood. But I refused to beg to be released or for Q to be careful. This was a battle he had to win with himself.

Every shallow breath was a hardship as Q slowly cut off my air supply. When I grew lightheaded, Q licked his lips and bent to kiss me. The rough dominance of his fingers didn't match the soft, sensual kiss he bestowed.

He didn't kiss me. He worshiped me.

Every whisper of his tongue paid homage. Every hitch of his breathing sent my heart speeding until it was a blur in my chest.

Strapped to the cross, all I could do was let Q give what he wanted. His erection sprang harder against me as he thrust his tongue deep, licking my mouth, devouring me.

Breaking the kiss, Q stepped back, holding up the cat-o'-nine-tails. He draped it on my shoulder and very, very slowly let it fall, so it tickled and trickled down the left side of my body. I shivered as a bead caught my nipple, sending it peaking into a painful tip.

Inch by inch, Q watched the trail of his whip on my belly and hip, falling like a waterfall of leather to kiss my welted thigh.

Thoughts raced in Q's eyes, and I wished I could decipher him; unriddle him and find the key to owning him heart, body, and soul.

Pulling back, he hooked his thumbs into his boxer-briefs and pulled them down. My mouth went instantly dry. Watching this man strip made every part of me combust into a rain of fire.

His cock sprang free, heavy and heated with need. The discarded boxer-briefs fell to his ankles, and he kicked them away without care. So proud and sure, almost cocky and arrogant, but the cool aloofness I mistook in the past was actually tightly reined passion. A will of iron that buckled and strained to stay human all the while urges beat him to submit.

Discarding the whip with a flick of his wrist, Q dropped his hand to wrap around his thick girth. He stroked once, twice. His long fingers fully encasing himself as he pumped strong and sure.

I couldn't breathe. I couldn't think.

Everything inside quivered. The just out-of-reach orgasm echoed in my pussy, clenching, calling to Q's perfect cock.

I wanted to be Q's fingers. I wanted to be his flesh. I wanted to be his cock receiving such pleasure. I wanted everything about him, and yet he gave me nothing.

I trailed my eyes up his physique, over his rigid stomach, skittering over his intricate tattoo, along his chest, up his stubble-smooth chin and parted lips until I finally looked him in the eye.

It felt as if the world exploded on its axis, tripping, spinning, hurling me headlong into sin and debauchery.

"You want me. Don't you, Tess." Q's voice dropped to gruff and midnight. Still stroking himself with one hand, he came forward and cupped between my spread legs.

I moaned as his touch acted like gasoline on an already blazing inferno. "Q, please," I warbled, my tongue too heavy to form proper sentences.

His fingers were little sticks of dynamite, and I begged to light them for a cataclysmic explosion.

He swayed toward me, stroking himself harder, drawing drops of glistening pre-cum.

My heart roared in my ears. I fought the restraints. I needed to be free. I needed to lick and bite him. I needed to fuck him with an urgency I'd never felt before.

Q tutted under his breath. "You want to be free?" He nuzzled my neck, licking at the sore skin from his earlier bite. "You'll never be free again. *Je te garde pour toujours.*" I'm keeping you forever.

Oxygen no longer held merit as Q inserted two fingers deep inside me, pulsating in time with his strokes on his cock. I bucked, desperate to get closer. Fingers weren't enough.

Take me! Own me.

Q groaned as he fisted himself, working harder. "Fuck, I want my cock inside you. To be deep in your darkness, your wetness, your fucking sweet pussy." He pressed another finger deep, and my back bowed.

I moaned, eyes squeezed shut against the siege of euphoria. "Do it. Please, God, do it."

"So eager. So keen," he growled, his hand working harder, fingers throttling his cock.

I moaned, nodding. "For you, yes. Always for you."

He trembled, groaning under his breath. "Only for me, *esclave*. All mine." He fingered me harder. His thumb found my clit, swirling in time to the tempo he set. Rocking, possessing, mind-shattering.

His thumb was magic, conjuring swirling, sparking energy to centre on his touch. My stomach tensed as my core tightened around him, demanding to be filled, to be satisfied and taken, but Q just kept up the maddening erotic beat.

Thrust, swirl, thrust. His hand worked his erection, bringing more blood to his cock, so it heated and wept with clear liquid. Liquid I wanted to lap. His balls tightened, sitting high and full, straining with the need to come.

With his fingers still deep inside me, Q stopped stroking himself to fumble with one of the straps around my wrists. I groaned as the tightness released, letting blood gush into my hands.

He never faltered in his rhythm as he undid the cuffs around my neck and other wrist. When I was free, he placed my hand on his cock.

His velvety heat was like the trigger on my release. My body clamped around his fingers as the first ripple milked him hard. *So fucking good.* My hand squeezed Q tightly. He hissed, but I didn't care. All I could focus on was the heady thrill of finally giving in to the body-aching orgasm.

I felt eternally heavy as if gravity increased a thousand fold and then I let go, embracing the next wave of my orgasm, pulsing around my heart, wrapped tight around my spine and inner thighs, blazing with need.

Q slapped my hand away from his cock and withdrew his fingers.

No!

I gasped as the orgasm faltered, and, with no stimulation, receded like a pitiful wave.

"Why? Let me come. Please, let me come!" I begged, reaching for him with my freed arms.

He ducked out of reach, unleashing my ankles before standing again. Trailing his fingers over my torso, he turned his hands to claws, raking nails across me. He didn't break the skin, but the burn activated the whip marks, encouraging pain to smoulder. Reaching my waist, he undid the final strap and pulled me from the cross.

With a grim mouth, he murmured, "I'm not done with you yet. When you come, it will feel so fucking unbelievable you won't be able to move."

He gathered me into his arms, pressing his forehead against mine and breathing deep. "Promise to obey everything I say. If you even think of rebelling or speaking against me, I'll not be held accountable. *T'as compris?*" Do you understand?

I was speechless. For Q to demand I obey him, to allow him full control and acceptance never happened. He got off on fighting, on denial. I wanted to ask so many questions, but held my tongue and nodded.

I would've promised to do anything if it meant I could finally come.

Q backed away a little, crooking his finger for me to follow. "Come here."

My feet moved on their own accord. I wanted to pounce on him and tackle him to the ground. Yet Q made no move to finish what he started.

My eyes darted between his intense gaze and heavy cock. Q pointed at the ground by his feet. "Kneel."

With a racing heart, I obeyed, folding to the floor as gracefully as I could with ten tonne lust-riddled limbs. The thick carpet welcomed, easing some of the soreness from the cross.

Q placed a hand on my head before walking slowly behind me. His fingers stayed locked with my hair, tugging it a little. With powerful hands, he gathered the strands. I shivered.

He captured every wisp and unruly curl, then twisted the thick strands until he made a blonde rope.

With a jerk, he pulled my head back until my heels jammed into my ass. "I like being able to control you this way, *esclave.*"

His mouth descended on mine from above. The upside-down awkwardness added a new dimension to our kiss, and I opened wide to let his tongue possess me. Controlling me with my hair, Q stole my breath, making me squirm.

My hands clenched into fists on my thighs, and I wanted more than anything to touch myself and come. I couldn't stand the ache much longer—the unbearable need to explode.

Withdrawing from the kiss, Q wrapped my hair around my neck. The tickling strands wrapped around my throat made me claustrophobic. Small pops of panic burst in my bloodstream. I didn't think I could stand to be strangled again.

Q stalked back to stand in front of me; my eyes fell to his cock. Pre-cum smeared down the underside of his velvety skin. I licked my lips.

His belly rippled with need and he groaned, taking a step closer. Our eyes burned holes in each other and we didn't say a word. He stood still, apart from the slight twitch of his hips, the unconscious plea to give him what I desperately wanted.

I sat higher on my knees, reaching with shaky hands to clasp his hot length. My fingers latched around him, tight and unforgiving.

His head fell back, and the moan dragged from his throat vibrated in my pussy. If he kept making sounds like that I'd come from the power of his voice alone.

I stroked him once and his heavy hands landed on my head, exerting a little pressure, giving me a request.

My mouth watered as I bowed my head. The hair tightened around my throat. The moment my tongue touched his cock, I knew why he'd lassoed my hair around me. My airway was already compromised. Sucking his cock diminished it even more. Breathing thorough my nose didn't help—every breath became a struggle.

My nostrils flared in fear, but I opened wide and sucked Q's girth deep into my mouth. He threaded his fingers into my strands, holding my head prisoner as my tongue lapped from beneath and my lips clamped tight around him.

He rocked deeper into me, pressing down on my head. "Take it. Fuck."

My pussy clenched, and I could've cried with how much I wanted his cock deep inside me. Anger and frustration bubbled, and I dared scrape my teeth along his length, testing him, showing him how on edge I was.

He thrust harder, causing my jaw to lock and teeth to mar

such delicate flesh. The thick head of his cock hit the back of my mouth and the urge to gag suffocated me. I tried to take a deep breath, but my hair didn't allow my lungs to fill.

Desperation grew and grew until my chest ached and my heart galloped. And yet I kept sucking, kept stroking. Q was in a different dimension, petting my head, taking my mouth with his eyes tightly closed.

"Your mouth is fucking heaven," he grunted.

His cock rippled as I sucked harder, determined to make him truly mean what he said. I wanted him to unravel. I wanted it to be over so I could breathe again.

Anxiety made me bold. I slid one hand between his legs and cupped his balls.

He jolted. His hips stopped their searching rock. For a second, I wondered if he'd stop me. Maybe I wasn't allowed to touch him there, but the second passed, and he relaxed again.

I squeezed the tender flesh, rolling them in my fingertips. He twitched, and his muscular thighs quivered.

Looking up, I imprinted how he looked in that moment. His eyes squeezed shut, his mouth in a grimace. He looked like an evil demigod. A living relic of sinful sex.

Opening wider, I slid him in and out, licking and laving while I cupped his balls harder. I wanted him to come. I wanted to steal the fine edge of his control and make him lose it.

I'm going to drive you wild, Q Mercer.

Growing braver, I darted my hand further between his legs. He stilled, but I didn't give him an opportunity to decide if he liked it. With two fingers facing upward, I pressed hard on the ridge of skin between his balls and asshole.

He jerked as I found the thicker node of skin, the small walnut-sized erogenous zone also known as the male g-spot.

I pressed it again, sucking his cock deep into my mouth.

Q gasped and wrenched back, but I went with him. I kept my lips glued around him and my hand firmly between his legs.

I suffered black spots in my vision as my hair slowly

asphyxiated me, but I kept a rhythm: suck, press, suck, press—
a thrusting motion between his legs, my touch firm and
unyielding.

Q let out a loud groan. "*Merde.* Stop!"

I didn't stop.

I added teeth to my suction. I flexed my fingers, ignoring
everything else but getting Q to lose control.

"Fuck fuck fuck." It was a match to a cannon, a lost pin to
a grenade. Q lost it. "Fuck me, *esclave. Merde.*"

His fingers gripped my head, holding me hostage as his
hips thrust violently into my mouth. I never let up on the
pressure between his legs, coaxing his g-spot, pinching the vein
feeding his balls with blood.

"*Tu vas me tuer. C'est tellement bon. Mon Dieu.*" You're going
to kill me. It feels too good. My God.

My mouth leaked saliva, unable to do anything but accept
Q's motion. My neck grew wet as I dribbled and my arm
erupted into fire from keeping the pressure.

Q grunted like a feral animal. His throat rattled with
curses, his body vibrated with aggression, and the entire room
filled with the thick scent of sex.

I teetered on the brink of passing out, my body numb and
weak. Q groaned from the tips of his toes. His belly stiffened,
his legs froze, and his g-spot surged.

Then he came.

"Fuck…" he snarled, spurting down the back of my
throat, cascading warm and salty on my tongue. Wave after
wave I swallowed, and still he kept coming. I choked and he
pulled out, fisting himself.

With angry strokes, he milked the last of his orgasm,
panting as he kept spurting, dousing me in white sticky droplets
all over my breasts.

The picture of Q towering over me, his face furious and
red while eyes blazed with his release, was a sight to behold. I
wanted to capture the moment, sear it on my brain, remember
the ink of his tattoo, the musky taste of him in my mouth, and

the knowledge I drove him to break.

With shaking hands, I unravelled my hair from around my throat, and removed as much spit as I could.

My entire mouth ached, and my pussy felt wronged— slighted for not being fucked and given the same sort of release Q experienced.

Taking gulping breaths, Q smeared a droplet of warm come over my nipple.

Instantly the orgasm blazed alive again, sparking, begging, setting my teeth on edge. *Please put me out of my misery.*

Never taking his eyes off mine, Q reached under my arms and helped me stand on unsteady legs. His face shut down, unreadable.

"Do you need me, Tess?"

I jolted with the power and ragged sex appeal in his voice. My eyes fluttered, needing to close; I was drunk on the need to come.

I nodded fretfully.

He ducked, so we were almost eye level. "Do you need my tongue on your cunt to come?"

My eyes snapped shut, battered by the image of Q licking me, biting me, making me unravel. "Yes," I moaned.

His fingers caressed my other breast, giving it the same treatment as the first. "Will you walk around in constant agony if I don't fuck you?" His thumb and forefinger pinched my nipple, sending waves of need through my belly to my core.

Anger rose again. What the hell was he playing at? It wasn't fair. It wasn't right. "You know I will."

He grabbed my breast hard, making me groan and shudder. I swayed toward him, trying to touch his still hard cock. If only he'd let me use it. He wouldn't have to do anything. I could ride him to satisfaction.

But his voice was a whiplash. "Don't touch me."

Shock wrenched my eyes wide; my skin flushed with embarrassment and hurt. I looked deep into his gaze, searching for the reason of his denial.

He shook his head. "You broke a cardinal rule. You disobeyed me." His back was ramrod straight, shoulders tight and tense. "You took away my control, *esclave*, and that's something you just don't do. Making me lose it is the worst kind of disobedience. You rushed me. You took what wasn't yours to have." His tone shimmered with warning. "I told you I wouldn't be responsible if you didn't do as I said."

I gulped. I couldn't handle another session on the cross, not unless I came first. My mind was scrambled. I needed to relax, unwind, and save my sanity.

He ran a thumb over my bottom lip, trembling with control. "Your punishment isn't whips or chains or any other torture you seem to enjoy."

I couldn't stand it. I had to know. "What do you intend to do?"

Q smiled. He was two sides of a coin—one moment remorseful, the next revengeful. "I intend to do nothing." Pressing his hand between my legs, he speared two fingers deep.

My forehead crashed against his chest as I buckled in his arms. My hips moved on his hand, my breathing quickened as my orgasm built super-sonically fast.

Withdrawing his fingers, he licked them clean. I stood wobbling, a throbbing mass of nerve endings.

"If you pleasure yourself, I will know. If you come before I say you will, I'll deny you pleasure for a month. You're to stay on edge until I give you permission." He bent to kiss my cheek so tenderly. "Only then will I fuck you like you want to be fucked. Only then will I let you scream my name."

The sentence was torture. Tears sprang to my eyes, and I reached to grab Q's hand. "Please." I shook my head. "Q, please. I'll do anything you want."

He smiled softly, running his fingers through my hair, fanning it out like a blonde curtain over my shoulders. "Don't do it again, Tess, that's what I want from you."

"I promise. Cross my heart. Never." I tried to capture his

cock, but he sidestepped me, heading toward the bathroom. "Remember you brought this on yourself. Get dressed. We're late."

Surprise made my voice squeak. "Late for what?"

Q chuckled before disappearing into the bathroom. "We're going to work. I told you I wanted you to work with me. Today is that day."

Three
Quincy

You're my obsession, I'm your possession,
you own the deepest part of me...

I ran.

I ran away like a fucking girl. My body felt foreign—thick, sated, but angst ridden and ferocious. I wanted to punch something. I wanted to scream at Tess for what she did. I wanted to attack anyone stupid enough to come within grabbing distance. I had to get the hell out of there.

She forced me.

She made me lose control.

I *never* lost control.

Slamming the bathroom door, I stalked to the black twin-sink vanity and put my hands on either side of a basin. Bowing over, I sucked in ragged breaths, trying to calm the rapid tempo of my heart.

My cock still seeped even after blowing two loads in one. I almost drowned her when I exploded down her throat. It wasn't satisfied. *I* wasn't satisfied. I was a lot of things, but satisfied didn't come fucking close.

The instant I thought about her touch, her fingers pressing so hard between my fucking legs, my stomach trembled and my cock—the bastard—grew thick and heavy.

Never before had a woman stolen what was singularly mine. Never before had someone made me come before I was ready. They knew better than to be so bold.

Tess knew better, yet she didn't give me a choice.

My eyes squeezed shut, and all I could see was a replay.

Her hair was spun gold between my fingers as I guided her mouth over my cock. Her warm, wet lips sealed around me, my back tinged with fireworks, and my balls tightened painfully.

The rope of hair strangled her little by little and I waited for her to gag and pull away; to glare at me with accusing blue eyes and refuse to pleasure me.

But she didn't.

She leaned further, strangling faster. Her mouth filled with delicious lubrication and she added the sharp thrill of teeth.

Everything she did was perfect, and my orgasm started slow and promising. Then she ruined it by shoving her hand behind my balls and finding that fucking spot that turned me to mush.

I flinched when her hand went where no one had touched before. Her fingertips pressed up, rubbing me directly into torment.

My orgasm shifted gears from slow to ultrasonic. Merde, *it felt amazing. Beyond amazing—body-shattering, mind-blazing, backbreaking.*

I jerked away, digging my toes into the carpet, trying to hold off the release, but she moved with me. She didn't let me go. Her goddamn hand stayed pulsing, rocking, and her mouth became the perfect vessel to unload into.

My thoughts turned into one long stream of curses as I battled two conflicting emotions.

Lust.

Terror.

Lust because she drove me fucking insane. I forgot who I was. I forgot why I had to stay in control. I forgot everything but grabbing her head and making her swallow my come.

Terror because the walls between me and the beast were obliterated. Extinguished by a fragile girl bent between my legs. No one was safe when that happened.

I opened my eyes, glowering at myself in the mirror. *You're a bastard, Mercer.*

I should head right back into the bedroom and order Tess to spread her sexy little legs and plunge deep inside her. She'd almost cried when I denied her. It was a cunt move to let her stay on the edge after she gave me the best orgasm of my life, but I was pissed. Beyond pissed. Confused.

My fingers clawed the marble countertop, and I fought the other emotion I tried hard not to acknowledge.

Resentment.

Resentment toward Tess, but mainly toward myself. I couldn't stop it. All my life, I prided myself on having ultimate control over my body, over my thoughts and needs. But in one move, Tess shredded those conceptions, annihilated my prized restraint, and turned me into a fucking Neanderthal.

She stole my control and instead of fighting it, I relinquished myself into her touch, allowed her to spell me, trap me; allowed my body to rule my mind.

How could I ever trust myself again?

I sighed, turning around to enter the black marble shower. The surfaces were so highly polished my reflection stared back at me.

Haunted.

My eyes were haunted, and the truth of why I was so angry shone bright. Tess drew more than just come from me, she took an element of dominance, and if I was honest, I hated it.

Wrenching on the shower, I flinched as cold droplets turned instantly hot. The pinpricks of heat helped leech away my rolling emotions, and I grabbed the soap to lather on my chest.

Memories of taking Tess in the shower the very first time sprang to mind as I dropped my hands to spread bubbles onto my cock. She'd been so hurt and mentally ruined from the rape. But I liked to think my untraditional way of replacing the memory with myself helped remove the pain and shock from her eyes.

Water sluiced away the remainder of Tess's spit, and I groaned when I squeezed a tad too hard.

Gritting my teeth, I stroked again. Angry, violent strokes—taking punishment out on the part of my body that failed to obey.

I wanted more. I wanted to drive deep inside her and make her promise never to make me feel so controlled again. She made me feel…weak. Not the man I knew. It made me soft, and I'd never had a soft moment in my life.

My hand worked harder, gripping too tight until the head of my cock throbbed. Spreading my legs, I settled in for a quick release, but I paused.

This wasn't fair. *Why should I get to come again, when Tess is probably living a nightmare right now?*

It took discipline and a tight jaw, but I uncurled my fist and let my cock free. My muscles bunched tight, and no matter how long I stayed in the shower, I couldn't relax.

Twenty minutes later, I strode from my bedroom dressed in a dark grey suit. The sombre colour reflected my mood perfectly: tense, horny, and entirely fucked up over a woman who had me by the balls. Literally.

Stalking through my home, I found Tess in the carousel room where I'd put her after the horrible incident with Lefebvre. The clothes I'd bought her remained down here. We hadn't made the move to relocate her to my bedroom. That final step toward admitting our lives were merging together hadn't been taken yet, and I didn't know if I was thankful or annoyed.

Tess sat on the end of the bed, rolling pantyhose over her

smooth skin, snapping it into place with a lacy garter belt peeking from beneath a tight skirt. She'd gathered it around her hips, so it looked more like a belt, and fuck, I wanted to rip it off her.

Tess was right about me enjoying ripping her clothes. It was a symbol. A way to tear and destroy without killing her.

She looked up and jumped straight to her feet, holding her chest. The perfectly cut blazer hugged her curves while the flimsy cream shirt underneath showed shadows of skin and bra.

My mouth watered; I swallowed hard against the urge to throw her over my shoulder and cart her back upstairs. Screw punishing her. It was fucking punishing me, too, and I'd had enough for one morning.

"Q. Crap, you scared the bejesus out of me." She rolled her shoulders, shedding the shock in her eyes, replacing it with interest and attraction. "I'll never get used to you moving so silently. You're like a freaking ghost."

I gave a rueful smile. "My silence comes in handy when I want to be unheard." I stepped toward her, already sporting a rock-hard erection. "I like watching you while you think you're alone."

She bit her lip, prickling with energy. Her eyes locked onto my lips and I threw caution and resentment and every other fucked-up emotion I felt out the goddamn window.

I grabbed her by the back of the neck, jerking her toward me.

She gasped; her hands came up to steady herself on my chest. My skin electrified beneath her touch. I growled, "Turns out I'm punishing myself by punishing you." I ran my tongue over her bottom lip, nipping at her, teasing her. "I don't like it."

She sighed, pressing herself hard against me. She trembled as she rocked her hips against my leg. "Does this mean you'll let me come?" Her voice was a thread, aching with need.

I picked her up to throw her on the bed. I couldn't think straight; all I wanted was her pussy around my cock.

"Merde. Je suis désolé!" I'm sorry.

Tess froze in my arms, looking over my shoulder toward the open door. An embarrassed smile bloomed on her face; her cheeks flushed bright pink. "Morning, Suzette."

I groaned. That woman had the worst fucking timing in the world. I let Tess down, dragging out the moment, slinking her over my body.

She tried to stay composed in front of the staff, but her heartbeat thrummed in her neck and my eyes latched onto the small bite I'd given her. Her skin slightly shadowed from my ungentle fingers.

The moment Tess stood on her feet, I spun to face Suzette with eyes narrowed and frustration darkening my voice. *"Qu'est ce qu'il y a?"* What is it?

She ducked her head, smiling shyly at Tess behind me. Damn the sisterhood bond they had going on. I liked that Tess had friends. I liked that my staff loved her. But I didn't like being the third wheel, the one they'd talk about the moment I was out of earshot.

"The helicopter is waiting to depart. The captain asked me to come and find you. You missed takeoff over an hour ago."

Pushing up my cuff, I checked my Rolex—the same Rolex I stole from my father after I shot him in the head. Shit, I'd missed a morning meeting, too.

"Tell him we'll depart in fifteen minutes," I ordered, falling into hard-assed CEO mode.

Suzette scurried off, and I spun to face Tess. I couldn't stand to be around her; the need to molest her was too strong. Swallowing the urge, I pointed at the bite on her neck. "Cover that. I'll meet you downstairs in five minutes."

And I ran again. Like a fucking pussy.

I found the one I searched for in the reading nook on the second-floor landing. It overlooked the foyer, bright and airy—it was the perfect illusion of ultimate freedom, all the while remaining in the house.

"Morning, Sephena."

She flinched, hugging the latest fashion magazine to her chest and cowering in the chair. Her knee bones jutted starkly under the jeans I'd bought for her, and she refused to wear anything but baggy sweaters that hid her gaunt frame.

My hands curled into fists as anger seeped into me. The night Franco brought Sephena here she'd been dressed in a bikini that wrapped around her body like an Egyptian mummy. The sick bastards who sold her liked to unwind her, make her dizzy, poke and prod until she was naked and forced to do God knows what.

"Morning, sir." Her timid voice never rose past a whisper. She refused to make eye contact with me, preferring to dog-ear the corner of the magazine and hunch into a ball.

I hated the stench of fear, appalled by her destroyed soul and beaten body. The beast in me tucked its tail between its legs when faced with prey that was already broken beyond repair.

Damaged girls brought out the need to protect them from harm, but they also turned me off completely. I waged with wanting to save them and wanting to kill them just to put them out of their misery.

I stayed my distance, heading to the banister to give her some space. "Did you want me to call your husband? I'm sure he'd love to talk to you."

She shook her head violently, sending matted brown hair all around her face. Tears spilled instantly, tracking down her cheeks. "No! I can't. He can't see me like this. I can't. No... Please, don't make me."

I held up my hand, fighting the urge to run from such desperation. I couldn't run from this. This was the reason I existed. My one redeeming quality to make up for the evilness living in me. "You can stay here as long as you need. However, he does know you're here."

I called him the moment I learned her identity. The local police located her loved ones through a missing persons search. Sephena had been stolen from her husband while on their honeymoon in Greece.

Three fucking years she belonged to a whorehouse for upmarket businessmen. A place where no questions were asked, any freakish perversion was permitted, and all lips were sealed.

Sephena sat with tears dripping into her lap. In a horrible daydream, she morphed into Tess. Broken, undernourished, and shattered beyond my reach. The thought of Tess ever being that way choked my heart with such fear I couldn't breathe.

Tess will never be like Sephena. Tess is mine. I'll protect her forever.

I needed to leave. "If you want anything, please don't hesitate to ask. I won't rush you to talk to your husband, but soon you'll have to face your past and move on if you want to have any chance of happiness. You need those who love you, not to stay hidden in a rambling house like this." I gave her a soft smile and descended the stairs.

My thoughts turned to Tess. She would work for me and it would be a relief of sorts. It would be good to have a diplomatic relationship. Purely business. I wouldn't be able to touch her. She'd be my employee—completely off-limits.

Maybe then my brain would finally see her as something other than a strong-willed woman who I longed to break. Maybe I could force myself to change by acknowledging she was my equal.

You'll still want her blood, you bastard.

I sighed heavily.

Even if we did work harmoniously together, it meant a whole other issue of office gossip. How would I ever explain to my staff why the woman I lived with couldn't sit down without wincing, or why she had to apply makeup on her neck to keep certain marks hidden?

"I said I'd fight for you. That you deserved to be fought for. You're worth every fight. Every argument and bump in the road. I'll fight because I'm falling for you, Q." Tess's voice popped into my head.

Did she truly mean that? I couldn't be honest with her though. I'd murdered my father, buried my drunken lout of a mother, and fucked a slave when I freed her, all because my willpower had an expiration date. She'd hate me. *I* hated me. No. Tess would never know. It was better that way.

The one person who knew everything was Frederick, and one was more than enough. Even Suzette and Franco didn't have a clue what had truly happened.

I preferred to live in the dark. On my own. I didn't want Tess to know the real me. She'd run. She'd break her promises and leave. And that was completely unacceptable.

Giggling greeted my ears as I entered the lounge, heading for the kitchen. I kept my face blank, even though I wanted to scowl when I found Tess and Suzette, leaning close, hands around steaming coffee cups.

"So you're going to *Moineau* Offices? Are you scared?"

"Scared? Why would I be?" Tess asked.

"Well, dealing with Q at home is bad enough. Working for him—" Suzette's eyes flew up, connecting with mine.

This time I didn't hold back and glowered with every fucking annoyance I felt. "Are you quite done, Suzette?"

She flushed a bright shade of maroon and darted into the pantry.

Tess laughed, taking a sip of her cappuccino. "No need to laser-beam the poor woman with your eyes. She was only making sure I was mentally prepared."

I huffed, stalking toward the already poured and perfectly made latte. Suzette may not know when to keep her bloody mouth shut, but she made a damn good coffee.

The sun warmed the top of my head and shoulders through the skylight and the kitchen glittered in the morning light.

Tess never took her eyes off me as I sipped the hot liquid. I kept myself guarded. The way she sat with her elbows on the table and cup to her lips caused her shirt to gape, showing glimpses of her bra and barely covered breasts.

Teases of red from whip marks made my cock thicken in my pants and all I wanted to do was grab a knife, slice off her clothing, and fuck her.

My legs locked into place as the need to savage her built behind my eyes. Every part of me felt wrong—not complete until I took her. Took her screaming and moaning and crying out for more.

Fuck, I wanted her pussy to clutch around me. I wanted to douse her insides with cum so she smelled like me all day long.

Think of something else. Sephena. Think of the poor broken women who dealt with bastards like you and didn't survive.

That put a stop to my lust, but only enough so I didn't fuck Tess in front of the staff.

Goddammit, I'd have to keep my distance the entire day to resist fucking her in public.

Suzette wandered out of the pantry, her arms laden with flour and other ingredients. Her body rolled in on itself, trying to be as small as possible.

She sucked in a shaky breath. "I'm sorry, master. I didn't mean to speak out of turn." Her hazel eyes held the same crippled terror that used to haunt her when she first came to me.

I'd worked so hard to remove that fragmented look, the part of her that was defective—shattered by bastards who broke her bones for pleasure.

I put the coffee down and pinched the brow of my nose. I was on a roll today. Pissing everyone off and being an asshole. "I'm not angry. Everything's fine." I dropped my arm to pat her on the shoulder, but she shied backward, trembling.

Goddammit, she'd regressed. "Don't you *dare* fear me, Suzette. I will never hurt you."

Tess froze on the barstool, never taking her eyes off

Suzette. Anyone with half a brain could see she wasn't the same carefree woman who'd giggled only moments ago. She was a ghost of her former self. The beaten slave who was so badly mangled internally she would never have children.

My words seemed to sink in, and Suzette slowly nodded. Gradually her shoulders relaxed, and she placed the ingredients on the counter. "Sorry. Momentary lapse, that's all."

"Are you okay?" Tess whispered.

My eyes shot to her. Her body had mirrored Suzette's—tense, hunched, protective from whatever enemy they feared. Tess hadn't told me what happened in Mexico, but if she ever did, I wouldn't be responsible for the string of corpses that would be left behind.

We'd made a vow to hunt the cocksuckers down, and I planned to start that journey today. We'd already waited too long.

Suzette shook herself, shedding the last remaining fear. "Of course. Ignore me. Pretend you never saw that." She waved her hand, laughing. It sounded genuine, if not for the brittle edge. "I'm going to get started on my to-do list. I'll see you when you come back tonight."

Without another word, she bolted from the kitchen and disappeared.

The second she left, the unfinished lust between Tess and I erupted into spine-tingling awareness. Tess took a breath, her coffee forgotten.

"You're the reason she's better. You're the reason she can laugh and enjoy life again." The awe in her voice touched me deeply. I'd never been proud of the man I was, but Tess's approval meant everything.

"It wasn't just me. She cured herself by finding another interest. Her healing hasn't been easy."

Tess shook her head, eyes glistening with reverence. "She wouldn't be alive if it wasn't for you." Her voice dropped to a husky rasp; my cock instantly reacted.

She hopped off the stool, moving toward me like a perfect

doll: blonde halo, porcelain skin, and thick lashes guarding the most stunning pair of eyes I'd ever seen.

The look she gave undid me.

She accepted me. She wanted me. She made me feel worthy.

I was struck dumb. I lost sensation of the warmth of my coffee cup. I forgot how to blink and breathe. All I could do was stare at the woman who was successfully breaking me into smithereens just by being alive.

What the fuck is happening to me?

The need between us crescendoed, arching like static electricity.

Tess's lips parted, and I couldn't look anywhere else. We took a step in perfect unison, compelled to be closer, unable to live with any distance between us.

I licked my lips, almost in physical pain with the need to kiss her. To whip her. Fuck her. Flay her. *Possess* her.

My chest pumped as I reached to capture the back of her neck. Her hair coiled upward, freeing her snowy skin. The urge to yank her into my embrace vibrated my muscles.

Images of ravaging her in the pantry flashed across my thoughts. We'd never make it to the bedroom. I needed her. That. Fucking. Second.

Tess was immobile, breathing shallow, the little buttons on her shirt strained against her breasts.

"I meant every word," I whispered. Ducking my head to nuzzle her throat, drowning myself in frost and scent that was uniquely Tess.

"Umm…" she moaned, reaching for my lapels, dragging me closer. I lost my footing, crashing into her, forcing her to back up and collide with the kitchen bench.

"You're my gravity. *Je suis à toi,*" I murmured. I'm yours.

How could I fuck this woman, sleep beside her, and care for her when I didn't even *know* her? My heart knew hers, my body belonged to hers, but I didn't own her mind.

And I wanted to. *Needed* to.

Grabbing her hips, I positioned her square with my cock. Her taut belly quivered as I pressed hard against her, pinning her against the counter. "I need to know you, Tess. I need to own every last thing about you."

Possessiveness snarled deep in my belly and muscles locked with anger. I wanted to own her past, her present, her future. I wanted to be her first and last and fucking forever. I wanted to wipe everything from her life where I wasn't the centre point of her evolution.

Fuck.

My lips crashed down on hers, and we moaned loudly. Her hands disappeared around my waist, frantically trying to pull my shirt from the waistband.

Her tongue entered my mouth with no apology, stealing every rational thought. She demanded anger. She demanded feral and brutal, but for once—for the first time ever—I wanted to kiss her sweetly.

I couldn't stop the low chuckle escaping me.

She broke the kiss, an eyebrow quirked.

I shook my head, still lightheaded from the taste of coffee and Tess in my mouth.

"Nothing," I muttered.

"You can't laugh mid-kiss and refuse to tell me, Q." One of her hands came around the front of my trousers, dropping to cup my cock.

I flinched, bowing closer as she tugged me hard. "I want to know."

The beast inside roared, and I fought the urge to slap Tess's hand away. She was getting too bold around me. She wasn't frightened enough to satisfy the sickness inside, but at the same time, her touch turned me on beyond belief.

Gone was the compulsion to be sweet. Sweet, tender... I spoke three languages, but I failed to understand those words. Whatever lurked inside would never learn them. It was a moment of insanity to think otherwise. But I wanted to keep Tess in one piece and to do that, I had to tame myself. No matter how much the leash would hurt.

Rocking back, I broke Tess's hold on me and picked up my coffee. I gulped it back, welcoming the scald on my tongue—the pain helped ground me. It wiped away frivolous emotional thoughts and made me regroup.

Work.

I had to focus on work. Not this woman who turned my thoughts and body against me. Avoiding Tess's gaze, I placed the empty coffee cup in the sink. "We have to go. We're late as it is, and God knows what's happened with my company these last four days."

I buttoned up my blazer buttons and smoothed the silk teal tie.

Risking a look at Tess, my throat closed taking in her glare. Her face was flushed, feverish; her eyes bright, shooting blue-grey lightning bolts right into my cock.

"I'm in agony, Q. I need some relief. You can't expect me to spend the day by your side and not go out of my mind." She came closer, but I captured her hands, keeping them from destroying my self-control.

"Please, *please*, fuck me."

Goddammit, how could I refuse that? How could I refuse my own body?

Red haze tinted my vision and the beast snarled deep within.

Fuck everything.

I'd give her what she wanted. What *I* wanted. What we needed.

"Sir, your flight is ready to take off." My chin whipped up to find Franco, head of my security and annoying son of a bitch, in the middle of the lounge. He bowed his head, brushing a hand over his amused grin. His green eyes never looked away though, knowing exactly what we were up to.

Merde. I'll have to fire all my staff if I want to have Tess naked again. All of them were determined to keep me from her.

"Fine. We're coming," I growled.

Franco covered his chuckle as he turned and left. Bastard.

Turning to Tess, I asked, "Are you ready to go?" My voice was gruff, cold. But only because I had so much frustration inside. All I wanted to do was slide deep inside her. I wanted to hang her from the ceiling in the harness and lick her pussy until she cried.

Tess narrowed her eyes, her hands curled into small fists. Small tremors of need skittered over her skin and her entire demeanour flared with annoyance. "As ready as I'll ever be."

My eyes shot to hers, trying to read her second meaning. I had no doubt there *was* a second meaning.

Her face said nothing, but her body spoke volumes.

And it said fuck me.

Four
Tess

Save me, enslave me, you will never cave me.
Taunt me, flaunt me, kill whatever haunts me...

Two words.

Love: The most spectacular, indescribable, deep, euphoric, unconditional acceptance of someone.

Hate: An intense dislike; an elevated level of anger; an unnatural emotion of inexplicable temper.

Both those words were defined, but if I existed this way for much longer, I would lose the meaning completely.

Love and hate.

Love and hate.

I both loved and hated Q with an ever burning passion.

Love was something I'd only ever had glimpses of: brotherly love for Brax, my girlfriendly love for friends at university. I never felt love for a family member. Not once did I have a rush of kinship in my entire childhood.

I existed in a loveless void until Q bulldozed his way in with his anger and twistedness.

What I felt for Q exceeded the realms of love in my mind. I *wanted* to love him. I wanted to crack his cruel façade and help him learn to love me back. I wanted to love his darkness, as well as bring him some light.

I swallowed back the weird giggle bubbling in my chest. *I'm the love cripple trying to teach a loveless monster.*

But none of that mattered, because he was set on torturing me. Twice he almost gave in to the gravity-altering pull between us and twice he let an interruption halt it.

An interruption shouldn't matter! He should've demanded more time—after all, he was the boss—and finished what he started this morning.

His punishment was the worst I could've ever imagined, and my stomach growled with hunger and indigestion from being so tightly wound. I couldn't eat. I couldn't think. I could barely sit still or walk straight.

My head pounded with excess energy, body twinged and throbbed with the need to release. My hands itched to touch myself. He shattered my willpower.

"Be careful." Q took my hand as I climbed the helicopter steps and entered the first chopper I'd been in in my life. The sleek black machine, emblazoned with Q's initials and a flock of gold-gilded sparrows, was stunning, but the inside was incomparable.

I slammed to a halt, my jaw hanging wide.

Everything about Q vibrated wealth. He wasn't flashy, he wasn't ostentatious. It was ingrained into his pores as much as his heady citrus scent. So why I let the interior of a helicopter floor me and make me hyperaware of Q's bank balance, I didn't know.

Q pushed me forward, moving me out of the way.

I looked around in wonder at the four impeccable black leather chairs. They faced each other in pairs with crimson stitching and armrests full of dials for massages and who knows what.

"Do you like it?" Q smiled, taking a seat in one of the huge chairs. "I was lucky enough to secure one of the prototypes. It's a Bell 525 Relentless." He stroked the leather while his face softened. "I may spend the majority of my wealth on other hobbies—" his voice tightened mentioning the sex trade industry—"but I like nice things. And I like procuring things others haven't owned before."

The ulterior message that Q liked unsullied—that he prized what was untouched and pure—wasn't lost on me. Too bad I wasn't a virgin for him—did he hate that I'd been used before? I stopped that train of thought. It hurt too much.

Ignoring his gaze, I tottered forward in my stilettos, the heels sinking into the thick, dark strands of luxury carpet. I couldn't think of a more aptly named helicopter: the Relentless. Exactly like its new owner: relentless in breaking me, owning me, *torturing* me.

A flatscreen TV graced one wall along with a panel full of dials and gadgets that I daren't touch.

"It's lovely," I whispered.

A loud masculine laugh rang around the enclosed cabin. "Just lovely? Hell, if you don't respect the bird, you can catch a cab to Paris."

Q chuckled, flicking his gaze to a man who'd appeared at the top of the steps. Decked out in full pilot regale, his black hair was covered with a beret and his dark brown eyes twinkled.

"It's nice to know you appreciate her as much as I do, Mr. Murphy." Q's voice echoed through my bones, activating my trembling core all over again.

I bit my tongue to stop the low moan and forced myself to smile. "It's a gorgeous piece of aviation. I'm looking forward to flying in style."

Mr. Murphy bowed his head, touching the edge of his pilot's cap. "I should think so, ma'am." He flashed me a smile and turned his attention to Q. "If you're ready to depart, I suggest we leave now, sir. Winds are good, and flight time should be about thirty-three minutes."

Q nodded, waving him away. "You're free to take off." His sharp jade eyes darted to me, and I suffered an instantly dry mouth. The taste of him lingered on my tongue. I wanted nothing more than to have him use me again.

His lips twitched and the cabin pressurized with whatever thoughts Q indulged.

"Please don't disturb us, captain. I have a lot of work to catch up on. I trust you'll get me to my office in time, without needing to communicate."

The captain shot me a quick stare before nodding and backing down the stairs. "No problem, sir. As you wish."

"Oh, and Mr. Murphy?" Q ran a fingertip over his bottom lip, deep in whatever thoughts he entertained.

The captain paused, his body poised. "Yes, sir?"

"I'm locking the connecting door." His head tilted, body language projecting a simple warning. "We aren't to be interrupted. Understand?"

The captain didn't look at me this time, for which I was thankful. My heart raced a gazillion beats a minute, and I couldn't suck down gluttonous breaths without swimming with need.

Q didn't move a muscle, locked tight in his chair.

The captain nodded again. "No problem at all. I'll see you in Paris." He swung the fuselage door closed. The sound of the lock stole the ability to stand up. My knees wobbled sending me sprawling into a chair.

Locked inside a tiny space with Q for half an hour.

Oh, God. *I'll end up humping his leg, or worse, sitting on his face.* I started to hyperventilate. I wasn't strong enough to endure his punishment. I'd crack. No doubt. *I'm already cracking.*

The chair enveloped me in five-star comfort, but I could've floated in gossamer and clouds for all I cared—it would've still irritated my skin, set fire to my extremities. Just like the hated tight skirt and silky pantyhose. Every twitch, every movement, flared the whip marks on my thighs—a direct link to the burn between my legs.

I would never feel normal again. I descended into the realm of lunacy.

Lunacy.

That's what I felt for Q.

Love and hate entwined so intrinsically, plaiting together into one sharp-edged, life-consuming feeling.

Q had created an entirely different emotion—one I'd never be free of: utter madness. I would never be free from the craziness of falling for a beast.

I dropped my eyes, realizing I stared at Q with my face projecting every racing conclusion.

"What are you thinking?" he asked, keeping his voice low and coaxing. If anything, it was worse than his normal volume. It whispered under my clothes, licking around my nipples.

I clenched my thighs together, glaring at my hands in my lap. Tears bruised my eyes; self-pity made me shake. I'd never wanted an orgasm so much in my life.

The sound of heavy machinery cranking shook the helicopter. The rotor blades picked up speed within a moment.

"Tess…" Q shifted forward in his chair, linking his hands between his open thighs. The position was so like when he put the tracker on my ankle when we first met that I whimpered. Even that first meeting, I'd been wet for him. My body had no self-control toward this man. He made me weak. He made me *dependant.*

"Nothing. I'm thinking nothing." My stomach swooped into my feet as we took off with an all-powerful soar. The helicopter acted as if it had wings, not metal blades keeping it airborne.

Q never took his eyes off me, frozen into position; the only thing that changed was his fingers. They grew white with how hard he clenched.

His proximity made me shiver and ache and scream inside. My body was swollen and driving me to the point of insanity with the need to release.

I'm sick. I must be. No person could make another exist in heightened flames of lust. I had a temperature, my mind consumed with my fucking obsession that was Q.

Q sucked in a breath before unlocking his unsteady hands

and reclining into the chair. "Are you feeling okay, Tess?" His eyes were guarded, face closed to me, but his body fermented with tightly reined lust.

I snorted loudly, twitching in the chair, cursing the lashes on my thighs, hexing Q for leaving me this way. "What the hell do you think?"

Q didn't move for a full minute. One torturous minute while our eyes locked and our minds connected and our subconscious bellowed at each other. Our minds made love, we ravaged, we ruined, all while not touching. But it wasn't enough.

It accelerated my heart. It made my pussy seep eager wetness. It pretzeled my mind into someone I no longer recognised, but it didn't give me what I needed.

"Why did you tell the captain not to disturb us?" My voice was barely noticeable over the rotor blades, but Q heard me.

He stilled, surging with carnal tension. He watched me from a lowered brow, letting me trap myself, walk right into whatever web he cast. "Why do you think, *esclave*?"

Esclave. The one word that was hyperlinked to my pussy.

My eyes snapped shut as a wave of my denied orgasm clutched my entire body.

Oh, fuck. Fuck me, I couldn't do it.

"I'm done," I choked, twisted with longing and fogged with confusion. "I'm going insane!" I grabbed a handful of hair and pulled, trying to find some relief from the ceaseless buildup.

But the pain only amplified my desire, sending another throb pulsating through my body.

The helicopter blades whirred and wound the cabin with sexual tension. Q sucked in a breath, straining against his suit. He sat so still and looked so unaffected. It wasn't fair. He came. He came all down my throat and all over my breasts. *It's my turn, dammit!*

I was too far gone—too consumed by a bodily need. Scrambling out of the luxury leather, I dropped to the carpet and crawled.

I fucking crawled in a two thousand euro designer skirt, zeroing in on the one person who held my cure.

Q's face shot to unreadable, pale eyes glowing in the morning sunlight from the window. His lips parted, sucking in a noisy breath. "Get up," he growled.

I whimpered and shook my head, keeping my shoulders hunched as I traversed the small distance. Every whiplash, every bead bruise, every cell in my body throbbed.

He sat straighter, using the armrests to hoist himself upward. His fingers turned white around the leather, gripping hard. "Stop. Have I ever asked you to crawl or be any less than a woman?"

His face grew black with fury as I slowed and knelt between his open thighs. His body heat murdered the rest of my coherent thought. He wanted to own me? He *possessed* me in that moment.

I raised my eyes, fearful of what I would see in his. Then I jumped as he reached down and grabbed my triceps.

"Fuck," he muttered, his fingers biting deep. But I didn't care. I didn't care because my master was touching me, and my body was too swept up in pleasure to be scared of Q's wrath. He teased me, used me, and denied me this morning. I couldn't be expected to work, or function as a human being without him saving me from this pleasurable agony.

Soaring high above patchwork farms, quaint villages, and thatched cottages, I bared my soul to him. "I didn't mean to take control away from you. I wanted to give you pleasure. I wanted to show how much I care, how much I believe in you."

Q shook, his face darkened further; his fingers turned to talons, cutting off the blood supply around my arms. "You took away my control. Do you know what happens to women like you if I lose it?" He shook me. "It's the one thing I've been able to rely on my entire life, and yet you shattered it with my balls in your hands." No other man had a voice like Q. Dark, dangerous, laced with a melodic French accent. Being reprimanded by him was pure audio perfection.

He stood suddenly, hauling me to my feet. I wobbled in his grip, staring into his turbulent eyes. *"Pourquoi tu dois me pousser comme ça?"* Why must you push me so?

"Because I need to break you to make you mine." My voice thickened with strength. It was true. More than I knew.

Not caring that Q might make my punishment worse, I wriggled in his grip until his fingers loosened. The moment my arms were free, I reached for my top button and undid it with rattling fingers.

Q's eyes dropped to my chest, absorbed by my jerky fingers.

My body was heavy, melting, sparking with the closeness, the threat of being taken. I would make Q fuck me. I would.

He didn't try to stop me as I unclasped the remaining buttons and pulled the soft material from my waistband. I stood in front of him, shirt spread to reveal the black lacy bra with tiny diamantés on the straps.

With my pulse skyrocketing, I traced a cross over the swell of my breast, directly above my heart. "I give you my oath that I will obey you. I won't force you to give me what you're not ready to give."

Q stopped breathing; his eyes locked onto my exposed skin. His wet tongue licked his lips, tasting me from head to toe without even moving. My eyes dropped to his trousers, a heady thrill heating me at the hard bulge straining against the material.

The helicopter banked to the left, sending us leaning into the curve. His gaze connected with mine and the lust simmering in his eyes changed from pale to glowing, burning, searing.

His hand shot out and captured my chin, holding me tight. His chest pumped and the cords of muscle in his neck shot into stark relief. *"Esclave—"* His voice positively stroked my pussy, rippling over my skin.

My mind swam, and I rushed to finish what I wanted to say. "I promise to obey, but I don't promise I won't make your life hell. You swore you'd give me what I needed. You broke your oath because I need you now. I need you so much I can't think straight. I need your tongue. I need your fingers, your cock, your voice, your scent. I need you all over me, in me, and around me." I panted by the time I finished.

He didn't move, eyeing me as if I were a messy business merger that refused to go his way.

"Did you stop to think for a moment why I asked the captain for privacy?" Bowing his head, he kissed the concealed bite he gave me earlier. "It's because I know the pain you're in. I'm just as tortured. If I didn't fuck you before we got to Paris, we would both end up in national news for public indecency. I'm done, too, Tess."

He ran his nose up my neck, heading toward my ear. I shivered when he nipped at my lobe. *"Arrêter de me supplier, je vais te baiser"* Stop begging, I'm going to fuck you.

It wasn't Q who lost it this time. It was me.

I launched into his arms, climbing him, scratching in urgency. My lips descended on his, and for the first and probably only time, I initiated sex between us. And for one precious moment, he let me take from him.

The moment my tongue entered his mouth, he snapped.

My stomach rolled, and I found myself flat on my back on the helicopter's carpeted floor. Q cradled my head so I didn't knock myself out, and somehow he kept the brunt of sprawling backward to a minimum. But that was as far as his chivalry went.

The moment he had me beneath him, he kissed me like a monster possessed. His tongue speared my lips and stole every last drop of oxygen in my body. My eyes slammed closed, and I clawed at his immaculate suit.

I need this off. I need his skin.

Every part of me boiled; desperation made me feral. I grabbed his tie, pulling him so hard against me, my breasts bruised and my neck, already tender from strangulation, spasmed with pain.

Q bit my lip, not drawing blood, but in a warning to let him go. He reared back on his elbows, digging his hips harder into mine. "You're determined to make me hurt you. I'm trying so fucking hard, but you don't seem to care. You're reckless with your life, *esclave*, so why should I hold myself back?"

My blood thrilled, summoning every dark recess to gush with want. "If by hurting me I get to possess you in return, then yes, I'm reckless, but only because I need you like I need air."

"You need this?" His eyes glinted as he rolled his hips against my pinned legs. The tight skirt held me hostage when all I wanted to do was open my thighs and welcome him to take.

I wished Q had a pair of silver scissors to cut me free, tear off my fanciful knickers, and fuck me like the slave I wanted to be for him.

"How much do you need to be fucked, Tess?" His head lowered to graze along my cheek, breathing me in. "How crazy does it make you, thinking about my cock deep inside, pounding you, stretching you?"

My complete education flew out of my mind. Speech was an impossibility as images of Q slamming into me berated my thoughts.

I cried out as he shifted and caught my barely covered nipple in his teeth. I bowed as his hot mouth closed over the highly sensitive nub, and my pussy squeezed.

"I think you need me badly. I think I need to show you how good my cock can feel."

"Please. God, yes. Show me. Now."

He collapsed on top of me, lips crushing mine. I opened my jaw wide to submit to his all-demanding kiss. Q panted, running his hands all over my body. His five o'clock shadow acted like match paper to my spark. We detonated. Had the helicopter plummeted to earth, we wouldn't have noticed. We were wrapped up, consumed by each other.

Q broke the kiss, levering himself off me.

Breathing ragged, he ordered, "Get on all fours."

When I didn't move fast enough, he grabbed my hips and flipped me over, hoisting my ass up until I rested on my hands and knees.

The second I was steady, urgent fingers pushed my tight skirt up and up, forcing it higher until the cute slit on the side split with a loud *crack*. "I want to rip this into shreds, but I can't have you showing the world what's mine." Q gave a final push and the skirt gathered on my hips.

The moment my ass was exposed, he spanked me hard, sending jolts of pain radiating through my body, but I existed on a painful plateau already, and his palm print bloomed into deliciousness.

My eyes glossed even as I pushed backward, imploring Q to strike again.

Vibrating with lust, he leaned closer and licked my smarting ass cheek, soothing away the sweet pain.

With a growl, he plucked the small G-string with his fingertips and pulled. The material tightened around my pussy, pinching my clit, making me burn. Then with a jerk of his head, Q sliced through the lace with his teeth and the G-string existed no more.

He brought the fabric to his nose and inhaled deep. "Fuck me, you smell *incroyable*." With a dark glint in his eye, he balled the scrap of lingerie and shoved it in his pocket. He caught me watching over my shoulder and said, "Now I'll always have you close, *esclave*."

My cheeks flared, but my heart fluttered just the same. Q wanted a part of me on him at all times. I wanted the same thing. I wanted to wear his scent. To wrap myself up in everything Q.

Q cocked his head and reached for his fly. Never dropping eye contact, he undid his belt buckle and slid it slowly from the waistband.

I started to shake. My fingernails clawed into the carpet, expecting another round of belt abuse. It'd only been four days since Q welcomed me home with the aid of his belt and some ice-cold champagne.

Q bared his teeth, eyes flashing with irritation. "I may be a lot of things, but I'm not such a bastard to hit you on top of bruises that are barely healed." Deliberately he tossed the leather to the side.

I didn't relax, and didn't know if I suffered regret or relief at his decency.

"I'm going to punish you in other ways. Face away." He motioned for me to look down and I unwillingly dropped my head.

Not seeing him was worse to my oversensitive body. Without knowing what he was doing, my imagination ran overtime.

The sound of a zipper coming undone sounded loud, even over the whirr of rotor blades. Q's hot, hard flesh connected with the back of my thighs as he pressed against me and jerked down his boxer-briefs in one swipe.

I moaned, rocking toward him. I thought his thighs were hot, but they were Antarctica compared to the inferno of his cock. It hung heavy and hard between my open thighs, teasing me to the point of mania.

He groaned, fisting his erection, dragging the head through my folds. "Fuck. Will I ever get enough of you?" As he spoke, he captured my clit with his thumb and forefinger.

I jerked and liquefied. My pussy rejoiced at finally having stimulation. Normally I'd need more than a simple touch, but this time just the thought of his hand on me summoned the orgasm that lived behind my eyes, in my blood, and deep in my core.

"Q…yes, Q."

He inserted the tip of his finger inside me before pulling back and replacing it with the thick head of his cock.

The heavenly bliss of being entered, expanded and stretched, sent my heartbeat whizzing. My head was too heavy to hold up, and I let it dangle, giving in to the overwhelming exquisite anticipation of Q fucking me.

He sank in another centimetre, his thighs rigid against mine. Another groan wrenched from his chest. "How is it I'm about to fucking come when I exploded in your mouth an hour ago?"

I bit my lip at the ragged wonderment in his tone. He wasn't asking me the question. It was rhetorical. He truly didn't understand the compulsion between us—I knew I didn't. There weren't words or rationality to explain our bond.

Happiness scorched through me like a sunrise. Me, Tess Snow, a woman from no worth or recognition, had a power over a sadistic legend like Q. And fuck, that turned me on.

Q spanked me again, slicing his large hand right across my ass. The previous belt marks awoke, tingling, searching for relief. Then he caressed me, leeching the heat away.

He repeated. Spank. Caress. Until my head swam and my pussy contracted around the small fraction of cock he let me have.

"Q!" I moaned. "Please. No more. I need you so much."

His fingers dipped between my legs. I cried out as he smeared wetness around my clit.

"Shit." Q's muffled curse caused sparklers and fireworks to fizz in my blood.

I pushed back, arching my spine. My lips parted; I didn't recognise the girl panting as if she'd run a marathon. All I cared about was coming.

"*Merde, esclave,* stop. For fuck's sake, you're ruining me." Even with the ferocity of Q's anger, I thrilled with the knowledge I was winning in some small measure—the former slave training the master. If I'd been a poet, I would've written how serendipitous it all was. How fate entwined and cursed us both.

Q gripped my hips, propping me higher. Pulling out, the heat of his erection nudged my ass; I jolted with urgency.

Sitting higher on his knees, Q muttered, "This is going to be fast and hard, and I don't want you to say a word, do you hear me?"

I nodded, breathless already. "I'll do anything you want, as long as you let me come."

"You can come, but only when I say." His nails imprinted crescent moons into my skin, digging deep. "But if you come before, I'll punish you worse. I won't feel regret or remorse. I'll find a way to punish you that doesn't make me suffer, too."

He rocked, and his cock eased down my ass, between my spread thighs, nudging my core.

Words were beyond me. I nodded wildly, scrabbling at the carpet. The strands wrapped around my fingers and I held on for dear life.

With urgent hands, Q untwisted my coiled ponytail and grabbed a handful.

With a jerk, he forced my head back. My spine arched as he plunged inside me.

Deep.

Hard.

Excruciating fullness.

I opened my mouth to scream, but he clamped a hand over me, riding me, containing my cries. "Shush, *esclave*. Not a sound, remember?"

The intrusion was pain personified, the rocking endless bliss.

The way he took me held no remnants of the sometimes sweet man beneath the blackness. This was purely brutal and dark and animalistic.

I loved it.

With his cock deep inside, his fist wrapped around my ponytail, and his other hand clasped over my mouth, he fucked me. Bucking so hard, carpet burn incinerated my pantyhose in a matter of seconds.

But every time he thrust, I pushed back to meet him. I bowed more than I'd ever bowed before, relishing in the burn of my hair being tugged. My lungs strained as Q grunted and rutted, taking me true to his word.

Little whimpers and mewls sounded low in my throat, but

Q captured every one.

My fingernails ached with how hard I dug into the carpet, and I flinched when Q let go of my hair to dig his nails deep into my hip, wrenching me backward, so his hipbones collided with my ass.

I groaned as his fingernails suddenly broke the thin barrier of skin, imprinting claw marks. Yet another autograph, another claim of ownership.

It unravelled me.

My pussy swelled and welcomed, it sparked and heated and melted. The orgasm started in my heart, working its way over my jaw, scalp, and spine. Every scorching trail it travelled, I trembled.

Don't come. Don't come.

The mantra was no use when every thrust of Q's cock overrode my commands. He owned me—it would be his fault I came.

"Take your punishment, Tess. Fucking take all of me." My mind screamed that I *had* taken all of him. His darkness, his worst, but he didn't mean spiritually. He meant purely physical.

He tugged on my hair again, pulling me onto my knees. Once upright, his arm latched around my chest while fingers twisted my nipple through the flimsy lace of my bra.

I reached back to weave my fingers into his hair, loving the silky thickness, the shortness, the manly feel of his scalp.

The moment he pinched my nipple, the first wave of my long-awaited orgasm swelled deep and strong in my belly. "Oh, God."

Q froze.

His cock twitched inside, throbbing with blood and unshed come, but he held himself dead calm, causing my orgasm to pop and fade.

I grabbed his ear, wanting to twist and scream that he finished what he started, but I didn't dare.

"Did you come, *esclave*?" His voice was breathless, sinfully hot on my nape.

I shook my head. "No, but, please. Let me, Q."

"You said those same words when you were chained and whipped in my bedroom. Remember how I fucked you with my tongue? How you rode my mouth with your legs on my shoulders?"

His voice painted far too vivid pictures in my head. I rocked back, sitting hard on his cock, causing his length to hit the top of my womb.

He gave a startled curse before his arms banded around me, forcing me to still. "Remember?"

"I remember. I want to do it again. I want your mouth on me."

"You'll have to earn it," he whispered, biting my ear, causing me to jolt in his hold.

He let me go with one arm and fumbled behind him. A moment later a flash of turquoise caught my eye as he captured my wrists, positioning them behind me.

My centre of gravity shifted as Q bound my wrists with his tie. With him deep inside and my hands restrained behind my back, I toppled forward. But Q caught me, helping steady me while lowering me to the floor. "Put your cheek on the carpet."

Letting me angle my head, Q waited before releasing me. Blood rushed to my temples, and my tender neck screamed, but I didn't make a peep.

My heart rate ratcheted as the helicopter swooped to the right. How close were we to Paris?

"Fuck, you look amazing like this. Tied up, impaled, completely at my mercy." He trailed a fingertip along the crack of my ass, working down until he touched where we joined. Warm wetness smeared both of us. He stole some of it to swirl around my clit.

My legs flinched, trying to close against the sudden intensity. "Q!"

"I'm going to fuck you now, Tess. Do not come until I tell you to."

True fear rose. I didn't have control of my body to

promise. I'd come on the first thrust. I bit my lip, preparing myself for the hardest obedience yet.

Q linked his fingers around the tie binding my wrists. Discomfort flared in my shoulders as my back arched, and legs splayed even further. The burn in my knees from the carpet turned my legs to fire.

The pace Q set was contradictory to what I expected. He started long and deep and slow. Luxuriating, languishing, pulling out almost to the tip, before slowly entering me again.

The thrice denied orgasm built again, coiling tighter with every stroke.

"Tonight, I'm going to tie you upside down and force you to drink my come, *esclave*. Then I'm going to eat you until you forget your own name."

Shit, Q's voice was an aphrodisiac. One more sentence and I'd explode.

"I'm going to do so many things to you. So many fucking sinful thi—" Q groaned, stopping mid-word as he thrust deep and hard.

He shattered the gentle rock, increasing the tempo until his balls slapped against my clit. I squeezed my eyes against the brain-warping need to come.

As Q lost himself in me, I lost myself to him. The sound of the helicopter faded away, and the most important thing in the world was the connection between us. The intrinsic link of male and female.

Q pinched my clit as he thrust violently, sending us forward a few centimetres. His hip bones bruised my ass as he turned savage. Gone were the long and measured thrusts. These were short and sharp and entirely explosive.

"Fuck, *esclave*. Fuck, yes." He let go of my bound wrists and spanked me once—hard and biting as he rippled inside; jets of hot come set off my own reaction, and I combusted.

The orgasm thundered into being but then teetered on edge, almost as if it expected to be denied again. The pain of being held in limbo made me cry out.

I writhed and bucked against Q's relentless pace.

"You have my permission. Come. Squeeze around my cock." Q thrust harder, stroking my clit until I had no choice but to fall.

I plummeted over the edge.

I surrendered to the pulsating waves of bliss.

My entire body contracted, and every part of me supernovaed into tiny particles. The little pieces of my soul collided, before reforming into something new.

My past no longer existed. My future was uncertain, but one thing was for sure, Q tumbled me headfirst into vulnerability, stripping me bare.

When the last tremor quaked through me, it ripped me apart, leaving my head swimming, lungs screaming, and my body completely limp. The sensation of being put back together after a world-altering orgasm brought me to tears.

I'd been reborn.

Q chuckled, still rock hard inside, but his voice sounded off as if he forced himself to speak. "I could come just from you milking my cock."

He pulled out and gently undid the tie from around my wrists. My body refused to move from the face-plant-ass-up position, and I moaned in pleasure as he wiped his come from between my legs with his expensive silk tie.

What just happened to me?

Once he finished, he stood and gathered me from the ground. Not meeting my eyes, he quickly secured his trousers and stuffed his tie into the same pocket that held my knickers.

His body was supple, sated, but his eyes were tight.

I reached to pull my skirt down, but he stopped me with his large hands. "Let me."

When our eyes connected, I stopped breathing. Whatever happened to me, he sensed it. He saw my confusion, my fragility.

His face danced with confliction along with a trace of self-loathing.

With aching tenderness, he smoothed down my skirt, frowning at the tear in the fabric he'd caused. We breathed each other as he carefully fastened the delicate buttons on my blouse. His hands were gentle and reverent as he repaired the damage, his knuckles brushing the sensitive flesh of my breasts.

His lips stayed tight in concentration, and I fell a little more.

Fell further into lunacy for this man who made me live.

When the last button was done he paused, not moving away. "Tess…"

I shook my head. Now was not the time to acknowledge what happened between us. I wanted to savour it. Protect it.

He nodded, eyes troubled. He guided me into a chair and did up my seat belt. Leaning over me, he gave me the sweetest smile, whispering, "I think we just joined the mile high club."

I laughed softly as he sat in his own chair and glanced out the window. He looked pensive, completely wrapped up in his thoughts. The air between us no longer seethed with sexual tension, it hummed with emotional connection.

I knew why Q looked quiet—it was because something deeper than just sex had happened. My mind felt it, my heart welcomed it—in the moment where Q made me splinter, I let down an unconscious wall. A wall that had been there my entire childhood—a foundation so I could have some sense of happiness, all while being unloved by my parents.

Q shattered that wall, and he felt it, too.

Something soft webbed between us, and I hoped it was the beginning of our future.

I sighed, resonating with bruises and aches.

High above the world, we were in perfect twisted harmony.

Five
Quincy

You crawled into the darkness, set my monster free,
so scream, bleed, call out to me, but never say stop,
never flee...

I'd done it.

I did what I was after—what the beast was after.

I broke her.

I damaged something deep within Tess, and it fucking butchered me. I wanted to apologise, to slam to my knees and beg for her forgiveness, but she shook her head when I began, shutting me out.

I didn't know what the fuck happened. Nothing outwardly changed, but something had crumbled—some barrier between us—some ledge we hadn't crossed.

As the helicopter began its descent from clouds to city, I beat myself up for punishing her. For demanding too much, too soon.

I fucking broke something deep inside her. *What if I've ruined everything?*

Risking a look at Tess, I flinched at the shadows around her neck and the fading carpet pattern on her cheek. Her eyes were closed with a tiny smile on her pink, perfect lips.

She'd removed her pantyhose to get rid of evidence of our in-flight entertainment and her skin was flushed.

My heart thudded hard, spreading foreign warmth through my body. The longer I stared, the more I wanted to wrap her up and keep her safe, but in the same thought, I wanted to kill and ruin anyone who came near her.

I wanted to highlight her bruises, mark her skin, so everyone knew she belonged to me. I wanted to brand her, to scar her, to wear her blood as a blatant warning to any man who ever looked in her direction.

Shit! I'm fucked up to want to hurt her so badly. I was right to send her back to Brax, and wrong to accept her back. She would never be free now. Not now I'd tasted her submission, felt the break in her psyche.

The delicious snap had sounded like a gong in my heart. I felt her break; I wanted to crawl deep inside her and find out what part of her yielded to me.

It was a sick addiction, and I wanted more. More. More. *More.*

I wouldn't be satisfied till I broke every barrier, consumed every thought.

Leaning forward, I put my head in my hands, trying to massage away the rapidly forming headache.

I'd always thought of myself as steel. Forged in hatred for my own father, sculptured by a will of iron to never bend to my heinous family traits. I'd always believed I was invincible. But I wasn't.

Turned out Tess was a furnace—the fucking kiln and smelter who gave no choice but to buckle and melt and turn into liquid.

Steel didn't change. It couldn't change its molecular structure, but liquid metal...it could. Other elements could be added, minerals removed, impurities purged, until an entirely new composite existed.

That's how I felt.

Melting, changing, evolving.

I just hoped I survived the transition.

"Bonjour, Mr. Mercer. *Directement au bureau?"* Straight to the office?

I scowled at the chauffeur. In his penguin suit and slicked-back hair, he looked like any other member of my countless staff on call to run me around, do errands, and make sure the fucking scary CEO of *Moineau* Holdings was happy.

I was never happy.

But today I was worse than normal. I was wound tight and confused, but I kept my tangled emotions hidden beneath a blank angry façade. *"Oui."* I smiled tightly in thanks, all the while wondering how the hell I was going to get through the day.

Ushering Tess off the helicopter and into the back of the Rolls-Royce Phantom, I tried to keep my hands soft instead of grabbing her and shaking the crap out of her. *Tell me what broke! Tell me if I ruined you.*

I wanted her to admit I ruined her as much as I hoped to fuck I hadn't. Would I ever have one thought that wasn't schizophrenic?

Tess slid onto the side seat, looking serene and content against the beige leather. She looked around, taking in the crystal bar, the big-screen TV, the decadence of such a vehicle.

"It's a morning full of surprises," she whispered.

I didn't think she meant for me to hear, but as I settled onto the backseat, I asked, "Care to tell me what the other surprises were?"

Perhaps the bit where you came undone, and it snapped so loudly, I heard it in my fucking soul?

I kept my balled hands hidden between my legs, portraying

the picture of calm and stability. When really I wanted to slap her and demand the truth.

But her entire demeanour turned languid and hard to read. She moved as if she had a delicious secret. She didn't move like a woman I'd destroyed.

Trying to tame my rapid heartbeat, I waited for her to answer. But she shook her head and looked out the window as the chauffeur started the car and pulled away. We were on a landing pad on top of a parking garage I owned. My office was next door. The inconvenience of driving the final three minutes paid in dividends for the use of roof space.

Tess picked up a champagne flute with a sparrow flying over a skyscraper etched into the glass. She ran her thumb over the engraving, turning to look at me. "Have I told you how much I love your logo?"

My lips twitched a little. I loved it, too. It took countless days, sketching frantically when I was sixteen, trying to figure out a sigil that I would wear with pride.

Every time I saw it I sat taller, embraced the hard work I did, all because it allowed me to free so many women.

Blondes, brunettes, young, and old.

Without this company—without my success—I wouldn't have been able to send so many home after a lifetime of torture. It wasn't often I felt proud. A man like me with so many demons lashing at his soul could never be truly proud of the human he was, but in that moment, I let myself be content.

"I'm glad you like it."

Suddenly, I regretted the four days with Tess I'd squandered. Instead of taking advantage of having her to myself, I'd buried myself in fucking paperwork, avoiding her questions, her requests for connection.

I'd blocked her off emotionally because I wasn't ready. *I'm still not fucking ready.*

But now it felt like such a waste. I could've found out everything about her—asked her multiple questions, until I possessed every inch, every thought.

And now it was too late. I let her free. She was no longer my prisoner, secreted away in my house to whip and fuck. She would become known by my staff. She would become a part of my business world.

My throat closed up. Sickness rolled in my stomach, and for the first time since I was a boy, I felt loss. The terror that Tess would find others better than me. That she might one day grow to hate me and share my darkest secrets with the world.

I hated myself for the thought. I could trust her.

But I didn't, and that one confession made me worse than every other fault combined.

Tess had accepted both me and my beast. She was falling in love with me. She had a power over me that no one else had before. And I didn't trust her.

Shit, I'm scum.

"I want to take you out to dinner tonight," I grumbled, trying hard to battle back the darkness.

Tess's eyes flew to mine. "Dinner? As in a date?" She laughed quietly. "It's a bit backward, don't you think? After you owning me and all."

My back stiffened and the blackness billowed, welcoming me back into its embrace. "I can take you to dinner without your permission. All I need to do is starve you until you fucking yield." The moment the words were out of my mouth, I rubbed my face, pressing my eyes with stabbing fingertips. *Goddammit.*

Sucking in a heavy breath, I amended, "I never owned you. I always intended to free you. I just—I couldn't. Not before I—" I couldn't finish, couldn't admit to wanting to completely destroy her before returning her to her tame little fuckwit of a boyfriend.

"I broke my own law by keeping you, but I gave you back to him before I took everything." I looked up, snarling. "I did the right thing!"

The same crushing weight I'd felt when I stalked from my bedroom the morning I sent Tess away, pushed me into the seat. I'd never felt so hopeless, so helpless, so alone as I did when I watched her plane take off.

Tess slid toward me, capturing my hand and running a gentle thumb over my knuckles. "I know you did the right thing. You wanted to protect me from you." Her voice helped ease the immobilizing weight in my chest. I risked looking at her.

"The thing is I didn't need protecting." She flashed me a bright smile, dispelling the angst between us. "I would love to go to dinner with you, Q."

Gravity shifted. Again. I dragged Tess into my lap, wrapping my arms tight around her. In my embrace, I held the moon and stars and planets. I held my future fucking happiness, and I'd kill myself if I ever fucked it up.

Tess wiggled in my lap, doing crazy things to my already swelling cock. "You don't have to starve me either, you know."

I snorted, dropping my head to inhale her crisp scent. In a moment of blinding honesty, I whispered, "Thank you. I'm still learning the correct etiquette for asking a woman out on a date."

She shifted, looking at me with wide eyes. "You've never—"

I shrugged. "How can I when I save broken slaves and pay professionals?" *Merde, I just admitted to using whores. Fuck me.*

Thoughts scattered over her face, a minor trace of disgust flickered in her eyes. She swallowed, visibly chasing the thoughts away. With an unsteady hand, she caressed my cheek, murmuring, "In that case, I'll make sure this is the best date you've ever had."

"Wow. This is amazing," Tess said, eyes wide as she took in the lobby of *Moineau* Holdings.

The floor was covered in tiny mosaics in greys and browns and blacks, depicting a perfect cloud of sparrows. The walls were white marble, so polished they bounced sunlight into every corner, highlighting a mishmash of paintings, sculptures, and water features.

I encouraged local artists to display and sell their work. I charged no commission, and it had become an unnamed art gallery and place to be seen.

Tess bewitched me as she inched forward, soaking in the impressiveness of the lobby.

Tonight.

Tonight I would take her out to dinner, and we'd have our first deep conversation about trivial things. I wanted to hear all her dreams and make them a reality. I wanted to crack her open and know every dark secret.

"This is all yours?" Tess broke into my daydream. Her face held awe while her eyes hid pain and unhappiness.

Why the fuck is she unhappy?

"It belongs to my company. Yes." I motioned for her to go to the left, and placed my hand on the small of her back to propel her forward. Such an innocent touch. So why did my cock twitch and my mouth water to taste her again?

We strode through the semi-crowded lobby to my private elevator. She asked, "Just how much do you own, Q?"

I swiped my clearance identification and pressed the lift button, before turning to face her. "Does it matter?" I cocked an eyebrow, watching her closely. It obviously mattered a big fucking deal.

Her eyes darted from mine as she bit her lip.

My stomach twisted. "Whatever is mine is yours. I signed the contract in blood, remember?" The memory of her arriving from Australia, sprouting all sorts of delicious promises, and slicing our palms with the paperknife to seal the deal, entered my mind. The confounding connection I'd felt when our blood smeared together had rocked me to my bestial centre.

The lift pinged, and Tess stepped inside in a daze.

The moment the doors closed, I imprisoned her chin with my fingers. "Don't. Whatever you're doing. Stop it."

She gave me a sad smile. "I'm just blown away. You'll have to give me time to get used to it." Her eyes dropped, but then met mine again with a vivid question in their grey depths. "Why me? Why did you let me into your life?"

I scowled, wanting to strike her for ever asking such a dumbass question. I never thought a woman could make me hate my wealth. My ability to do what I did was the one thing I lived for. But right then, I wanted to be penniless if it made Tess more comfortable.

I let go of her chin, running my fingers down her throat, along the valley of her breasts, over her stomach, veering toward her hip. I clenched my fingers hard around her hipbone, making her squeak.

Instantly the awareness between us sprung to a fever pitch. The lift filled with thick tension and my body grew heavy with lust. "You already know the answer, *esclave*." I rocked my hand against the five perfect fingernail marks. I knew they were there; I watched them bleed as I fucked Tess in the helicopter.

I branded her with yet another mark, all in the name of taming the beast, reminding him that she may hide our violent nature from others, but her skin bore the truth beneath her clothes.

"Q…" Tess battled with giving in to the burn of my fingers, or fighting me off. I didn't know which would win, and we stared, glared for a millennium, while I waited for her decision.

Taking the decision from her hands, I growled, "You need to accept this is all yours. I need you too badly to let you go." I backed her up against the mirrored wall. "Tell me why I need you, Tess. You know the truth."

Tess lowered her eyes, her thick lashes causing shadows to dart over her cheeks. She looked so demure, so innocent and fucking fragile.

My semi-hard cock thickened to full mast in a millisecond.

97

I would never be satisfied around this woman. All I wanted to do was push her against the wall and wrap her legs around me. I wanted to be buried so fucking deep inside her, she would never contemplate asking me *why her* ever again.

Why her? Because she made me fucking happy for the first time in my sorry existence. She made me stronger, more grounded...more *right*.

Her gaze connected with mine, glazing with glittering lust and need. Her breathing grew shallow and my eyes dropped to her breasts, seeking out her hard nipples beneath her flimsy shirt.

"You need me like I need you. I get it," she murmured.

I ducked and nuzzled her throat, teeth aching to break her skin and lick. "And why is that?" My hand reached to cup her neck, not squeezing—just a gentle coax, reminding her she was in my power.

Her mouth opened and her body melted against mine. "Because..."

My body burned for her; my ears strained for her answer. "Because..." I licked her lips, begging her to finish her sentence. I had to hear why she cared. It meant the world to me.

My stomach tensed, recognizing yet another change in me. I would never have cared about another person loving me before. Now, I needed it more than anything. I would never be able to remove the dark tendencies I'd lived with all my life, but I slowly grew a capacity for calmness.

Almost as if the monster took what it needed, then gave me a brief respite where I could be the love-struck, considerate man I wanted to be for her.

Tess kissed me back, whispering into my mouth.

"Because you're my monster in the dark, and I'm yours."

Six

Tess

Strip me bare, pull my hair, I don't care, just take me there.
I need that high, I need that pain, it's the only thing that keeps me sane...

The lift doors opened, breaking our moment.

Q sighed, letting me go with a grimace. It looked as if he couldn't stand the thought of not touching me.

I knew how he felt. Whatever existed between us was growing fast, and I didn't want to move. I wanted to stare into his eyes and try and decipher him.

Q stepped out first, opening another door only a metre or two away. It wasn't pretty. It wasn't designer. In fact, the heavy riveted metal looked tarnished and weather worn.

"Where are we?" I asked as I disembarked the lift.

He smiled and undid the door handle, pushing the metal open. Instantly, sun beamed into the gloomy space, and I squinted in the glare.

"Come on. I'll show you where I spend most of my time."

Q beckoned me to follow, and I couldn't believe my eyes. I'd died and gone to heaven. Literally.

I stepped over the threshold and gasped. The entire Parisian skyline was there for my viewing pleasure. I ghosted forward, not aware of moving until I stood on the edge of the roof with the cosmopolitan city spread before my feet.

My eyes popped wide. I hadn't walked over concrete, but the softest, brightest green grass I'd ever seen. Wildflowers, bonsai, and fully grown fruit trees ringed the roof, shading little sitting areas and water features.

Nestled in the middle of such an urban wilderness was a white sparkling building with glass walls all around.

Q came toward me, bringing with him the noise of wingbeats and small updrafts of feathers.

I ducked as a flurry of pigeons, blackbirds, and sparrows took flight over my shoulder, scattering from the garden into the limitless sky.

I spun to Q, trying to understand this place.

He grinned, eyes glowing with such blazing intelligence it floored me. This man ran a worldwide company. He dedicated his life to helping others, all the while hating himself for his downfalls.

I meant what I said—why me? What did I ever do so special to deserve him?

Only someone perfect and worthy and conflicted enough to understand him was worthy of all this. I hated my doubt—hated my need to hear him say he was falling for me, too.

Some part of me worried I'd never hear those words from him.

"Welcome to my office." He fanned his arms wide. "I think it's a much better use of space than a boring helipad." He strode toward the building, sitting so proud, like a crown on top of his empire. "Shall we?"

I nodded and followed Q to his domain. A few brave birds alighted on the grass as we left them in peace.

This place was a sanctuary for wildlife in the heart of the city. The analogy didn't escape my mind—Q built an oasis wherever he went, looking after those that needed the space to heal and be free.

As enamoured as I was with Q, and as much as he fulfilled me, gave me everything my sick, twisted little soul could want, he drove me insane. I wanted into his head. I wanted to know every minute detail about him, and yet he didn't trust me. That splintered my heart, and I wished I could prove my devotion to him. That I would never spill his secrets or cast blame on his perversions. I didn't like that he might never fully open up, that I may never completely understand the man who possessed my heart.

Q stopped just outside the building, holding out his hand.

I stopped short, eyeing it warily, so conditioned to expect pain or pleasure from his touch.

He huffed, gritting his jaw. "You refuse to do something as simple as hold my hand?" Hurt shadowed his gaze, and he let his arm fall.

I rushed closer and took his palm, squeezing it hard. "I'd never refuse you anything. I'm just not used to something so…normal from you." I gave him a shy smile, linking my fingers with his until we were locked together.

Holding Q's hand was so completely different to anything I'd experienced. Brax used to hold me sweetly, our palms a little sweaty—a boy and a girl fumbling with growing up.

Q held me with possession, and the rough-softness of his skin set my teeth on edge and my pulse catapulting. He was pure man. A dominant male who expected explicit compliance, all the while searching for a thread of retaliation. A complete contradiction—a man with two desires.

He held my heart, rather than my hand.

Q tugged me closer until our hands were wedged between our torsos. "I'm glad you're here," he whispered.

I gulped, drowning in his citrus and sandalwood. Most of the time we fought with dagger and claw, and yet in that moment, the intensity simmered to flowers and petals.

For the first time ever, our connection was sweet.

"Don't go dreamy eyed on me, Tess. I'm feeling

sentimental. That's all. Don't get used to moments like this. You'll be sorely disappointed." He untangled his fingers from mine and stalked into the building, leaving me shocked and alone.

Had I done something, or had Q realized how tender the moment was and freaked? I guessed the second one was more likely.

I had a good mind to steal Franco's gun and hold Q hostage so I could stand a chance of getting into his head. Every time I was close to breaking through, he ruined it.

Sighing, I entered the open and airy office and froze on the spot.

Ice.

Terror.

Utter, heinous foreboding.

My limbs locked in place, and my instincts blared on high alert. The message was simple:

Run.

Run far, far away, and don't come back.

Run, Tess!

It was the same body-steeling compulsion that made me so afraid in Mexico. My body quaked as I locked my legs from turning around and throwing myself off the building.

Q didn't matter. The sun or knowledge that nothing evil resided here didn't matter. All I saw was darkness and blackness and the stench of death.

Run!

I cried out, clamping a hand over my mouth, crumbling into a ball.

"You've got nice tits. You can't hide them forever. Get in the shower and wash your filth." Leather Jacket's voice roared into my head. My healed rib bellowed in memory of him kicking me.

"Accept that you are no longer a woman. You are merchandise. And merchandise must have a barcode for sale," Jagged Scar muttered, just as the pain of the tattoo gun shredded my wrist.

No! Stop.

I'm safe. I'm safe. It's not true.

"Shit, Tess. What the fuck?" Q plucked me from the ground, hoisting me off my feet. Cradling me, he carried me further into the building before sitting on a white canvas couch.

Let me go. I couldn't be there. I couldn't. Ice cubes lived in my blood, greyhounds raced in my legs, wanting nothing more than to sprint.

I tried to get my panicked breathing under control, but my mind was back in Mexico, back with countless other women whose fate might have ended by now. I wanted the assholes who took me to die. I wanted to be the one who stole their lives, just like they stole others.

"Tess. Tess!" Q's voice was far away and I latched onto it, gulping in oxygen, swimming hard against the panic.

Something fierce and hot struck my cheek; it helped chase my nightmares back into the depths.

Q rocked me, crushing me against his powerful chest. "That's it, *esclave*. Come back to me. Don't you dare fucking leave me."

My ear pressed against his suit and the loud rush of his pounding heart brought me back to reality. I sucked in one last wavering breath and opened my eyes.

I tensed, waiting for the room to send me reeling back into a psychotic breakdown, but it stayed bright and airy and completely innocent.

Q froze, letting me go, watching me with piercing eyes. *"Est ce que ça va ?"* Are you all right?

When I didn't answer, he launched into a string of angry French. *"C'est quoi ce bordel, esclave? Est-ce que tu peux me dire pourquoi tu as eu cette absence? Est-ce que tu me caches quelque chose? Tu as besoin d'aide? Pourquoi tu ne me dis rien!"* What the fuck happened, *esclave*? Care to tell me why you had a breakdown? Have you been hiding this from me? Do you need help? Why didn't you tell me!

I flinched against his anger, hanging my head. "I'm sorry. I don't know what happened." Images of Suzette suffering her own attack flickered into my mind. "Maybe it's an episode? You know, leftover feelings from my past?"

He scooted me off his lap and onto the couch. The moment he was free, he moved to sit on the coffee table, shoving away large folders and binders.

He kept his hands to himself, almost as if he couldn't touch me without wanting to break me in half.

"Have you had them before?" His nostrils flared, his entire frame trembling with aggression.

I shook my head, telling the truth. I'd never suffered so violently before. Sure, I had nightmares of the kidnapping and rape, but Q was always there to save me. This was entirely new.

I hated the feeling of being so afraid. I cursed Brax for taking me into the café and for not being strong enough to save me. I wanted to tear each bastard who hurt me into little tiny pieces. I wanted their hearts on a stick. I wanted to live without the awful memories.

But if you didn't suffer, you would never have been sold to Q.

My eyes widened. After everything—dealing with beatings, degradation, and being tagged like a dog—life rewarded me with my deepest desires. Did fate extract a horrible toll, all in the name of granting my ultimate wish?

"Suzette lets my temper affect her. What was the reason for yours?" Q exploded upright, pacing away, jamming hands deep into his pockets. "It's me, isn't it? Being alone with me up here. You're afraid. There's no staff. No Franco to stop me if I go too far." He looked at me with tortured, haunted eyes. "Tell me the truth!"

Heat and temper travelled up my spine, eradicating the last remaining chill. I stood up, pointing a finger at him. "Don't make this about you. How many times do I need to say it? I'm not afraid of you!"

He threw his hands up. "Maybe you should be fucking scared of me. I'm the worst you'll ever be with. No one else will come near you as I won't allow it." He thumped his chest, breathing hard, straining his immaculate graphite suit. "I'd kill for you, Tess. I *have* killed for you. Don't undermine me by fearing others. Fear *me*. Let me rule you!"

He rushed forward, capturing my nape. "My life guards your life. *Tu es à moi.*" You're mine.

His passion, his rage, chased the rest of my panic away. But no matter how touched and honoured I was about his vow to protect me, he couldn't stop the residual instinct that something wasn't right.

My heart kicked into high gear as I noticed the wide corridor behind Q's shoulder, leading off into the unknown.

I swallowed, trying to ignore it. An innocent hallway, nothing more, but my eyes latched onto the entrance, and the slow creep of spiders began anew.

Q followed my eyes. He frowned, then realization shone on his face. "You're afraid of somewhere new."

Rushing, he added, "Have you been anywhere else, other than your home in Melbourne and places you'd visited before?"

My brow furrowed, thinking of his question. Finally, I shook my head. "No. You're right. This is the first place that's completely new to me."

He slouched before rubbing the back of my neck and letting me go. "I know what triggered it. You're terrified of a new location because in the last one you were beaten and kidnapped." His voice sharpened with anger and his muscles bunched, but he gave me an encouraging smile. "I've seen it happen with countless slaves that arrived. They all despise newness—newness is full of horror because you can't mentally prepare for what you don't know."

I blinked. I didn't think I'd ever grow to be completely comfortable around Q. He saw too much, knew too much about what happened in the sex slave industry.

The property business wasn't where Q's heart lay. It was consumed by broken birds. Healing wings, granting purpose to otherwise dead women. He was the glue to so many fractured families finding happiness again.

I couldn't stop staring at him in a mixture of awe and

uncertainty.

He frowned, placing his hands on my shoulders, branding me, his thumbs stroking gently. "You're safe here, Tess. I won't let anything hurt you. You have my ultimate word on that." He lowered his head, eyes unreadable and fierce. "You need to rest."

I shook my head, horrified at letting him down on the first day. "No, I'm fine. Give me a moment and I'll be ready to become your doting employee." I smiled, but it was watery.

Even though I forced myself to be rational, to acknowledge that this was a safe place and Q would fend off the devil for me, I couldn't stop the froth of fear curdling in my stomach.

Get a fucking grip, Tess.

Q's body tensed, his jaw flexed. I swore he had some overactive sense that knew when I lied and was truly afraid. He had the nose of a predator, and in that moment I was weak and strung-out prey.

"Maybe you're right. I'm so sorry, Q." The thought of going anywhere else and meeting a bunch of new people gave me the hives.

He dropped his hands, nodding. "No need to apologize."

Slowly, some of the tension uncoiled from my limbs, leaving me shaky. Would I always suffer repercussions of what happened? I thought I was stronger than that. All along I thought I wasn't broken, but maybe they fractured me just enough to stop me from healing completely.

I felt like a coward. I let my instincts override rational thinking, making me fear an illusion.

Q took a deep breath, ridding himself of the angst visible in his shoulders. He smiled softly as his pale eyes warmed. "I have a meeting I'm late for. I want you to stay here and relax. Watch a movie, feed the birds, go for a bath. Do whatever you want."

He captured my hand, tugging me closer. "The moment I'm done, I'll come back, and we'll go for a nice dinner, or order up, I don't care. Tomorrow is soon enough to share you."

I smiled, looping my arms around his powerful back, letting him make me forget that I made a fool of myself. "You don't want to share me?" I murmured against his chest. A rush of gratitude filled me once again for being sold to such a strange, but moral man.

My fate could've been so, so much worse. I was eternally lucky.

He chuckled; the sound resonated in my ear, making my world right again. "No. I wished I never said you'd work for me. I'd rather keep you chained and subservient to me at home."

I laughed, and the last of my apprehension melted away.

Q wanted me, Q would protect me, and eventually Q would love me.

Me, the girl with nothing but a broken mind.

Q left me alone in his heaven-high office, heading to his meeting, donating his attention to something greater than me. I kissed him goodbye by the elevator before walking reluctantly back into the building.

Why he had to go downstairs for the meeting was beyond me. But watching the birds flying free, and the manicured gardens, I could understand him wanting to keep this as private zone where only he was allowed to enter. And now me.

I clenched my hands as I re-entered Q's space. The wash of instincts screamed at me, freezing my limbs, but I ignored it. For the first time in my life, I willingly told my instincts to shut the fuck up.

Q's office was simple, elegant. No heavy wood like his

library at home, or the over-decoration of animal hides in the lounge. This was purely him. A place untouched by his father, an uninherited space.

It seemed he liked cold and stark—if his furniture was to go by: a glass desk with four skyscrapers holding up the corners, white artwork with silhouettes of all types of birds in flight, and a massive skylight completed the space. Splashes of colour came from scattered cushions and strategically placed scale models of hotels and building complexes.

It was perfect, but empty. A feeling of abandonment rose and I squashed it. I had no reason to feel abandoned. Q told me to relax and, to be honest, I needed to.

For the next half an hour, I paced in Q's office. I stared at the artwork, flipped through some of the folders full of building permits and regulations, and went for a stroll outside.

Anxiety made me jumpy and twice I thought I saw a shadow lurking out of place, only to find a cloud had rolled in over the sun.

I couldn't keep this up. My heart hurt from racing so much, and my mouth was dry. My entire body shivered from being damp with nervous sweat.

I have a date tonight with a man I desperately want to know. I couldn't go smelling like a homeless woman.

Taking Q's suggestion, I headed back inside and swallowed my fear to head down the corridor in search of the bathroom. I came across a bedroom which was four times the size of my old apartment with a crisply made bed and a mountain of fluffy cushions. The entire end of the bedroom opened with bifold doors to bring the outside courtyard in.

Innocent and white perfection came to mind. It was so unlike Q's tower room it was laughable.

I found the bathroom off the bedroom and smiled in anticipation.

If the helicopter, Rolls-Royce, and Q's incredible building hadn't impressed me with his wealth, the luxury in every corner of this bathroom did.

One wall was completely covered in mirrored tiles, giving the sense of never-ending space and repeating possibilities. The two-sink vanity was laden with small soaps and tiny crystal bottles.

The shower could've held a football team with a metre-long showerhead, but it was the bath that called to me.

Tuscan inspired with steps leading upward before disappearing into a heavenly deep plunge pool. Silver jets for bubbles riddled the sides and plush pillows lined the rim.

If anything could rid me of my anxiety, it would be this bath.

Turning on the waterfall tap, I headed back into the bedroom to see if I could borrow something of Q's to wear after my soak.

The walk-in wardrobe buffeted me with notes of citrus and musk. Q's signature scent wrapped its arms around me and took away my loneliness. God, he smelled delicious.

My body hummed, missing him, looking forward to when he returned. Every shirt I rifled through sent my mind swimming.

Deciding on a pale jade shirt, the same colour as Q's eyes, I held it to my nose and inhaled. Q's darkness, his temptation, shot up my nose and deep into my heart.

My pulse increased, needing him. My body belonged to him, set alive by his scent, touch, and voice.

Damn you, Q, for leaving. I wanted nothing more than to take a bath together. Maybe when he returned, he could join me.

I needed to reaffirm that all of this was real. This wealth, this future, this life I now lived. Without him to remind me, it all seemed like a ridiculous dream.

The mirrors were fogged and weeping with condensation when I returned. Clouds of hot steam enveloped me, instantly saturating my skin with airborne droplets. The last of my irrational fear receded, turning me limp and eager to slip into the water.

Removing my clothes, I redid my ponytail into a messy

knot and stepped into the scalding hot bath. It blanched my skin as I submerged. Gritting my teeth, I bore through the temperature, letting my skin grow accustomed to the onslaught. Every whiplash sparked with extra agony, irritated by the heat.

The instant I was fully covered, the water lapped and coaxed, easing the last remaining kinks from my body.

The entire bathroom wept around me; dew even dripped from the ceiling. It was like being in a private water world where nothing but happiness could reach me.

I went from sleep to drowning in two seconds flat.

One second my head was above water, drifting in dreamland and fantasies, the next I was pushed deep in the tub and pinned to the bottom. Reflexively I inhaled, filling my lungs with useless, killing water.

I kicked and squirmed, trying to get purchase on whoever held me down, but the fist in my hair wouldn't allow any leeway.

What the fuck?

It's not Q. Please don't let it be Q.

I knew he had black desires, but I didn't believe he would drown me just for kicks. I didn't believe he'd be that cruel. Not the man who raged when he thought he couldn't protect me from my panic attack. Not the man who smiled so sweetly when we finished fucking in the helicopter.

All the rage and anger that I embraced when I was kidnapped raced into being. I lost the softness, the dependency Q gave me and revved with survival energy.

I scratched at the wrist holding me down, digging deep with sharp nails.

My assailant jerked, trying to un-pry my fingers with his

other hand, but I didn't let go until blood grew slippery under my fingernails.

A moment later the hand on my head loosened, and I shot upright.

Water erupted from my mouth as I choked and heaved, gasping for breath. Twisting in the water, I snarled. My heart pumped once and died.

I wished I'd stayed under water.

No. No, no, no. It can't be true.

Leather Jacket sneered, his black eyes filled with the same atrocious evil they'd held in Mexico. His body leered toward me as he wriggled his dirty fingers. "Hello, slut."

The panic attack.

Shit, Tess. It wasn't a panic attack—it was real! My instincts knew. They knew all along, and I ignored them.

Hot furious tears threatened to fall as I bared my teeth. "Get the fuck away from me." My eyes darted around the bath, looking for a weapon. Nothing but fluffy pillows and bars of moisturising soap.

Leather Jacket laughed, running a hand through his greasy hair. "That's no way to be nice. I've missed you and your nice tits." He cocked his head, tutting under his breath. His eyebrow raised taking in the red lashes on my stomach. "I hear you're proving to be a bad investment, and my boss *hates* bad investments." His Spanish accent thickened as his eyes slithered down my body. "Looks as though someone else decided you needed punishing too, huh?"

Wrapping my arms around my nakedness, I shouted, "I'm no longer yours to torture. I belong to another. Someone who will be extremely pissed if you lay one finger on me." My teeth started to rattle, despite the humid air and hot bath.

I can't let him take me. I can't.

"If you leave now, I'll forget you were here. I won't tell my owner to hunt you down and rip you apart." All I wanted was for Q to appear and blow Leather Jacket's brains all over the bathroom walls. Killing him had been my intention ever since I left Brax.

Leather Jacket threw his head back and laughed. "Don't worry your pretty little head about me, slut. Your so-called owner won't be a problem for much longer." He inched closer, leering down at me. "He did a very bad thing. Time for him to pay."

I pushed off to the other side of the bath, but Leather Jacket moved like a demon. He jumped into the tub, clothes and all, and grabbed a chunk of my hair. His metallic stench filled my nose as he forced my head under the water again.

I thrashed, I wriggled, I tried not to scream, but the sheer terror erupted my lungful of air into hot water.

The heavy *thud, thud* of my heart went wild as I inched closer to drowning.

The agony lasted forever while my lungs screamed and died a painful death, but at the last second, he hoisted me up, dragging me to the edge of the tub.

Clinging to the side, I sucked in hungry gasps, choking on droplets running over my face.

"Now that you're clean. Get the fuck out. We have somewhere to be," Leather Jacket ordered.

"What—?" I couldn't finish, heaving for breath. "I'm not going anywh—"

With a savage jerk, he pulled me upright. I screamed, trying to free my hair from his claws. He tugged so hard chunks tore from my scalp. "Let me go!"

I twisted, trying to get his wrist to bend enough to get free. He was too strong. My weak body wobbled and weaved after nearly drowning. I cursed my body for failing. I couldn't fight.

He hauled me from the tub and against his horrible body. The cold zipper of his jacket dug into my naked breasts as he breathed rancid breath over me. "Not gonna happen. Time to take a little ride."

I lashed out and kneed him square in the balls. He dropped me, clutching at the towel rail in agony. I didn't wait another second. With my head pounding and strands of hair falling to the floor, I bolted.

Straight into another man.

His arms whipped around me and his unnatural broken smile crushed all my hope of freedom.

Jagged Scar.

The man who held me down while the bitch tattooed and inspected me. The same bitch who inserted a tracking device into my neck.

Fuck.

The tracker! I wanted to kill myself for being so stupid. The moment I arrived in Australia I went on the waiting list for a day surgery to remove. But they kept pushing me back— emergencies bumping me down the line. There was nothing I could do, and then I went back to Q.

For four days I romanced and teased the man I'd returned to. I didn't even stop to think about such a life-threatening device tracking my every move.

Shit, Tess! I should've told him. I should've made sure it was removed straight away. I should've butchered my own body to remove it.

This was all my fault.

Jagged Scar clicked his tongue. "Just realized, didn't you? I have to admit, people tend to forget about that part." He sighed, sounding almost apologetic. "It really is a shame to do this, but your circumstances have changed."

My brain couldn't focus on one thing. *Run, fight, run.* Trembling, I said, "They were paid for me. Let me go. Please."

Leather Jacket limped toward us. I cringed as Jagged Scar spun me to face him. I didn't care about being naked, I only cared about killing these men and running to Q. Tears bruised again at the thought. I didn't know where Q was. I had no clue which floor, or even which building he was in.

Oh, God. I'll never see him again.

Leather Jacket scooped up Q's shirt on the seat in the corner. He threw it at Jagged Scar. "Dress her."

He nodded and let me go to open the shirt. The thought

of being dressed by these bastards was too much. They had no right to touch Q's clothes.

I snatched it off Jagged Scar, growling, "I can do it myself." It took a few attempts to undo the buttons and shrug it on. It hung on me like a dress. The whiff of Q's aftershave crippled me, and I wanted nothing more than to give in to the huge wracking sobs building in my ribcage.

But I didn't have that luxury. I had to be brave and fierce. I had to stay sharp and ready to maim.

Jagged Scar didn't capture me again, and I stood trapped in the middle of them as Leather Jacket pulled something from his trouser pocket. His black eyes glinted, enjoying my fear. "Do it." His gaze flickered behind me to Jagged Scar.

My heart lurched into my throat and I ducked, trying to avoid whatever was coming, but it wasn't enough. The punch to the side of my head sent stars exploding behind my eyes; I slammed to the marble floor. My knees screamed and I braced myself on my hands, trying to shake away the agony.

"Fuck me, look at you," Leather Jacket muttered. "We thought the man who owned you was a pussy, but looky here." A disgusting finger trailed along the base of my spine where the shirt had risen and poked the bruises on my ass. He prodded the fresh fingernail cuts Q gave me in the helicopter. "Kinky bastard, isn't he."

Jagged Scar laughed. "At least we know she likes it rough. That'll entice a few others to buy a secondhand slave."

My ears rushed with horror. "I'm already sold! You can't do this!"

Both men laughed. "It's not up to you anymore." Leather Jacket squatted in front of me, brandishing the item from his pocket. He kept it hidden in his large meaty fist.

All the hatred I felt for them burned my heart and soul. I'd planned on hunting them. Tracking them like animals and making them pay for what they did—bring retribution for all the women they hurt. Now all of those goals were dust.

Because of one stupid error, my life was over. For good

this time. I'd had my second chance and blew it.

"Give me your arm." Leather Jacket smiled. "I have a present for you."

I didn't want any fucking present. Gritting my teeth, I snarled. "Fuck you."

Jagged Scar chuckled behind me as Leather Jacket smirked. "I've missed your fight, *puta*. Just wait till I've got you all alone. You're gonna pay for breaking my finger."

I swallowed hard as memories of him coming to find me in the dark threatened to pull me under. "You shouldn't have tried to rape me."

Leather Jacket stopped smirking and glared with so much hatred it was like standing in a cauldron of hell. He lashed out and stole my arm. "You'll regret that."

I fought. Of course, I fought, but Jagged Scar grabbed my shoulders and held me in place while my arm was straightened and locked between Leather Jacket's body and elbow. "I'm gonna enjoy this. Say goodbye, slut."

With snake-like reflexes, he jabbed something sharp and painful into my arm. Almost instantly a foggy cloud descended, turning my brain to custard, my limbs to candyfloss.

No!

I clung to lucidity, but it was no use. Second by second, my heart silently poisoned me by allowing the drugs to ooze through my bloodstream.

My eyes went first—wonky and unclear. Then my limbs disappeared from my control until I fell headfirst into Leather Jacket.

He cradled me in his rapist arms as the final stretch of my nightmare closed in on me.

My thoughts shrivelled up, my breathing went shallow, and the last thing I heard sent my hopes directly to hell.

"Welcome home."

Seven
Quincy

I long to see your creamy skin blush, welted and marked it gives me a rush...

I stifled my groan as I rounded the corner to my office to find Frederick slouching against the doorjamb. Arms crossed, dark hair slicked back with gel, and sporting a tweed jacket with slacks, he looked like a poster boy for Country House and fucking Garden.

How we ended up being friends I didn't know. We roomed together at boarding school, and when I went back to finish my exams after murdering my father, he knew something major had happened in my life. Not because I was gloomy and my normally snappy self, but because for the first time, I sported a smile and an air of relief. I finally did the world a favour by killing my old man, and I wanted to share my good fortune.

I never told him exactly what happened, but somehow he tripped me up enough to give away my history. To unveil most of my secrets and give me someone to confide in.

The moment he saw me, his lips twitched into a smirk. He ran a hand through his glossy gay-ass hair.

Glowering, I pushed my way past into the boardroom, eyeing up his carefree smile.

"Quoi?" What? I demanded when he put his arm up to barricade me from entering.

I only knew five people in this entire building. And those five people I trusted only so far. Frederick was one of them, but he was also the only one who got away with driving me batshit crazy with his antics.

"Bonjour." He clicked his teeth. "I wondered when we'd be graced with your famous presence again."

I knocked his arm away, and stalked toward the large oval table. Picking the head seat, I sat with my hands steepled on the tabletop. "Get to your point, Frederick."

"Well, I assumed with a hot piece of ass at home you'd take longer than four days before coming back to this chaos."

My temper exploded. "Don't. Ever. Disrespect. Her." I squeezed my eyes. Not for the first time I regretted stringing Tess up from the ceiling for the impromptu business meeting. I hated that Frederick saw her like that.

I'd been a fucking bastard to do it, but I had my reasons. Reasons that didn't add up with the way Frederick Roux gloated at me.

He threw himself in a chair next to me, holding his hands up. "Hey. Just stating a fact." He shuffled forward eagerly. "So…you're finally letting a woman tame you, huh?"

"She didn't tame me, she—" I stopped mid-sentence, swallowing back the pansy thing I was about to say. She didn't tame me, she set me free. Definitely not appropriate for my fearsome reputation.

I seized the huge pile of paperwork that I'd requested to catch up on, and pretended to ignore him. I couldn't deal with his shit right now.

Leaving Tess alone had been the hardest thing I'd done since making an oath to never become my father. I left my capacity to breathe upstairs with her. Only the knowledge that she was completely safe and untouchable allowed me some relief to get to work.

What the fuck was with her panic attack? She was so strong. It didn't make sense for her to let memories get the better of her. I'd seen enough women lose their entire lives to reliving what happened. The switch that sent them spiralling into depression and destruction never turned off.

I would never let that happen to Tess.

"Stop gloating. I can feel your smugness from here," I grumbled when Frederick refused to look away.

"Hey, man, I'm allowed to gloat when my long-time friend finally comes to work looking well-fucked and a tinge happier than every other day of his sad little life."

I dropped the paper and took a swing at him. Half-hearted, but I missed all the same.

He ducked, laughing. "I'm pleased for you." Inching forward, he slapped me on the back, grinning. "Welcome to coupledom. You're no longer a sulky bachelor who has to get his wallet out to get his kink on."

"For fuck's sake, keep your voice down." My eyes darted to the door. Any moment we'd have company, and people did *not* need to know what I did with the cash in said wallet.

Frederick nodded. "I'll stop now. Just happy for you, that's all."

Warming a little, I leaned back in the chair. "What makes you so sure I'm keeping her? I sent her back the first time. I could do it again."

He snorted, covering up a loud laugh. "Seriously, Mercer? You were a fucking wreck the day you sent her back. Or are you forgetting I found you almost comatose, lying on your pool table, mumbling about God knows what?"

It was unfortunate that he'd found me. I'd planned on getting a lot drunker. I needed something to numb the pain.

He ducked to sniff my shoulder. I managed to deck him, not hard, but enough to make my point. "Plus, you smell like sex. You reek of it, my friend, and that little glow you've got going on tells me that you've kept her, and you're finally going to stop kicking yourself in the balls for needing what you do."

"Back off, Roux. I get it. You're happy for me." I narrowed my eyes, gathering the papers once again.

He smirked and his blue gaze, so bright that I always secretly wondered if they were fake, glinted. "You've got a wrinkle."

I paused, rubbing my forehead. Great. A fucking wrinkle. It was only fitting, I supposed—I felt ancient. Ever since Franco forced Tess to bow at my feet, I'd aged a little every day, worn down by the monster inside, cursing my urges that would end up killing me one day.

Or killing the one you care for.

The thought stopped my heart, and I glowered at Frederick. "Is this another one of your fucking analogies?"

He nodded, chuckling. "Wanted to see if you cared. Bet you'll care if I tell you there's a crusty tie and a pair of what I'm assuming are panties sticking out of your pocket."

Merde!

I hastily shifted in the chair and stuffed Tess's underwear, along with my come-encrusted tie, back into my pocket. I couldn't stop my smug grin at the vision of Tess on her hands and knees while I pile-drived my cock deep inside her. Goddammit, I wanted to do it again.

I wanted to fuck and hurt her right on this boardroom table.

As much as Frederick drove me nuts, I liked that he wasn't afraid of me. He knew how far he could push. Whispering under my breath, I said good-naturedly, *"Va te faire foutre."* Fuck off. "Stop being a dick about it."

Frederick chuckled . "Fair enough." His eyes darted to the door, looking to see if we still had privacy. My hackles shot up when he leaned forward, bowing his head. "I heard from the Russian mob. The man you shot for touching your slave, he's out for blood."

My hands fisted, and I shot forward into his personal space. "She's not my fucking slave. Her name is Tess and she's a part of my life now. You'll never discuss how she came to be that way. Am I understood?"

Frederick nodded, non-repulsed by my temper. He had the disposition of an unflappable pilot. Always smooth, forever calm. I wished I could steal some of his serenity; maybe then I could stop the swirling mess of feelings inside me.

"You have my word. But can I ask one question? You made it your life's work to save so many women from situations that you put Tess into. Why did you string her up to be eye-fucked if you hate it?"

Trust Frederick to see through the ruse. Yes, that night had been fifty percent selfish. I wanted to do something as horrid as my father. I couldn't help it. Just once I gave into the beast and did something I deplored. I got hard watching Tess struggle and put her in a situation that fucked with her mind. But I also knew the Red Wolverine wasn't happy with me.

Too many times I accepted his bribery—agreed to an underhanded real estate permit, or provided my name as collateral against a mob enterprise—all to get my hands on the women he traded.

My reputation was sick and tarnished in the underworld—exactly the way I wanted it. They didn't know I used black money to fight filth; every penny went into saving slaves. But Tess. Shit, I wanted to fuck her so badly that night. I wanted to cut off the dress and take her so many fucking ways.

And with the darkness running thick in my veins, I knew it would be a good opportunity to show the minion of the Red Wolverine that I did enjoy my bribes.

Whispers had begun. Foul gossip that I released the bribes I accepted. That I turned them loose and never touched them. Something had to be done.

I couldn't let that information leak. It would mean all the girls I'd saved would be rounded up, tracked like vermin, and sold once again into nightmares. So, I gave them a show. I put Tess on stage and fucking forgot it was all a pantomime to calm the gossip and halt one of the largest mafias involved in trafficking from suspecting me. I let myself get achingly hard, entertained visions of fucking Tess like the slave she was, and allowed other men to drool over what was mine.

She was too perfect. So amazingly sexy hanging from the ceiling, tempting me like the apple tempted fucking Eve.

The entire dinner I couldn't concentrate as Tess hung like a gold-imprisoned doll, completely helpless, completely defenceless, completely at my mercy.

Frederick slapped my shoulder. "Stop gouging the table, Q. Your temper is getting out of control."

Fuck. I placed my hands into my lap, cricking my neck from the overwhelming tension in my back.

"I did it to protect other women. I sacrificed Tess's dignity and fucked with her mind in order to put on a show for the cocksuckers we do business with." I glared at him. "Happy?"

He nodded as if it made perfect sense. "I thought as much. If you weren't emotionally invested, you wouldn't have ruined the show by shooting the same cocksucker you were trying to impress in the fucking leg."

I snorted, remembering how satisfying it'd been to pull the trigger and cause bodily harm. He dared put his hands on Tess—hurt her, torture her. I would kill him next time I saw him.

Then my heart died with black repulsion remembering how Tess fainted from pain and shock. That night would go down as one of the best and worst of my life.

Shaking away the memories, I asked, "Have you heard anything? Did you rush through that bastard's paperwork?" I wanted to confirm the building permits he requested as soon as possible. After all, the approval of his application represented Tess's freedom. Her life for a piece of concrete and glass in the heart of Moscow. A front for laundered money, weapons, and women.

"Yes. The permits have been approved thanks to some carefully greased palms. But I don't think that's the end of it. The guy you shot wasn't just his minion. It was the Wolverine's son."

My eyes popped wide, and I choked on my own spit. *"Merde."* Just my fucking luck. I put Tess in harm's way to protect the truth, and I go and shoot the fucking mafia's golden child.

The blond idiot in his ridiculous white jumpsuit sprang to mind. I'd thrilled with pleasure when his blood seeped through his pants. He'd been taught a lesson, and Franco gave him an extra little something to remember us by when he kicked his ass out of my home.

What the hell did it mean? Would the Red Wolverine come after me for hurting his only offspring? I needed to pre-empt him before he got any wild ideas about retribution.

Frederick interrupted my plotting. "I want to meet her, Mercer."

My eyes shot to his. "You think I want you talking to her? Telling her to run as far as she can away from me?" He never would, I knew that, but my chuckle held too much pain and stark truth to be ignored.

Je suis un faible idiot. I'm such a weak idiot.

Frederick laughed, dispelling the awkwardness. "I won't divulge your secrets. But I do want to talk to her. I want to make sure she's worthy of my friend."

I rolled my eyes, ignoring his sappy comment. Damn idiot.

The door swung open and in siphoned the managers we'd been waiting on.

Frederick shifted from happy-go-lucky-friend to strict-second-in-command, facing his underlings with an iron grip. The hierarchy in the room included me as the big motherfucker and Frederick as my right-hand man. He was the link between my orders and making sure that the thousand plus staff did as they were told.

I sat silent as Katya, a long-legged fiercely intelligent woman who had bigger balls than most men, strode in. Her talents lay in project managing and sourcing new contacts. Kevin, with his balding head and spectacles, was in charge of accounting, Samuel, with his dreadlocks and scruffy clothes, worked mainly with trade staff and hands-on affairs, and last but not least was Sandra, the stern, grey-haired woman in charge of human resources.

They smiled and murmured greetings, but no one dared talk to me outside a business level. And that's the way I liked it.

Once everyone was seated, I clapped my hands once and said, "Now we're all here. Let's begin."

Two hours into the debrief, an ache formed relentlessly behind my eyes. The headache I'd fought since the helicopter nagged stronger and stronger.

Logistics and figures swarmed in my head until I couldn't hear anything but a gentle buzz. I battled through it.

Turns out I had two weaknesses: control and fucking migraines.

I poured some water, hoping it was just dehydration. Forcing myself to focus when all I wanted to do was go back to Tess and curl up to rest.

Ten minutes later, the numbers on a new acquisition in Hong Kong bounced off the page and slithered onto the table. My vision fuzzed then sharpened like I took a strong hallucinogenic. A sure signal I'd left the realm of headache and ploughed straight toward a migraine.

"Yes, but what if we bought the building next to it. We could consolidate the lots and secure the permit for a thirty-story hotel," Frederick said to Katya, chewing on the end of a pen.

I shook my head, trying to dispel the overwhelming thickness taking over my brain. Shit, this couldn't come on a worse day. What with the stress of Tess's panic attack and hearing the Red Wolverine wasn't happy, I didn't have time to be fucking sick.

Katya said something and the entire table turned to stare at me.

I couldn't move my tongue to make a proper sentence. *Merde*, I never got this bad so fast. It normally crept over me, stealing a little of my senses, giving me time to get the hell out of there and hide my one bodily weakness.

"Mercer. You all right?" Frederick patted my hand. My eyes shot to his, but I had to squint against the pain of bringing him into focus.

I can't do this.

The only way to break it was a dark room, and Tess's heavenly fingers to massage away the agony.

Tess.

All I wanted to do was be with her. I needed her. She'd help cure me—just like she cured me of everything else.

The beast inside whimpered, agreeing that in this circumstance, it didn't want to hurt her. It wanted her to be gentle and nurse me.

Shaking my head, I swallowed back the rush of nausea and stood. Forcing myself to act cool and fully in control, I said, "It sounds as if you're more than under control here. If you'll excuse me, I have other business to attend to."

Frederick frowned, but nodded. "No problem. I'll keep you up to speed with what we decide on the Hong Kong and London development."

I nodded approval, which sent the world suffering a bout of turbulence. I hated when it got this bad. I hated being so weak.

Keeping my lips tightly together, just in case my morning coffee decided to make a reappearance, I strode firmly out of the room.

The second the door closed behind me, I leaned against the wall and took a deep breath. It felt as if no oxygen existed inside this goddamn building. I fumbled with my collar, trying to undo the top button.

The door clicked open, and I spun painfully to face whoever it was.

Frederick watched me with concern. "Another one? That's one a month for a while now, man. You promised you'd go to the doctor."

I didn't have the strength to tell him I *did* go to the doctor. And for me to admit I had a problem was a big fucking deal. But on paper there was nothing wrong with me.

The headaches were stress related, apparently.

In my painful haze, I mumbled something incoherent and headed on the marathon journey to get back to my private office.

Don't think. Just get to Tess.

Frederick followed me to the elevator, and I swiped my identification to activate my private lift. It was the only elevator that went to the roof. I didn't want anyone else going up there without my permission.

The whir of the arriving machine cut off as the metal doors swung open. Frederick's arm stuck out, barring my way.

Fiery hot shards poked my brain, stealing my colour vision, making him look as if he dripped with sienna and taupe. "Get out of my way, Roux."

He lifted his arm and let me enter, but jumped in a millisecond later. He eyed me, prodding me in the temple with a finger.

I winced and swung at him, but my perception was way off; I punched the mirrored wall instead.

"Yep, you're having a full attack, man. Not good."

Agony flared in my knuckles and I growled, nursing my hand. "Thanks for the advice. You going to charge me for that?"

He smiled. "Nope. That's on the house." He pressed the top button and we rode in silence before he said, "Don't bother wasting your breath telling me to fuck off. I'll stay until you've had some painkillers and that woman of yours has got you on the couch and resting."

I didn't want to argue with that. It sounded fucking perfect. But I hated being told what to do. The last time I obeyed anyone I was eight and let my father kill a slave for sneaking out to find food for her starving bed mates.

Fuck that shit. I never wanted to take orders again.

Frederick snuck glances at me, but I ignored him, focusing on curling my fists so hard my fingers threatened to break. The chance of a fracture prevented the fog of pain from devouring me completely.

I stepped back a little and skidded on a puddle of water. I figured my brain was playing tricks on me. I discounted it, but then froze. I could smell it.

Frost.

Orchids.

Tess.

My body locked down as panic charged through my limbs. Why the hell had she been in the lift? And without me? She wouldn't be able to get back without my keycard.

Frederick raised an eyebrow, noticing my trembling muscles. "What the hell, Q?" He came forward but slipped, too.

His eyes shot to the floor, reaching out to grab the side rail to avoid slamming to the floor. "Huh. That's strange. There shouldn't be a leak in here."

My instincts roared to life—trying to tell me something—something I should've noticed the second I entered the lift.

The beast inside sniffed and howled. Something was seriously fucking wrong.

The conclusion kept darting out of reach. I slapped myself in the head, trying to get my brain into some sense of working order. The migraine curled around my neurons, making me dumb as a piece of concrete.

I inhaled deep, trying to calm my crazy pulse. The scent of Tess swam in my pounding head, making my heart thud and cock twitch.

And that's when it fucking hit me.

My entire body felt as if knives dragged along my skin, flaying me alive. The world screeched to a halt.

"Shit." *Tess!*

"What is it? What's wrong?" Frederick asked, eyes flying around the lift, looking for some unseen threat.

The rush of panic shoved the migraine away as it darted down my spine. Rage followed hot behind, filling me like a cannon. They fucking dared touch her! My body coiled with the need to attack, to turn animalistic and rip apart anyone who touched my woman.

I sniffed again, dragging the horrible stench of cigarettes and grease into my lungs.

Must and body odour.

Men.

Something malicious wrapped around my stomach, dragging images of every bastard I'd dealt with in the trafficking industry. I didn't understand how I recognised the stench, but I knew.

Evil had been in this lift. With Tess.

I needed out of this metal box that travelled way far too slow. I needed to scale the building like King Kong and smash every last asshole into pulp.

Snarling, I punched the mirrored wall so hard it shattered. Cracks radiated from my fist, splintering into tiny pieces and tinkling to the floor.

"Mercer, wh—"

The elevator doors opened, and I bolted.

I slammed my shoulder into the metal door and gulped in a breath as I stumbled and fell to my knee. The sun was a dagger, a fucking bazooka to my head with its brightness. My vision turned completely white as I battled to stay lucid.

Gritting my teeth, I forced my body to obey and half-lumbered, half-ran across the minefield of sunlight. Birds took wing, squawking at my interruption.

With my heart in my throat, I exploded into my office.

"Mercer! Tell me what the hell is going on! You're fucking scaring me." Frederick chased after me. I didn't waste my breath answering. I couldn't afford to waste any part of my rapidly failing body.

I had to know Tess was here. Safe. Protected.

It's all in my mind. It's a horrid daydream. My brain is playing tricks. It's not real.

But the stench was worse here, the carpet wet with large puddles. Shit.

The energy of the office wasn't tranquil anymore, it was tainted. Brittle and tense, it lurked with a nasty undercurrent: something black and hellishly cold—evil and putrid.

The migraine throbbed around my skull, squeezing my thoughts in a never-ending vice. I sensed death and unhappiness. Tess's strength and pureness were nowhere to be found. Some chasm that had been full before was now empty and dark.

Don't be such a fucking drama queen.

I stomped on the fear, crushing it. The stink of cigarettes permeated the lounge, guiding me down the corridor and into the spare bedroom.

I followed the reek, but retraced my steps to unlock my HK P2000 pistol from the sideboard. Frederick skidded into the office, gawking around like a maniac. Considering he was supposed to be the calm one of our duo, he looked wired and ready to kill.

"Do you think I should take that?" He eyed the gun in my unsteady hand. My vision wavered in and out. One moment full colour, the next black and white. He had a point, but screw my head. Screw my shitty eyesight. I was in charge of Tess's safety; I'd use the fucking gun.

Ignoring him, I crouched and moved silently down the corridor. I'd never been so thankful for being deathly silent on my feet before.

The urge to shoot some fucktard who dared breach my space and take what was mine consumed me. The beast inside roared and raged, ready to go nuclear with fury.

I swung my arm wide, finger pressing the trigger as I entered the bedroom.

Nothing.

The bed was untouched, the room perfect as I left it.

Frederick fell back, keeping close to me with his legs bent, ready to fight at a moment's notice. If I had to have anyone at my back, it was him. He looked like a pussy, but he fought with the best of them.

Frederick was my wingman, my confidant, and ally, but he didn't have the same blackness in his soul, or the blurred lines of right and wrong.

"Tess, *où es tu?*" Where are you? I whisper-growled, inching into the walk-in wardrobe.

A single empty hanger lay on the floor.

My heart exploded through my ribs; my headache stole my vision, leaving me completely blind for a second.

I grabbed hold of the shelf holding my shoes, trying to stabilize myself and bring my heart rate into submission.

Frederick didn't say a word while I suffered and blinked, coaxing my eyesight to return.

Finally, a scramble of images came back to me, and I motioned for him to have my back as I moved toward the bathroom.

On the carpet, leading the way like a sinister path, were droplets of water. Staining the beige carpet a darker brown. It started off as a trickle, until splashes grew bigger and drenched the carpet outside the bathroom door.

Gulping back nausea and violence, I nudged open the door with my toe and charged in, waving the pistol into every corner.

Only once I knew the room was clear did I let myself take in the scene of my worst fucking nightmare.

"Q, don't move. I'll call the police."

I stood in a puddle, staring at a bath full of water and no Tess. The towel rail dangled from the wall, and Tess's clothes from that morning were on a chair.

The migraine swelled to epic proportions. I stumbled against the wall, shaking off the blackness, the cloak of unconsciousness. I wouldn't let a weakness stop me from understanding.

Slapping myself, I managed to shake away the stupor long enough to move forward and dip my fingers into the water.

Lukewarm.

Tess had taken a bath like I told her, and while I sat in a meeting she suffered a fucking nightmare.

My broken eyes found Frederick's. "How did they get up here, Roux? What happened to the goddamn security cameras and guards?" My heart beat thickly, sending more pressure to my skull.

I wobbled, but righted myself before Frederick could help. I didn't want his help. I wasn't an invalid! I was a bastard of an idiot for thinking Tess was safe.

How the hell did the motherfuckers find me? How did they manage to capture Tess right from under my nose!

I sagged against the wall as the migraine seized control. The mirrored tiles reflected a man with demons snarling at his heels and his world imploding around him.

"I don't know. But I'll find out. We'll get her back, man," Frederick said, his voice low. He left the bathroom, leaving me with horrible images: images of Tess beaten, raped, and sold. Ruined, and broken. Gone.

I couldn't let that happen. Disregarding the fact I could barely see, I lurched out the bathroom and collided with Frederick, who'd stooped to pick up a piece of paper from the floor.

I snatched it off him, trying to read the scrawl, but the writing turned into insects on the page, scurrying away from understanding.

"Q. You really need to lie down. You'll have a stroke at the rate you're going."

I snarled, "Don't tell me to fucking calm down. A woman

who was supposed to be in my protection has been taken. A woman who has lived through so much already has been snatched from my very fucking arms, and I failed her! So don't tell me to fucking calm down until I find her and make the bastards pay."

Shoving the note back under his nose, I demanded, "Read."

Frederick took the paper, swallowing hard.

"Deal's off, Mercer."

My heart seized, and the room warped, squeezing in on me, crushing me.

Something smashed free inside, tearing at every bar, every lock I'd ever created. The last few days I'd tried desperately hard to tame myself. Brainwash myself into being a better man for Tess, but with those three words, I shrugged off the falseness that I could never be. I growled and welcomed the feralness, the raging psychotic temper.

The beast sprung free, and I breathed hard. This was who I was. A man who craved blood. A man who laughed when breaking a bone, and didn't flinch when shooting a bullet into a rapist.

Frederick continued. I didn't want to hear anymore.

"I've taken back what was mine and sold for a better deal.

Fuck you.

Gerald Dubolazov."

Gerald? In my moment of migraine weakness, I couldn't remember which cockroach he was.

Frederick smoothed the crinkled paper, muttering, "The seal is the Red Wolverine."

I spun and punched the wall so hard my fist disappeared through the drywall. I wished it was someone's head.

That fucking Russian bastard. Dubolazov. The man who practically owned all of Russia. The Russian president thought he ruled, the mafia thought they controlled, but they were in the pockets of one man: Gerald Dubolazov, the king of everything dirty and wrong.

"Merde!"

Stalking back into the bathroom, I searched for clues. Anything that might shed light on how they found Tess and where they took her. The window of time to get her back was terrifyingly small.

Blonde strands littered the floor, and I clenched my jaw. Just the thought of someone hurting Tess made me see litres of blood and acres of fucking carnage.

In my mind the sound of a huge, ominous clock began to sound. Tick, tick, ticking the seconds away, marking the moments Tess's life hung in the balance. I had to find her before it was too late.

Something crunched under my shoe, and I bent to investigate. The moment I set eyes on it, my migraine left the realm of excruciating and amplified into kill-worthy.

I toppled sideways as Frederick appeared over my shoulder. "Fuck me, that isn't good."

He could say that again.

The evidence of what happened to Tess enraged the beast, clawing at my mind. I forgot everything but the need to plunge my hands deep into the kidnappers' chests and rip out their fucking hearts.

I want blood. I want corpses. I want to dance on unmarked graves for this. I wouldn't rest until every single person involved died a slow and bone-shrivelling death.

My hand closed tight around the object of my rage, and I made an oath. I would find Tess, I would save her, and I would kill every last son of a bitch who took her.

The gentle clink of breaking glass sounded over my harsh breathing. The broken syringe sliced my palm, and one lonely drop of blood landed into a puddle of water.

The same syringe that drugged Tess and stole her away from me.

My *esclave*—so strong and fierce and sexually feral—was gone.

Her cage wasn't me anymore.

It was them.

Eight
Tess

Don't show me mercy, don't cut me loose, I need you to tighten that noose.

"*I told them to take you,* esclave.

"*Did you honestly think I could want you?*

"*You aren't enough for me. I was kidding myself, and it's time to end this. Time you went to an owner who wants you.*"

Tears rained down my cheeks as I huddled on the floor by Q's feet. He stood proud and regal, entirely closed off and robotic. No cares, no feelings, no love or need in his eyes.

Just pure, calculated indifference.

"*You don't mean that. You don't. I know you, Q. I know you—*" *I sucked in a huge breath, sobbing at his rejection.*

"*It's done. You're dead to me.*" *He spun on his heel and prowled to the door. With a parting glance, he sneered, "Don't let the wolverines shred you alive.*"

The door slammed, and I was left in a pit with twigs and mud facing three pacing, starving wolverines. Looking half-wolf, half-badger, and full demon spawn, they slobbered and stalked, their yellow eyes glowing with the thought of an easy dinner.

"*Q!*" *I screamed, scrambling backward. The wolverines twisted into dinosaur size, all of them with barcodes stencilled across their furry chests.*

They growled and blood spewed from their mouths, creating a river of red, lapping at my feet.

I'm in hell. I'm dead, and this is my penance.

"Stop screaming, *puta*. For fuck's sake, trying to sleep here." Something sharp kicked my thigh, and my gritty, heavy eyes opened.

I tried to sit up, but my body no longer belonged to me. It belonged to the chemicals blocking my brainwaves. It succumbed to the sweet fog, stealing my consciousness, and evoking horror-filled nightmares.

Giving up the fight to corral my limbs into working order, I lay back. My vision was glassy, and the cracked mouldy ceiling above gaped wide and spoke in slow motion. No words. No sounds. Just speaking silently with its weird ceiling teeth.

Someone poked me in the cheek; I couldn't do anything to stop him. He laughed. "Fuck, you're high."

The voice turned my heart to lead, and I fought harder to move, to get far away, but every part of my body was weighed down by whatever they'd injected into me.

Hot, cold, numbness, sensitivity. I couldn't distinguish anything anymore.

Fingers landed on my thigh, squeezing hard. "There, there. You'll get used to it soon. It's a fucking trip when you let the drugs take over." Leather Jacket loomed above me, licking his foul lips. "You wait till we get where we're going. I'll make you feel *real* good." He ducked and dragged his foul tongue up my neck.

I rattled with grotesqueness. Unable to move from the slime, my eyes gushed with tears. They cascaded down my cheeks, filling the shell of my ear with salty liquid. I wanted to tell him to leave me the hell alone, but my tongue was bound in lethargy.

"Dammit, Ignacio. You were told not to touch her until we arrived."

Leather Jacket reared back, wiping his mouth with a sneer.

"I didn't touch her." He gave me a wink. "I licked her. And I'll be fucking her too before the week is out."

My heart died and rotted in my chest. This was it then. My life was over. I'd never see Q again. Never be free. My mind was shackled with chemicals; my body would become a plaything until I died of some horrible malady.

"Crap, turn her neck. I forgot to deactivate it," Jagged Scar said.

Leather Jacket exploded into abusive Spanish, ranting and raving at him.

I tuned him out. Wishing my other senses, hearing, and eyesight would abandon me, too. Living as a blind, deaf mute would be better than living through the awfulness when Leather Jacket finally raped me.

My mind flew back to another kidnapping—being owned by Q. He'd slowly turned my eyesight, hearing, and senses against me, but he did it in a way that I accepted, wanted.

I tried to conjure Q, to find some sense of peace even while tears poured from my eyes.

Harsh fingers twisted my neck to the side, and the same iPhone-looking contraption from when I was first tagged, waved over my throat before emitting a painful shrill.

Once again, I tried to shift, to wriggle away from his grip, but nothing worked. Every command fell on fogged receptors, rendering me a vegetable.

"It's done. If they thought to chase her by the tracking number we provided, they won't have any luck now."

The first jolt of life came into my body at the thought of Q coming for me. He'd never rest until he found me. I knew that in my soul. Q had his downfalls, but saving those who needed saving wasn't one of them.

Please find me. Before it's too late.

"Shit, man, they could've been tracking us for two days." Leather Jacket glared at Jagged Scar. "That was your fucking job to make sure it was taken care of. The Wolverine is gonna be beyond pissed if we fuck this up. You heard what he told the boss." He cuffed him around the ear, and something clattered to the floor. "You incompetent little worm; I'll show you how to make sure that bastard doesn't sniff her down."

The sound of a switchblade snapping open sent panic overriding the fog of narcotics. I tensed as Leather Jacket sat beside me and grabbed my throat. He put the knife tip against my skin. His black eyes burrowed into mine. "Gonna cut you, bitch."

I whimpered—it was the best I could do. Screaming required muscles that were no longer in my control.

"What the fuck? Don't, you idiot." Jagged Scar grabbed the knife and tore it from Leather Jacket's grip before he could stab me. "I already deactivated it! It needs to stay in so we can reboot when she's sold again." Jagged Scar huffed, rolling his eyes. "Fucking moron."

Leather Jacket roared upright and decked Jagged Scar in the chest. "*What* did you just call me?"

My heart raced faster as the two psychotic kidnappers wrestled and cursed. If they couldn't work together without killing each other, there was no hope for me.

I closed my eyes, ignoring the raging argument. My forehead furrowed as I coaxed my fingers to move, straining to override whatever they'd pumped into me.

Nothing happened. The bizarre feeling of being untethered from my body caused more panic to race.

I needed to look around, to figure out where I was. I needed to keep track of everything Leather Jacket and Jagged Scar said so I could spy an opportunity to run. But all I could do was float in a sea of sickness, staring at a cracked talking ceiling.

I'm weak. I'm terrified.

The thought of what would happen almost caused me to throw up.

Leather Jacket appeared in my vision again, smiling with his disgusting teeth and pockmarked skin. "Not long now. I've arranged a special welcome-home party just for you."

Images of rapists and murderers filled me with dread. *Oh God, I don't want to survive.*

I mentally slapped myself for the thought. I was stronger than that. I would eventually be coherent enough to fight back. My body betrayed me and my mind was slush, but I had to stay focused and ready to run. Run back to Q and watch him detach these bastards limb from limb. My hand twitched into a fist on its own accord, and a flare of pride filled me. I overrode the drugs.

Leather Jacket frowned, his eyes falling to my hand. "Well, that's just fucking annoying." He turned to Jagged Scar, holding out his hand. "She's coming round. Give her another dose."

Jagged Scar inched closer. I forced every cell in my body to get moving. To launch upright and punch their vile faces in. But it seemed my fist curling was the extent of my progress.

Jagged Scar pulled out a syringe but paused. "I don't know. If we give her too much she might coma and not wake up."

My heart charged, head became clearer. *Give me more time!*

Leather Jacket snarled, grabbing the syringe from him. He uncapped it in an angry wrench and plunged the needle deep into my arm.

The sharp pierce dragged a scream from my lungs, and my last thought was of Q as I was flushed into hell.

"I told you I didn't want you. Stop fighting the inevitable, esclave, and let these men resell you."

I hated his icy aloofness, the confidence in his tone. *"But, I don't understand. You want me. I'm yours."*

"I wanted you for a time, and now I don't. Goodbye, Tess." His form faded from solid to smoke and wisped away as I fell and fell and fell.

I cried and I begged, but Q never came back for me.

And then the blackness swallowed me whole.

The drooling, yellow-eyed wolverines waited for me every time I fell into the deep.

I lost count how many times I awoke and quickly succumbed again. A constant battle waged in my mind—trying to keep me awake, trying to knock me out.

But every time I dropped into the dark, the wolverines were there. Mauling me, gnawing on my arms and ankles, they drained me of blood, turning me into leather.

Distant voices came and went, broken conversations. Sounds of engines and dreaded transport taking me further and further from Q.

Q appeared in my catatonic state. *"I'm coming for you, esclave. Keep fighting. Wait for me."*

Hope dazzled through me, waking me up, giving me something to latch on to.

"So you do care."

He leaned over me, his eyes full of pain and guilt. *"Of course I care. You're my gravity. I'll find you. I'm coming."* Q's voice resonated in my body, warming me from the bone-deep chill I suffered.

Images of his home, the conservatory with all his birds, filled my mind, granting me a reprieve from horror for too short awhile.

Then sleep grabbed me with its sharp-tipped claws, dragging me back to the wolverines.

The next time I woke, I could move my arms. The heavy cloud of blackness dissipated, letting little rays of myself shine through.

The strength and will to survive returned slowly, quietly—meek and timid. I didn't want anyone to know I no longer lived in limbo.

I held my breath for eons, making sure I was alone. Every time I opened my eyes either Leather Jacket or an unknown trafficker pierced my skin and drowned out my tentative awakening with drugs.

My gaze went wobbly, trying to focus on the room around me. I couldn't distinguish anything and random thoughts kept distracting me.

What would the walls taste like if I licked them?

What sound would the floor make if an elephant jumped up and down?

I shut my eyes, trying to get control of my haywire brain. I hated drugs. I'd never used substances in my life. Never dabbled with marijuana or sampled something harder. Now I knew why. Control: drugs took away control, granted nightmares and hallucinations. They spaced me out, stole time and my wits.

My mind turned rogue, hurtling me back to hell—making me forget how to fight, how to care. It turned Q into a monster. One moment he cared for me, the next he left me to the den of snapping wolverines.

He came for me when I was raped. He'll come again.

I wasn't an idiot. Of course, Q would try. But he would fail.

With no way of tracking me, he would lose the trail quickly. I had to give it to Leather Jacket. I'd never been on so many airplanes as I had in the last few days.

I had no clue how long we travelled. Time ceased to have meaning. I vaguely remembered being carried, engines whirring, tyres squealing. I slept in cellars, and dungeons, only to wake up shivering and cracked out of my mind.

Starving, dehydrated, it was only a matter of time before my body gave out. In fact, it was the fifth time they injected me when I got sick.

The drugs couldn't hide the racking shivers as a fever wrapped its false blanket around me. Nor could it compete with the wacko visions that now plagued when I was awake.

I shivered and ached and wished to God I could see a doctor.

My brain felt squished inside a skull full of cement and fog, my mouth parched drier than a desert, and my heart thumped, heavy and broken.

Noise came from behind me; I snapped my eyes closed.

"Wake up, *puta*. We're finally home." Leather Jacket grabbed my arm and hauled me off whatever I lay on. My body, so useless after days of lying inert, slid off the platform and sprawled at his feet.

I bit my tongue at the impact, wincing as blood trickled down my throat. Hunger pangs tore into my stomach, growling loudly. Trembles from hunger spread through my limbs, adding to the shakes from my fever.

My tongue stopped bleeding, but a sickness rose in me, and I ached for more of the warm metallic. It was the first thing I'd tasted in days—it was beyond delicious to my perishing body. The blood reminded me of Q. I missed him. Needed him. So much.

Leather Jacket kicked me, just for sport. "You like that? Do ya?" He kicked me again, growling. "Get to your fucking feet. I'm not a taxi. Get your sorry ass walking."

A wracking cough jangled my ribs, sending me gasping for breath. Fiery pain from his kick radiated outward like a bomb.

I tried to move, I really did, but I was a useless body with no life.

"Move!" Leather Jacket kicked my leg; I cried out.

Oh God, I can't move.

A peculiar calm fell over me, relaxing my trembling muscles. I slumped into a further drug-messed puddle and refused to obey. After fighting so hard in Mexico, after surviving Q and the rape, I had nothing left to give. No matter how hard I fought, or how much I refused to give in—it was never enough. So why bother?

Is this it, Tess? You're just going to give up?

"Oi, bitch!" Leather Jacket kicked me again.

I moaned, cursing him to hell, but I still didn't move to obey. If he killed me from sheer rage, so be it. I wouldn't walk to my own demise. I wouldn't put myself through that again.

"I'll break your neck if you don't get up right now, slut." He ogled me, his boot raised, ready to deliver his promise.

"Get up, esclave! Give me time to find you before being reckless with your life. Your life belongs to me, no one else." Q manifested in my feverish brain and I groaned.

I didn't want a pep talk from my cracked-out subconscious. I just wanted to lie there and give up.

"Lève toi!" Get up. Q leaned down and brushed tangled hair from my cheeks. His face contorted with grief, darkened with sorrow. "Please, Tess." His pleading wrenched my heart, and I moved.

I moved on my own.

Leather Jacket chuckled. "Didn't like the thought of a broken neck, did you, slut." He crossed his arms, watching my slow progress as I pushed off from the ground.

Lack of food tore my stomach, the fever rattled my teeth, but I bore through it all to stand upright for the first time in days. The drugs receded, not that it made a difference to my swimming head.

"I did this for you, Q. Don't make me regret it. Find me."

Wobbling, coughing, I stood as tall as I could, but the bruises from his kicks kept me hunched. The pride in the small victory blazed bright, giving me courage that I could fight. That I could battle against the drugs and win.

Leather Jacket smirked. "Not so hard to obey, is it?" He pulled out a dog collar from his pocket, and with calloused fingers secured it around my neck. His vile fingers deliberately squeezed the buckle one notch too tight. I struggled to swallow.

I didn't move a muscle, or let my face portray my hatred for him. I nursed my anger like a small flame, coaxing it to flare brighter, ready to explode.

I let him believe he owned me. All in the name of self-preservation.

"Good dog. Time to go and meet your new master." He attached a chain to the collar and yanked me forward. I stumbled, following him from whatever mode of transport we'd been in—a large black van with no decals—and entered muggy night air.

I looked around greedily, imprinting as many details as possible.

Water lapping. A harbour. Bright lights in the distance. The reek of fish and salt. The balmy weather suggested somewhere tropical, and my heart curled in terror at the thought I might be back in Mexico.

If you are, who cares, Tess. It doesn't matter where you are because you'll be leaving soon.

You're a survivor and today is not the day you give in.

That was yesterday.

Today was entirely different.

I awoke to an ocean of icy water. It came from nowhere, drenching me, causing Q's pale shirt to cling to my rapidly depleting curves.

Gasping with shock, I sat up, scooting to the end of the pallet. My eyes darted around the cell—dank, freezing, reeking of dried fish.

Three goons stood staring, raping me with their heinous eyes.

Whatever sickness I'd contracted had evolved into a full-blown attack last night. My skin burned, my throat felt like I'd swallowed a bunch of machetes, and my lungs wheezed with every breath. I couldn't stop coughing every few minutes, and I was hungry. *So hungry.*

Leather Jacket stood to the side of his troop of traffickers, holding an empty bucket. "You awake now, bitch?"

Trying not to show my fear, I swiped my face free of excess water and wrung my hair out. I swear steam curled off my skin thanks to my fever. I coughed hard, smashing my hands against my mouth in the hopes of keeping my lungs in my body.

Once my coughing fit subsided, Leather Jacket muttered, "It's that time of day. Guess what that is?" He tossed the bucket into the corner, putting his hands on his hips. When I didn't answer, he gloated. "The answer is fucking time for your medicine."

He nodded at the two next to him, and they rushed forward.

No! Not again.

I cried out, scurrying backward, pressing against the freezing cold wall. I wanted to burrow my way through the concrete and run. Oh, how I wanted to run.

Four large hands dragged me down the bed and pinned me to the hard surface. "No!" A cough exploded out of my mouth, and every inch pounded like one giant headache. Bile rose in my throat even though I had nothing in my stomach to reject.

With no reserves and a wasting frame, I knew I didn't stand a chance, but I couldn't let them drug me again without a fight.

I fought because I couldn't do anything else. I had to stop the inevitable, even if it killed me.

The men grunted, fingers digging harder into my body while Leather Jacket slapped me around the head. He laughed. "You haven't changed a bit. I must say, I didn't expect to see you again, but it proves wishes do come true."

His black eyes glinted as he grabbed my upper arm. "You might as well give up, slut. I've been given orders to break you. Hurt you. Fuck you. Ruin you. Degrade you to the point where you're nothing but a confused sack of shit who wishes daily for death, and then we'll sell you."

My throat clogged; I wanted to cut my ears off. I didn't want to listen. I didn't want to believe. I also hated myself because I saw the truth. Everything Leather Jacket promised would come true. And there was nothing I could do to stop it.

He licked his lips, pulling another syringe from his pocket. "Turns out your fucking master has enemies in high places. What did he do, *puta*? Who did he piss off, the stupid cunt?"

"*Je suis à toi, Tess.*" Q's voice whispered in my head. I latched onto it, giving me courage to face whatever was coming.

Q would come for me.

Q is coming for me.

One of the thugs jerked my arm up, imprisoning me.

"Stop! You don't have to drug me."

Leather Jacket pressed his lips against my ear. "Oh, but we do. That's the fun of it." He pulled back and tapped a vein, then stabbed the needle into the crook of my arm. The sharp prick heralded more doom.

Instantly, the heat of my fever was replaced with numbness. My head lolled on my shoulders as liquid horror made its way around my body—stealing limb control, turning the volume down on my soul.

My personality faded, muted by distance and echoes. The drug stole my thoughts on why I should care, blurred boundaries of right and wrong.

I screamed silently as I drowned in venomous smog until finally I sighed, completely dead inside.

Leather Jacket chuckled, speaking in a string of words that made no sense. His head seemed to swell to gigantic proportions, and I giggled.

He's a fucking idiot—he can't even speak properly.

Visions of dancing alphabets kept me company. Vowels pranced by in drag; consonants strutted past in dominatrix wear. An S tangoed with an X, while the Q—

Fuck, the Q.

Why did I hold such fondness for that letter? Such a lifeless character and yet it dragged hot, determined emotion from the dregs of my heart.

That letter belonged to someone else, someone worthy, not the drugged captive.

A heavy wall of nausea slammed into me, chasing lethargic blood, trying to remember.

I flinched as Leather Jacket squeezed my breast and breathed hot on my face. "Forget everything you ever knew, bitch. You thought Mexico was bad? That was fucking Disney World compared to this carnival ride. You aren't human anymore."

His slimy hands twisted my nipple, cutting through the haze like a whiplash. "I'm going to enjoy every moment we have together. You'll never know what's coming, you'll never heal. The drugs will turn you against everything you've ever known. They'll tear your brain apart with hallucinations. I'm gonna fuck you up, pretty girl, and there's nothing you can do about it."

His touch dropped from my breast to between my legs and squeezed. "Then let's see you fight."

Roast chicken.

The smell of delicious food roused me from my drug-coma, fluttering my eyes back to the world of the living.

The moment I woke, I wanted to descend back into the

fog-filled abyss I'd lived in since Leather Jacket made promises that made me want to slit my wrists and paint my cell red.

"Hello, girl. How pleasant to see you again."

The man who ran the operation—the same one who ordered me to be drugged and stuffed on a plane bound for Paris—sat on the edge of my pallet. His sky blue eyes, so like Brax's, reminded me how drastically my life had changed. His perfect clothes and blond shaggy hair looked as if he'd stepped from an Aussie beach and needed a surfboard under his arm.

"Here, let me help you up." His hands scooped under my arm, levering me into a slouch. I wiped away drool from the corner of my mouth as fumbling life came back into my body.

My eyes latched onto the platter of chicken, vegetables, and bread. Gone was the ability to think. My stomach roared and stabbed with a thousand desperately hungry knifes.

White Man chuckled, nodding. "That's for you. If you do what I say."

Shit. What the hell did he want? What more could I give?

"Esclave, don't give up. Stay alive. For me."

Tears pressed and every regret I felt for pushing Q too far choked me. I should never have made him come that morning. I should've thanked him for every bit of attention and fair treatment he gave me. Why would he come for someone who promised to make his life hell so she could own him?

Why did you push him away?

My mind couldn't focus anymore—everything was upside down, back to front.

Suddenly, no matter how hungry I was, I couldn't stand the thought of eating. My heart was empty; my stomach should be, too.

White Man ran a fingertip along the back of my hand. "Stop thinking. It gets easier if you let the drugs take you."

A loud cough stole my oxygen, racking my body with barks. Once the spell was over, I looked up with watery eyes, begging him to let me go. "Please. I'll do whatever you want."

He stiffened, and shadows lined his face. "You didn't do

what I wanted the first time. I must say, I've never had a client demand us to collect his purchase before. I almost didn't agree—after all, it's not my business once monies have been exchanged—but the Red Wolverine had a very valid point."

I gulped, hanging my head. What did I do wrong as a slave? I fell for my master. I taught him that two people could be perfect for each other. What was so wrong about that?

White Man continued. "I grow rather close to the clients who buy merchandise from me. So you can imagine I want to maintain a happy relationship with them. This particular buyer sent us to collect you for a rather unforgivable reason."

He stopped, buffing his fingernails on his trousers. "Do you want to know what you did wrong?" Not waiting for my reply, he carried on, "He bartered you for a business transaction. That same business transaction met with…difficulties." He laughed. "Of course, it does help that he paid double what you cost with strict orders to ruin you."

My eyes shot to his, trying to unscramble the mess of sentences. Drugs clouded me, leaving me in a stark reality where I could only hope death was short and fast.

As a last resort, I asked, "How much did I cost? I'll buy myself. You're a businessman, let me make it worth your while."

Q would give me the money. I had no doubt about that.

White Man stood, throwing his head back in mirth. "You're worth more to me than money now, girl. You see, my orders are simple." His eyes narrowed and all humanity dissolved—I stared into a killer's soul. "You are to be unrepairable. And after your little stay with us before, I know your strength lies in your mind. You won't be broken by physical abuse—your key to breaking is something harder. Something I haven't come across, but I'm looking forward to seeing put into action."

He leaned down, eyes looking deep into mine. His cologne gagged me with its cloying, syrupy stench. His blue gaze ripped me into bleeding pieces. "You will work for me. You will do what I say, when I say it. You will beat other women. You will hurt them so fucking bad their minds will shatter and you'll wear their lives on your soul. If you don't do what I tell you, I'll kill them to make you obey." He grabbed my chin; his Mediterranean accent snapped every word into violent shards. "Do you understand?"

I understood. I understood that I would become well and truly deformed as a human being. I would be made to abuse other women in order to keep them alive.

No.

I wrenched my face out of his iron grip, glaring. "I'll give you a million dollars to release me. Give me access to a phone and the money can be in your account tonight."

And then Q will rip your intestines from your stomach and burn you alive, you bastard.

He stood, smoothing his black shirt and jeans. "You're a fighter to the end. I respect that. But the next time I see you, if you speak back, you'll regret it."

I had every intention of fighting back. I would make them hurt me. I would never be responsible for another woman's spiral into madness.

"You're worth more than dollar signs now, girl. Better get used to taking orders."

He pushed the plate of food toward me before striding toward the door. "Enjoy your last meal as a free woman. Tomorrow you belong to me, and you'll have a full day's work ahead of you."

The door slammed behind him, resonating in my barren cell. The fever roared in my blood, making me weak and terrified.

I was no longer merchandise. I was an employee.

Nine
Quincy

I can't contain him, you set me free. This isn't a role I play, the monster is me...

"Anything?" I demanded as Frederick hung up the phone.

"Nothing. He says he's been banned from their operation for months, ever since he won a knife fight and killed one of the Wolverine's guards."

I stared at the ceiling, struggling with my anger. The rage bubbled in my blood, never granting peace. All I wanted to do was tear through the globe and kill anyone who stood in my way. I wanted goddamn answers. I wanted a victim I could string up and torture names from. But nothing.

Fucking nothing in two long days.

Two long fucking days where I turned my entire book of contacts upside down, and nothing. I harassed, I cursed, I pleaded, I threatened. Every single trafficker, every single man I'd ever accepted a bribe from and not *one* of them knew a fucking thing.

Tess had vanished. No one knew anything. No one would talk.

"Try harder, Roux. We're running out of time."

Frederick scowled, tapping the phone in his hand. "I know you won't rest until you find her, man, but you've been awake for forty-eight hours. You barely survived a migraine that kicked your ass, and your blood pressure is through the roof."

I stopped rifling through some old transaction files. I wanted to rip his fucking head off for suggesting I sleep. As if that was an option when Tess could be God knows where, dealing with fuck knows what. "I'm not wasting energy telling you to piss off, Roux." I waved angrily. "Go and help Franco. Be useful or leave. I have shit to do."

I didn't have time for anything but searching. I ran purely on vengeance and the need to kill.

I'd never had people in this space before, but now I didn't give a shit about having a private zone. All I cared about was finding Tess.

If it meant I had to demolish every building I owned to do so, then so be it.

Standing abruptly, I grabbed the stack of files from my desk and strode into the bedroom.

For two days I hadn't left my office. The rooms were a mess with strewn paper and scribbled notes. I had a small army of people in the lounge, overseen by Franco. The moment we looked at the security footage and saw how two black-haired men bypassed the coding on the lift, we knew it had to be a trafficker with money. They'd had the password—only someone with a substantial bank balance and knowledge of how I worked could figure it out—or buy it.

They strolled in, bold as fucking day, and took an unconscious Tess to the basement level where another accomplice had been waiting.

The only people who had security clearance on my private lift were head of cleaning and head of building security. Both were being interrogated right now. I didn't fucking go to all the trouble to keep my office out of bounds for the fail safes not to protect it.

And the bitch was, I *knew* who would've bribed or

tortured to get the passkey, but I daren't move until I had proof Tess was there. If I was wrong the entire company would come crashing down. The real kicker was I didn't care about the company, but I did care about the women who hid in its protection.

"Fuck."

I slapped my cheeks, trying to stay alert. It was hard fighting through the sludge. The residual brain-crushing pain of my migraine had stolen more from me than just coherent thought and vision.

It stole time.

For twelve hours, I was useless. Finding Tess's hair ripped out on the bathroom floor with the syringe had been the final bullet, and I'd blacked out.

My body had reached its limit—turns out I wasn't invincible after all—and if it hadn't been for Frederick, I would've lost the plot entirely. I vibrated with loathing; I ached with the strength of a thousand beasts to cover my hands in blood.

I needed to make the cocksuckers pay; I'd never rest until I did. But the headache cursed me to be a useless invalid, hogtying me to a long-suffering sentence.

I physically hit a fucking wall. And it gutted me.

Frederick organised the team to help search. He ordered Franco to arrange his top men to leave at a moment's notice. He made a thousand calls, sent a hundred emails, all the while I lay dead in the dark.

My vision completely deserted me, and I was sensible enough to know I was a hindrance, not a help. But it still fucking hurt to stay out of their way, concentrating on myself rather than Tess. It was wrong, and I cursed the weakness in my blood.

I let Tess down. I left my woman to suffer at the hands of bastards all while I huddled in a fucking corner and popped painkillers like Tic-Tacs.

It wasn't until Frederick snuck a sleeping tablet into a

handful of codeine that I fell asleep, and the migraine lost its power over me.

But the sleep wasn't restful; it robbed the rest of my sanity.

Images of blood and broken bones and Tess screaming ceaselessly for my help. Her voice stabbed my heart over and over, full of accusation for letting this happen to her.

The moment I woke, I'd thrown myself headlong into tracking down the cunts who took her. But I hadn't stopped to use my useless brain.

Breathing hard, I perched on the end of the bed and fanned out the files. Now that I had no one prying down my neck, I opened the paperwork that might hold some clues to finding her.

The records on all the girls I saved.

Tess's details were at the back and I cracked the folder open.

Subject: Blonde Girl on Scooter
Barcode reference: 302493528752445
Age: Twenty to thirty
Temperament: Angry and violent
Sexual status: Not virgin
Sexual heath: No diseases
Ownership guidelines: Recommend strict punishment to break temper. Trim body, fit enough for extreme activities.
History: No living relatives

My eyes fell to the number. I'd tried to track Tess using the device when I sent her back to Australia, but it didn't work. I always thought she removed it when she went home to Brax. I'd been pissed and proud at her for cutting it out because it meant she was safe even though I couldn't spy on her whereabouts.

Try it anyway. You ever know.

My mind spooled back to letting Tess go. My sacrifice hadn't been voluntary. I wanted to keep her forever, but I

153

didn't want to crush her. Tess was my phenomenon. The once in a lifetime dream that I never thought I'd get. *And I've fucked it up.*

Motherfucker, screw it. I wouldn't sit here holding my cock while the Red Wolverine had Tess. He'd left his note— deliberately to get me to hunt him. If it was a trap, I didn't care anymore. No one was more important than Tess.

Grabbing the spare laptop I kept in the bedside table, I called up the program associated with the tracking number and entered in the code. It was a waste of time, but I had to check.

The connection took a while, and I placed my hand on the lid to close it. *See, she did remove it.*

Then a small map appeared, followed by zooming in, faster and faster until it zeroed in on the one country I'd suspected and hoped to avoid.

Intense anger throttled my limbs. I wanted to howl. A month she'd been back in Australia. A full fucking *month* and she didn't remove it? What a moron. An idiot. Did she enjoy playing roulette with her life?

I wanted to kill her for being so stupid. She gave them the perfect way to find her!

When I get my hands on her, by God I'll make her pay.

If she'd been standing in front of me, I would've cut it out myself and wrung her neck for being so stupid.

At least I now had proof.

The Red Wolverine had her—it was undeniable.

I wanted to ruin him. I wanted to take away his business, his money, his very flesh and blood. And only when he had absolutely nothing would I torture him until he begged me to kill him.

That's how much I hated Gerald's guts.

Tess was in Russia.

"Frederick, get your ass in here!"

Footsteps charged down the corridor, soft on the carpet. "What is it? What'd you find?"

I threw the laptop to the side. "I've confirmed he has her

in Russia. We're leaving." I brushed past him, but he stopped me.

"But we asked the contacts we have in his team. They said they haven't seen a girl matching Tess's description. If we barge in and start shooting, you're ruined, Q. The rest of your contacts will come after you. Think clearly for a moment. Are you sure he's got her?"

I bared my teeth and rushed back to the bed. Grabbing the laptop with the flickering red dot in Moscow, I shoved the machine into his arms. "Enough fucking proof for you?"

Leaving him to worry that my company was about to dissemble and fall into ruin, I careened into the lounge to find Franco.

I moved like a fucking whirlwind of male fury.

His dark brown hair hung over his forehead and lack of sleep made his eyes raw and brutal. He looked up as I crooked a finger for him to come to me. When he was away from the other staff, I muttered, "Call up nine of your top mercenaries. Meet me at the airport in an hour. We're going in. I don't care if we have to kill every last bastard if it means we find her."

No element of surprise or pause; Franco knew when to just obey orders. His eyes glinted with pleasure. "Yes, sir. I'll see you at the airport."

Frederick, with his old fashioned style and friendly personality was the polar opposite to me—he lived a tame life, married the sweet girl, lived in a presentable house—while Franco, the man I hired because I saw how efficiently he killed, indulged in the same hobbies I did, just on a more acceptable scale. Franco and I never talked about our similarities, but we knew. It was easy to spot the monster in others. He may look like a gentleman: moving sedately, speaking eloquently, but beneath the sleek façade lurked a killer with a temper. Franco had no remorse for dealing out vengeance to those who deserved it.

And that made him fucking perfect.

I may be going to Moscow, to the den of the Red

Wolverine, but I went with armed men whom I trusted with my life.

My cell phone rang in my pocket. I grabbed it with one hand, nodding at Franco to go and fulfil his orders.

"Mercer," I snapped.

Frederick came back into the lounge and gave me the thumbs-up sign. The tightness in my chest unwound a little. His approval for smashing the reputation of *Moineau* Holdings meant more than I wanted to admit. Who knew what we would be able to salvage from the rubble once this was all over.

Once it got out that I accepted women as bribes, my true contacts would dry up. And when the knowledge that I let those women go and I was on the war path for the fucktards who sold them to me landed on evil ears, I was painting a massive bull's-eye on my back.

"Frederick just told me you're heading to Russia. I must advise you that our intel won't back you up if anything goes wrong. Think carefully, Quincy. We can't help you if you leave our protection."

The chief of police, also a close confidant, lectured me. The same man who encouraged me to see how deep my emotions went for Tess. The same man who told me he wouldn't arrest me if I decided to keep Tess indefinitely.

I didn't like that he gave me double standards—I didn't deserve it.

I swallowed back the curses I wanted to throw. His heart was in a good place. "I won't do anything stupid, Dubois."

He chuckled. "I don't believe that for a second. But I had to call and say my piece. Just…just promise me you won't put your life on the line for one woman."

My finger twitched on the hang up button. "She's more than just one woman, Dubois." *She's my life.*

Silence reigned before the police chief sighed. "In that case, you have our backing. If and when the newspapers get wind of what you've done, I'll try and issue a gag order to the best of my ability."

"Merci." I hung up before he could sprout some other bullshit wisdom. I didn't need wisdom at a time like this. I needed a semi-automatic and a rocket launcher.

Pressing the number on speed-dial, I called Hans, who lived on standby to fly my G650 private jet. He answered on the first ring.

"Arrange a flight plan to Moscow. Leaving in sixty minutes. I'll see you soon." I hung up, watching the commotion in the room. Soon this would all be over, and Tess would be safely back with me. That moment seemed too distant to contemplate. I couldn't imagine ever feeling human again until I had her back in my bed.

My phone rang. I answered it on autopilot. *"Quoi?"* What?

"Master, please give me some news. Any news! Have you found her yet?" Suzette's sweet voice came down the phone, high with panic. I regretted telling her yesterday. She'd caught me off guard, complaining I hadn't given her instructions for dinner, asking if Tess and I were returning home that night.

I snapped and told her of course I wouldn't be fucking coming home that night or any night, not while Tess was stolen and in danger. That just opened a huge barrel of fucking problems.

"You have to let me work, Suzette. I'll call you the moment I've got her."

A sniff came down the line followed by a hard-edged promise. "You find her, and you make those bastards pay. She belongs with us. Find her quickly."

I couldn't speak; my throat snapped closed.

Tess touched all our lives, and we'd all be ruined if she never returned.

There was nothing I could say. Nothing I wanted to say. I just grunted and hung up.

Half an hour later, we pulled up at the private wing of the airport. I went to open the car door but paused. Turning to Frederick, I said, "You've done more than enough, Roux. Go home to Angelique." I slapped him on the shoulder in gratitude. In all honesty, I didn't know what I would've done if he hadn't been there that first afternoon. My migraine rendered me incapacitated while he orchestrated a worldwide manhunt.

"I'm coming. No questions or arguments." He smiled. "I told you; I want to meet the woman who wrapped you around her little finger."

I shook my head. "I don't know what's going to happen. I don't expect you to give any more than you already have."

He nodded, glancing out the window. "I know. But you'd do the same for me. I keep putting myself in your shoes, and it's a fucking painful place to be, Q. I love Angelique, we've been together for ten years, and the thought of suddenly being without her...it's excruciating."

I shifted uncomfortably. "That's why you should go home to her. I don't want to be the reason why you don't return."

His forehead furrowed as his temper filled the car. "I'm coming. Shut up."

There was nothing else I could do. I'd tried to protect him—this wasn't his battle, but I wasn't going to waste time or resources by arguing. I shrugged and exited the car.

Franco stood by the plane steps, giving me a hard grin. "Don't worry. She was strong enough to stand up to you. She's strong enough to stand up to whoever took her."

A proud smile tainted my sorrow-tugged mouth. "She's the strongest woman I know." Memories of whipping her, fucking her, heated my blood. Throughout everything I did to her, she never broke. I had to hold faith that she'd remain strong.

I nodded to Franco and entered the plush interior of the Jetstream. Down the back, nine men had already buckled up ready to go—an army of cloned power, ruthlessness, and severity. Black suits, black ties, and white shirts, I had an entire cast of James fucking Bond at my disposal.

As I sat down, a single thought popped into my head. *I'm not frightened she won't fight, I'm worried she'll fight too hard.* If the Red Wolverine had her she wouldn't stay in a singular piece for long, especially if this was revenge against me.

My hands wrapped around the armrests as the monster inside me went wild with the need to kill.

"We'll find her in time, boss." Franco patted my shoulder as he headed down the aisle to his colleagues.

The pessimistic part of me—or was it the realistic part—wasn't so sure. I knew what Gerald was capable of. I'd rescued enough slaves from his stables to hear countless stories of torture and rape.

My skin crawled at the thought of Tess in his clutches. I forced myself to stop thinking about it. I shifted in the seat, hating sitting still, hating the feel of not moving, not hunting.

Hans appeared in the doorway. He wore an understated suit and cap with gold wings embroidered on the front. The moment I saw him, I demanded, "Get us airborne. I want to be in Russia yesterday."

He nodded, his bright red hair sticking out the sides of his hat. "I have clearance to take off in fifteen minutes, sir. Our flight plan has been approved. We'll be there in approximately three and a half hours."

It was three and a half hours too long, but it would have to do.

Tess, stay alive. You fucking stay alive, or I'll hunt your ghost and whip you stupid for leaving me.

The animal inside hadn't calmed down. It wanted to gallop across the earth, sniffing, tracking, hunting the fucking bastards who'd taken Tess. I wanted to pull out their guts with my claws and howl to the goddamn moon when I had their blood on my hands.

Sighing, I closed my eyes and tried to keep my stress level under control. But as the engines whirred and we shot down the runway, I stayed tightly wound, tense as a fucking loaded slingshot.

And I would stay that way till I found Tess.

We touched down, and two black vans met us at the flight of stairs. Half the army of guards disappeared into one while Franco and the remaining crew came with me.

Moscow was cold, but not wintery. No snow graced the cityscape, no ice layered the roads. But damn, the wind bit through my suit like daggers.

The dark evening was broken by spotlights on the airport and a huge silver moon.

I'd been to Russia more times than I could count, but I never lingered. Something about this country didn't sit well with me. And it wasn't the prettiness or the quaintness that tourists were allowed to see.

No. I didn't like Russia because the dark underbelly indulged in far too many sins—sins I'd committed and wanted to commit over and over. I could control myself only if temptation was far away. And Russia welcomed corruptness with open arms. I'd never psychoanalyzed myself before, but I knew I was an addict for sadism, and Russia was sweet tantalization.

I wasn't strong enough to endure such a place.

No one spoke as the van whirred down semi-vacant streets. Slipping beneath the moon, coasting through streetlights, and past cute little store-fronts. The closer we got to the kingdom of Gerald Dubolazov, the more the atmosphere in the van thickened until every breath tasted of anticipation and hunger for blood. We morphed from businessmen to savage hunters, and I never wanted to tame myself again.

We weren't on our way to sign paperwork and indulge in mindless chitchat. We were going to war on behalf of a woman I was falling for. A woman who would be the catalyst for my business crumbling and my fortune draining away. But I would give it all away in a second if I could have her back intact.

The beast inside snarled and ripped holes in my soul. The darkness billowed, and I no longer had the strength to fight it. I would never fully repress it again. But I didn't care.

I liked acknowledging this part of myself. I loved being free for the first time in my life.

Even running on no sleep, barely any food or water, I revved on a higher plane. I was strong enough to find Tess, but only if I embraced the monster inside me.

Consequences would come later.

The van swung around the last corner, tyres squealing. "This one, boss?" one of Franco's men asked, slowing down to pull into an alley. Beside us rose a huge majestic hotel. Designed in typical Russian beauty, it stood out like a ruby glinting in the night. Red accents on windowsills and plasterwork looked as good as the day it was painted. The pale pink turrets looked like a cupcake, iced by some fucking fairy.

I was proud of this project but wanted to tear it the fuck down with my bare hands until nothing remained. And I would if Gerald had hurt Tess. I'd blow it up, with him inside.

"Yes," I said, glaring out the window, looking for onlookers.

No one walked past the alley, no one disturbed us. "Let's go," I muttered, twisting in my seat to face Franco. He was already prepared, leaning forward, tension palpable in his tight muscles.

The moment his eyes met mine, he placed a semi-automatic into my awaiting palm and snapped a radio watch onto my wrist.

"Frequency is set, all you have to do is speak into it, and the team will hear you." All business, he pushed a few extra clips into my blazer breast pocket, and fumbled in the black canvas bag beside him for a wicked sharp hunting knife. "You have enough rounds to kill most of the staff inside, so you should be covered, but keep the knife on you, just in case."

I took the handle, running a thumb over the sharp blade. A strange haze came over me, removing me from the van, hurtling me into darkness.

Franco knew my aversion to carrying a knife into a tense altercation. Guns kept me human—impersonal, remote from taking a life. But a knife? A knife spoke to the beast. It made my mouth water at the thought of slipping the blade between an enemy's ribcage and piercing their heart. To be so up close and personal, to feel their last breath, knowing I stole it from them. It made me fucking hard and twisted my brain into something monstrous.

The temptation was exquisite, filling my mind with ruthless power. My hands shook with the need to gut Gerald the Wolverine. If I took this there would be no turning back. I would be admitting that Tess was gone, and I was sacrificing not just my livelihood and countless of freed slaves, but my sanity, too.

I'd fought my battle for twenty-eight long years. Exhausted myself into believing I could be just a man—a human without the savagery of a monster. If I let myself slip now, it was all over.

You have no choice. Embrace the black, recognise the truth.

Gritting my teeth, I tucked the knife into the back of my waistband. The moment it was out of my grip, I breathed normally again.

"You know what I want." My voice didn't resemble a man anymore.

I might as well pretend I never was one. I was nothing more than a creature with the urge to bathe in his enemy's blood. I'd never felt such baser needs or the compulsion to stab and mutilate so keenly.

Franco nodded. "I know what to do. Don't worry, we've got your back, and we'll make sure your exit is clear…" His eyes darted away before settling back on mine. "Look, if anything does go wrong, there's a man called—"

I held up my hand, cutting him off. "I don't want to know. Nothing will go wrong. *T'as compris?*" Understand?

Franco gave me a tight smile. "Of course, but…" He snapped his lips closed. Avoiding my eyes, he passed a Glock to Frederick along with a matching knife. "I know you probably won't use these, but it's best to be armed."

Frederick grimaced. "I've managed to work with Q for years and kept my hands clean. But I'm not squeamish if I have to."

Franco smiled, but his body language frustrated the fuck out of me. He had something on his mind, and if he didn't spit it out who knew if he'd be compromised.

My eyes narrowed. "Speak, Franco. What the fuck do you want to say?"

He glared, before looking away briefly. "I'm just worried that we're walking into a building full of murderers and drug dealers and Tess might not be there. What's the next step?" He dropped his voice so only I heard it. "Sir, what if she's run… What if others have her?"

The memory of Lefebvre rutting between Tess's legs collided through my mind. Would I never be free of that fucking image? The hatred for myself for hurting Tess so much she ran into the clutches of a rapist hammered me into the ground.

I clenched my fingers so hard, I pressed the trigger on the gun. Luckily for everyone in the van, the safety was on.

"They won't give her an opportunity to run. She'll be there." *She has to be.* Otherwise, I didn't know where the fuck to look, and that terrified the shit out of me.

Franco nodded. "Fair enough. You know this cocksucker better than I do." He straightened. "Let's get this ball of fun on the road, shall we?"

I nodded and slid open the door. Franco spoke to his men. "Alpha squadron with me. Beta team you're with Dean, and Charlie outfit you're with Vincent. Everyone, you have your orders. Follow them meticulously if you want to stay alive."

Frederick climbed out to stand next to me as Franco's clones disembarked the van. They moved like a legion of shadows, armed to the fucking teeth and dying to bloody their weapons.

No one spoke as Franco took the lead. With a few finger codes from him, we fell into formation. Half the team melted into darkness as if they evaporated into the night. The other half plastered themselves against the rich architecture of the Wolverine's hotel. The same hotel I owned shares in, arranged permits and consents for. The same hotel that gave me two slaves as bribes.

I prided myself on remembering every girl's name, linked in my mind to the building or acquisition that allowed me to save them.

Sophie and Carmen were collateral for this particular building. Polish, and English, both beaten within an inch of their life, both forever unable to walk properly with what was done to them.

The familiar rage compounded on top of the already black blood in my veins. I pitied anyone who was my enemy—I would have a tally of deaths after tonight.

I wanted to drive a wrecking ball through every floor and crush the hotel to rubble. Fucking Russian bastard.

Within a matter of milliseconds, Franco's team spread out and camouflaged into the night, leaving Frederick and me to stroll casually the rest of the way. The small semi-automatic weighed down my blazer's inside pocket, and the knife pricked the top of my ass every time I stepped.

Every movement felt different: smoother, sleeker. I no longer owned my body—the beast inside did.

"Try and pretend you're still human, man. You're freaking me out, and I know you won't hurt me."

I shot a look at Frederick, who'd hidden the Glock in his suit and smoothed his gelled hair, so he looked presentable.

"I don't know what you're talking about," I growled.

"Course you don't. But I'm telling you, lighten up, try and think of pleasant things. Your eyes are positively savage."

Words were delays, and I wanted none of it. Glowering, I strode forward and headed toward the main entrance. The street held a couple climbing into a taxi, their luggage littered around the curb.

The doorman gave us a curt nod as we walked in. My back stayed ramrod straight thanks to the knife down my pants, and my hands ached to clench into fists and start tearing up the place to find Tess.

She has to be here. She has to be.

The lobby looked like the Renaissance period threw up on it. Scrolls and gold leaf, pretentious and ostentatious.

Trying to act normal, I eyeballed the concierge. I didn't pay any attention to the private alcoves or carefully arranged seating nooks, nor did I listen to the gentle notes of a piano playing. I focused entirely on the man who would be my first victim if he didn't take me to Gerald.

I demanded, "I'm here to see your boss. And before you ask if I have a fucking appointment, I don't, and I don't need one. Mention my name. He'll see me."

The elderly concierge looked down his nose, peering over half-moon glasses. "I know who you are. And he said to let you up when you arrived."

I didn't register shock. That would be a weakness; I was anything but weak in that moment. I was ready.

"Lead the way," I clipped.

The man handed me a keycard and pointed at the elevator

reserved for the penthouse floor. "Be my guest. I've been told not to disturb your meeting." He gave me a sneer and my fingers twitched to punch him.

Frederick came to the man's rescue by tugging my arm. "Great. We'll head up." He plucked the keycard from my grip, hauling me to the lift. "Wait till we're behind closed doors before you go berserk, Q."

I jerked my head in some sort of acknowledgement and followed him into the elevator. The doors began to close, and Franco appeared from nowhere, jumping in beside us.

"All clear as far as we can tell. I'm guessing he has his penthouse fortified. I recommend we wait till Alpha squadron can catch up."

They were lucky I wasn't scaling the fucking building with my bare hands. Wait longer? No fucking way.

I didn't bother answering as the lift soared upward. I reached into my breast pocket and pulled out the gun.

Frederick eyed me warily, but then followed suit. Franco pulled two guns from his holster beneath his jacket. We nodded at each other then stared at the doors, waiting for the moment when they would open.

The three clicks of safeties being taken off helped mollify me for a moment.

Not long. Hold on, Tess.

The gentle ping of arrival sent every muscle in my body vibrating with tension. I was coiled, armed, and fucking ready to create some carnage.

The doors glided open. We crouched and moved forward.

"I expected you twenty-four hours ago, Mercer. You're losing your touch." Gerald chuckled the moment we stepped into the lounge.

I froze, battling back the urge to let loose the entire round of bullets into him.

The penthouse was five hundred square feet of pure decadence. Not only had I designed the hotel suite's floor plan, but hired an interior designer who knew the value of great lighting, subtle wall tones, and elaborate wallpaper.

It was a perfect palace, sullied by the fucking gutter rat who lived there.

Gerald sat in a large weathered chair, nursing a goblet of liquor. His prosthetic leg cocked to the side awkwardly from a former gunshot, courtesy of a disgruntled business associate.

His pink scalp and wispy blond hair didn't do anything to help his gob for a face, or the nasty scars on his cheeks. His nose was red and large, identifying him as a drunkard, and his large gut strained in the ridiculous paisley shirt. It made him look watery eyed and almost ready for the grave, but regardless of his sickly appearance, his control over his empire was legendary.

"Where the fuck is she?" I snarled.

His son appeared. My heart thudded with thick hatred and I wanted to shoot him all over again. He wore an exact replica of the jumpsuit he'd worn when he hurt Tess, only this one was a horrifying yellow. His gold-capped teeth looked garish when he smiled and waved a wooden cane in my direction in a salute.

"I never got a chance to thank you for the goodbye gift, cocksucker. Your dog over there dragged me out before I could repay the favour." He pointed at Franco. "You'll pay for kicking me when I was fuckin' shot. Only way you could get one over me. If my leg hadn't been gushin' blood, I would've had you dead in a moment."

Franco snorted. "Didn't sound so tough when you fucking pissed yourself after I slapped you." He leaned forward, eyes narrowing. "How about I slap you again and you can cry to Daddy?"

I swallowed hard, tasting the threat, the underlying violence in the room.

The man launched forward, and I didn't give Franco a chance to deliver his promise. He deserved more than a fucking slap. My fist collided with his jaw, cracking in the silent room. The throb started in my knuckles and radiated up my arm, but for the first time in days, I felt like things were finally going my way.

"Come near us again and I'll not only cripple you like your old man, I'll redecorate your insides."

"Enough!" Gerald demanded, throwing the goblet at my head.

I ducked, encroaching on his space. "Tell me where she is. *Je ne le redemanderais pas.*" I won't ask again.

Gerald laughed, his big gut jiggling with every guffaw. "Why the hell would I know?" His eyes went from mirthful to hate-filled in a second. His entire body settled heavier in the chair as he glared at me from beneath his overhanging brow. "You shot my only son for sampling the present we gave you. Not exactly hospitable behaviour."

My jaw ached I clenched so hard, but I didn't move; I didn't speak. I let him get on with his little fucking speech. The sooner he finished, the sooner I could get my hands on Tess.

"I had planned on using her myself—after all, the great fucking Q Mercer kept her as a pet, there must be something special about her cunt to warrant such a prize."

I flinched and gripped the gun harder, imagining it was his fat-riddled neck I wrung.

"However, a better deal came along than fucking your sloppy seconds."

My legs spasmed, dying to rush the bastard and slash the knife into his throat. My voice echoed with hatred. "Stop wasting my time." I aimed the gun at his crotch. "Where is she, Dubolazov?"

Gerald laughed and wheezed, before answering. "That, my pussy-whipped friend, is no longer your concern. I like keeping secrets. Consider this my notice that I will no longer do business with you." He looked at his oaf of a son, huddled by the wall, nursing his bruised face. "After all, I can't deal with a man who severely injured my own, can I?"

Something slithered over me. Something cold and sinister and normally I would fight. I would stop the shutting down of my emotions and the remainder of humanity receding like a wakeless tide, but I didn't. I let the conversion happen, and the gun grew heavy in my hands.

Did he honestly think I wouldn't kill him if he had nothing to offer me?

Dubolazov seemed to track my line of thought as he swallowed, a trace of fear ringing his eyes. "You can't kill me. It would be business suicide. You so much as look at myself or my son again and I'll crucify you."

I shrugged. I honestly didn't care. All I cared about was finding Tess and giving her the best life I could.

Shuffling sounded behind me and Franco yelled, "Stay right fucking there. Just having a conversation, boys. No need to get your cocks out."

I looked over my shoulder at the three guards who'd arrived, all waving guns, trying to decide who to train their sights on. Deciding I was the greatest threat, they pointed the muzzles in my direction, even as Franco and Frederick trained theirs on them.

Raising an eyebrow, I held up my gun, letting it dangle from my finger. "All good. Just finishing up our little chat, then we'll go."

No one moved as I placed the gun on a side table and inched forward.

Gerald glared, but didn't order the men to kill me.

I stopped within grabbing distance and gave him a thin smile. "So, you mean to take your secret to your grave, Dubolazov?"

One chance.

One last chance to give me Tess's location. Then I'd grant mercy. I would walk away. I would cage the demon inside me and not fucking maim him.

He leaned forward, sending a whiff of vodka into my face. "I'll never tell a fucking prick like you. You pretend to be one of us, but you free merchandise. Slaves we've dedicated time to break, women who, by right, belong to us until their godforsaken little pussies wear out. Fuck you, Mercer. We're done here." He lowered his voice to a hiss. "I hope she's dead already."

The switch inside sprung permanently free, and I moved.

Time slowed as I reached for the knife in my trousers. I existed in slow motion as the blade came free, my arm swung forward, and the obstruction of gristle and windpipe gave way under the sharp metal.

The thrill, the rush, the heady fucking pleasure rippled through me and I smiled. I fucking smiled as I watched Gerald blink in shock, wondering what the hell happened.

I moved so fast, it took a moment for blood to well and cascade down his throat.

"No!" Gerald's son threw himself off the wall, colliding with me.

Gunshots rang out and something hot nicked my arm. Franco called out, and Frederick yelled. Gerald's son punched me in the ribs, but his meaty hands were no match for my blade.

I stabbed him deep in the kidney and twisted.

I waited for horror, for self-hatred of loving the hot splash of blood and the dying gurgle of my victim, but for once I was free.

The rush and fire and righteousness doused my veins; I shuddered with black delight.

Murder.

It was fast becoming a new hobby of mine.

I stood, pushing the convulsing body off me, drenched in hot blood. I honoured Tess's wish to bring down the bastards involved with trafficking.

I killed a father and son.

I killed…

And the beast inside fucking loved it.

The memory of taking my father's life filled my nostrils. The stench of his bowels loosening, the sharp tang of blood and brain. It all mixed in some sort of morbid perfume, resonating with the feral part of me, making me proud to be a killer of evil.

Slowly sensation came back into my body. My arm burned. Twisting my neck, I fingered the hole in my blazer, poking the slippery wound beneath. Fucking fantastic.

I'd been shot.

Frederick appeared, reaching for my jacket. "Oh, shit. How bad is it?" He ripped off my jacket before I had a chance to push him away.

"Don't worry about it. I'll be fine." The bullet had gone right through my bicep. Fairly clean and tidy considering. It didn't even hurt.

I looked toward the entrance where a mound of corpses lay. Puddles of blood dotted the white tiles.

Franco met my eyes. "Five dead. Four shots and one stabbing." He motioned for us to leave. "We have to go. Who knows how many more guards are on their way."

I shook my head, feeling strangely lightheaded. "We're not leaving until we search the place." Scooping up the gun and clenching my jaw against the sudden flash of pain in my arm, I took off in direction of the bedrooms. "Fan out. Meet back in here in ten minutes."

Picking up my pace, I jogged quickly down the long expanse of corridor, trying to ignore the chills of eerie silence and mound of bodies behind us.

Gerald normally only had three to five guards in his private residence. He said they cramped his style when I asked a few years back why he didn't surround himself in security. We were alone. For now. I just hoped we'd stay alone for a bit longer.

Keeping my finger tight on the trigger, I swept room after room. Strode through decadent parlours and bedrooms fit for a prim aristocrat, not a raping, murdering mobster.

But I only found emptiness. No women. No Tess.

I opened cupboards, searched under beds, even smashed a few floorboards to see if a secret room had been added since the original blueprints. But nowhere did I find a bound and frightened woman. No evidence of a struggle. No trace of Tess at all.

After a full circuit of the apartment, I met Franco and Frederick by the elevator. "Anything?" Three pairs of eyes were better than one. Especially seeing as I'd been fucking shot. *Please let them have found something.*

Frederick hung his head. "Nothing." He sighed, adding, "But it doesn't mean she isn't in the building."

I had a better idea. Pulling out my phone, I entered the same website that tracked Tess the first time and waited for the little red dot to appear on the map.

Nothing.

Heart racing, I tapped the device against my thigh. *"Viendra sur, toi merde."* Come on, you piece of shit.

I looked again, wishing, praying for the little red dot to show me where Tess was. It was the only connection I had to her. It had to work. It had to.

Franco looked over my shoulder as the screen flashed and came up with an error message. *The tracking device you have requested is no longer in service. Please check the number and try again.*

"Fuck!" I threw the phone across the room, trembling with rage. My eyes fell to the bodies, and I wanted nothing more than to stab and stab and stab, take out retribution and funnel my rage.

Frederick put his hand on my uninjured arm. "We'll find her, man. Don't worry. With or without a beacon."

Franco nodded. "He's right. We'll find her, sir. We'll just have to mow down some bastards to do it."

Ten

Tess

Tie me, tease me, let your pleasure please me. Hurt me, love me, but please don't ever leave me...

My employment began immediately.

Trapped in a world of drugs and insipid fog, White Man plucked me from my bed and threw me at Leather Jacket.

I cried out as I collided with his creaky leather and stench. I cringed as he smirked, holding me tight against him. "Hello again, *puta*. Time for some fun." He spun me around, trapping my wrists.

His dirty fingers wrapped around my skin, hoisting my arm back till my shoulder bellowed. Even the foggy stupor couldn't save me from the pain of a dislocated limb.

"What the—" he muttered.

"Let her go, Ignacio. I need her to be able to use her arms."

"But look at what the little bitch did. Stupid slave." He ran a thumb over my modified barcode, no doubt seeing the sparrow and the number fifty-eight. He chuckled and shook me, breathing hard against my ear. "You idiot bitch. You fell for the bastard who bought you." His chuckle morphed into a laugh, shaking both our frames. "This is too good. I've heard of slaves becoming attached to their masters, but you went to a whole other level."

He grabbed my chin, digging his fingers into the hollow of my cheeks. "You were like a fucking queen in that bathtub, thinking you'd landed on your pretty little feet. Well, live it up, princess, 'cause you're in servitude now."

His head cocked to the side, and he kissed my cheek with dry lips. "Then again, if you fell in love with one asshole, you can fall for another. Maybe you'll want to fuck me before the week is out. Huh?"

I flinched as he stroked my hair, then sighed in relief as White Man pulled me from Leather Jacket's embrace. "You'll have plenty of time to mind-fuck the poor creature. But first I want to see just how strong she is."

He held out his hand as if he'd asked me out on a date; blue eyes twinkled as I gawked at his palm. I couldn't remember what I should do. I couldn't remember anything. The alchemy of chemicals in my bloodstream slowly stole everything I knew.

"Come along, little one. No time like the present to start your initiation."

I tried to step back toward the pallet. I ordered my limbs to move, to run, but nothing obeyed. I just stood there swaying until White Man grabbed my elbow and guided me from the room.

His perfectly ironed clothing contrasted against the sinister grime as we made our way down a long musty corridor. I wanted to scream and punch him in the eyes, but all I could do was coast along like a good belonging. The fog imprisoned my mind—turning me into the worst sort of captive—the one who obeyed without duress, who didn't even need shackles to keep her down.

They'd taken my will, and soon, they'd take my mind.

White Man spoke to Leather Jacket as we stopped outside a door and pushed me inside. "Don't go too far, Ignacio. Remember…little is key. They become more pliant that way."

I stumbled like a brain-dead zombie, screaming silently for my body to do *anything* but fumble. Everything was so heavy and soupy and unresponsive.

Please. This is your last chance! Obey!

I managed to twitch enough to inch backward, shuffling toward the exit.

But all it took was a hand between my shoulder blades and I was pushed forward.

I blinked, looking around. Concrete walls, concrete floor with dampness climbing the corners and puddles resting in cracks. Three chairs, white and sun-worn, faced each other in a circle.

White Man guided me by the shoulders to sit in one of the chairs. It creaked under my weight and my head flopped onto my chin. So tired. So confused.

I'm hungry. I'm tired. I'm cold. I just want to go home. Where am I?

He patted my cheek, saying, "Have fun, little girl. Happy initiation."

I wanted to hurl myself out the door; my heart bled as he clapped his hands and looked behind me. "Great. The others are here. You'll no longer be alone, little one. I'll see you later."

He slipped out the door and the lock clicked into place behind two girls who'd entered on a leash, tugged by Jagged Scar. He gave me a snide smile before jerking the girls forward and pushing them into a chair.

I couldn't comprehend what I saw.

Both girls were naked. Both trembled and shook as if an earthquake had replaced their hearts. Their eyes were full of horror and terror, but it was their hair that terrified me.

Blonde. Both of them. The same honey straw as my own. Oh, God.

I wriggled in the chair to stand, but the chemicals blocked the signal from my brain and I sprawled to the floor instead. My cheek pressed against slimy concrete and I groaned as a flash of pain spread through me.

Leather Jacket laughed, coming to my rescue. Grabbing a

chunk of my hair, he hauled me upright and threw me onto the chair. "Clumsy bitch."

My eyes smarted from the agony of his grip, but I swallowed back the heaviness of tears. I was foggy enough without adding grief to the mix.

The girls sniffed, trying hard to stay silent even as tears tracked their dirty faces. I refused to look at them. I hated seeing the shadows of bruises on their arms and ribs. Why were they here?

They're here for lunch. We're going to have lunch, and then we're going to have a nap and dream of whimsical things.

I shook my head, snapping out of the druggie daydream.

Leather Jacket gave a sadistic smile, bending to lick me. Once again, he dragged his foul tongue up my cheek and into my hair. "Trying to figure it out, aren't ya? You won't be able to. Not with the mixture in your blood. You're going to do as I say, when I say. Got it?"

A small flash of my normal self wrenched itself from the dirty puddle that was now my soul. I forced past the weakness, whispering, "You're a fucking cocksucker and I'll ch—chop off your balls before you die."

He laughed and clicked his fingers. "Is that a fact?"

A guard I didn't know appeared next to me. He looked like a sack of potatoes. Big gut, lumpy clothing, and a face only an ogre could love. He smiled, wriggling his fingers in my face. "Hello."

I must be pleasant. Be polite. How many times did my parents tell me they could only love a polite, quiet child?

"Hello," I repeated, wishing my head wasn't so heavy so I could keep eye contact longer.

Leather Jacket moved forward, heading behind the two girls in front of me. He rested a hand on both their shoulders and they whimpered.

Don't. Don't touch them. I shook my head. *Why can't he touch them again?*

"Ryan here is going to make sure you obey." Baring his

teeth, he jerked the girl's heads back with their hair. "He is the consequence of not listening. Understand, *puta*?"

Should I nod? *I don't know. I don't understand.* The drugs pulled me further into their web the longer I sat there.

Leather Jacket shoved one of the girls to the floor, cocking an eyebrow in my direction. "Pick her up. Go on."

The will to save another blazed through the fog and I fell off my chair to crawl to her. The girl moaned as I touched her wrist and our eyes connected in a brief moment of lucidity. In her green gaze I saw all my dreams and hopes shrivel to dust. We would all die here. It was just a matter of how much we had to endure before we would be free.

Grunting, I tried to help her up. But I wasn't strong enough.

Someone smacked me out of the way and I crashed into a chair. Ryan the ogre picked up the blonde as if she was a dirty sock and hurled her into the seat.

I climbed upright, using the chair as support. Drugs swirled. *I'm hot. I'm cold.* A racking cough crippled me and it was a while before I could breathe again.

I couldn't understand what just happened.

Leather Jacket said, "If you can't do it right the first time, Ryan will do it better than you." He came closer, leering into my face. "He'll make sure to do it ten times better than you. Understand, *puta*?"

I gained enough minor motor control to nod. Just to get him out of my personal bubble.

"All right then, let's get this party started." He nodded at Ryan. "Go ahead."

Everything exploded.

The girls screamed as Ryan launched himself at them. Dragging them toward the concrete wall, he pinned one with his forearm while holding the other immobile for Leather Jacket to cuff.

For the first time, I noticed iron manacles dangling by chains from the wall. Rusty and ancient, they looked like they belonged in a medieval torture chamber.

Leather Jacket worked fast and before I could move, the girl's arms were spread wide and her ankles trapped with more iron cuffs attached to the floor.

She looked at me and my heart died for her. What the fuck was happening!

Once the first girl was secure, Leather Jacket proceeded to shackle the other. He slapped her when she tried to pull away. She squealed and thrashed, causing more abuse to rain upon her skin.

I found my voice in the fog and screamed, "Stop!"

But Leather Jacket just laughed. "We're the ones doing the ordering. You just wait your turn."

Once the girls were chained to the wall, bodies pressed against icy concrete, both men came toward me, sandwiching me between them.

The girls pleaded with me to help them. I wanted to. I would. But how? I could barely function, let alone save us.

One girl wailed, "Please. Don't do this. Let us go. What did we do? We just want to go home!"

My own misfortune from the first time I'd been Leather Jacket's captive came back to haunt me. I'd never begged. I'd fought and it landed me in more pain.

Why did I fight again? *Because it isn't right. None of this is right!*

I'm hungry. I'm tired. I'm cold. I just want to go home. Where am I?

Leather Jacket roared at them in Spanish and I trembled, unable to look, but I couldn't look away either. I wanted to imprint them to memory. Their survival was on my shoulders. I would get them free.

Leather Jacket put an arm around my neck, sticking his gruesome tongue in my ear. "Ready for day one of training, bitch?"

I squirmed, but it was too late. A needle disappeared into my arm and another hot wave of all-consuming mental oblivion sucked me deep. Down and down I went, spiralling heavier and heavier until I existed on the bottom of a rubbish-filled ocean.

Sounds warbled. Smells twisted. My vision darted from place to place, never locking on anything, always moving, making me sick with vertigo. But it was my brain I worried most for. My sharp intelligence and fierce awareness no longer existed. It'd been suffocated into tiny clouds, floating uselessly in my skull.

Leather Jacket pushed me forward and I wobbled on uncoordinated legs. "Hit them."

Hit them. *Hit them.* Of course, why didn't I think of it? Hitting them makes total sense.

No, wait.

It doesn't. What? Why would I hit anyone? I didn't want to inflict pain.

No!

I swallowed thickly, licking my oversized lips. "Wh—why?"

He frowned, bouncing around in my crazy funhouse vision. "Did you just ask why, *puta*?" He shook his head, looking at Ryan. "Rule number one. You *never* ask questions. Ryan. Please show this bitch what I expected from her."

"Sure thing, boss."

I watched in horrifying slow motion as Ryan sucker-punched a girl in the gut. She bent over, jerked to a halt by the manacles. She screamed, crying uncontrollably.

Why did he do that?

Because she's been naughty. A child needs discipline. Yes. A child needs discipline. I should know. I suffered enough slaps while I grew up.

No. this is different. Don't forget. Never forget this is wrong. So wrong.

Leather Jacket pulled me forward. "Let's try this again. Hit them."

"Hit them?" I repeated. My voice sounded far, far away as if I lived in a dark tunnel where no light existed.

"Hit them, or I will," he ordered.

I shrugged. Did it matter to me? Why did it matter to me?

Because he'll kill them! At least if you do it, you'll be as gentle as you can. Do it. Protect them by hitting them.

The small nucleus of who I was wailed at the injustice. How could I stop this?

Leather Jacket said something in Spanish to Ryan the Ogre. I blinked and weaved on the spot.

"Be my pleasure." Ryan moved at lightning speed, and the action didn't register in my slow brain until the bone-crunching *thwack* of his fist connected with the other blonde. She doubled over, puking instantly.

Fuck! Get it together.

Hit them. Hit them. Stop this!

Some frantic part of me doggy-paddled against the riptide of drugs, dispersing it a little, enough so I could see glimpses of reality. Oh, God. I had to torture these women. I had to abuse women who looked like me. I had to break and do as I was told in order to save them from a worse punishment.

Hands flew to my mouth, trying to contain the rising bile. I reeled backward. "You're sick. Let them go!" My wide eyes flew to Leather Jacket in horror. "Please. Do what you want with me, but leave them alone!"

Leather Jacket shook his head. "Goddamn, you are strong. You should've buckled under the mix by now." He ran hands through his greasy hair, thoughts racing in his eyes. "Ryan. Give me the stick."

Ryan gave him a baton. The same type police used on bad guys and men like Leather Jacket. "Take this, *puta.*" He held it out to me.

I growled like a feral cat, backing toward the door. I tried the knob, knowing full well it wouldn't turn.

He didn't try to stop me, just watched with a cocked head and twisted smile. "I won't ask you again, bitch. Take this." He waved the stick in my direction and I shook my head, succumbing to the drugs again.

Why didn't I want to take the stick?

No reason. Stop fighting. It's such a waste of energy. You're right. I'm hungry. I'm cold. I want to go home. Where am I?

My mind turned traitorous, leaving me in the dark completely. Q had turned my body against me, but these bastards were doing it to my mind.

Leather Jacket nodded. "Have it your way." He passed the baton to Ogre. He didn't say a thing. The man accepted it and in one fierce strike broke a blonde girl's leg.

Her screech echoed in my ears and I knew I would never forget it. Never erase the pain and horror of her voice. I would live the rest of my days listening to her scream. *I could've prevented that. I could've stopped that!*

"Stop!" I sobbed, tears waterfalled down my cheeks. "Stop. I'll do it. I'll do it. I'll do it…" I couldn't stop repeating and repeating. The thought ran around and around in my head. "I'll do it!"

Leather Jacket grinned, coming toward me to tuck me under his arm. "Good, bitch. Now that we've broken through. Let's have some fun, shall we?"

The fog sucked me deeper, and this time I didn't fight. I allowed the clouds to smother me. I let the blankness and strange soothing softness ransack my mind and prevent myself from ever remembering what I was about to do.

Agonising centimetre by centimetre, I let Leather Jacket guide me to stand in front of the two sobbing women. He patted my head, murmuring. "Good girl. Now, do what I say."

I hung my head. A brutal headache formed and I welcomed the pain.

I deserved pain.

Pain was terrible.

Pain was awful.

I would always run from any form of pain from now on.

Oh, God. *I'll always run from pain.* Gone was my future with Q. Gone was any hope of finding happiness with him.

The drugs sucked me deeper. *You'll never see him again, so there's nothing to grieve.* I would die here. And I would rot in hell for what they made me do.

"Hit the blonde on the right. No hesitation or else Ryan will have a go."

I didn't move; I just stared at the two women. We became trapped in our own little blonde cocoon. Their hair colour was symbolic. By beating them, I beat myself. I willingly helped Leather Jacket break me. And the realization did nothing but send me spiralling deeper into insanity.

I'm cold. I'm hungry. I want to go home. Where am I?

A huge barrel of coughs erupted from my throat as I stood shivering from head to toe. Leather Jacket prodded my back, and I stumbled into the blonde on the left. I fell against her; we flinched. She had a belly button piercing of a star and hanging diamantés. Her eyes were green, her breasts soft against my body.

More tears fell from my eyes as I surrendered to everything. "I'm so sorry." My words slurred and thick.

Leather Jacket murmured, "Hate to break up this lesbian party, but you have five seconds, *puta*."

Five seconds to hit this woman in order to save her more pain. Five seconds to grant her my destruction, to ruin both of us.

Kill her and be done with it. If she represents you, kill yourself. It's the only way to be free.

I struck and slapped her. Her eyes glassed and tears spilled, but she bit her lip, and in a heartbreaking, mind-tripping, life-ending move, she nodded. Fucking nodded, accepting what would happen. What I would do to her.

The other blonde sobbed quietly, her small breasts rising and falling with panicked breaths.

It didn't matter how many drugs Leather Jacket forced into me, I would never do this willingly. I would never hit another or take a life.

He gave me no choice. If I was weaker, I might've given up and let Ryan take my place. Their blood would be on his hands, not mine. But I couldn't do that. Their lives were mine to protect.

Leather Jacket pulled my shoulders, moving me to stand in front of the blonde with small breasts. She didn't have a belly button piercing, but she had a small tattoo of a hummingbird on her hipbone.

A bird.

I was about to crush a bird that Q would do everything in his power to protect. I was about to become the exact opposite of the man I loved.

Leather Jacket whispered in my ear, "Punch her. I'm sure there's more vomit in her gut."

I stood for an eternity, trying to befuddle myself out of the drug-fog. *There must be a way out of this. Think!*

I'm cold… I'm hungry…

Leather Jacket growled, "Five…four…three…two…"

The drugs roiled and I punched the girl in the stomach. Even though the drugs cushioned the horribleness of what I did, I shattered inside.

A whirlwind of sparrows filled my head and their tiny talons grabbed my last remaining sanity and flew me far, far away. Either to heaven, hell, or limbo—I didn't care. All I knew was I'd never be whole again. My mind had protected itself by flying free, soaring back to Q, leaving me to die.

My muscles shut down and it wasn't the girl who threw up, it was me. I splashed Leather Jacket's shoes with my roast chicken lunch and collapsed into the warm mess.

They'd finally done it. They'd found my weakness.

They could do what they wanted to me. Torture me. Rape me. And I would always have inner fire—the strength that drove me onward. But make me hurt and torture someone else? That was a recipe for me losing my sanity.

The recipe that would well and truly break me forever.

I moaned, cringing at the crick in my back from lying on a hard pallet. I tried to move but every part of my body ached.

My knuckles were scratched and bruised. My teeth hurt from clenching. My head pounded with a never-ending headache and my side screamed from the kick Leather Jacket gave me for not obeying.

You're turning into one of them. You hurt others. You're becoming a devil.

I did it to protect them! I hurt them a lot less than Ogre would have done.

No excuse. You're breaking. They're winning.

You need to run. Run. Run. Run. Run.

I clutched my head, trying to stop the swirl of words from making me sick.

I couldn't move, let alone run. That was an impossibility.

Hours ticked past and I couldn't sleep. My brain never granted me peace, echoing constantly with curses and blames, telling me to run even when my body could never obey. The girl's scream lived in my ears, always ringing.

Every time I closed my eyes, Q appeared.

"How could you, Tess? You became one of them. I thought you were better than that. I thought you were pure." He hung his head, eyes glittering with remorse. *"There's nothing left to love about you. You're a traitor. A monster. I'm going to have to kill you."*

I ran to him, but something held me back. Some wall of air, or invisible imprisonment. *"No! I'm not like that. I didn't want to do it. I did it to save them!"*

He laughed, throwing a look of such hatred, I shrank to the floor in shame. *"You're weak, Tess. So weak. I underestimated you. I saw someone fierce. Now all I see is a ruined little girl."*

"Save me then! Please. I need your help. So much." I couldn't stop crying.

Q shook his head. His powerful body encased in a black suit looked fit to attend a funeral. My funeral. He was saying goodbye to me.

"Q!"

He refused to make eye contact. Turning his back, he walked slowly into the swirling mist. *"Goodbye, Tess."*

Q hated me. I hated me. I wanted to die.

More time passed.

My cell door opened and the same woman who'd tattooed me strolled in. She moved boldly, relaxed and happy. She smiled wide, holding an uncapped syringe. "Ready for another dose, *cariño?*"

I shuffled upright, cursing my heavy head. "No…pl—please, no more." My words slurred, tripping and sliding over each other.

She perched on the edge of the bed, reaching for my arm.

I flailed around, managing to avoid her grip. "No. I said no mo—more."

Her smile slid from her face, replaced with black anger. "Mateo!"

The door opened and in walked Jagged Scar carrying a baseball bat. He kept coming until his knees touched the end of the pallet. "Don't make me use this." He slapped the bat into his hand, threatening me. "Be a good employee and let Sofia give you your medicine, okay?"

His voice was so smooth compared to Leather Jacket. Always giving the impression of civility, all the while he was the worst of the lot. He was a true psychopath.

My throat closed and I twisted my unresponsive fingers in my lap. "Please. Money. Jewellery. I'll give you…"

What was I talking about? *I'm hungry. Ask for some food. I'm cold. Maybe if you take the medicine, they'll give you a blanket.*

Oh, I loved that idea. A blanket. It felt like forever since I'd been warm.

I coughed hard, gasping as my lungs struggled for breath.

Someone pushed me back until I lay down and soft fingers took my arm, spreading it flat. A gentle tap in the crook of my arm sent my heart racing. "No! Wait!"

Too late.

The needle pierced my skin and the woman pressed the plunger. Instantly hot, cold, tingling, stinging liquid entered my body and began its journey to poison me.

Compounded onto whatever else they gave me, I didn't stand a chance.

My eyes no longer worked and I floated into darkness. My head was the weight of a twenty ton bowling ball.

I sighed, listening to the heavy *glug-glug* of my heartbeat. There was no other noise apart from my shallow breathing. The woman and Jagged Scar had gone.

How long ago? I didn't know.

Now is your time to run! Get up. Do it! Freedom!

I didn't know how I moved, but one moment I slouched on the pallet, the next I lay jumbled on the floor.

And that's where I stayed for hours. I spent God knows how long living in a horrific circus of freakish hallucinations while I lay shivering on the freezing concrete floor.

My parents who never loved me made an appearance.

"Look at the sight of you." My mother with her blue-rinsed hair bent to my level, tutting under her talcum powdery scent. *"We always knew there was something wrong with you. But now? We're repulsed. Doing drugs, beating up women, and indulging in rough sex? Ugh. Look how far you've fallen, child. Only hell is good enough for you now."*

I didn't bother to retaliate or care.

My father in his tweed suit and leather cap looked down like I was shit on his shoe. *"I disagree with your mother. Beat the shit out of those girls. You're a killer. Embrace it. You're not one of us. You're one of them."*

The iciness in my bones was replaced with sickly heat. The room transformed from grey concrete to bright red, flowing with blood.

Gallons of crimson—blood from my victims. Litres and litres of scorn stained my hands.

No! I didn't mean to do it. I didn't want to do it. Forgive me. Please, forgive me.

Time continued on without me while I died slowly on concrete and became a gelatinous, mind-fucked blob.

Leather Jacket came for me one day. I'd been on my own for so long, my mind craved human contact. Any human contact.

My heart actually jumped when he came for me.

"Time for your next training session, *puta*." He nudged me with his foot. "Get up."

I no longer knew how to speak or move or pretend to be human. I was cold and hungry and I desperately wanted to go home.

I tried to conjure images of Q. Remember his house and Suzette's warm embrace. But I came up empty. All those happy memories were blank.

Tears tried to form in my eyes, but it'd been so long since I'd had anything to drink only a single droplet formed.

Someone hoisted me to my feet. Cold concrete was replaced with frigid air as Leather Jacket scooped me up, holding me against his repulsive frame. My body, so, so cold, huddled into him even though my drug-fogged brain fled in repulsion.

Leather Jacket chuckled. "Starting to like me? Huh, bitch?" He licked my cheek, walking us to the door. "You'll like me even more after today."

My heart tried to race, terror tried to kick-start adrenaline, but my fight was stolen. Gone. Disappeared.

One moment we were still in my room. The next we were half way down the corridor.

Then we were in another room.

Then in another corridor.

Blocks of time disappeared, leaving me with a splattering of photographic images.

How much longer before I completely lose my mind?

One moment someone tossed me onto the floor of a shower and sprayed me with a hose. A second later, I was clothed in a red dress, short and slutty. It was meant to cling to curves and accent sexiness, yet it didn't do any of those things—only amplified how skinny and sickly I'd become. But at least the fabric was clean. After decaying inside Q's damp shirt for days, it was heaven. Loneliness wrapped around my heart as Leather Jacket yanked the material from my hands and threw away the only thing I had left of Q. The last connection I would ever have to the man who owned me completely.

"Give it back." I shuffled forward, trying to get to the rubbish bin behind Leather Jacket.

He pushed me to the floor, laughing. "You get nothing that you want. Unless you want my cock."

I curled up on the wet tiles, trying so hard to keep my mind from skipping off into some other dimension. A dimension where I no longer had to fear every time I woke up and suffer every time I went to sleep.

Time flickered and the bathroom no longer existed.

Something starchy was forced down my throat, followed by fresh, delicious water.

Then I was standing over a girl with a club in my hands.

Time flickered again. I blacked out.

Spray. Hot, wet, metallic spray. It splashed across my face and I instantly gagged.

Oh, God. *No!*

I dropped the club, clutching my stomach as my retching turned into racking coughs. The blood on my lips entered my mouth and I scratched frantically at my tongue.

I couldn't have her blood in my mouth. I couldn't!

Someone grabbed me, hoisting me upright. I kept coughing and bucking and I finally snapped completely. Words strung from my mouth, interrupted by huge barks. I made no sense. I didn't need to make sense. They understood. They knew that my breakdown marked the beginning of the end.

My mind wanted out. I reached the end and the taste of a girl's blood in my mouth was the last straw.

I hurt her. I didn't know how. I didn't remember. But I did something horrid and she suffered at my hands.

I can't live with that! I tried harder to get loose, wriggling, biting, coughing, snarling.

"Fuck, someone give her something. The other dose isn't doing jack."

I twisted and bucked, only seeing compressing walls and being suffocated by the horrible cough hijacking my body.

Someone grabbed my legs and I kicked out.

"Ouch, you bitch!" A cuff caught me around the head, but I was no longer in my body. I was in some other world where I wanted with every wish to die.

A needle punctured my flesh and administered the ghostly ice I'd grown to know so well. Spreading its white smog through my blood, stealing my body, killing my mind.

My coughing stopped and I hung utterly spent in someone's arms.

"That's better. Let that kick in. She'll be cutting them up like Picasso again in half an hour."

The image of me slicing off body parts and arranging them in some terrible piece of art kept me occupied while I floated into demise.

When I came to, I lay flat on my back, wheezing like a ninety-year-old smoker. My ribs shrieked with agony and my lungs felt as if someone had filled them with pond scum.

I tried to move, to make sure I no longer had blood on my face, but my arms once again weren't mine.

"She's alive. Bring her here."

Time fractured and suddenly I'd gone from lying on my back to standing, swaying with a baton in my hands.

Fast forward through time and my ears started working again; I immediately wished they hadn't. Whimpers and wails filled the small dungeon.

The tiny blonde with the hummingbird tattooed on her hip lay at my feet. Her face was black and blue, distorted from swelling. Her eyes held mine as I gasped in absolute horror.

I slammed to my knees when I saw the bloody tooth on the concrete.

"I'm sorry! I'm so sorry. Sorry. Sorry!" I couldn't handle it. The old passion in me rose, giving a reprieve against the drugs, only to hurl me into sickness.

Hugging the club, I rocked and rocked. "Stop. Make it stop. Please, God, make it stop. Q. Please. I'm sorry. I need you. Q!"

Something fissured deep inside. My soul folded inside me like a tattered piece of origami, taking everything good left in me, leaving me with nothing.

My memories, my happiness, my strength, and passion for Q all vanished. Just like that.

Oh, my God. Oh, my God.

It's happening. It's happened. I'm done. I literally stared at the end of my life.

Time blacked out and I came to as Leather Jacket pushed me over, sprawling me on top of Blonde Hummingbird. She didn't move, didn't make a sound.

He laughed. "You were doing so well, bitch. Taking orders like a pro." He squatted in front of me, grabbing my hair to look me in the eye. "You beat her until we told you to stop. You swung that bat like she was vermin you wanted to kill. Do you remember, *puta*? Do you remember what you did? Huh?"

I retched and buckled over. The coughing started with vengeance. Maybe I could suffocate from coughing, drown from whatever buildup existed in my lungs.

Ryan the Ogre kicked me off Blonde Hummingbird and dragged me away.

I tried to stay awake and not let the drugs swoop me away, but time flickered and crackled. *Why am I fighting it? The oblivion is better than reality.* With a drawn out sigh, I let the drugs consume me.

Corridor.

Room.

Another corridor.

Ryan threw me into a space different to the abominable dungeons and cells. A large grimy window let gorgeous sunlight stream in, highlighting the evil and dankness in the room.

A fist to my shoulder blades sent me straight to the ground.

A flare of red fire lit up my jaw and my eyes snapped open. I blinked when Leather Jacket appeared in my face. His greasy skin and stringy hair needed disinfecting; he stank like a dumpster. "Know why you're tied up, slut?"

I'm tied up? I looked down, noticing the bindings around my wrists and my legs imprisoned tight against chair legs. Another black-out. Another fragment of my life stolen.

I didn't answer. I no longer had the energy to care. The drugs for once were on my side—cushioning me from the outside world, turning me introvert until nothing else existed.

He whispered, "We're going to do to you what you've done to the girls over the last few days. But we're going to show you how hard we expect next time. No more timid little pussy hits. We expect a beating...so take notes."

I couldn't breathe.

Days? I've been doing this for days?

Ryan mumbled something in Spanish, hoisting the baton in his hand and slapping it against this palm. "Ready to see a pro at work?"

He gave me no preparation; he attacked.

I sucked in a breath as he hit me hard in the stomach.

I doubled over, almost falling off the plastic chair. The shackles around my wrists were the only thing keeping me upright.

Pain resonated like a marching band in my tummy, but I welcomed it. This might be the end. They might kill me.

Please kill me.

The next blow was to my thigh, cracking so loud I was sure my leg was broken. I welcomed the pain, adding it to all the rest. Compounding it until my heart raced and pumped, hurtling me closer to blacking out.

Someone hit me around the ear.

Then punched my breast.

A kick landed on my ankle.

A fist connected with my cheekbone.

They hurt me beyond hurt—they catapulted me into agony, but they never went too far. They restrained from killing me.

Each punishment hurt more than the last and I sobbed freely in my bindings. Every part of me wept for freedom.

I can't do this anymore. I want out. I want to die.

Finally, something sharp pricked my skin, and another dose of medicine sent me cartwheeling into nightmares.

Eleven
Quincy

You call me maître but I am the esclave—slave to inflict the pain I crave...

Time was my enemy.

I wanted to shatter every clock, dismantle every tick. Every second was a ceaseless moment that I let Tess down, every minute an eternity in missing her.

I ran only on hatred and the undying need to find her. I couldn't eat. I couldn't sleep. Everything I did felt like a betrayal.

Every day that went past, my temper frayed further until I lost sight of the cool businessman who owned the world and morphed closer to the beast I truly was.

No one wanted to be around me. I swore and yelled and raged. Every day, I dropped a little further into hell, and I didn't care. I welcomed the numbness, the emptiness, because I deserved it.

I'm not good enough.

I wasn't even strong enough to hunt the woman I loved.

I'm a fucking loser who deserves to be alone.

I wanted to gut the Wolverine and read his intestines like

tarot cards. He had answers but I'd been too stupid to make him talk. I was too hasty, and now he was fucking dead along with the chance of ever finding Tess.

I slouched and poked at the wound in my arm. The dull pain wasn't enough. I deserved more. I deserved to be electrocuted, to be mauled by rabid tigers. I deserved every horrible way a man could die. I deserved to be put down for failing my *esclave.*

My fingers plucked at the stitches. Some lucky pre-med student got a free flight in a G650 to patch me up on our way out of Moscow. We'd managed to get out before word had spread, but I had no doubt a bounty hung around my neck from more than one trafficking bastard now.

Sitting at some desk, in some office, in some city, in some country, I hung my head and wrapped my fingers around my skull. I squeezed, digging harder and harder, inflicting pain, inviting a migraine. I wanted to crack open my brain and stop all the emotional pain.

Some moments I couldn't breathe with the thought of what was happening to Tess. I wanted to suffocate all thoughts of her from my head until I no longer had to endure such agony.

But on the heels of such self-pity and loneliness, came furious anger. Livid hot temper that she left me. I hated that she made me care. I cursed her for the way she turned me into this tangled, twisted creature and then disappeared.

Six days passed.

Then a week and a half.

Twenty-four hour blocks all stacked on top of one another creating an unmovable mountain, barricading me from ever finding the one person I ever cared for. Time obstructed me from finding my fucking other half.

I would live alone. I would die alone. I would exist in the netherworld all fucking alone because Tess had been stolen and I was too worthless to save her.

Fuck. Where the hell are you, Tess?

"We just had a tip-off. We're flying to Singapore in an hour," Frederick said from the doorway.

I looked up, still clutching my head.

I couldn't even remember what country we were in. We'd been everywhere. Russia, Spain, Saudi Arabia, Thailand. Following whispers of rumours. Hints that someone knew someone who knew where Tess had been taken.

It'd been a fucking rabbit chase. All lies. All of them hiding the truth.

The truth would be found only by finding the source. Not bribing underworld contacts, or threatening to turn their precious names into local authorities. I had power, but it didn't mean shit when no one knew a thing.

Goddammit. *You're a fucking imbecile, Mercer!* The truth can only be found at the source! Why didn't I see it?

It was as if someone wrenched back the curtains, inviting piercing sun to chase away the gloom of a disused room.

I stood up so fast the chair fell back and clattered against the tiles. I remembered now. This office belonged to Lee Choi. A man I'd built two casinos for in Macau in return for four slaves. Hong Kong was sleek and money-shiny, but beneath the surface—just like every cosmopolitan city—lurked the dangerously sick and twisted world.

Lee Choi no longer ran that world.

Lee now rotted in a foetus position stuffed in his closet.

"I don't care about a tip," I snarled. "I know where we need to go."

Frederick frowned, coming closer. "Q, when was the last time you slept? You need to eat. You're gaunt. You can't live on revenge and bullet casings."

The urge to hit him rose, but I swallowed it back. "No more leads. They're useless."

He shook his head. "One of Choi's underlings gave up a name of a man who has a harem in Singapore. He might know where Tess is."

I rubbed my face, trying not to snap. "It's a waste of time.

He won't have Tess. We need to go to the source."

"The source?"

I moved fast, pushing past Frederick. No one in the usual circle would've bought Tess. Gerald wouldn't have sold her to be used so...kindly. He was out for blood. Where was the payback if she was sent to a sick fuck, but someone who would ultimately keep her alive? No, he'd send her to someone who would ruin her. Break her. Someone who would stand to earn just rewards for destroying her.

Fuck. Why didn't I think of it before?

It felt right. My gut knew I was on the right path.

"Pack up. We're flying to Mexico."

Four days.

Four long fucking days we'd patrolled the sin-stained world of Mexico. Hunting drug dealers and spineless thieves, we lurked in dives and sniffed around illegal enterprises. No matter how many men Franco tortured, or how many palms I greased, no information was forthcoming.

No one knew who kidnapped a blonde girl on a scooter four months ago.

"Eat this, boss." Franco skidded a plate of noodles under my nose, obscuring the map of the slums of Mexico I'd been studying for the past three hours.

Tess could be anywhere in this filthy city, and I might walk right past whatever building she was imprisoned in and never know.

As much as I was starving, the thought of eating, of surviving, when Tess might not even be alive, ate at my soul.

I ignored him, shoving the plate away.

Franco clasped my shoulder as Frederick came over from

the bar with three mugs of icy beer. "You need your strength. For her. Your brain will work better with fuel."

Frederick sloshed the beer onto my map, taking a seat.

I glowered, swiping my hand over the paper before the liquid could ruin it.

Frederick nodded. "I agree. Eat and recharge. You're no good to her if you're passed out from hunger."

The animal inside didn't need such petty things like nutrition. It only needed blood. *But you're not a fucking superhuman, so eat up.*

Sighing hard, I tried to return to the land of men and sat taller. Acknowledging they had a point, I dug into the noodles and forced myself to swallow. I was a world traveller. I'd lived in cities around the globe, but the man I was at heart was French, and I missed Mrs. Sucre's duck and homemade baguettes. I missed simple perfection. I missed my regimented life. I missed Tess with every fucking part of me.

Half-way through my meal, I gave up and growled, "There has to be some other way."

I slouched, scowling at the droplets of condensation on the beer mug. Frederick mumbled something around his mouthful of food and Franco cocked an eyebrow. "Like what? We've tried bribing men we know in the sex trade, we've tried beating it out of others. We've argued, we've threatened, we've pleased. Either no one knows who took her, or they're too terrified to say."

I rubbed my chin, letting my brain race for clues, answers, conclusions that might work better than our current methods.

"All Mexicans are linked somehow. I read that the city is one of the friendliest on earth," Frederick said, wiping his mouth and swigging some beer.

Yeah, apart from the raping trafficking bastards.

"It's said that it's a matter of pride to have the largest family possible. I'm talking cousins upon cousins upon cousins. You need to go for a—"

"Cousin." I bolted upright, smiling for the first time in

fourteen days at Frederick. *"T'es un putain de génie."* You're a fucking genius.

Franco stood, glancing around the crowded, dirty bar, making sure my abrupt standing didn't attract unwanted attention. My muscles were rock-hard at the thought of a bar fight. I craved to use my fists, to pull out the knife and lose myself in anger.

Once he deemed the coast clear, Franco said, "Care to share?"

No, I didn't care to share as that would be a waste of fucking time.

Instead of answering, I strode right to the bar and jumped on top. Men nursing their beers looked up with their mouths hanging open, their hands guarding their precious alcohol.

"What the hell are you doing up there?" the barkeep asked.

I threw a hundred euro bill at him. "Turn the music down."

The barkeep grumbled, but shoved the bill into his dirty apron and reached down behind the counter to mute the volume. In the sudden silence people stopped mid-sentence. All eyes trained on me, and I waited until complete silence reigned.

The moment I had everyone's attention, I said clearly, "I will pay anyone who has knowledge of a band of men who kidnapped women in the downtown area four months ago. They targeted women from a café and may have had other operations around town."

My hands curled and I willed myself to continue in a calm voice. "I'll pay thirty thousand euros to anyone who can give me a name. Totally anonymous. I don't need to know anything about you. Provide information, and the money is yours."

Giving incentive, I pulled out a couple hundred euros from my blazer pocket and fanned it out in my hand. "In gratitude for your attention, your dinners and drinks are on me."

Franco appeared by my feet, looking up with tense awareness. His eyes scanned the room while his hand hovered over his chest holster, ready to pull his gun free in a second. "Time to get down. You're a sitting duck up there."

I nodded, saying to the crowd, "I'm sitting at the back. Come find me if you have a name." I jumped off the bar.

Franco's eyes bugged out of his head. "What the hell. You were a perfect target up there. Anyone could've popped you."

I brushed my suit and handed the money to the barkeep, whose eyes lit up like a fucking firework. "That's for everyone's tabs for tonight, understand?"

He nodded. I doubted he would be trustworthy, but I really didn't care.

"Someone will squeal, Franco. They always do when money is involved."

"What if they just kill you expecting to find more than thirty G in your pockets?"

I smirked, brushing past him to go and sit down. "That's what you're here for. To keep me alive to do stupid shit like this."

He huffed and the music increased to deafening decibels yet again.

I moved back to my seat and settled in for my prey to come to me.

Six hours later, the barkeep tried to kick us out.

No one ventured near our table, and there were only so many beers we could drink before our concentration faltered.

We paid off the barman to stay overnight. I didn't want to move. In my mind, the nugget of information I needed was on the way to me, heralded by the allure of thirty thousand euros. I visualized the news being spread from mouth to mouth, making its way through ghettos and impressive neighbourhoods, passed cousin to cousin. Eventually someone would know. Eventually someone would come to me.

I refused to think otherwise.

By the time morning peeked through the filthy windows, my ass was flat from sitting and my back screamed bloody murder. But a new day had arrived.

The day I found Tess. The day I brought hell on earth to the men who thought they could steal what was mine.

Instead of being desolate and incompetent, I felt eager and on track. *This is right.* For the first time in days, I was one step closer to finding Tess and putting this entire hellish nightmare behind us.

At ten in the morning, the kitchen staff arrived to prepare for the lunch crowd. By eleven, the doors opened and some early punters trickled in for some pub grub.

Considering I hadn't slept a wink in over fifty hours, I revved with pent-up energy. My eyes never left the door, and every person that stepped through sent my heart racing.

This was it.

It would work.

Any second.

Any second turned into another fucking hour, and my heart went from racing to thick with fury. It had to work. It was the last chance.

What the hell would I do? Go home and live my life like Tess never existed? Pretend she hadn't made me a better person or taught me how to be happy?

My mind turned inwards at what my future would mean. I

would never go back. Never return home without Tess by my side. I would leave Q Mercer behind and—

"Shit, Q," Frederick mumbled, his eyes glued behind me. "It fucking worked. I don't believe it."

I spun and came face to face with a dirty child who I guessed was about ten or eleven. The little girl had matted dreadlocks down to her waist, and her skin might've been clear and innocent but was covered in mud and a nasty scar on one cheek.

I didn't know how she snuck in without me noticing, but I instantly knew. This was the girl who would lead me to Tess.

My hands twitched to grab and shake her, to demand to know what she knew. But I curled my fingers and kept them out of sight under the table.

It took every conceivable control in my body to smile gently and lean to her level. My voice was gruff and unused, but I kept my tone even. "*Bonjour.* Did you come to see me?"

She looked toward Franco, who brooded menace, and Frederick, who had a soft smile on his lips. All three of us hadn't shaved in days, and our eyes were red rimmed and far too intense with grief and anxiety.

Poor kid would be petrified, but I didn't have time to soothe her.

"We won't hurt you. Tell us what you know, and I'll make sure you and your family are looked after for a very long time."

She bit her lip, shuffling with bare toes on the sticky beer-covered floor. "I know who you want. My mama used to clean over at the warehouse, before they moved, and I used to sneak in for food when the guards weren't looking."

My stomach twisted into knots. A warehouse. How many fucking girls did they sell? I wanted to ask so many questions; I wanted to save every single woman.

I swallowed hard, pushing the questions from my head. Only one question mattered here. The rest I could come back for. Tess was mine. She needed me and I would be there for her before the day was out.

"The man scares me, but he gave me candy if I let my mama work in peace and I sat in the corner. But he touched other girls my age. He tried to touch me once, but my mama stopped him."

Her big black eyes met mine, so innocent, but not naïve. She knew what she was doing by telling me this man's name. She knew he wasn't fit to live. Even in her young heart, she smelled the vileness.

"Tell me his name." I leaned forward, unable to restrain my urgency anymore. It radiated from my pores, bunching my muscles. "Tell me, and I'll make sure you never have to see him again."

She dropped her eyes and gulped. Seconds ticked by while she shifted on the spot. Finally, her eyes flickered round the bar and she shuffled closer. Putting her little hand around my ear, her lips brushed my flesh as she whispered, "His name is Smith and he isn't in the city anymore."

Smith?

Fucking *Smith*? The most common name in the entire world. How many dead-ends must I run into?

Rage and satisfaction were two equal counterparts. I had the bastard's name, but I was no closer to finding him. "That's very good, *ma chèrie*." I smiled, bristling with tension. "Do you know where he lives now?"

She shook her dreadlocked head, mumbling, "I know where he works though."

I tried so fucking hard to keep my patience, nodding slowly. "Fantastic. Can you tell me? I'll pay you extra so your mum never has to work again."

Her eyes popped wide, and once again she cupped my ear. "I heard my mama say he moved to a place called Rio. But I don't know where that is."

Rio.

Mother fucking Rio.

Tess was in Brazil.

I couldn't help myself. I grabbed the child and squeezed

her before passing her off to Franco. "Pay the girl and make sure you take her wherever she wants. Buy a house, I don't care, just repay her."

The girl squealed as Franco hoisted her into his arms and strode out the bar, heading toward bright sunlight.

At last the sun wasn't mocking me. It wasn't saying life would go on without the woman of my dreams; now it was telling me to go on the final hunt. The final battle to free her.

Striding out the door with Frederick at my heels, I muttered, "You should leave, Roux. You don't have to be a part of this."

I planned on having copious amounts of blood on my hands tonight. I would dance in hell for what I would do to motherfucker Smith.

Frederick muttered, "I'm not going anywhere. I want to see you tear this bastard limb from fucking limb."

My soul burned with the urge to kill. No ounce of humanity existed—tonight it was all about death.

I'm coming for you, you bastard.

And I'd make damn sure he'd fucking cry before I was through.

Twelve

Tess

Save me, enslave me, you will never cave me.
Taunt me, flaunt me, kill what haunts me...

Two days? A week? A month? A Year?

I no longer knew how long I existed in this hell.

It no longer mattered as my body was broken, my mind unrepairable.

I existed in turmoil and grief. I lost weight as I no longer ate. My bones stuck out in stark relief and my mouth was always desiccated. The drugs never granted me a moment's peace—taking me from a monstrous reality to a nightmare encrusted subconscious. The fog, the smog, kept me from realizing just how close I was to the end.

Leather Jacket kept taunting me—making me hurt the two blonde women until I obeyed without question. If I didn't hit them, he did.

If I didn't wallop them with the baseball bat, he did.

If I broke down and cried, he hit them harder, breaking a bone or drawing blood.

I wallowed in drugs and apologized and cried. He laughed and prodded and thrilled to hurt.

He made me hate myself for being alive. He made me doubt everything that I was and all the good things I thought I'd been. There was nothing left.

Who could love me when I was a devil's protégé?

My mind tortured me with visions of a happier place: of Q's bed, Suzette's laugh, and warmth.

I wanted to be home. I wanted to sleep in a patch of sunlight and never be cold again. I'd never been so cold.

Sparrows visited me often in my dreams. At first they helped fly me away, taking me upward and beyond Leather Jacket's reach, but the longer I tortured and mutilated others the more their black eyes went from condolences to hatred. Now their wings weren't my salvation. They pecked my flesh with sharp little beaks, hopping around me like tiny vultures.

Every time my thoughts turned to Q, I shut down. The pain was insurmountable, and I couldn't handle the hard hatred in his eyes.

"Your soul is rotten, esclave. *Bound by darkness and I can no longer save you."* He leaned over me, smelling so fresh and citrusy pure. "Je ne suis plus à toi." *I'm no longer yours.*

It was those words that unthreaded the rest of my ragged mind. I was no longer Q's. I was unbelonging once again and instead of old hurt, all I felt was relief. Relief because soon, I wouldn't exist. Soon I would die, and then I would no longer have to suffer hurting others.

Something shot me back into the present. I looked down at my shuffling feet, my arm braced in Ryan's meaty grip.

Another block of time. Gone. Never to be recalled or remembered. What was I doing before walking?

Forcing my tongue to work, I mumbled, "Wh—where are you taking…" My strength left and I could no longer remember what I wanted to know.

My mother appeared in front of me, watching with her arms crossed as I shambled closer to her. *"Look at you, child. You need a bath. You look like a homeless ragamuffin. How many times did I tell you to eat?"* Her concern for my wellbeing felt nice, until she snarled. *"If you are all skin and bones, what will be left for the Wolverines at dinner?"*

The illusion shattered as Ryan jerked me into a room at the far end of the eternity-long corridor. "Time for your final lesson before you graduate, lovely." He patted my head like I was his favourite pet. "I'll miss our fun and games. Your nails are fucking sharp. Loved watching you scratch like a baby kitten."

I swayed on the spot, mortifyingly enjoying his petting. After so long in the dark with only freezing concrete for company it was heaven to feel the comfort of another's hand. Even though the same hand had beaten a girl within the inch of her life.

Deep inside, I managed to find the strength to stumble away.

Leather Jacket appeared from nowhere, chuckling. "Still fighting, even after all this time, slut." He grabbed my face and I closed my eyes. I didn't want to see him and his piercing black gaze.

"Tessie, why did you leave me? For this? You left my kindness and respect for this? To chase a life of pain and ruin?" Brax swirled into being before me; I swallowed hard. Brax represented everything I no longer was.

He was untouched and pure and sweet, and I wasn't worthy for him to talk to me.

"Don't look at me! Please." I buried my face in my hands, but Brax came forward and unpried my fingers to look into my eyes.

His sky-blue gaze rendered me helpless. *"I may not understand your decisions, Tessie. But I'll always be your friend. I'll always be a safe haven for you."*

Leather Jacket shattered my drug-induced daydream by grabbing my hair and throwing me to the floor.

It hurt. It degraded. I didn't care; I just lay there.

Someone threw something heavy at me. It bruised my spine before bouncing off and clattering to the floor.

I curled into a ball, wracked with shivers from whatever fever I'd caught. The coughs were getting explosive, and slowly my lungs filled with more and more liquid until I felt as if I floated in an ocean as well as fog.

"Pick it up, *puta*." Leather Jacket nudged my hip with his foot. "Now. Don't make me ask you again. You know what will happen."

I didn't think I had the strength to obey, but one moment I was lying, the next I sat on my knees, staring blankly at the cracked floor.

Something cool rested in my hands.

Something heavy and black and sinister.

A gun.

My heart rate peaked for the first time in days, racing fast against the comatose of the drugs. *Why am I holding a gun?*

"Final lesson." Leather Jacket pointed at the girl in front of me. The gentle blonde with the small breasts and hummingbird tattoo on her hipbone.

She was gagged and her red-rimmed eyes were dry. She'd stopped crying days ago when Ryan broke her left arm. It was as if her mind had already gone.

I tried to smile at her, both of us locked in this horrible prison, but she just stared blankly at me.

"Kill her, cunt. Or I'll cut her fingers off and then her toes until she dies slowly."

The drugs couldn't hold down my horror. I dropped the gun and crawled away. "No!"

"No," he chuckled. "Did you just say no?" He stood in front of me, his legs barring my passage. "You really should've said yes." He looked over my head. "Ryan."

The glass-shattering scream made me retch as Ryan cut off one of the girl's fingers.

I couldn't look.

I can't look.

Don't look.

"Tessie, leave this place. It isn't what you want," Brax murmured.

"*Esclave, you're not one of them. If you even think of giving up and dying, I'll hunt you for eternity.*" Q's passion shocked me. For days he'd been telling me to die. To give up and let myself go. Was it my mind telling me not to be so weak? Could Q really still care for me after all I'd done?

"Shoot her." Leather Jacket pushed me backward. "Go on."

Another moment ticked past and another scream rose.

I kept my eyes downcast, but it didn't stop me seeing the puddle of blood forming around the girl. Even though she screamed for mercy, she still didn't cry.

My heart squeezed to death at the thought that she couldn't even find relief in tears. Her life was gone. Whether I shot her or not, her life was over.

She wouldn't survive.

Save her. Shoot her. Set her free.

"One last time, slut. Shoot her." Leather Jacket crouched to my eye level, placing the gun in my grip. "Do it." He stood and backed away.

Every last shred of decency in me imploded. To save a girl from horror, I would steal her life.

With shaking hands, I raised the muzzle and pressed the trigger.

Some divine guidance took hold of the racing bullet, lodging it directly in her forehead. The life in her eyes instantly extinguished and a small smile tugged her lips before she fell sideways into silence.

I did it. I killed a bird that Q would've given everything to save. I was truly the devil and I couldn't live with myself anymore.

Do it again, Tess. You set her free. Set yourself free.

Yes. I could escape everything.

I angled the gun into my mouth, sucked on the sulphur-laced muzzle, and pulled the trigger for the second and final time.

"So, you punched her because she tried to kill herself?"

"Yes, boss. I did as you said and only put one bullet in the gun, but she still tried to swallow a fast one."

"Good work. You succeeded. A strong bitch would never try to take such a chicken-shit way out."

The voices weaved and plaited together, making me dizzy.

A steady throb in my temple brought me back from serene blankness to a freezing, emaciated reality.

"She's coming around. We need to end this tonight. I have no more use for her."

I cracked my eyes open just as White Man loomed above me. He smiled his crocodile smile. "I hear you tried to put yourself down like a dog, little girl?"

I moaned, reaching for my head. The pain was stronger for some reason, the fog not as thick or syrupy.

The drugs…they were wearing off. Clarity started coming back along with a terrible racking shiver. My jaw locked as I fought the trembles.

"Ah, do you know what that is?" White Man caressed my cheek. My reaction time was quicker and I jerked away. "That's the first stage of withdrawal. You're dependant on what we've given you. It's the perfect key for any master to keep you inline."

He sighed, grabbing a lock of my dirty hair and twirling it around his finger. "Do you know what would happen if you didn't get a fix in an hour or two?"

"You'd shake so hard you'd probably bite off your own tongue," Leather Jacket announced happily, adding, "You'd be so consumed with the need for a fix you'd pick at your own flesh. You'd climb the walls. Tear off your fingernails… You'd willingly sell your body for a meagre drop of what you need."

I shoved White Man away, hunching with my head in my arms.

Is it true? Would that happen?

But I didn't have to believe them for it to be real. Already my skin itched for relief and my mouth watered for something other than food. I couldn't exist in this world. I wanted the endless smog, the warm comfort of oblivion.

I looked up. I sat on a desk in the corner of a large room with threadbare carpeting and filing cabinets. A tatty cobweb-covered lightshade hung in the centre of the room.

I squinted, trying to focus. I didn't know if it was the drugs or lack of food, but my vision was fading. My hearing was dulling. My body failing.

Coughing loudly, I almost fell off the desk with the wracking episode. I wheezed and every rib dug into my skinny sides. I didn't need to be a doctor to know I had pneumonia.

The constant chill, the heavy, lethargic limbs, the sloshing in my lungs when I went from lying to standing all pointed to the illness.

White Man clucked his tongue. He stood over me looking regal and collected in his baby blue polo and jeans, belying the true evilness inside him. At least Leather Jacket wore his intentions on every inch of his body. White Man looked like a favourite uncle or distinguished businessman.

"You passed your final lesson today. How does it feel to be a killer?"

I sucked in a breath, trying to stop the memories from overtaking me.

The loud *boom* as the gun went off.

The kickback of the heavy weapon.

The smell of gunpowder and bloom of red on the innocent girl's forehead.

I squeezed my eyes shut as my fingernails scratched my forearm, finding some relief from the slowly building itch.

White Man didn't leave me alone. "Did you enjoy breaking

that girl's leg?"

Slamming my hands over my ears, I forced myself to forget.

Forget the *thwack* of the bat against her femur.

The *snap* of bone as it gave way under the force.

I whimpered, rocking on the desk.

White Man grabbed my hands and inspected my fingernails. Broken, dirty, a thick layer of filth wedged under the tips.

"Did you like scratching that girl until her breasts ran red? It's her blood under your nails."

My mouth hung open as I stared at the horrible evidence.

Images of scratching her, sobbing as I dragged my claws across her stomach and breasts haunted me. By the time Leather Jacket let me stop she looked like she'd gone head to head with a cheetah.

I wanted to collapse into a puddle and cry. I wanted my soul to leak free from my eyes and escape this ruin. These memories of what I'd done.

White Man stroked my cheek. "You did well. And your action today proved to me that you're ready." His lips twisted in a sadistic bow. "Do you want to know what you're ready for?"

I shrivelled inside. My heart chugged with terror. I didn't know and I didn't *want* to know. I couldn't listen to more atrocities. A salty tear escaped my scratchy eyes.

Kick her.

Punch her.

Scratch her.

Kill her.

And I did.

Over and over.

I relived the moments where I became Leather Jacket's toy—his obedient monster. Oh, my God, I remembered their agony. Their terror. The sound of their bodies breaking, repeating like a horrible symphony in my head.

More blood. More screams. More…more…

"Get out! Get out!"

White Man cooed, "There, there. Do you want something to take the edge off? Make it all go away?"

Yes!

No!

They owned me. Drugs were now my deliverance. My reality was something I could no longer endure as I'd dirtied it, torn it to smithereens, and filled my soul with corruption.

Seconds ticked past, and I shook so bad my entire body jiggled like a flesh-picked skeleton.

"Tell me what you want and I'll give it to you." He stroked my hair, trailing his hand to my breast.

I moaned a little, tugging free, but he pinched my nipple, keeping me in place. "You can try and fight it, but ultimately you know you won't win. Already you're craving. We've given you a high dose…you have a long way to fall, little girl."

"Wh—what d—do you w—want?" I chattered, scratching openly at my dirty arms. The itch was spreading, consuming me.

He licked his lips. "Such a sweet question. But you know what I want. I want you to beg."

I shook harder, trembling as ramifications bowled into me. He wanted me to beg…for what? Drugs? Sex? For him to do whatever he wanted to me?

I can't.

I won't.

But you know you will…eventually.

Icy panic turned my shivering into quaking. I dry heaved as my lungs ached with liquid and sickness. "Please. Just let me go."

He stroked my hair, pulling me against his chest until my cheek rested on his shoulder. "Soon, little girl. Soon we'll sell you, but you aren't quite broken yet. I made the mistake of selling you whole and it landed me in a lot trouble. I won't make the same mistake again."

His voice soothed me even as his words signed my death warrant. "When I sell you, you're going to be so dependent a master will be able to do anything to you and you'll want it. Your mind will be so fragmented you will accept orders as life-lines, as you can no longer think for yourself."

I cried silently. Hating the promise in his voice. Hating that all of this would come true. I was so close to being the perfect slave. My addiction to Q was overshadowed by the need to have the fog and jittery warmth. I'd never been this close to losing myself.

I'm already lost.

It petrified me.

"Please...please..." I no longer knew what I begged for.

"That's close enough," White Man murmured. "Ignacio."

Someone grabbed my arm, and the small prick of the needle was pure elation. I wouldn't have to listen to bones snapping or see blood gushing. I would drift uncaring and remote.

"Precious, I've enjoyed this journey with you. You're not ready yet, but after tonight...perhaps you will be." White Man kissed me on the forehead as my body gave out and I hung lifeless in his arms.

False warmth welcomed me and I sighed, letting my body sink deeper, faster.

At the bottom of the fall, Q was waiting.

His arms crossed over his powerful chest, his suit glistened black, looking like velvet. *"This isn't you, esclave. My Tess wouldn't be this weak."*

I giggled, rolling in the fog, letting it cuddle me in its chemical embrace. *"I'm no longer your Tess. I'm nothing anymore."*

"Don't say that. I'm coming for you. Fucking fight. Don't waste my journey to find you."

"You're too late. You're too late." A fluffy cloud danced in front of me and I reached for it, falling flat on my face.

A livid Q paced, his perfect shoes kicking up wisps of fog. *"Fight dammit! Se battre comme vous le faites toujours!" Fight like you always do!* His voice seeped through my stupor, making me hate myself.

Instead of screaming back, I hung my head and let his wrath crash over me. *"I can't. I can't. I'm done."*

"You're not done. You hear me. Fight!" The command forced some sort of energy into my body, only to amplify my wounds and reinvigorate awful memories. I deflated further to nothingness. I closed the door on Q's beautiful face. I cut myself free so I no longer had to endure. *"I'm sorry. I wasn't strong enough."*

The world went dark as the smog whisked me away.

"Goodbye."

Cold woke me first.

A biting freeze on my nipples.

I groaned, trying to swallow the thick furry aftertaste in my mouth. My entire body felt foreign, frigid.

Where the hell am I? I thought hell was supposed to be unbearably hot.

I could do with heat. My lungs were heavier with liquid, and every breath I wheezed with a struggle. The punishment of beatings and abuse turned my body into a wasted object, no longer useful for anything apart from the garbage.

"She's awake. You may precede, Ignacio."

My heart raced, chasing away the last of the smog I lived in. My brain kicked into gear and I looked around.

Shit.

I was in some sicko's idea of a bedroom: a satanic bedroom. Black curtains hung lopsidedly over a boarded-up window, peeling wallpaper hung off the wall like dresses half shed, and a red lightbulb in the grotty chandelier turned the entire room into nothing but sick shadows.

My stomach twisted as I looked down. I was shackled to a scratchy bed, naked, wearing only gnawing rope on my wrists and ankles. The knots held my legs open, completely vulnerable.

Vomit rose in my throat but I swallowed it down. If I threw up I might choke and drown.

Good. Drown. Death would be a far better existence than what's about to happen, Tess.

A whimper sounded beside me and I looked to my left. The blonde with the barbell and scratches down her chest lay in the same prone position. Our eyes met and her mouth wobbled as she fought back tears.

"Help," she whispered.

I wanted to reach out and hug her. I wanted to protect her. Tell her all of this would be okay; that it was just a horrible dream.

I shook my head, biting my lip so I wouldn't cry.

She squeezed her eyes, dispelling a waterfall of liquid. She sniffed, trying to bury her head into her shoulder.

"Which one do you want first, Ignacio?"

My eyes flew to Leather Jacket as he prowled at the end of the bed. White Man sat in a fancy faded chair by the peeling wall.

Leather Jacket smirked, his eyes slithering over every exposed inch. "I'll go with chubby. Let the *puta* bitch see what's gonna happen to her once I'm finished."

Oh, God.

I thrashed my head, twisting my limbs, trying to get free.

I cried out as the woman who'd tattooed me waved from beside the bed. She gave me a horrid grin. "Time to go to a happy place." She sat on my shoulder and inserted a needle into my overused vein. As she pressed the plunger, White Man murmured, "This is a different concoction to what you're used to, little girl. It's going to…well, it's going to play with your mind. After all, that's the part we need to break."

The icy heat already threaded through my veins, heading to my heart to be shot around my body.

White Man stood and came forward. Patting my naked foot, a shred of pity appeared in his gaze. "After today, you'll be sold. I've kept my side of the bargain. I will miss you, though. I've grown rather fond of your strength. It's been a privilege to ruin you."

He moved forward to cup my cheek. "Don't worry. I've told your new owner that you like it rough. You'll be well taken care of."

I gasped as the worst feeling in my life started.

Beetles.

Spiders.

Insects with teeth and tiny claws shredded my intestines with rapid gnawing. My entire body itched and burned and I screamed. Then I coughed because my lungs couldn't hold enough oxygen. I cried and coughed until I wheezed for breath and still the insects grew worse.

What's happening?!

"Make it stop!"

Leather Jacket and White Man looked on as the sensation crept up my arms, into my fingers, my toes, my stomach, my chest. My heart became infested with cockroaches. My tongue chewed on by locusts.

And then it hit my brain.

I screamed as if my soul could fly free and evict itself from this prison of a body. This prison fast filling with murdering beetles and bugs. White Man morphed into a giant rodent, his perfect teeth elongated into yellow fangs. Leather Jacket evolved into a jackal, slobbering and laughing, growling and raging.

The girl next to me stayed pure and virginal, glowing white and silver with all the goodness in the world while the room began to dissolve, walls melted, paint dripped from the ceiling, scalding me as it landed on my naked body.

Leather Jacket with his jackal head started undressing. He

removed his black jacket and slung it to the rapidly eroding floor. Flames licked the awful carpet, singeing a fiery path toward us.

I couldn't breathe. *I can't breathe. This can't be real. It can't be real.*

Once Leather Jackal removed his shirt and trousers, he eased off his disgusting underwear and stood with his small bent cock jutting out from a thicket of black hair. His groin crawled with spiders, a mass seething between his legs.

I closed my eyes but the visions found me there, too. If possible they were worse.

Q featured and he morphed from naked perfection with his sparrow tattoo, into a raging black-winged angel. His back sprouted three-metre-wide wings, glistening ebony with oil-slicked raven feathers. His pale jade eyes glowed with ferocity.

He shook his head in weighted disappointment and turned his back on me. His wings encompassed him into a black cocoon until he exploded into a million birds and took wing.

He left me.

Left me with Jackal and Rodent.

Something grabbed my ankle and my eyes flew open. White Man Rodent trailed his fingertips up my shin, my thigh, right to my hipbone, cutting me like a dagger even though he had no weapon. Phantom blood wept from where he touched, crying with red.

"This is for your own good." He raised his fist and punched me in the jaw.

My head snapped sideways and I latched onto Blonde's eyes. She panted, looking manic and wild. Undrugged, her eyes were clear and panicked. She looked like an angel, and I went from wanting to protect her to wanting *her* to protect *me*.

Please save me.

Another punch, but this time to my stomach. Lying down made the hit resonate through my tummy to my kidneys and liver.

Leather Jackal climbed onto the bed and came forward on

all fours, gawking at Blonde Angel and me. His knee went between my open legs, and I cried out as he slurped his horrible feral tongue into my belly button and down. He nipped at my clit, dripping with burning saliva.

I screamed and screamed as his saliva ignited into flames, burning me to a cinder. It hurt. Fuck, it hurt. *Make it stop!*

White Rodent ordered, "Pay attention to the other one. Let the drugs fade a little. She won't cope otherwise."

Jackal nodded, breathing deep and gruff. One long paw grabbed me between the legs, probing me, raking me. He groaned as he forced a shredding nail inside. "You won't be dry for long, *puta.* You wait for those drugs to switch. Soon you'll be begging me." He removed his touch and clambered on top of poor Blonde Angel. She keened as he settled between her legs. His hairy, untoned ass thrust hard as he rested his elbows on either side of her face.

"Lesh her go—go—you bastard!" Was that me? That slurring, broken, wild-sounding thing?

White Rodent punched me again, this time in the ribcage. I cried out as my old cracked rib wailed in agony. Did he rebreak it? It felt like it—every breath punctured my lungs, letting the build-up of liquid trickle out, filling my body with slime.

"Every time you tell Ignacio to stop, I'll hit you. Do you hear me? You have to learn that speaking without permission equals pain. You have to learn that obeying is the only thing left for you. Do you understand, little girl?"

I raised my heavy eyes to look at the massive rodent standing over me in his blue polo and jeans.

Why is a rat dressed? It's speaking to me.

"It's here to rape you, Tessie. Do things to you that I would never do. You left me," Brax murmured in my mind.

I knew it wasn't real, but no matter how hard I tried to snap out of it, I couldn't. The horror wouldn't let me free.

Leather Jackal kissed Blonde Angel, rubbing his horrible snout all over her face. She cried and wriggled.

"St—stop it!" I yelled.

Instantly, a sharp ringing slap blazed my cheek. "What did I just say, precious?" White Rodent shook his head, admonishing me. "You need to learn."

He said something about pain. Disobeying? *Don't disobey?*

"Disobey. Fight. I'm coming for you, Tess!" Q raged in my head.

But if I fight, I get hurt. Why would I keep inviting such pain? That's stupid.

"It's who you are. You're too strong to let them do this to you."

Q fizzled away, replaced with White Rodent again. He asked, "Are you still with me, little girl?" He peered into my eyes, but I couldn't bring him into focus. He stayed blurry and furry and vague.

Jackal spat on his paw and rubbed his claws between Blonde Angel's legs. Her whimpers turned into ragged gasps and pleas. "Stop. Please. I'll do anything you want. Please. Don't do this!"

"L—listen to her! S—stop!"

A punch to the breast.

Fuck, that hurt the most. The sensitive tissues yelped and burned.

"Learn, girl. Retaliation equals pain. Next time, I won't be so kind."

Next time? Next time what?

Coherency left me and I swam deeper into fog.

I'm cold. So cold. Insects have taken over my body. I feel them creeping through my blood. They're chewing on my brain.

Blonde Angel suddenly bellowed and screeched. I watched in horrified terror as Leather Jackal plunged his putrid cock inside her. He groaned deep and licked his lips, looking deep into my eyes. "You're next, fucking bitch. See how I'm fucking her. That's gonna be you." He thrust again and again. "Oh, yeah. You're gonna take me. I'm gonna pay you back for fighting."

The fear swelled over me, bringing with it more spiders and locusts.

Blonde Angel fell deathly silent. Her body rocked with Jackel's pummels and her eyes never stopped leaking, but her face went slack as shock stole her mind. I literally heard the snap as her mind broke.

No!

I went crazy.

I bucked and cried, uncaring that my body couldn't withstand movement with its injuries. Nothing else mattered but getting free. I wanted to kill Leather Jackal. I wanted to rescue poor Blonde Angel.

Get off her! It wasn't fair. The poor girl. The poor innocent girl. Ferocity blew the drugs clear for one precious moment and I screamed, "Get the fuck off her! Get off her, you bastard."

Pain.

Intense, radiating pain.

I retched, activating aches in my chest. The agony swirled in my head, threatening to knock me out.

White Rodent stood above me with a pair of pliers. His eyes were grim, jaw set. "See what you made me do. Learn!"

I looked down, already back in the pit of hallucinations.

My middle finger was snapped in two. Bone protruded from skin and blood ran freely. Worms appeared from the wound, wiggling in the air.

The throb grew worse and worse. I wanted to tear my hand off just to be free of it.

"Nooooooooo!"

"Yes. Fuck yes." Leather Jackal panted, rutting harder into his victim. She squeezed her eyes and endured.

I cried. It was sick, so sick. I opened my mouth to tell Leather Jackal to stop. To leave her be, but a lasso of panic noosed me.

Retaliation means pain.

My tongue lodged in my mouth and my eyes flew to White Rodent. He waved the pliers in my face. "Are you learning yet?"

Against everything, yes, I was learning. My body had been

reconditioned. My mind enslaved to chemicals.

Everything I thought I knew had been reprogramed. Pain was hideous. Pain was atrocious. I wanted to run away from pain and avoid it forever. Never again would I crave the fine line of passion and sweet, sweet agony.

Never again would I want Q to touch me.

Never again would I find myself in the mess I'd become. I was utterly, truly lost.

Leather Jackal groaned, pumping harder, shaking the bed as he came. Blonde Angel half-sighed, half-sobbed as he pulled out of her.

The small relief that he'd finished with her was ruined when his gaze fell on me. "Give me five minutes, *puta*. Then I'm all yours."

My lips pulled back to snarl, but the cold bite of metal encircled my pinky. White Rodent murmured, "You sure you want to say whatever you're about to say?"

I squeezed my eyes. If I said yes, I might force them into killing me. I could make them give me my freedom.

Say it, Tess. Be done with this.

"She probably doesn't, but I'll say it for her."

That voice.

The echoing softness, the fine edge of violence.

I knew that voice. From another life. A happier life.

My heart picked up its sluggish beat, so downtrodden by weariness it barely functioned. It took all my remaining energy to twist my head to the doorway.

The magnificent black raven angel from my hallucinations was back. His three-metre wingspan filled the room, sparking with ebony fire and murderous rage. A flock of crows fluttered around him, turning the melting room into a whirlpool of feathers.

White Rodent spun and faced this new vision. I sighed and wished with all my heart he was real. I wanted him to be real so I could finally relax and be safe again.

"How the fuck did you get in here?" White Rodent

growled, pacing toward the figment of my imagination, wielding the pliers. Crows squawked and attacked from above, raining little black bombs with beady eyes and yellow beaks, but it didn't stop him.

Ryan the Ogre appeared from behind my apparition, launching himself at the angel. But Q spun too fast and a loud bang filled the room.

Ryan's skull exploded in a fine mist as his body crumbled to the floor. White Rodent backed up, throwing the pliers down as more angels spilled into the room.

Black-winged Q soared toward me, feathers rustling as his eyes drifted over me in horror. I wanted to tell my dream to take me away. To save me. I didn't care if leaving meant death. Not if I could go with him.

Take me. I'm ready to leave. I'm ready to go with you.

"Franco. *Attrape ce fils de pute.*" Grab that son of bitch.

I blinked as a man appeared around Q's black wings. His muscular chest glittered with gold fur and emerald eyes blazed like twin moons.

"It would be my fucking pleasure," Gold Man muttered.

"Wait. Don't," White Rodent said, pressing hard against the weeping mould-riddled wall.

Gold Man punched him square in the jaw, grumbling in satisfaction as he slammed to the ground.

My eyes darted from Gold Man to Angel Q as he sucked in a ragged breath. "Tess…" His tortured voice caressed my body. I shuddered.

"Fuck. I'm so sorry." He reached out to touch me, but stopped himself. His face twisted as his shoulders bristled with self-loathing. "This is all my fucking fault."

Another man appeared beside him. Glowing with a sapphire light, his old-world beauty made me smile. "Q. Not here. Stay together, man. It's not over yet."

Q stood upright and shoved him back, screaming in rage. "Do you see? Do you see what they've fucking done?"

The Sapphire Man grabbed Q's face in his large hands,

forcing him to look him in the eye. "Yes, I see. But you have work to do, remember?"

For a moment it looked as if Angel Q would tear the man apart, but eventually he gritted his jaw and jerked away. "You're right."

He spun to face me. The agony in his eyes shut down until nothing existed but grim determination. His large hand landed on my wrist, fumbling with the rope.

I sighed, watching him, wanting to stroke his feathers, feel the softness of his wings.

Once my wrists were free, he ran a thumb over my tattooed skin, his face spasming with such awful regret. "I'll make it my life's work to keep you safe, Tess. *Tu es à moi.*" You're mine. "And I'll never let you down again."

Releasing me, he turned to my ankles.

"He came for you, Tessie. That's nice. He did more than I ever did." Brax stood over me, smiling softly.

I shook my head. *"He isn't real. I've finally cracked, Brax. I'm not returning after this. I'm leaving. Dying. I don't care as long I don't have to live this life anymore."*

He shook his head. *"You'll survive. You always do."*

The vision shattered as Q leaned over me, pressing his forehead against mine. I breathed in his deep scent, drowning in musk and something heady—a dirtier smell of sweat and blood and toil.

Q's face twisted with heartbreaking grief. "I'm going to murder the men who did this to you. I'm going to make them fucking scream." His anger buffeted me, sending my heart rate spiralling.

"He's going to hit you. And you deserve it for what you've done." My mother appeared.

Q touched my cheek softly, but I cried out. Expecting more pain. Expecting more torture.

He jerked back, eyes glassing with remorse. "Someone get me a fucking blanket!"

His face came over mine again, pale eyes searching mine.

"Tess. I'm going to pick you up. I swear on my mother's grave I will not hurt you. You have nothing to fear. I promise."

Nothing to fear.

Nothing to fear.

"How can he say that when he whipped you, Tessie? He drew blood from you." Brax scowled at Q, crossing his arms.

"I asked for that, though. I wanted it. I begged for it." Even as I said the words, I couldn't remember why I would ask for such agony.

"Did you, Tessie? I'm not so sure…"

Time shot forward and another block of awareness was stolen.

Stabbing, intense pain from my finger consumed me. Someone wrapped a piece of bedding around it, but already blood stained the cotton.

Swallowing hard, I noticed something warm and scratchy covered me, chasing away the icy chill I'd lived with for weeks. Hard muscle cradled me; Q murmured, "I'm going to take you home and fix this, *esclave.*"

Esclave.

The word shocked me from my drug-stupor; I blinked. Q carried me toward the door, his ebony wings shimmered with every colour as he strode beneath dangling lightbulbs.

His jaw was covered in a thicker shadow, lines etched his mouth, and his eyes were aged and sleep-weary. The strain wasn't in keeping with the perfection of my illusion.

Why did my angel look so…so human?

My eyes distorted, flickering with another vision. An image of Q in a dirty rumpled suit, carrying me as if I was a long ago misplaced possession. Something he had no intention of ever letting go again. Anger permeated around him while sadness wept from every pore.

My heart picked up its sad little rhythm.

Q found me. He's here.

"Don't be so stupid." My mother sneered. *"He wasn't looking for you in the first place. No one wants you, Tess. Stop making up such*

fanciful stories."

My lungs faltered in the quest to breathe as pain ricocheted around me.

Why would he come? After all, I was an enemy now. I hurt women. I had blood beneath my fingernails and a kill staining my soul.

"Are you r—real?" I whispered, wincing at the ache in my lungs.

Q faltered, pale eyes connecting with mine. For a never-ending moment he just stared until his mouth tightened and he murmured, "I'm real. It's over, Tess. You're safe."

I tried to smile but centipedes chewed my lips off. I shuddered, slurring, "That's n—nice. See, Brax. He did come."

Brax appeared, running a gentle hand through my hair. *"He did, Tessie. But you can't be so naïve to think you can go back to the past. Not now. Not after what you did."*

My heart smashed into pieces. He was right.

Q's muscles bunched beneath me, hoisting me higher, bringing my chest to his face. He trembled as he whispered tortured words into my neck. "Your mind is not broken. Your mind is not fucking broken."

Somehow, I didn't think he spoke to me.

He rambled in French. *"Si vous me l'enlevez, je le jure devant Dieu je vais ... Je vais ..."* If you take her from me, I swear to fucking God I'll... I'll... He didn't finish. Instead, he lowered me in his arms, bundled me tight, and roared at White Rodent, "Did you fucking think you could get away with this? Rape women? Traffic them? Drug them? You're a fucking dead man and the only place you're going to is hell. I guarantee your corpse will be chopped into little pieces." Q chewed on every word. His anger was palpable, filling the room with thick tension.

I looked up, bewitched with the way his wings rustled with ferocity and he stood so rigid and unswerving. He looked toward Franco. "Bring them. The pliers, too."

Q turned on his heel and strode out the room. I curled

225

tighter into his body as the corridor contracted around us, making me feel like I lived in the belly of a ginormous snake. My snapped finger threatened to send me into darkness again, but I held on. More insects came to nibble on my brain and a procession of visions trailed after us. My mum, dad, and Brax all followed as Angel Q whisked me off to safety.

Q bent his head. "I'll pay them back like for like, *esclave*. Mark my fucking words, they'll wish they were dead before I've finished."

A burst of heat filled me as black wings fanned around us, entrapping us in a cocoon. His hotness was a bonfire against my chilled skin, and he carried me as if I was a feather.

A damaged and broken feather.

I didn't trust anything anymore. This couldn't be real. I'd done nothing to warrant such saving.

If only this *was* real. If only I was being taken away. Maybe I was dying. Maybe my brain created its own sense of finality. Saying goodbye to Q. Majestic Q with his raven wings and cloud of crows.

"You are dying. Confess your sins now, child, or you'll never be welcomed into heaven." My mother wrung her hands. *"Confess how you screwed up our life. How you ruined your brother's life. How you've ruined a man's heart. Just die already."*

I choked on the intense hatred gleaming in my mother's eyes. I couldn't believe the pain she caused.

"I never wa—wanted to be a burden." The tears I'd been holding all this time spilled. Once they started, they wouldn't stop.

Q jerked to a halt. "No, *esclave*. Stop it. You're not a burden. Never."

With a shaky hand, I reached up and caught a black oily feather from his wings. They quivered as he wrapped them tighter around us like a shield. I ran my fingers over the quill. "I confess to everything. I'm worthless and want to die."

Then I passed out.

Thirteen
Quincy

You're my obsession, I'm your possession. You own the deepest part of me...

Words lost all meaning.

I became a creature of suffering.

Tess wanted to die. My Tess. The woman who made my heart keep beating had resorted to the last option available.

She wants to die.

She wants to leave me permanently.

Whatever she'd lived through had been too much. Gone was the strong woman I knew, replaced with a shadow, a damaged hologram of who she used to be.

My arms tightened so hard I worried I might snap her in half. My entire body suffered jittery horror at the thought that even though I held her, I'd lost her.

I was too late.

The image of that fucking naked bastard with his rancid cock and the pitiful blonde girl beside Tess raped my mind.

My heart combusted with horror when I saw how similar Tess and the blonde looked. Their hair colour was so alike it tore my soul into pieces at the thought that I might've been too late. Too late to stop Tess being raped. Too late to stop her from suffering such tragedy again.

But I checked. When Tess passed out as I wrapped her snapped finger in some sheeting, I made sure to check she hadn't been used. It killed me to invade her privacy, but I needed to know.

I *had* to know. I wouldn't live with myself if she'd been violated again. Not after Lefebvre. Not after what I put her through. No one person should ever live through as much as Tess.

I wanted to howl to the bloody moon and shed my body in favour for something vicious with claws and fangs and no fucking conscience. I wanted to be the devil.

My mind dismembered from rational thought. I couldn't think straight. I doubted I'd ever be sane again. The fact that Tess wasn't bleeding between her legs helped me stay human for a little longer.

Tess weighed nothing in my arms as I carried her back the way we came. She'd lost so much weight she looked like a wraith. A blonde, delicate wraith with so many black bruises all over her she looked like a fucking domino.

My body wouldn't stop trembling as every emotion went on hyper-drive. I wanted to kill. Fucking kill and kill and *kill*.

Tess thrashed, her face scrunched up with whatever hallucination she suffered. The track marks on her arms gave a vivid story of just what she'd endured.

I kept begging over and over. *Her mind isn't broken. Her mind isn't broken.* Once she detoxed, she'd be fine. I had to believe that.

My teeth clacked hard as I remembered what she'd said. She fucking talked to Brax. He lived in her mind, whispering to her, offering all sorts of comfort. Why didn't she dream of me? I would give anything for her to think of me. To find solace in my memory.

You were never comforting. You were her master who played with her mind. How could she ever think of you fondly?

I couldn't answer and it killed me all over again.

Coming to the fork in the corridor, I turned left, heading toward the large factory floor where we'd snuck inside.

We found the old fish-processing warehouse after a day of bribing the head of police. He'd had morals and refused for a time, but then we'd found out via other means that Smith paid off airport officials to transport his cargo.

I admit I went berserk at the thought of Tess flying away from me again. I grabbed the police chief by the throat and pulled out my trusty knife, all while Franco kept watch so we weren't disturbed.

Faced with losing his life, the police bastard spilled his guts. He knew Smith. He knew enough to make me want to exterminate him, too. However, once he squealed, we walked. Someone else would kill him. I had other men I wanted to bleed.

My skin wouldn't stop crawling as we entered the compound, moving in shadows and silence. When I found Tess, my heart spontaneously exploded into shards.

I'd never felt this way before. So weak. So afraid. So helpless.

The tightness around my throat squeezed harder as I looked at the unconscious woman in my arms. Blood oozed through the sheet around her finger, and I would never be able to erase the image of her bone sticking through her skin.

Her jaw was swollen and shadowed while other abuse marked her perfect skin. Every mark punctured a hole into my soul.

If only I never went to work. If only I was strong enough to be open and tell Tess I cared deeply for her. Be brave enough to share every secret and swear every promise.

If only I'd asked her for proof that she removed the fucking tracker.

Because of me the Red Wolverine saw through my act and took revenge on Tess. He managed to cut my balls off and bury me alive by taking the one thing I couldn't live without.

I did this by being selfish. I wanted her too much to let her go, but at the same time she lived in constant danger thanks to me. And it would only get worse. The word was out that I killed cocksuckers who traded women. Death threats were coming and I knew I had to kill them, before they killed me.

I cradled Tess closer, willing my heat to enter her freezing form. Franco appeared, striding toward me, carrying the other blonde girl who had blood smeared on the insides of her thighs. She was white as a corpse and her eyes held an expression I knew all too well: the expression of no return. An empty shell where a soul had flown free to escape reality.

So many slaves had come to me with that look. They were the hardest to fix. To coax back into their bodies and not let them whither into nothingness as they lost the will to live.

Franco set his jaw and didn't say a word.

I hugged Tess ever harder and strode toward the back of the warehouse. The whole place was black with filth and stank. Unused for years, it'd found a new purpose: trafficking.

Normally, if I found a place like this, I would dispatch Franco and a few of his best men. I would let them infiltrate and get their hands dirty. My profile as CEO was too well known to risk becoming a vigilante.

But that was over now. I could indulge in a little 'kill the fucking rapist.'

This time I would tear every motherfucker into pieces. I would dance in the cooling puddles of their blood as I burned the entire place to the ground. Q Mercer no longer existed. I didn't care about my company or image.

Now all I cared about was smashing every single fucker who hurt women. Who hurt *my* woman.

Gone was my act. This would be the first time I'd fully let myself go, and I didn't want witnesses. I planned to savour the kill. Drag it out, taunt my prey until he begged. And then, when they could no longer speak from such agony, I'd dispatch them with no mercy.

"Frederick has taken Alpha team to round up the remaining assholes while Beta squadron has found over twenty girls in numerous rooms."

Tess coughed, wheezing loudly in my arms. My heart lurched at the sound. It wasn't good. She was sick. Her pallor and fever scared me shitless.

Franco muttered, "She'll be fine. We just need to get her home."

Home.

A place where I used to be free, but not anymore.

The moment Tess walked into my life she owned me. I would never be free again. I never *wanted* to be free again. If Tess thought she'd leave me by killing herself, she'd hate me for eternity when I kept her alive.

Footsteps sounded behind us. Franco and I turned to face the crowd of people as they arrived from the corridor. The cavernous factory floor with old rusty machinery and decrepit conveyor belts welcomed both traffickers and slaves.

Frederick ushered in the malnourished and dirty women. They blinked when they came closer to me.

Franco murmured to the girl in his arms, "Can you stand on your own?"

The girl took a while to reply, and even then it was a vacant nod. Franco settled her on her feet, making sure the blanket covered her.

The girls all came to a stop, clutching each other's hands, looking frantically around the room.

Now his arms were free, Franco strode toward his team who had guns trained on the ten or so traffickers who moved forward in a mixture of hatred and guilt.

When the naked asshole who'd raped the blonde girl walked past, Franco slapped him around the head. I'd never seen such a black look of rage in Franco's eyes. He'd always been so good at hiding it, but I guessed tonight was a first for all of us. He would kill and love it and I'd let him. There were enough for both of us to sate our murderous hunger.

Violence was permitted when such fuckers existed as these.

"Where do you want them?" Franco asked, looking at me with anger glowing in his eyes.

I jiggled Tess in my arms, positioning her higher all the while I itched to go and finish what I promised.

Surveying the best place for a massacre, I pointed with my chin. "Line them up over there." Directly in the middle of the factory floor, with the conveyer belt to their backs and spray-painted windows to the front. No one would see and at two a.m. in the morning, I doubted anyone would hear. But just to be sure.

"Gag them. All of them."

Franco smiled tightly. "No fucking problem."

I stayed frozen with a fitful, unconscious Tess in my grip while Franco ordered everyone onto their knees and directed his team to stuff old packing material into their mouths before sealing with duct tape.

"Take the women outside," I ordered one of Franco's men. They shouldn't have to see this.

The man nodded and motioned for the women to leave. They shuffled away, looking over their shoulders, seeing their kidnappers for the last time.

Once they were gone the naked rapist tried to stand and fight. "You won't fucking get away with this. People will come and slit your throats in your sleep. They'll put a bounty on your head."

Franco pushed him back, almost forcing his fist inside his mouth as he stuffed him like a Christmas turkey. "We're counting on it, you dickshit. The more of your kind we can cull the better."

The man in the blue shirt and jeans—obviously the fucking ringleader—said softly, "You're making a huge mistake, my friend. Just take your girl and go, but leave the rest with us. I'll pretend this never happened and I won't tell the Wolverine a thing."

My hands clenched around Tess. This was the bastard who ordered every diabolical thing that'd been done to my woman. I trembled with ferocity, forcing myself not to break Tess's fragile form.

"You're not my fucking friend and I will take my girl and leave, but I'm not leaving you alive." I took a few steps closer. "The Wolverine is already dead. Just like you."

A woman whimpered; my heart hardened to rock. Her long black hair was tangled, her cheeks stretched with the duct tape over her mouth. A woman involved with trafficking women? I couldn't think of anything more traitorous. She'd be the first to die.

Some men cried, some moaned, others pleaded, warbling around their gags, but it fell on deaf ears.

Not one of my team held any compassion. We were there to do the human race a favour by obliterating such evilness.

My jaw clenched. It was time to get dirty. Time to bloody my hands in honour of the woman who owned me.

I moved toward Frederick. He gave me an understanding nod as his eyes fell on Tess.

Her head lolled like a floppy doll against my shoulder. I couldn't bear the thought of putting her down. But I had no choice.

Frederick made eye contact, asking silently to take her.

I looked away, wanting so badly to kiss Tess and make everything disappear from her mind. I wanted her to wake up whole and undamaged. But I would never live with myself if I didn't kill every last bastard. I had to relinquish her…for now.

Slowly, I angled my body toward him. Frederick moved closer, brushing my arms with his as he readied himself to take her weight.

"Wait," I snapped.

Frederick didn't say a thing, stepping away. I rolled my neck, centring myself.

I cleared my throat, facing the men and women who made their living stealing the lives of others. Police hadn't punished them. Karma hadn't cared. But me? I cared a shitload, and they were about to get their just rewards.

"See this woman?" I held Tess higher, raising my arms like she was on a pyre ready to burst into flames. "You did this to her." My eyes glazed recalling the fighter, the amazing woman who captured my heart, and not the flightless bird in my arms. My voice came thicker, roughed with hatred. "You stole everything from her. You stole her entire life not once but fucking twice. I don't know what goes through your head. I don't fucking want to know. I've always classified myself as a fair man even though every day I battle black desires. I see the satisfaction such a trade can bring. I see the temptation for money and the dark call of lust. But what I don't see is how you lost so much of your humanity that you let yourself give in. You sicken me. You disgust me, and I promise no one will care when you rot in your unmarked graves."

The line of ten or so men squirmed on their knees, testing the ropes around their wrists, working the gags. The woman hung her head, but kept glaring at me with black evil. She was a true psychopath. No feelings or sense of right and wrong.

I motioned to Frederick to take Tess. He came forward and opened his arms, easing them beneath mine. My body ripped into pieces as Tess's gentle weight transferred from my arms to his. He cradled her with such compassion I suffered a bolt of hot green jealousy.

I lashed out, clamping my fingers around Tess's arm.

Frederick froze, watching me carefully. "She's yours, man, I get it. She'll always be yours. I'm just keeping her safe for you while you avenge her honour."

It took everything I had to relax my grip and nod.

I held out my hand to Franco, who stood to my right. "Give me the pliers, Franco."

Frederick sucked in a breath and stepped hastily back, cradling Tess's head on his shoulder. Immediately Franco obeyed, passing over the tools used to break my woman's finger.

I stalked forward until I loomed over the line-up of traffickers. The psychopath woman stiffened—too stupid to be afraid. "Cut her ropes and stand her up."

Franco obeyed without question, slicing through the binding. Grabbing her long black hair, he hoisted her to her feet. Her nostrils flared above her gag and the first sign of fear glimmered in her gaze.

Franco wrapped his large arm around her shoulders, keeping her in place.

I inched closer, tapping the pliers in my hands. "How does it feel to be a traitor to your own sex? Do you enjoy it?"

She glared, tilting her chin in defiance.

Smiling coldly, I placed the pliers in my pocket and reached to my waistband. I pulled free the knife I'd used to kill the Wolverine and his son. The hilt felt righteous in my grip, urging me on. Using the tip of the exceedingly sharp blade, I sliced through the duct tape. She flinched as I nicked her and a small line of red appeared.

I had to hear her reasoning before she died. I had to understand what drove people to such things.

Spitting out the burlap sack, she hissed, "Go to hell, asshole. I see you for what you are. You think because you wear a fancy suit you are different to us. You're lying. You're the one who wants to hurt and sell women."

Not the answer I wanted.

I backhanded her. Her head snapped sideways and she stumbled.

Frederick moved further away, protecting Tess in his arms.

"Do you believe in redemption, cunt?" My voice was detached, killer-cold, precise.

She pursed her lips, denying me an answer.

I belted her around the ear. She muttered, "Yes. I will be forgiven."

My lips curled in a snarl. I grabbed her hand, jerking it forward. She struggled, but it made no difference. Franco held out his palm to take my knife while I grabbed the pliers from my pocket. In one fast move, I inserted her finger into the nasty tool.

She sucked in a breath, wriggling in Franco's grip, but it was no use.

I whispered, "I'm taking your life. You will die and become nothing. Not even a speck of thought, or whisper of second chance. I want you to know that as I take your life, I'm cursing you to the bowels of the underworld. I'm wrapping you in curses so your soul will never rise again."

My hand twisted the pliers and she let out an ungodly scream. Her finger gave way as I snapped the bone and Franco pushed her away from him. He tossed me the knife and in one short slice, I cut her jugular. Just like Wolverine.

For one millisecond her neck stayed intact, then her flesh gaped open in a red angry gash, spurting my chest with red glowing blood. Hot and tangy, it spewed as if it couldn't stand to be in her body any longer.

Her hands flew to her throat, her finger bent to a horrible extreme, trying to staunch the blood. She gurgled rather than screamed.

Her rapidly beating heart hastened her death as litres of crimson evicted through the cut.

The bound and gagged traffickers all froze, staring in horrified realization. The realization that there would be no walking away from me. That they'd met their fucking maker and had minutes left to live.

The woman toppled to her knees, before crashing onto her face as the last pump of life-force drenched the concrete.

She twitched her last. My voice rang loud and clear. "Your blood will mingle today. All of you. You worked together, you'll die together."

I looked to Franco, who nodded.

"Gentlemen," he said to his team. Instantly, the black-clad mercenaries ringing the space unholstered their guns.

Shaking my head, I said, "Too impersonal." Holding up the bloody knife, I added, "No guns."

"You heard him. Put your guns down," Franco snapped. The sound of knives being pulled free from scabbards hissed around the room.

I pointed at the fucking ringleader in his pouncy blue shirt. "Not him." Then I looked at the naked fuck who'd raped the blonde girl. "Him either. Both are mine."

The mercenaries moved forward, standing behind a victim. Blair, one of Franco's trusted men who looked like a Norwegian god of war, placed his knife across a trafficker's throat, his shoulder tense and ready.

Darkness yowled inside, swarming thick and fast; I let myself be consumed. *This is for you, Tess.*

I never felt the need to be so barbaric, but the beast called the shots. And it wanted blood. It wanted an Olympic swimming pool filled with blood.

"Joined together in death, you will be entwined in purgatory. I have no mercy for you." My eyes met Franco's. "Do it."

It was a morbid floor show gone horribly wrong as the mercenaries severed their victim's neck in one swoop. Dying bleats and prayers smothered by their gags.

Waterfalls of red gushed forth, splashing wetly against the concrete. One by one their bodies twitched and convulsed, sending blood from veins to floor.

Franco moved closer and mumbled in my ear. "Can I have the rapist?" His eyes flashed black, and I felt a camaraderie like never before. Monster to monster.

I nodded.

The gruesome death scene played out. The air grew rife with metal and rust. The sweet stench of death followed not long after as their hearts gave out.

My eyes shot to Tess still unconscious in Frederick's arms. Her hastily wrapped finger lay broken on top of the brown scratchy blanket. Her cheek pressed against Frederick's black polo. If anything, she looked worse than before—her skin pallid, ashen.

I needed to touch her. Affirm she was still alive and would stay that way. Stepping through the pools of blood, I headed to

Frederick and placed as delicate a kiss as possible on Tess's forehead.

Frederick held her steady, while I caressed her cheek and tried to get my heart to stop hammering against my ribs. *She's still alive.*

Her blue-grey eyes flickered open, her pupils so far dilated, I was afraid the drugs in her system might kill her. But her gaze latched onto mine with intelligence, fighting hard to be free.

"Y—you're covered in blood—" She stopped short, wheezing and whooping with racking coughs. Goddammit, I had to get her to a doctor.

Seeing her so sick sucker-punched me in the gut. I smiled gently. "*Esclave.* We're leaving soon. I'm extracting revenge and then we're going home."

Frederick scowled. "Seriously, Q? Calling her slave at a time like this?" His look of disapproval pissed me off.

"*Tu ne sais rien.*" You don't know. I tried to keep levelheaded but anger made me mutter, "Don't judge me." He didn't get it. *Esclave* had become an endearment. Aching with tenderness, encapsulating everything that had happened between us.

Tess mumbled something incoherent and I brushed my fingertips down her feverish cheek. "Tess, what would you have me do? What sacrifice would give you closure?" I bowed my head against hers. "Tell me, *esclave,* and I'll make it happen. Tell me what will halt your nightmares and bring you back to me."

For a while she didn't respond. Then her eyes flickered open and her voice trembled with rage. "They don't have h— hearts. I want to see if it's true."

Frederick tensed. "Q...don't take that literally."

What a fucking stupid thing to say. Of course I took it literally. All I could see was holding a black-threaded heart in my hands as the ringleader perished.

My eyes narrowed as Tess slipped back into limpness. She looked so innocent, so broken in her slumber, but the black part of me recognised the black part of her. *How dark do you run? How alike are we truly?*

Her one request told me more about Tess than any questions I could've asked. She wanted their hearts. She wanted the most integral part of a person—the one symbol that represented compassion and love. She wanted it carved out of the men who hurt her.

It would be my fucking pleasure.

I stood straighter, mouth watering at granting her request.

Frederick stepped back a bit, shaking his head. "Q. Don't. Just put an end to this and be done with it. She won't remember."

I snarled. "It isn't the point that she won't remember. It's the fact she asked and I promised. I swore I'd lay her kidnappers' corpses at her feet. And I mean to deliver them in pieces."

Tess's request echoed in my skull: A heart for a heart. A life for a life. A thrum of living for the last beat of death.

It was only fitting. Only fair. Time to deliver the heart of the man who stole her, to put the past behind.

"Leave, Roux. I don't want you here. Take Tess back to the plane and get ready to leave."

"You won't be able to run from the memories if you do this, Mercer. His death will be good enough."

"What would you fucking do if Angelique asked you to cut off the cock of the man who raped her?"

He hung his head before answering, "I would slice off his cock and feed it to him."

"Exactly. Goodbye, Frederick."

He turned to leave and I raised my voice to the room. "Everyone go. Wait for us at the airport."

The men cleaned their blades on random sacking on the conveyor belt and disappeared silently from the room.

Frederick left with Tess cradled in his embrace. Once they'd gone, I stalked back to Franco. He had the ringleader and the rapist in his grip, both bound and gagged, glaring at me.

Grabbing the ringleader's shoulder, I said, "Do whatever you want to him. But don't come down the back of the warehouse. I'll return when I'm done."

"Understood."

We went our separate ways, and the ringleader struggled as I pushed him toward the gloom. It wasn't far to the back, but it was deep in shadows. Perfect.

I threw him at the conveyer belt.

He twisted to face me, eyes flaring wide, trying to articulate around the gag.

I ripped off the tape, cocking an eyebrow. "Any last words before I butcher you?"

Spitting out the sacking, he sneered, "So you're the master who doesn't let himself play."

My hand curled harder around the hilt of the knife; sweat and blood made it slippery. "I'm the man who knows right from wrong."

He chuckled. "No, you live in denial. One day you'll see the truth. But for now, you'll kill others who have bowed to the needs they have." He leaned forward, but I shoved him back.

He smiled. "It will happen. You can't ignore who you truly are forever. One day the decision won't be yours anymore, and when that happens operations like ours will be your saving grace."

His words shot bullet after bullet into my heart. I shouldn't let it affect me, but it did, because he was right. He was right and that's why I fought so hard.

The thought of what these places offered in broken, subservient women enticed the blackness and made me tremble with sick wanting, but I was also stronger than I'd ever been.

Tess taught me that I may need to hurt others, but her strength restrained me.

Every day, I worried that I would give in, that I'd snap and become my father. I could finally fit in. Belong with these soulless bastards and no longer fight against a constant war.

But I had more faith in myself now. Thanks to Tess. She

proved there must be something good inside me to deserve such a creature as her.

She saved me in so many ways, and I didn't even realize until now.

My chest swelled with pride. "I'm stronger than you will ever be. I have a woman who sees the light inside me. And I'll never stop trying to be the best I can be for her."

"It's not enough. Sooner or later you'll crack. You'll kill her and become like us."

I trembled with rage. "The day I give in is the day I kill myself." I meant it as a threat, but it resonated with an oath. I swore on my soul to end my life if I ever became like these men.

The man's eyes narrowed and he pressed harder against the conveyor belt, looking for a way to run. "Just let me go and I'll give you anything you want."

"There is nothing I want from you." I ran the blade through my fingertips, adding, "Apart from your heart."

He gulped. He knew what was coming and finally concluded it wouldn't be quick.

The moment the glow of horror filled his eyes, I launched myself at him. Punching him in the jaw, I threw him onto the conveyor belt. Old strapping for fish crates littered the floor. Grabbing a few, I made short work of tying his dazed body to the belt.

He jerked, testing the strength of my knots. "Wait. I'll give you anything!"

Screams filled the warehouse from the other end of darkness. Franco had begun work on the rapist and his cries soothed my soul. He deserved everything Franco gave and more.

I grabbed the collar of the guy's shirt and with a quick slice, slit it in two with my blade.

"Please. I'll give you anything. You name it. You want to save women? Fine, I'll give you all the names and contacts of the men we sold to over the year."

I didn't rise to the bait. I knew Franco's men would've already raided the offices and found every last shred of information in this godforsaken place.

Everything I needed for future rescue missions was already mine.

I listened detachedly to his rambling begging as I shrugged off my bloodstained blazer and undid my cufflinks.

Each move was predatory and unrushed, dragging out the last few minutes of his life. I rolled up my sleeves, taking care not to wipe too much blood from my hands onto the black shirt.

Another scream rang around the walls and a merciless laugh followed quick behind. My heart beat thicker, slower. My mind sharpened until all I saw was the man in front of me.

I didn't think about Tess.

I didn't think about repercussions of such brutal retaliation.

All I thought about was blood.

I dropped my eyes and let myself be free. I smashed through my walls, unlocked the cage, and snarled like the rabid animal I was. The false me ceased to exist. The real me was ready.

The ringleader trembled, his skin shocked to white. "I was wrong when I said you're like us. You're not."

I laughed, picking up the blade. I dragged the tip down his sternum, circling around the thing Tess asked me to retrieve for her. "No, I'm not like you." I pressed on the blade and the man screamed as I punctured his ribcage inch by inch. There were easier ways. I could slice his diaphragm and reach upward for his heart. But I wanted the hard labour of breaking his ribs as I worked toward my goal.

He wasn't going to die an easy death. I wanted him to be alive the entire time I butchered him.

"Je suis pire." I'm worse.

Fourteen

Leave your mark, scar my skin, I will bow down to you, my king.

"*Well, I hope you're happy. You're probably not going to die,*" my mother whispered in my ear.

I ceased to know what the hell was happening. I lived in constant pain from my finger and the chilly ache in my lungs. I didn't know where I was any more, or if I'd dreamt Angel Q or not.

"*Don't listen to her, Tessie. I'm so glad they found you in time.*" Brax glared at my mother. He never liked her. I didn't blame him. She wasn't very likeable.

Time spaced out again and broken images came in little puzzle pieces.

Warm arms—1920s man carrying me.

Men—hordes of them. All sitting in some fancy place with their hands bloodied in their laps.

Engines and loss of gravity as a jet carried me far, far away from nightmares.

"Stay with me, *esclave*. We're almost home." Q stood before me, his black shirt glistening with red dampness. His hands were stained and sprays of crimson camouflaged his face.

He looked like a monster. A man who killed for me.

My heart raced with fear. Would he kill me, too? After everything I did, I deserved the same fate.

"You did it?" *Did what…what am I asking?*

Q held up something demonic. Something riddled with fat and sinew, dripping horribly in his palm. "I took his heart. I took everything from him, Tess." He bowed at my feet, placing the grisly muscle on the floor. "For you. May it give you the strength to come back to me."

Whirs of helicopter blades shattered my little daydream and for the first time in ages, I thought of sex. I thought about Q spanking and fucking me in the helicopter. I thought about the way he captured my wrists and made me so vulnerable.

No slow, sensual burn started in my belly. No need to have Q's touch rendered me lust-filled. I only felt empty.

Time merged into one big jumbled hallucination where helicopter blades tore me to shreds and plane engines gobbled me up to spit me out, burned to a char and on fire.

A jolt woke me and I moaned with the terrible pain in my hand. *Someone, please cut it off.* I couldn't stand the excruciation anymore.

"Get her inside," someone said. "I've already called the doctor."

I couldn't focus on anything. I couldn't escape the prison my brain had become.

"Learn, girl. Retaliation equals pain. Next time, I won't be so kind." White Man roared inside my mind. The memory of being hurt took centre place in my stupor, replaying, hitting me around the head with the hard-learned lessons over and over until I became afraid of my inner thoughts. I couldn't speak. I couldn't even think. What if I spoke out of turn? The poor blonde would be killed and I'd be hurt.

Slowly, the fog turned into tremors and pinpricks of agony. The itch from before crept back under my skin and I moaned. I couldn't go through withdrawal. It would be used against me. They'd withhold the drug until I did whatever they wanted. And I would do whatever they wanted, as I was weak. So fucking weak.

"She's convulsing. Hurry!"

I bounced and jiggled in some weird sort of transport. The bruises screamed and my lungs sloshed with liquid. I coughed hard, tearing my throat up with phlegm. I didn't know what was happening, but my body didn't like it.

My skin temperature developed schizophrenia. One second chilling me to deep Antarctica, the next turning me into a bubbling volcano.

The bugs were back; their little feelers and legs tickling my insides, making me wish I could scratch my brain out.

"No!" I thrashed and someone slammed to a halt, tightening their grip on me.

"Tess. Stay with me. Please. Help is here. You'll be fine soon." Q's voice cut through the beetle-laden fog and I latched on to it.

"Put her down. I can't work if she's in your arms."

I felt sick and nauseous one second, then ravenous and ready to fight the next. The drugs faded, leaving me in a turmoil. My system couldn't find an equilibrium no matter how hard it tried.

"Hold her down. She's doing more damage by moving."

Something pinned my shoulders and I lashed out. "Don't touch me. Not again. Please not again." Tears erupted from my eyes and I sobbed, remembering the snaps of broken bones and blood of other girls beneath my nails. "No! Please. I won't do it anymore. I won't hurt any more hummingbirds. I won't. Kill me. I want to die." I coughed and coughed and coughed, unable to breathe past the thick liquid in my lungs. My fingers bent and I scratched my face, trying to peel the skin back to get at the gnawing bugs in my brain.

A band of pressure landed on my chest as someone pressed me onto something soft. "Fuck, I'm so sorry, Tess. Forgive me." Q's tortured voice murmured in my ear as he caught my hand and I felt a needle puncture my skin.

Him.

He was just the same as them. Keeping me drugged. Keeping me dependent.

I drifted into dreamland cursing him to the depths of hell.

Fifteen
Quincy

*You crawled into the darkness, set my monster free,
so scream, bleed, call out to me, but never say stop,
never flee...*

Suzette wrung her hands as the doctor administered the anaesthetic.

Franco waited in the doorway, watching me come apart. I couldn't see straight, my heart was a fucking rabbit in my chest, and my body felt like it would never calm down.

I held Tess's hand as she slipped away into sleep, and I wanted to throw the heart I'd cut from the ringleader into the fire and watch it fucking burn.

"Move away from my patient. I want this room to myself while I work," the doctor said, pushing me aside.

"No fucking chance. I'm staying right here." I crossed my arms, daring him to argue. The rage inside was ready to smash him if he tried to separate me from Tess again. We scowled at each other before his eyes dropped to my bloody clothes.

"It's not sanitary for you to be near while I operate. Go have a shower and come back. Your maid can keep watch."

Suzette blinked, coming out of her shock at the state of

Tess. I didn't blame her for looking like a ghost—Tess was no longer recognisable. Her golden hair lay dank against the pillow in clumps. Her collarbone pierced her skin with hunger, and her beautiful bruised cheekbones looked too stark for her beauty. The sheet wrapped around her broken finger was crusted dry with blood, and that was without seeing all the contusions.

I stumbled away from the bed, holding my head in my hands. "Fix her, goddammit. Just fix her."

I couldn't be there while the doctor stripped Tess and inspected her injuries. Just the thought of another man touching her set my blood to boil. I did the sensible thing. The only thing I could do.

Pointing a finger at Franco, I ordered, "Watch him."

Franco nodded, stepping further into my room. Without a backward glance, I stalked to the bathroom and slammed the door. The second I couldn't see Tess, anxiety twisted my spine. I itched to go back out there and make sure she was exactly where I left her—laid out like a fucking corpse on my bed.

My tower room, where Tess and I had indulged in blood play and whips, seemed like a joke now. It no longer gave me pleasure or satisfaction; all I saw was Tess so tiny and exhausted, bleeding and drugged.

I may never have my strong *esclave* again. I may never string her up and hit her because we both got off on belonging to each other.

I may have found her, but that didn't mean a damn thing.

"Fuck!" I roared, punching the tiled wall. Instantly, my knuckles screamed and I shook my hand to release the pain. The doctor was right. I shouldn't be around Tess when I was covered head to toe in another man's blood. Her immune system already fought so much.

Shedding my clothes to burn later, I stepped into the shower and proceeded to scrub every inch as if I could erase the last seventeen days from existence. Make it all disappear and pretend that Tess had been beside me all along, always safe, never hurt by anyone but me.

Once I was clean, I repeated the process until my skin burned from scrubbing and the bathroom wept with steam. The stitches in my arm from the gunshot irritated, but surprisingly didn't hurt. The scar would be a constant reminder of what I did to get Tess back. I would wear it with pride.

By the time I entered the bedroom again, dressed in jeans and a black T-shirt, the doctor had cleaned Tess with the help of Suzette and wrapped her chest with bandages.

He saw me looking. "She has two cracked ribs from coughing. She's severely dehydrated and needs to be put on antibiotics to stop the pneumonia."

Pneumonia.

Those raping fucking bastards.

I couldn't stand still. I gritted my teeth, dragging hands through my hair as I paced.

"She should be in a hospital, but because you won't allow that, I'll have a few nurses stay here and administer around the clock care."

Damn right I wouldn't allow her to go to the hospital. She needed to heal here. Where I had a top of the line security system and a crew of men ready to kill and then ask questions. She would never be out of my sight again.

"How long before she'll be well again?"

The doctor eyed me with annoyance as if I was a rabies-infected dog sniffing around his dinner. "Time heals everything. You need to be patient."

I stopped, glaring. "Don't give me bullshit answers. How long?"

He looked back to Tess, applying antiseptic balms to the shallow cuts and bruises all over her body. "It will take however long it needs to take. You're to be gentle with her until then. No rushing her. She'll be fragile as the drugs leave her system. She needs someone strong and collected, not—" He stopped and looked up, waving at me with the tube of antiseptic. "—not a feral animal who looks like he wants to rip her throat out."

Suzette shifted, anger radiating off her tiny frame. "My master found her and brought her back. Don't say he's—"

I held up my hand. Suzette was sweet but I didn't need her interference. "I'd never fucking hurt her, doctor. Just do what you have to do."

Suzette looked at me with tears shimmering in her eyes and I glanced away. I couldn't look at her right now. Not while I hung on to my sanity so delicately. If anyone showed me any pity or compassion, I would most likely do one of two things: beat them stupid or burst into fucking tears.

And I didn't do tears.

Ever.

No one spoke a word while the doctor set up an IV and started Tess on the course of antibiotics. "Without having the results of the blood work for a few days, I won't know what drugs they made her take, but I've added a few things to counteract the effects of withdrawal. She'll still feel pretty low, but it should be bearable."

Bearable? I didn't want Tess to bear through it. I wanted her to be repaired and given her wholesomeness back. I wanted her to rest in peace, not bear through agony.

"Give her something stronger."

The doctor shook his head. "I'll assess once she comes around again. Don't tell me how to do my job and I won't ask how you came to paint yourself in someone else's blood." His eyes hardened; we had a pissing contest of wills.

Suzette cleared her throat, breaking the silence.

I moved toward the window, glaring outside. I needed to do something—*anything* to stop myself going crazy.

The doctor took his time with the full exam, then turned his attention to repairing Tess's finger. He cringed once he unwrapped it.

"Who the hell were these people?" he whispered.

My chest swelled with pride. He used *were*. Past tense. Even the shiny doctor and his morals knew the bastards weren't alive.

That's right. I struck the match. I doused them in gasoline. I stole their lives and made them fucking burn in an old fish factory in Rio.

The memory of the blazing fire had helped purge my mind a little of what I'd done. Almost as if it put a giant full stop at the end of a dark and disturbing sentence. What happened in there would live with me forever, but the fire made it all disappear.

The doctor sluiced Tess's hand in orange sterilizing liquid and Suzette held a handkerchief to her mouth, gagging at the horrible sight. She bolted upright. "I, eh... I'll come back."

Franco sidestepped from the doorway, letting Suzette leave. I motioned for him to go, too. He nodded and disappeared.

I stayed right where I was as the doctor realigned the bone and added a few stitches where her skin had been pierced. Once completed, he smeared more orange stuff all over and wrapped it up with a splint and gauze.

"Will she be able to use it?" My voice was calm but I wanted to slam my fist into the wall.

The crushing weight of blame stole oxygen from my lungs. I did this to Tess. I let her be taken. I let her prance around with a fucking tracking beacon in her neck.

How was I going to live with this overwhelming guilt?

Tess fell for the wrong man—a useless man who would never *ever* forgive himself.

The doctor nodded. "In time, yes. Don't expect a miracle overnight, but the human body has an amazing ability to knit together and overcome injuries that look unfixable."

I exploded. "In time. In *time*! That's all you can say." I threw up my hands, glaring at the curtain that hid the St. Andrew's cross where I'd whipped Tess.

Normally my cock would harden. It would twitch and swell at the memory of hurting her, but nothing. Nothing because the strong woman who made me so fucking hot for her just by answering back was gone. She'd been replaced with someone incapable of receiving any more violence.

I lost the fighter and been given a broken fucking bird and I honestly didn't know what that meant for me.

The beast inside mourned heavily—dug a pit to curl up in because he would never be free again.

Yes, I'd rehabilitated hundreds of women, paid for their healing, coaxed them back to life—but I never stood by their bedside and nursed. It wasn't in me to tend to something so weak. Sickness and frailty were things I couldn't be around, and yet, I couldn't leave Tess to heal on her own. I would be with her every step of the way.

But by seeing her so weak, my lust would die, my need to hurt her would shrivel. I would distance myself to protect her all because she could no longer handle what I needed.

I have Tess back, but it's not enough.

The doctor stood, snapping his bloody gloves off, giving me a sad smile. "She'll survive. Now that she's warm and in a healthy environment her body will heal."

He gathered his things and headed for the door. "I'll come back and check on her in a few hours."

I never took my eyes off Tess. "You forgot one thing."

He raised an eyebrow, looking at his unconscious patient. "What?"

I pointed at her neck. "Cut it out."

His wide eyes met mine. "Excuse me?"

He probably thought I'd gone mad. I sure sounded like it.

"She has a tracker in her neck. That's how they found her. I want it out. This fucking instant."

"In order to do that, I'll have to make an incision. I'm not sure we should, given the state of her body."

I shook my head. "You're not listening to me. Now, doctor. I won't ask again." I let some of my anger show. I was ready to order him at gunpoint if that's what it took. I'd already lost her once to fucking stupidity. I wouldn't do it again.

He gulped. "Fine. But I want you out of here."

"Not going to happen." Giving him a consolation prize, I

headed to the far end of the room and sat in a wingback. "I'll sit right here and won't say a word, but I'm not leaving her."

The man sighed, heading back to the bed. "You sure don't make a happy working environment." He reached for his bag of tricks and placed a green medical cloth on the mattress by Tess's neck before laying a sterilised packaged scalpel on top.

Snapping on fresh gloves and opening the scalpel, the doctor brushed Tess's hair away, ready to begin.

She never moved, deep in sleep, and it took an eternity for the doctor to drag the sharp blade down Tess's neck.

I gripped the armrests until one of the leather studs popped and material tore from its seams.

Blood.

Her blood.

My mouth watered to taste, then a wave of nausea filled me. *You're a sick fuck. You'll never taste her blood again because you'll make it your life work to keep her safe from any more pain.*

I would protect Tess from me. I would care for her, tend to her, but never love her the way I needed. Never again would I hurt her.

The thin trickle of red as the doctor inserted a pair of tweezers into her neck sent me reeling back to the warehouse.

"Stop!"

"Never," I growled, digging my blade deeper. The knife sank through his ribs and I sawed through cartilage, sweating with effort. I cleaved him open inch by inch; he screamed louder with every slice.

I cut a hole in his motherfucking chest and licked my lips the moment he died.

The feel of his hot wet cavity as I pulled out his heart, rebirthed me to something monstrous. His heart grew cold while resting on my palm.

My first and only thought had been: I have to give this to Tess.

"What do you want me to do with it?" the doctor asked, clanking the tiny tracker into a surgical tray, shattering my daydream.

Shooting to my feet, I rushed toward him and grabbed the tray. Tipping it upside down, I let the life-ruining device land in my open palm. Streaks of warm blood stained my clean hands.

The doctor curled his lip in distaste, but didn't say anything.

I couldn't wait another moment. Striding to the door, I found Franco in the corridor. The poor man looked fucking beat. Eyes hollow, face gaunt, and a wiry edge that would petrify anyone if they'd known what he'd done to the rapist last night.

I'd seen the remains. I'd stepped over dismembered fingers, toes, and cock while holding a bleeding heart in my hands. We were a nasty pair of work, but through killing together we'd been granted a kind of peace that we wouldn't get if the pervert was sentenced to jail. We gave them fair justice. We ended it.

"Is she doing okay?" he asked, looking at my clenched hand.

"Yeah, the doctor is stitching her up now. I need you to stay with her till I get back. *"Vous, ça va?"* You good? I couldn't remember the last time any of us slept. It wouldn't be much longer till we all crashed and burned.

"No. I got it." He passed me, slapping my shoulder. "Pleasure working with you, Mercer."

"Likewise." I gave him a tight smile and headed down the stairs.

I managed to keep my calm all the way through the house. I managed to smile at a few of the girls we'd rescued from Rio as Suzette and Mrs. Sucre arranged temporary staff to make sure they all had rooms and whatever they needed.

I kept walking at a normal pace right out the front door and away from the house, but the moment I was away from view, I ran.

I fucking bolted across the grounds, heading toward one of the many outbuildings at the back of the property. Birds flew, squawking in indignation, and the freshly mowed grass filled my nose with freshness.

Skidding to a stop outside one of the many converted

barns where my father's priceless cars rested, I punched in the pin on the keypad and entered the hushed world of mechanics.

I hated these cars and never used them. I didn't want to sell them either, as in my mind locking them up in a garage was a way of sticking it to my father one more time. Plus when I got angry, I liked to take my rage out on the pristine panelling and immaculate upholstery.

I beelined for the back of the garage, toward the overstocked toolroom where any builder would've come in his pants with the top-of-the-line gadgets.

Bending, I placed the blood-smeared tracker on the concrete floor and paced toward the rack where all the hammers hung. I selected the baddest, heaviest sledge hammer from the rack and turned to face the electronic nightmare on the ground.

Howling, I swung with all the rage trapped inside and brought the wrath of the hammer on top of it.

It smashed into a billion teeny tiny fragments. It turned from small to microscopic dust, but I didn't trust its evilness was truly dead.

I hit it again and again and again. I swung until my back ached and sweat poured under my shirt.

All I could see was Tess tied to the bed in Rio. Her sweaty, sickly skin. Her protruding bones and dilated pupils. Her agony was caused by this shitty piece of technology.

Vous avez tout pris de moi! You took everything from me!

I hit and hit. Growling, straining, *cursing.*

It wasn't until I had a crater the size of a bowling ball in the concrete when I finally conceded it was no longer operational.

Breathing hard, I dropped the hammer and let it rest where it landed. The last two and a half weeks caught up with me in a rush and I stumbled against the wall. My head swam with tiredness; my bones screamed for a bed.

You can rest. Tess is safe.

I fucking thought she was safe last time, and she wasn't.

You've hit that wall. You have to rest.

I let my body crumple to the floor and bent over my folded knees.

For the first time in my life, I let weakness consume me and I grieved. Grieved for what I lost when Tess was taken. Grieved for myself for what was stolen.

Because one thing was for sure.

Tess had changed.

And I feared I'd never get her back.

Sixteen

Tess

Tied to a rack or down on my knees, it's you my master I long to please. Own me, take me, you can never break me...

The first thing I did was scream.

Sleep left me, dumping me into a world of severe pain. My finger, my ribs, my...neck. It was too much. Too much!

Then the bugs scurried from their hiding place, taking refuge in my skin, chewing me from the inside out. Maggots wiggled in my hair, termites bored through my legs.

I screamed as if my soul wanted to escape. I screamed as every single hellish thing I'd lived through crushed me with the force of a logging truck.

Unsurvivable guilt suffocated me, latching around my brain and heart, squeezing me to hell. Those girls. What I did. I couldn't live with myself.

"Shoot her, slut."

"Beat her harder. Harder!"

"I'm gonna fuck you next, cunt. Oh yeah, I'm gonna split you in half."

"See, Tess. No one wants you anymore. Die already."

"I'm always here for you, Tessie. Don't give up."

"*You ruined everyone's lives, Tess. You deserve to die for your crimes.*"

"*You're strong, precious, but that's her blood under your fingernails.*"

I couldn't breathe. *I can't breathe!*

"Get out. Get out. Get out!" I bolted upright, then immediately fell back down again. My ribs stabbed me and I saw stars, tripping into faintness. Wet coughs grabbed my lungs, drowning me even as guilt pushed me further into madness.

Drugs. I needed drugs. I needed something to dull this murdering emotional agony. I needed the smog to take me far, far away so my mind didn't crack.

"I want to die. I deserve to die. I hurt them. All those birds. I did it. I did what they asked. Give me something. *Anything!*"

Hard pressure landed on my shoulders; my eyes wrenched open.

"Shit, Tess. Calm down." Q's tortured gaze met mine. Seeing him only sent me spiralling into more madness.

He'd found me. Just like I knew he would. But now I could never be worthy. I killed. I hurt women instead of saving them. I was the exact opposite of Q and he'd kill me if he ever found out.

I hyperventilated, panting hard. "Don't. Please. I didn't mean to. I know you can't forgive me. But don't kill me. Don't."

The bugs chomped harder at my flesh, tearing another scream from my lungs. *"You need to beg if you want something to stop the craving, little girl."* White Man appeared and I knew what I had to do.

I grabbed at Q, fumbling with eager hands, so desperate for the calm fog. I'd do anything. Be anyone. Beg. Steal. Lie. Kill.

Oh, God. I'd kill again if I could escape this madness.

"Give me what I need. *Please!*"

Q cursed, hoisting me into a sitting position with his

strong arms. The liquid in my lungs drained from horizontal to vertical, making my cough even worse.

He clutched my shoulders. "Don't panic. Tess. Stop. You're safe. You're safe with me, *mon amour*." My love.

He lied. I'd never be safe. Never be free from the haunting of my villainy. *Don't look at me. Don't see the horrors I've committed.*

"Tess. Goddammit, *esclave*." He shook me, his fingers digging deep into my shoulders. His touch wriggled with beetles, nipping at me, devouring me alive.

If the guilt doesn't kill me the bugs will.

"Stop it. Relax. You're going to hurt yourself." Q captured my chin, holding me still and every single abhorrent thing I'd done smothered me, sending me into a free-fall.

I pulled the trigger.

I swung the baseball bat.

I scratched.

I tortured.

I inflicted never ending agony on those girls.

My heart destroyed itself with every memory, unable to withstand the pain. White Man entered my thoughts. *"What did I tell you about pain? Run from it like a good little slave. Do anything in your power to avoid it. Be good. Obedient. Otherwise I'll make it twenty times worse for you."* He threw away the pliers he held and brandished a welding torch, holding it near my body.

I wanted to curl up and die. I waited for the burn, the melting of my skin. I deserved to be set on fire—burned like a witch. I was a witch. Cursed and riddled with evil.

"Do it. Kill me! I don't deserve to live."

"Tess, fuck, you're killing me. Come back to me. Stop this now!" Q's voice changed from pleading to a roar.

I trembled. I'd never been so close to death. I felt as if I was one step away from my grave. All I had to do was let the guilt consume me and then I'd be blessedly free. Tarantulas crept over me with their furry legs and I gave up. I relinquished my sanity.

Q may have found me, but I lost my mind to what I'd

done. No amount of help or cure could save me.

I let go of my straining grip on life and fell. Falling, falling, surrendering to death.

But something happened.

A wall sprang up from nowhere. Soaring into being, faster and faster. Brick by brick, mortar by mortar, a huge impenetrable barrier sprang up between me and the horrible memories. Me and what I'd become. Me and Q.

I fell deep into the heart of this newly made tower. It was lonely. It was dark. It echoed with sounds of chains and irons—being fortified with barbwire—completely impassable.

The second the noise stopped and the tower was fully erected all I felt was heavenly release. Nothing could touch me. No guilt. No pain. No memories of what I'd done.

I was free.

Opening my eyes, I stared into deep into Q's gaze, trying to figure out what just happened. He searched mine, his face hard and tired and so, so handsome.

"Are you okay?" he whispered.

His hand on my face was so familiar, but his touch was never gentle. He'd caused me pain and misery. And my tower did not permit such things.

The rest of my soul withdrew to huddle deep in the structure, sucking every last emotion, every single thing that I'd ever felt deep inside.

A void grew wide, creating a moat between the outside world and my heavily armoured mind. The guilt was gone. The pain and memories hidden. But so had everything else.

I waited for the feeling of home. The love I once felt for Q, or even fear. But there was nothing but a large cavernous hole. Everything that made me *me*, had disappeared deep inside my bombproof barricade.

The moat filled with creepy crawlies as the steady itch of needing something came back. My mind might be safe, but my body was being eaten alive by insects.

Q sighed, stroking my cheek. His pale eyes never stilled—

swirling with so many emotions. "You're safe. I won't ever let anything happen to you again."

The promise reeked of guilt. It was a promise he'd made before and a promise he broke. My emotions were no longer accessible—hidden behind this thick barrier, and I sat there feeling nothing.

Nothing.

My trust in him was broken. My belief that he would always be there for me—my monster in the dark— was gone.

But although I knew it should rip my heart out, I only felt empty, cold, forgotten.

I wanted to ignore the coolness I felt toward him. I wanted the blankness and wall to disappear. I wanted to remember. But if I did, I'd die from the weight of guilt. I'd perish from everything I'd done.

Focusing inward, I rattled the door of this newly formed tower, looking for a way out. But there was no exit. No key to get free. Whatever my mind had done to protect me, it had shut down everything else.

My heart was boarded up and unfeeling. The same heart that tumbled with lunacy and need for Q. The same organ that ballooned with madness for this man who beat me, fucked me, wanted me.

Now it deflated, a shrivelled raison-like thing, hanging useless in my chest.

Q ran his hand down my cheek, avoiding the fresh bandage on my neck. His fingertips whispered down my arm before capturing my hand. He flinched when I curled my fingers, avoiding his touch.

I didn't want to be touched. I didn't want any sort of contact. I didn't need it. All I needed was to be left alone. Alone forever in my unfeeling tower.

Pain etched his eyes as he swallowed hard. His five o'clock shadow was scruffier than normal, his hair unkept and longer. He kept his eyes trained on my hand before leaning forward, bringing the shadow of his body over mine. His arm tucked under my shoulder blades, gathering me in a crushing embrace.

I squirmed as claustrophobia clawed, then stiffened as I forced myself to allow him comfort. I may not want this, but he did. And I wasn't such a shallow bitch to deny him.

Somehow, I'd gone from Tess who cared to a blank replica and I had no desire to go back. I wouldn't survive the past.

Q squeezed me harder, hurting my ribs, flaring my bruises. I didn't move away, but I didn't move to console him either. His large body pressed hard against mine and all I could focus on was the vacuum my soul was in. The vacancy deep inside. No longer did I suffer.

You deserve to be in pain. I had no right to forget what I did. Pain was my life-long affliction.

Pain.

"Pain is bad, little girl. Run from pain." White Man blazed into my mind, stealing me from Q's arms and the safety of his home and dumping me back into the rank dungeon.

The vacuum suddenly reversed and spewed every splinter of pain into me. The trauma of the drugs, the nightmare of doing their bidding—all came back with hammers, impaling me with stakes.

"No. I can't take it!"

My throat seized, my lungs drowned with liquid, and I went nuts. I couldn't go back there. I couldn't go through it again. I wanted my tower. I wanted to go back to the void and never feel such agony again.

The bugs roared and multiplied, scurrying over me, their pinchers and claws dragging me back to hell. I struggled to run, but something held me tight. Held me firm for the bugs to find me.

"You took my life. You're just like them." Blonde Hummingbird floated before my eyes with a bloody bullet hole in her forehead. *"You did what they asked. Why? Why did I have to die?"*

"Pain used to be your saving grace, didn't it?" White Man

appeared over Q's shoulder, waggling a finger at me. *"What did I teach you? Pain is bad. Don't make me get the pliers."*

Arms tightened around me and I flipped. "No. No. Don't. You don't need to do that. I'll behave. I promise."

"Fuck, *esclave*. Stop it!" Q shook me so hard my teeth rattled. "Stay with me. Don't listen to whatever figments are taunting you. Please, I beg you! I fucking beg you to fight."

I opened my eyes at the agony in his tone. Q's eyes were red-rimmed; shadows darkened his haggard face. His angled jaw was locked tight and forehead furrowed with over-whelming concern.

"Fight. Don't give in. Okay?" He bent his head, whispering his lips against mine. His eyes imprisoned me. I froze, trying to control my erratic gulps against his mouth. "I'll do anything. Tell me what I can do to make this better," he pleaded.

I searched my brain for answers. Something that would help me back from the scrambled eggs my mind had become. But nothing made sense. I saw no quick fix. No way out of the maze I was trapped in.

"Put her down. You're hurting her ribs."

Q glared toward the door where a man appeared in a white coat over a casual suit. I curled up, trying to become invisible. I hated strangers. Hated that I didn't know what to expect—that they might pretend to be nice, but they only wanted to rape and kill me.

Let me back into the tower!

Pain and fear crested and the guilt—shit, the guilt, came at me with the sickle of the grim reaper, hacking me into pieces.

Q looked down at me, dragging me closer, not listening to the man's orders. "She's freaking the fuck out. You have to give her something for the hallucinations."

The man came closer; I whimpered.

"He's there to finish you off. You disobeyed. He's here to hurt you." White Man laughed.

Never again would I go without a fight. Panic made me

crazy and I bit Q square on the shoulder.

"Let me go. I just want to go back to the tower!"

He sucked in a breath, but didn't push me away or strike. Instead, he looked at the doctor with such tragic weariness in his eyes. "Just give her something to ride out the worst of it. I can't stand seeing her like this."

The man nodded, and I tried to scramble out of Q's arms. Not even the pain in my ribs or neck or finger could stop me from fighting. I couldn't go through more. I couldn't. My mind was already dead—I'd never find my way back.

I moaned as clammy sweat sprouted on my skin, chilling me. Bright lights erupted behind my eyes as the craving intensified.

The mouth-watering, teeth-clenching *need* for something. Something thick and syrupy and foggy. Something that I didn't have a name for, but fuck, my body wanted it.

"Please. I'll do whatever you want. Give it to me."

"What's happening to her?" Q asked but his voice was far, far away.

"She's hit the second level of withdrawal. They must've kept her on a high dose for it to be this bad so fast."

A tidal wave of insects consumed me, all chittering and chattering as they scurried around in my brain. "Give me it. I'll fuck you. I'll do it. I'll do anything!"

Arms let me go and I collapsed against the mattress. I yelped against the pain, but it could no longer compete with the craving. "You have to give her something. I'm going out of my fucking mind listening to this."

"All right. I think it's for the best that she sleeps through the worst of it."

Sleep. Yes. I could do with sleep. Vacant, never-waking sleep.

Something icy trickled into my veins, moving stealthily through my body. Instead of the horrible smog, this was clear and fresh, and it granted me wings to fly away from the putrid memories and leave it all behind.

I found the tower and returned, locking myself deep inside.

I was safe inside. Protected.

I would never leave my sanctuary again.

After that first morning, my life became a patchwork of fragments.

Waking up with the consuming need.

Going back to sleep.

Waking up coughing my lungs out.

Going back to sleep.

Waking up in the dead of night to find Q sprawled out exhausted beside me.

Going back to sleep.

Each time I woke, the insects were fewer in number, and I no longer wanted to rape someone to get my hands on whatever I needed.

One afternoon I awoke to soulful, tortured music playing through the house.

You told me you were strong enough. You told me you were brave.
Yet now you lie next to me and all I can do is save.
I'm here for you. I'm there for you. I'll help you with every fight.
But no matter what I do for you, I see no end in sight.

The lyrics tugged at some numb part of my heart, but no emotion cut through my tower. Ever since that first day, where I almost died from the mental onslaught, I made sure to never leave. The tower was the only thing keeping me alive.

Was it shock or weakness that caused me to retreat deep inside? I didn't know. I didn't want to know because regardless of how I came to live behind my heavily fortified wall, I was never leaving.

I knew what awaited me if I ever did and I wouldn't survive it.

Q stayed beside me, never ending his vigil. Whenever I woke, he was there to fetch me a glass of water, or massage my temples if I had a headache from the medicine.

He tended to me with all the gentleness in the world.

I smiled and thanked him. I let him know I appreciated his tenderness, but I wished he would leave. Q wasn't a healer or nursemaid. To the old me he was a beast, a strong-willed man who would never let me ruin him this way.

Every time I saw him, he changed. His pale eyes lost the ferocious glow—they muted, faded, turned inward and unreadable. His body language morphed from itching to touch me, to withdrawn and self-conscious.

If I had locked myself in a tower, he had chained his monster up and forgot who he was. We both existed in another dimension—one that would never have a happy ending and one I wanted to leave as soon as possible.

I knew Q was pulling away from me, but I didn't care. I *wanted* to care. But I wanted to stay in my unfeeling tower more. And so I let him care for me, to nurse my body from broken to whole, all the while saying a silent goodbye.

I let him drift away from me.

Hours turned into days and my lungs gradually drained from sickness. Q hardly ever left my side, but we never talked. He sensed I'd left him. When he looked at me, he stopped searching my eyes, stopped bossing me around to snap out of it.

He didn't talk about his business, or what he went through to find me. We existed as strangers—our roles reversed from lovers to patient and nursemaid.

Thankfully, the bugs had transformed from gnarly insects into annoying moths and butterflies. The craving was still there, aching in my teeth, but I could ignore.

Even my dreams were vacant of emotion and thought. In fact, sleep was one thing that hadn't returned. I managed to nap, to catch rest here and there, but at night when Q lay twitching with nightmares beside me, I stared at the ceiling.

You know this isn't normal. You should grieve. Go through the stages of dealing with the guilt and find absolution.

I ignored myself. I was stronger this way. I stayed alive this way.

Q shifted beside me, mumbling in his sleep. "I'll kill you. I'll kill you, you bastard." His fist gripped the bedding and he snarled, "I fucking love—" His leg struck out hitting my foot. It didn't hurt, but the moment he made contact, I fell straight back into hell. My tower cracked, letting all the guilt and fear and never ending hatred for myself consume me.

"You think you're free from us. You're not. We're coming."

"He doesn't love you. Nobody could."

"Die, bitch. We'll cut you up nice and fine."

My head pounded, and my belly twisted with nausea; I dry heaved. The tower left me unprotected and in a bad, bad place to be.

"No. I want to go back. Don't make me remember," I moaned as another wrack of sickness crippled me.

"Tess?" Q murmured, half-asleep. "Shit." He shot to his knees, helping me sit up. He grabbed a bowl from the bedside table and gathered my hair back as I retched and retched. I wished there was something inside to purge. At least then I might've stopped. Each wave squeezed my painful ribs until my vision greyed on the edges.

"You killed me. How could you! Don't you know my family will never find my body?" Blonde Hummingbird wept.

In my mind, I hammered on the tower, my fists growing bloody with the need to go back in.

The guilt grew deeper and deeper, cracking my mind, making my heart race toward a dying beat.

"It's okay, Tess. Don't fight it. It's okay," Q soothed, his nostrils flared, scenting my panic.

After days of no emotion, I was sure he relished some sort of reaction from me. His eyes were alive for the first time, his body tense and hopeful.

Then the door in my tower opened wide, tumbling back into safety—granting me freedom from guilt. The retching stopped and I pushed the bowl away, dislodging Q's grip on my hair. "Thank you."

Q stared, shaking his head slowly. "How do you do that? You were feeling something. I could smell it. And now you're like a shell. You smile, you talk, you heal at a miraculous pace, and yet you're not really here." He tossed the bowl away, anger tingeing his moves. "Speak to me, Tess. Tell me what happened."

I looked away. "No. Don't ask me about it."

The darkness in the room seemed to grow as Q seethed with temper. Gone was the nursemaid; I saw glimpses of the monster who'd been covered in blood in Rio.

He gave me a heart. He placed the heart of White Man at my feet. The sudden memory made me ill and I fortified my tower even more. I'd stepped outside my safety twice now and all it brought was pain. I would never again willingly leave my safe place.

Not for Q.

Not for me.

Not for anything.

"You *will* talk to me, *esclave*."

My eyes rose to his. "I'm not your *esclave* anymore. I'm sorry, Q, but what we had is gone."

"Only because you refuse to fight. I've seen a lot of women come back from the shock you're living with. It will take time, but I'll be here for you. I'm not letting you go again."

I sighed, wishing I didn't have to do this. I didn't want to break his heart, but he had to understand. My life as I knew it was over. It didn't matter if a week past, a year, or a century. I was never stepping out of my tower again. I would explode with grief and I wasn't strong enough to deal with such pain.

"I'm weak, Q. And I don't want to hurt you. But I'm not in shock. This is who I am now."

"Bullshit. You're a fighter. So fucking fight, Tess. I'm getting tired of you shutting me out. Do you even know how long it's been? Nine days! Nine fucking days where I've watched your body heal and your mind drift further and further away."

He grabbed my hand, squeezing hard. "I'm not going to let you do that. Not after everything I've been through."

"I can't thank you enough for saving me, but you have to understand—"

"I don't have to understand a goddamn thing. All you need to know is, I'll make you come back to me. I didn't fucking kill the monster inside me so I could heal you and not have you whole." He dragged hands through his hair. "I didn't sacrifice everything just so you could live a half life!"

There was nothing for me to say. So I didn't. I had no urge to fill the tense painful silence. I had no yearning to kiss Q and take away his hurt.

"I need to be alone," I whispered.

Q snorted. "Alone. You need to be fucking alone. What about what I need? What about talking to me? Helping me understand what you went through so I can help you through it. Talk to me!"

I sucked in a deep breath and delivered my parting sever. "I'll never talk about it. Not to you, or a shrink, or Suzette, or anyone. It never happened. It doesn't exist. And if you keep forcing me, you'll only kill me."

Q's chest strained, the fluttering inked sparrows looked as stricken as the man.

I swallowed hard. "Do you want to kill me? Because if you do, keep pushing me. Keep forcing me to live with the guilt. I won't ever tell you because if I did, you'd kill me anyway. So, leave me alone. Go away. Let me to drift away in peace."

Q's shoulders rolled and his hand came up. *Will he strike me?* I sat taller just in case, ready to accept his blow.

But all the fight drained out of him and he climbed off the bed.

Without a word, he traversed the large bedroom and left. I didn't move as the door clicked behind him. I didn't feel relief or regret or any other emotion but blankness.

My mind, for the first time in forever, was clear. I had no residue of drugs, or agony of grief. My body was healing and I no longer wanted anything foreign in my blood stream.

Grabbing the IV in the back of my hand, I pulled it free and tossed it off the bed. It dangled and a single drip landed on the carpet.

Hours passed as I stared into the darkness.

Unfeeling.

Uncaring.

All alone.

"Master, it's been two weeks. You need to stop beating yourself up. It isn't your fault."

Something slammed against the wall and shattered into tinkling pieces.

Q raged, "All of this *is* my fault. Tess was the perfect person to go after in order to punish me. And it fucking worked because I want to kill myself for what's happened to her. Look at her, Suzette. She might as well be dead for all the life left inside her."

Suzette murmured, "She'll come right. You'll make her come back, you'll see."

"Don't fucking patronize me. I've tried. I've been gentle and patient. I've slept beside her. I've offered to listen and help. But none of it does any good because she's fucking blocked me out and I can't find a way in."

Something banged again and I kept my eyes tightly closed.

"I'm done. The moment we can send the girls home they're gone. I don't want to be reminded about any of this. I just want everything to go away."

I dared crack open my eyes. Q paced, running anxious hands through his longer hair. It wasn't the sleek pelt he normally favoured—now it was long and stuck up in all directions.

Suzette stood by the door with a tray in her hands. "Will you at least let me feed her?"

"She's not awake. Believe me, I've watched her all night. Waiting for her to open those blank eyes so I can force her to talk to me."

He told the truth. All night he'd stared, and all night I pretended to be asleep. Even though I told him every night that I needed to be alone, he never listened.

If he disobeyed me to get a reaction, then it wasn't working. I wouldn't argue. I had no energy to argue.

Suzette glided forward, smiling at me. "She's awake, master. I'm surprised you didn't sense she was faking."

If I had any emotions left inside, I would've scowled at Suzette.

Q whirled to face me, then dashed to the edge of the bed. He took my hand. I wished he'd stop touching me. He squeezed my fingers. "Tell me what I can do to fix this. Fucking tell me right now. I'm done waiting for you to snap out of it."

I waited for an urge to either squeeze him or pull away. But my tower kept me snug from everything. I hung in an eternity of nothingness.

"Just go. Return to work."

His eyes delved into mine, but they weren't soft and tender, they were agonizingly sharp. "My work is in ruins. Did you know that? I slandered the company's reputation all in the name of saving you."

"I'm sorry. Go live your life before you knew me then.

Before I ruined everything for you."

He looked away before roaring, "I *had* no fucking life before you. *You* are my life. Without you, I might as well take a shotgun to my head and join you in the dirt because, Tess, if you leave me—if you're so fucking weak not to fight, then that is what will happen to me. You'll crucify me."

He leaned closer, bringing with him the smell of citrus and desperation. "So go ahead, *esclave*. Take my life as I'm not fit for anything anymore."

Tossing my hand away, he stalked past Suzette and slammed the door closed behind him.

Whatever we'd had before was well and truly broken. *I* was broken. My soul tentatively touched the wall of the tower, wanting freedom to go after him. But I killed that part of myself. If I stepped free from my fortress, the guilt would find me. The ghosts would haunt me. I would die from an avalanche of emotion.

I raised my gaze to focus on Suzette.

She shuffled to the side of the bed with her tray. Up close it smelled like chicken noodle soup and fresh baguette. Her gaze was full of understanding painted on her pretty face. "Do you want to talk about what just happened?"

I shook my head. How could I talk about it when I'd been the devil? When I'd maimed and murdered? No one wanted to hear my plight. I didn't deserve it.

"I know you must hate me for hurting him, but I won't talk about it. Not to anyone." My stare was a forceful warning.

She didn't say anything as she placed the tray on my lap. When neither of us moved she whispered, "I don't dare presume what they did to you, Tess. But if you ever need to talk, I'm here. I haven't told you my story, and I don't know if I should, but your broken finger looks a lot like all ten of mine did when I was sold to Q."

My eyes flew to Suzette's in horror.

I blocked out the pain of the pliers with the help of my tower, but how did Suzette do it?

"Whoever took you will never take you again. Q made sure of that." Suzette added, "You don't believe me?"

"He said they wouldn't take me before, but they did. He lied, Suzette. But none of that matters because he found me. It wasn't his fault. I was the one who let life get in the way and forgot to remove the tracker. I ruined Q's business. I brought this on myself." My voice was a monotone, never rising with hills and valleys of emotion. "I know you think I'm being silly, but I honestly can't talk about it. A burden shared is a burden halved, or however that stupid proverb goes. But I'm deadly serious when I say the past is in the past and I refuse to think or feel or even acknowledge what happened."

Suzette brushed a strand of brown hair off her forehead. "I understand more than you know. And I can't force you to step out of that safety net you've created. Just try and remember all the things you're sacrificing."

"I'm—"

She held up a hand. "Let's not think about it. You're strong enough to have a shower. That will make you feel ten times better." She smiled gently. "After all, you do kind of smell like road-kill."

My lips quirked for her benefit only, and I let her move the tray and quilt so I could stand on wobbly legs.

She helped me upright, giving me time to cough wetly as the last dregs of liquid in my lungs sloshed around.

"Every step takes you closer to being well again, Tess. And I'll be by your side as long as you need me."

I smiled and let her lead me onward.

Seventeen
Quincy

Whimper and moan while I sit on my throne, we can
be monsters together so we're never alone...

I could no longer look at inane objects without wanting to
smash them to fucking pieces.

Everything pissed me off. My temper broiled constantly,
and the helplessness I felt when it came to Tess crippled me.

She shut me out. She flatly refused to talk to me—to tell
me what happened so I could help fight her nightmares for her.
She looked at me as if I was a fucking stranger.

I meant every word. If she gave up, gave up on herself, on
us, then I had nothing left. She might as well have died in
fucking Rio. I could've gone rogue and killed everyone until
someone put me out of my misery.

But that wasn't the worst of it. The worst part was the
nightmares and the skull-crushing pain of a migraine that
refused to break. I lived on codeine and anti-inflammatories to
try and function—to make sure I was there for Tess.

My one bodily weakness was determined to murder me all
while Tess ripped out my aching heart.

No matter what I did, nothing worked. I slept beside her,

nursed her. I died a little inside. The beast hated seeing her so meek and broken while the man learned a new compassion for caring. But day by day, hour by hour, the passion and need I felt for her turned from lover to brother. From consumed to confused.

I knew I could no longer hurt her and the sane part of me didn't want to. But the part of me that knew Tess would never come back wanted to kill her faster. Just so the agony would be over with.

She looked at me with such emptiness it only made me sink further into hell. I'd never be able to touch her again. Never draw blood or show her how much I cared with the use of a whip or flogger. That was all gone and I mourned for it. The beast lamented that I would never again have Tess panting in pleasure-pain, completely at my mercy. But now I mourned a deeper feeling.

I'd wrapped her in cotton wool; I'd doted on her for over two weeks. I watched as her body responded to treatment, how the bruises faded, and her lungs stopped wheezing. I stopped going to work so I could be with her every hour. I gave up my entire life to make sure I was there for her, but she didn't want me.

She didn't want the man with the beast who wanted to make her scream.

She didn't want the man who cared for her so sweetly and would never hurt her.

She doesn't want me.

Any part of me.

Frederick took over the company, and I had nothing to do with my time but lurk in my home, being confronted with so many injured and broken women. The beast inside trembled and huddled into a ball. It hated everything. It begged me to leave. To run.

Franco found me making my way outside. "Sir, the doctor and his team have finished their daily rounds for the women. Do you need them for anything else before they leave?" He came closer, eyeing me.

Franco hadn't left me alone since damn Frederick told him to watch out for my migraines. He ratted me out to my own staff to keep an eye on me. I tore into Frederick for overstepping the line, but he just hung up on me. Bastard.

Franco always looked at me with fucking respect; now it bordered on friendship and pity. Even after everything we'd done in the warehouse, he thought I was weak.

I fucking hated it. *I hate everything. I hate everyone. Tess did this. Tess cut out my soul and left me with nothing.*

"Tell him to go. I don't need him." If I died of a migraine so be it. Then at last I might find peace.

"Are you sure?"

I glowered. "Don't, Franco. Don't ever forget your place."

He dropped his eyes, taking a step back. "Didn't mean to piss you off." He left without another word, and I ploughed through the house that was no longer a private sanctuary but a convalescent home for over twenty women whom we'd flown over from Rio. I slammed the front door behind me.

Five were due to leave today. And two left the moment they arrived. A few were sick and four suffered withdrawals like Tess, but none of them had been hurt as much as her. It made no sense to butcher items bound for sale. The only casualty had been found by one of the mercenaries: a blonde in a shallow grave with a gunshot to the head.

I had no purpose as I paced around the exterior of the large manor. I had no compass or direction anymore. I needed to go for a run, or beat the shit out of some gym equipment. But all I could think about was Tess.

I didn't have the balls to go back to see her. I couldn't stand looking into her empty soulless eyes. I couldn't be told to leave again. I might strike her. I might hit her and then I'd be no better than the bastards who stole her.

Hit her. Whip her. Force her to face whatever it is she's blocked.

But instead of pawing at me, encouraging me to race back to tie Tess up, the beast curled deeper into the corner, hanging its pitiful head. It wanted to bolt. To leave and never come back.

The urge to sprint filled my limbs and I took off. I wasn't dressed for a run—in jeans and a black T-shirt—but I couldn't stand the angst anymore.

I took off toward the manicured fields, running from thoughts of Tess.

I charged under ancient trees, sucking in lungfuls of air as I outran my demons. Outran the memories of her hallucinations and fretful mumbling. I tried to forget that she talked to Brax in her sleep, her parents, too.

My hands curled and I slammed them into a tree as I darted past. Bark lodged into my knuckles, but I didn't care.

I didn't care about anything but running.

Two hours later, I could barely move and smashed the library door behind me. Throwing myself into a wingback, I tried to calm my breathing, wiping my sweaty face with the hem of my T-shirt.

I needed a shower, but I couldn't face going upstairs to my room yet. The thought of seeing Tess hurt like a motherfucker.

Scowling at the library, I remembered why I'd avoided coming in here. Too many memories existed: Tess standing up to the police when she thought they'd come to arrest me; Tess coming back to offer her love.

And now that fucking love was fading. If not already disappeared.

I picked up a heavy candlestick from the side table, hurling it at the fireplace. It bent and smashed against the bricks. The violence awakened the need in me, and I wanted to wring somebody's neck for stealing something so precious from me.

My jaw ground until my teeth almost turned to dust. I needed a fight. I needed to kill to purge myself of this...this...foreign emotion. This mind-twisting confusion.

Everything inside no longer made sense. When Tess woke up coughing and fighting her dreams, I called her my love. I called her the sweetest endearment I'd ever called anyone in my life, and she didn't react.

I willingly opened my heart to her and finally fucking admitted that I no longer merely cared for her. I no longer even fell for her. I'd hit rock bottom and loved her with every inch of my fucking soul.

And *nothing*.

Her fragility and sickness activated another part of me. The part that stood up to be a protector and provider. My need to wipe her brow and hold her while she healed encouraged dormant sides of me to grow.

I felt myself distancing, retreating from a harsh lover who wanted to hurt, to something softer. A man who would lay down his body, who would flay himself alive if it meant Tess would heal. But those caring needs crippled the beast and I no longer saw Tess as a fighter.

By her own words she was forcing me away.

She looked at me with no emotion, not as her lover who'd drawn her blood and been so deep inside her, I bruised both of us. She looked at me as if she'd said goodbye already.

I stood up, unable to sit any longer. Grabbing a pair of bookends, I threw them against the desk. The loud bangs as they dented the wood encouraged me to reap more anarchy.

Turning myself over to the beast, I brought an apocalypse on the room.

I tore off bookshelves.

It's over.

I shredded limited editions.

I've fallen in love only for it to end so fast.

I hurled figurines and kicked priceless artefacts.

She'll never be my strong esclave *again.*

When the room was in complete disarray, I threw myself into the chair.

Sitting forward, I massaged my temples, trying to dislodge the migraine.

Tess shot into my mind. How her head threw back when I licked her pussy. How she moaned when I fucked her. How her skin flushed when I whipped her.

I waited for the beast to snarl and demand I do worse things. To go up there and become her entire world while I hurt her.

But my cock shrivelled and I skated away from such things. All I could see was a woman I would die for, a woman who paid for my sins with her agony, and all I wanted to do was wrap her in silk and finery and never go near her again.

"Um, wow. I suppose I'll need a bit of help cleaning tomorrow."

My eyes snapped open, and the sharp swell of a headache welcomed me back to the world of unhappiness and horror.

Suzette moved through the dark room, stepping over rubble, dodging broken lamps.

"Are you okay, master? Can I get you anything?" She smoothed her pinafore, refusing to look at the mess around us. She probably thought I'd completely gone insane.

I sat straighter, dragging a hand over my face, trying to dispel the headache's grip on me. My clothes were crusty from sweat; I felt ancient. "Is she okay?" My voice was a growl. I cleared my throat.

Suzette bit her lip before answering, "She'll be fine. She just needs time."

I tensed at her tone. She lied. *"Qu'est ce qu'il y a,* Suzette?"

What is it?

Her eyes darted away before she inched closer. "She asked me if you'd let her use a laptop and internet."

I exploded upright. "Does she still think I won't let her talk to the outside world! She isn't my fucking prisoner. Of course she can have a laptop." I stalked toward my desk and grabbed the spare I always kept there.

If Tess showed an interest in something, perhaps she would find her way back. I couldn't crush the hope building in me—even though I knew it would probably end up hurting me more.

"Here." I shoved it toward Suzette.

She took it, but didn't move. Finally, she glanced up and my heart swooped to my feet. "What else?"

"It's not my place, but I don't think you should let her have it." She tried to give the laptop back, but I moved away. "I don't think it's going to help her recovery."

"What do you mean it won't help? I'll do anything if it means she'll find herself again." I shivered, remembering the cold blankness in her eyes. "If it's what she wants, give her the laptop, Suzette."

She bit her lip. "I'd like to give you hope. Say that the same thing happened to me and that time will heal, but... in this instance, I'm not so sure. I think something drastic needs to be done, before you lose her."

Suzette and I had always had a close bond. She got away with talking to me about things I shouldn't discuss, but as much as I wanted to problem solve Tess, to talk about what the fuck I lived with, I couldn't.

I wouldn't discuss my feelings for Tess, or the desperation I felt.

With a small sigh, Suzette left, taking the laptop with her. The moment she'd gone, I panicked. What if she was right? What if I did the wrong thing by letting Tess have access to the outside world?

You have no fucking choice, she isn't your slave.

Not for the first time, I wished she truly was. Then none of this would've happened as she would never have left my house. I could beat the shit out of her for being so distant. I could teach her to come back to me—her owner. She wouldn't have a choice.

But she wasn't my slave.

She was the one who stole my heart, and I doubted I'd ever get it back.

The migraine decided not to kill me when I called it quits a few hours later. I tried to work. To add some input on upcoming mergers with Frederick via the phone, but all I could think about was Tess upstairs in my bed on the internet, talking to who the fuck knows.

I wasn't a jealous asshole, but I was petrified she'd block me out even more. I had no power over her and I wasn't used to such a weakness.

The house rested in silence as I crept up the stairs. I didn't know what the time was; everyone had gone to bed.

When I arrived outside the door to my room, I suffered a horrible pang of loss. I may have Tess back but her heart had gone. I'd lost the woman I wanted to fight and whip and love for the rest of my days, and I didn't know how to act around the broken stranger in my bed.

I'd yelled at her before. Did she care? I wanted her to scream at me—to have a fight with her—anything to draw emotion from her dead soul.

My hand rested on the doorknob and I took forever to turn and enter.

Stop being a coward.
Stop my heart from hurting.

Go kill something, then you'll feel better.

Shadows swallowed the room as I opened the door and tiptoed across the carpet. Like a fucking spineless coward, I waited until Tess drifted off to sleep before returning.

I lurked in the darkness, not turning on any lights. She slept with her mouth slightly parted and hair tangled on the pillow. The matted curls were now nice and clean. Her body smelling faintly of my orange soap from the shower.

She no longer looked like a mental patient who needed serious drugs to cope. She looked so innocent. Yet beneath that porcelain skin and golden hair lurked a demoness, a temptress who I wanted so badly to see alive again. Did she still exist in this shell of a girl?

Could I draw the real Tess free? Show her what she was giving up by shutting me out?

At least watching her while she slept, I could pretend she still belonged to me.

The fiery passion she used to possess was gone. It cut me to my black soul and beyond into forever.

My hands clenched, wishing I hadn't buried the ringleader's nasty heart under one of the rosebushes outside. I wanted to tear it from his chest all over again. It was the only piece of him I kept. If Tess ever asked for it, I would be prepared to give it to her.

Maybe it would bring back her fight—the passion I needed to see.

It was late. I'd had a hell of time the last few weeks, and all I wanted to do was topple into bed beside Tess. But the mental strain compounding my headache guaranteed I wouldn't sleep.

My hands went to my belt, automatically undressing for bed. The leather was warm in my hands and I fondled it like I would an old friend. This was the same belt that welcomed Tess back into my world. Maybe it could do it all over again.

I froze. The animal inside rose its head, contemplating this sudden development.

If I woke Tess up with the bite of pain I doubted my *esclave* would welcome me. The broken girl who didn't know me might crumble even worse. I would be detrimental to her healing.

There's nothing worse than the emptiness she lives in already.

Maybe it was time for me to sleep elsewhere. To remove myself, just like she'd asked. But if I did that, I'd never get her back. I didn't want to admit defeat.

I've never been so confused.

Sighing heavily, I let go of the belt, removing the feel of tempting leather in my grip. Images of Tess in the gaming room spread over the countertop roared to mind. The sound of her skin being slapped by my belt echoed in my ears. I swallowed hard, watching the silhouette of the woman who made me live in constant agony—a tripwire of desire and repulsion.

Then the urge for that sort of kink flew away, leaving me cold and hating myself for being such a fucked-up asshole.

Tess was no longer strong enough for that sort of shit, and it shut me down until every last need filtered away.

I forced myself to look at her—really look at her, and I didn't like what I saw. The weight loss, the sense of sadness shadowing her even in sleep. Every inch of me wanted to climb beside her and hold her. To curl around her, offer the protection of my body, but I stood stiff instead.

My hands didn't unclench as I fought so many urges, not all of them making sense. I'd never been so vulnerable. So tamed. I hated the lack of control over the last weeks. I hated the fact that this delicate woman had a power over me like no other. She could break me in half if I failed to keep her alive. She'd already broken me into pieces by being so remote.

The beast inside, the one who craved her blood and screams, breathed heavy with perplexity. It still wanted to tear into her, to claim her and make her cry, but at the same time it wanted to run far away whimpering and forget she ever existed.

I want to hurt you, Tess, but now the very idea of hearing you scream makes me sick to my fucking stomach.

Q, you're changing. You never cared about repercussions before. Only the chase, the hunt, the pleasure.

Was this what love was? This soppy weakness? This mind-altering reality that left me lost and confounded?

If it was, I hated it.

I missed my straightforward, if not constantly battling life. I missed the coldheartedness I'd built like an impenetrable fort. I missed simplicity.

Tess groaned in her sleep, twitching violently away from some nightmare.

My heart raced as her eyes flared wide, only to close again instantly. "No, please, Q. You don't hate me. You don't."

My knees wobbled, threatening to send me to the floor. She thought I hated her? There was nothing further from the truth. Her body trembled, then she turned to the side, curling into a little ball.

The closed laptop on her legs shifted and I caught it before it slid off the bed.

The snowy bandage on her neck helped soothe me. At least the tracker that led to this entire mess was destroyed and out of her body. Those bastards would never hurt anyone again, but others would try.

Franco had been given exclusive rights to keep tabs on the traffickers who'd heard of me slaughtering Red Wolverine. The death threats were piling up and soon I'd have more blood on my hands.

Feeling like a creepy bastard watching her in the dark, I took the laptop and went to sit in the chair by the window. No moonlight graced the room, which was fine by me. I didn't deserve moonlight with what I was about to do.

Throwing a careful look at Tess, I opened the lid and waited for the laptop to boot. Immediately I went to history, and my heart seized when her email account opened.

Are you fucking sure you want to do this?

Of course, I wasn't. I wasn't a snoop. I hated that I had to know what Tess talked about. But I also couldn't live with never knowing. She hurt deep inside and wouldn't let me in. She refused to talk. This might be the only way I could understand. I might finally decipher how her mind had cracked and help her come back to me. I wanted to heal her, not just for her sanity, but for mine as well.

I wouldn't survive much longer without her.

From: Tess Snow
Time: 8:22p.m.
To: Brax Cliffingstone

My skin instantly broke out into a sweat. I shot a glance at sleeping Tess. Why the fuck did she email her ex?

With an aching heart, I read.

Hi Brax,

Long-time no chat, huh? It's weird cause I feel like I've been talking to you a lot lately. I don't even know why I'm messaging you. I just...crap, I don't know.

Let me start again. How are you? How's Bianca? Did you take her out on that date? Oh, and how's Blizzard? Is he still chewing my shoes that I left behind?

Anyway...just wanted to say hi. So, hi.

Such a rambling message with no point. Did she think she couldn't waffle on to me? I would gladly listen to anything she fucking said. I would spend the rest of my life listening to her talk about shoes and any other trivial thing if she let me.

My stomach rolled when I scrolled down and noticed the reply.

From: Brax Cliffingstone
Time: 8:38 p.m.
To: Tess Snow
Hey!

Wow, I know you said you wanted to stay friends, but I didn't know if you would. It's awesome to hear from you, Tessie. I have to admit, I've been missing the hell out of you. I keep waking up in a cold sweat, you know? Thinking you're still kidnapped and I can't find you. But then I remember you've run off to be with some guy you couldn't live without and are madly in love with and happy. Which I'm glad about. I want you to be happy. And in answer to your question, I took Bianca out for the first time a week ago. She wanted to give me time to make sure it was what I wanted. She's awesome and I'm starting to really care for her, but I'll always have a soft spot for you.

See ya!

It didn't offer any consolation that he'd moved on to another girl, not when he still missed her and had a soft spot for the woman fast asleep in my fucking bed. *She's mine, goddammit.* I wanted to throw the laptop at the wall. I wanted to shake Tess awake and demand an explanation.

Instead, I kept reading.

From: Tess Snow
Time: 8:45p.m.
To: Brax Cliffingstone
Oh, you're online. That's great that you're having a good time with Bianca. I'm glad one of us is happy.

Fuck if that line didn't cut my heart out. I couldn't help sneering at it. She sounded like a little drama queen. I knew she had a right to feel like that, but after everything I'd done, after everything I did for her, it lodged in my throat like a hard to swallow pill.

The email turned into instant chat. I couldn't contain the crushing sadness filling my chest.

Brax: Are you okay? That last comment was kinda weird.
Tess: Yes, I'm okay. Just had a rough couple of weeks.
Brax: Want to talk about it?

Brax: Tess, you there?

Brax: If you don't want to talk about it, you don't have to.

Tess: I don't want to talk about it. I can't. Sorry.

Brax: Is there anything I can do?

Tess: Not really. Just talking to someone normal is helping.

Brax: LOL. You're saying your new man isn't normal?

Brax: Helloooo…again, you don't have to answer if I pried. None of my business.

Tess: Q is everything I dreamed and more. He's perfect for me.

Brax: Why am I hearing a but in that sentence?

Tess: You're not. Clean out your ears.

Brax: Haha. What's up for real, Tessie? You're making me worried.

Tess: I…

Brax: Yes…

Tess: I'm empty.

Brax: Okay, wow, um, that sounds like you need to talk to someone. I don't have the training to deal with cryptic replies like that.

Tess: Sorry. Let's talk about other things.

Brax: Hang on. Don't change the subject. Did he hurt you? Are you okay? If he hurt you, so help me, I'll make sure he's fucking ruined.

Tess: It isn't him. He's been amazing. He's shown a side I didn't know existed.

Brax: Fibs and fakers, Tessie. Don't avoid the truth.

Brax: Look, I won't press you, but do you need me to come get you?

Tess: That's sweet but no. I'm fine.

Brax: Shit, I gotta go, but now I'm freaking out that you're not okay. Promise me you'll message again soon. Okay? Even if it's just to talk about how goofy Blizzard is.

Tess: I will. Thanks…

Brax: Anytime. Bye.

The clock on the computer dashboard ticked away the hours that I sat there. Too frozen, too consumed with pain to move.

Tess felt nothing.

Tess felt nothing for me.

Too fucking bad I felt enough to combust into agonising pieces.

Tess screamed at daybreak, hurtling me from dreamless coma into full killing mode.

My back bellowed from falling asleep in the chair, and I stood up so fast the laptop clunked to the floor.

Tess's eyes shot over to me; the residual emotion from her dream shut down to be replaced with emptiness.

Jumping over the computer, I dashed to her side. Her hair stuck to her clammy forehead and all I wanted to do was brush it away. To touch her softly, kiss her, stroke her. Remind myself that she was still in my bed, even if she'd run away mentally.

I'd never cared for anything in my life. Sure, I kept birds and fed the local wildlife but I'd never tended to a sick human. Never wanted to. The slaves who came to me hurt and injured were dealt with by an in-house nurse. I didn't want to be around weak things as I didn't trust myself not to finish the job and put them out of their misery.

But Tess. Shit, she was different.

"You're okay. *Je suis là.*" I'm here.

She looked at me with no emotion. "I thought you went to work. I told you, you don't have to care for me anymore. I'm feeling much better."

"You're not feeling any better otherwise you'd be talking to me."

She hung her head. "Not this again. I told you. I will *never* talk about it. So stop pushing me."

I leaned down, almost nose to nose. "I will push you every damn day if it means you'll crack and face the things you're hiding from."

I wanted her to slap me. Push me away, beat my chest, scream, cry—*anything.*

But she blinked slowly and didn't say a word. Her eyes left mine, looking toward the window. "Did you use the computer last night?"

I looked guiltily at the abandoned laptop on the carpet. I didn't want to lie, but I didn't want her to know just how desperate she made me. Swallowing hard, I said, "I checked the stock market. I'm watching carefully to see if the thing with Red Wolverine has affected shares in other investments."

Her mouth popped open as her eyes went saucer wide. "Wolverine. The man who ordered me kidnapped—for revenge against you?"

Motherfucker. She knew.

I ran a hand through my hair and stepped back. She deserved to know the entire story. Hear what happened. I had so much I had to tell her.

"We need to talk, Tess. About so much." I moved closer, reaching out to take her hand. "Can you please tell me what happened?"

She stiffened before I even touched her. My hand dropped, not bothering anymore. "I ripped out his heart for you. Just like you asked. I travelled around the world searching. I paid more bribes, tortured more people, and killed enough to land me in hell for an eternity. But I didn't care, because all I thought about was having you back in my arms." I looked down at my arms, finally realizing that they'd forever be empty of her.

"You're telling the truth. Aren't you?"

She cocked her chin, her entire demeanour cold. "Yes. I'll never go back. I can't. I'm sorry."

The woman I fucking loved was gone. My spine tingled with heavy regret. I could hit her. Cajole her. Bribe or beg, and it wouldn't make any difference.

I nodded, swallowing past the ball of sadness in my throat.

I couldn't be there anymore. I couldn't let her kill me inch by inch.

I slammed the door and left.

Eighteen
Tess

Choose me, use me, you will never lose me...

Another week passed.

Seven long days while I lived in limbo. The laptop was never far, and the soft ping of an incoming message gave me something to do. I lived via the internet world. Looking at jokes, funny videos, love scenes, drama episodes. I watched everything I could, waiting for some sort of reaction other than emptiness.

But nothing triggered a response.

I was sick of this bedroom. Sick of feeling nothing. My body was stronger. The coughing had subsided and I wanted to leave.

I needed to move. I didn't want to witness how Q hurt. This was his bedroom and all I'd done was sully it with sickness and bad memories. It was time to remove myself from his life so he could begin the journey of forgetting me.

Cracking open the laptop, I read Brax's message.

From: Brax Cliffingstone
Time: 2:25 p.m.
To: Tess Snow

Hi! Thought I'd touch base and make sure things are okay? Haven't heard back from you so I'm hoping you're still alive. (bad joke) Anywho… Bianca and I have officially started going out and I want you to be as happy as me, so let's get this show on the road. What do you need? Anything? Do you need some Aussie stuff sent over? I'm sure the French food has got to be crap after our award-winning pies.

Message me back.

Brax

I sighed. How much I wanted to laugh. To be a human again, but to share in happiness I had to let the guilt rip me apart. I just couldn't do it.

I existed in a rigid coldness. And for now, that was the way it had to be. Maybe forever.

Me: I do miss marmite, I admit.
Brax: Eww, gross. That stuff is nasty. Vegemite rules.
Me: Yuck.

How could I joke and pretend to be normal when I felt zero?

Brax: So…how you feeling?
Me: Okay.
Brax: Just okay?
Me: Still empty.
Brax: What would it take to make you whole again?
Me: That's the problem. I don't think it's fixable.
Brax: That doesn't sound like the Tessie I know.
Me: You never really knew me, Brax.
Me: I'm sorry. That was harsh.
Brax: No, I get it. I didn't. Not really. But only because you never talked to me. You sprang it on me and I acted like an ass.
Me: It was my fault. I never knew what I wanted.
Brax: And now you do. You want that man that you ran half-way across the world to see.

Me: I used to.
Brax: You will again.

I stopped typing, waiting for an unfurling of hope that Brax was right. That this cold emptiness would soon be filled with light and love again, but nothing happened. I looked around Q's bedroom and suddenly the need to leave was overwhelming.

I couldn't stay here. I couldn't be this invalid any longer.

Me: If I said I was coming back to Australia. What would you say?
Brax: I'd say you always had a place to sleep and Bianca and I will help you with whatever you need.

I smiled. I had no intention of gate-crashing their new romance. No one wanted an ex-girlfriend sleeping on the couch. I'd go somewhere else. It didn't matter where. I didn't care.

Suzette appeared, coming toward the bed. She carried a plate with a smoked salmon bagel and some iced tea. "Lunch. I hope you're hungry." Her eyes fell to the blinking message from Brax. She froze, skimming the text.

She shook her head, giving me a heart-stopping look of betrayal. "You're giving up so easily?"

"It's not what you think, Suzette."

She slammed the plate on the bed. "What do you mean it's not what I think? It's in black and white." She tapped the screen with an angry finger. "You're thinking of leaving! After everything. After *everything,* Tess. You're just going to leave!" She breathed hard, visibly bringing her sharp temper under control. "I get it. I really do. It took me years to get over what happened and I know you need more time. But you need to stay around people who love you."

I hung my head. "Time won't help. Something's happened to me. I'll never be free unless I let myself suffer what I've done. And if I let myself suffer, I won't survive the memories.

If you knew what I did, Suzette…" My voice dwindled and for the first time in days the crush of guilt managed to penetrate my tower.

I panicked, rushing to fill the crack, wrapping it thicker with chains.

The fear of what I'd done grew by the hour, trapping myself further inside my mind.

Suzette deflated. "What did they do to you? What's made you so afraid?"

"It's what I did to others that I can't live with." I was back to being vacant, thankfully free from the guilt.

"Don't go, Tess. Stay. Q is in agony. He loves you and yet you can't even bring yourself to touch him anymore." She stopped, brushing away a tear. "Stay for him."

"It's because of him that I'm leaving. It's not fair to torture him this way."

She sighed, eyes flashing with pain. "I suggest you think on your decision, because the moment you step out the door and rip out my master's heart is the day you lose me as a friend. You don't deserve him if you leave." She headed to the door, turning to face me one last time. "I know you're capable of coming alive again. You just need to believe you're strong enough." She closed the door quietly behind her.

Am I strong enough to face the women I hurt? To allow the drug-clouded memories to hurl me into guilt and misery?

No, I'm not strong enough.

This was the only way.

That night Q didn't come to bed.

I'd grown used to falling asleep and waking up in the middle of the night to find him asleep on his stomach, fully dressed. As if he wanted to always be ready to protect me. Even in sleep, I knew he suffered headaches. The tightness around his eyes never left him. Just another way I made him suffer.

But tonight, when I woke to shuffle to the bathroom, the bed was empty.

And just like the bed, I was, too.

The next day I made the decision to go.

My finger no longer hurt, only ached, and the doctor had removed the stitches in my neck. He told me Q ordered him to remove the tracker while I slept; I thanked him profusely. Having that devil thing out of my body was the first thing to give me a tiny feeling of relief.

My ribs were sore but nothing I couldn't handle and whenever a memory or vision tried to drag me from my tower, I promptly shut it down. I'd become a master at wrapping my mind with chains and padlocks—I doubted I'd ever find a way to unlock them.

After a shower and dressing awkwardly in a pair of Q's running shorts and T-shirt, I made my way from the room.

Shuffling down the corridor, I struggled for breath and my lungs strained with the remnants of pneumonia. The steps went on forever. I kept going, stopping occasionally until I reached the bottom. One at a time. Gentle and slow.

Maybe I wasn't strong enough to leave. My strength was seriously depleted.

The foyer was just as I remembered with its grand entrance and sweeping staircase covered in midnight blue carpet.

My eyes popped wide as I entered the lounge to find four

women sitting on the couch. Two were reading while the others had their heads bent in conversation.

The moment I appeared they all stopped and faced me.

Suzette slammed to a halt when she appeared from the kitchen, carrying a tray of drinks. "Tess." Her voice rested between cool and concerned. I gave her a quick smile.

"I had to get out of the room." Nodding at the women, I added, "Hello."

The girls diverted their eyes, pretending I wasn't there.

Luckily none of them were blonde. I didn't know what would've happened to my carefully constructed safety net if I'd come face to face with the girl who'd been raped by Leather Jacket.

Suzette lingered once she'd deposited the drinks on the table. Normally I would've fidgeted or rushed to say something to fill the silence, but I had no urge to fix the wrongness between us. All I wanted to do was be alone.

I gave her a nod, turning back the way I came.

Something crackled and popped; I froze as music rained from the speakers.

I'm a murderer, murderer, murderer. Bright blood stains my hands
I used to live for violence, violence, violence, but now I lurk alone
Forcing myself to be normal, normal, normal, trading my nature for always bland
Now I live in agony, agony, agony, left with relics, memories, nothing but bones

Q.

He'd used music to get to me before; he'd turned to it again. The songs he'd played previously made me fall in love with him. I understood his inner torment through the lyrics, guiding me to see the tortured soul he lived with.

I balled my fists as a roar of grief flattened me. I missed him. So fucking much. I wanted to hold him. Kiss him. Let him save me from my sins.

"You killed me. I'll never fall in love. You ruined my life!" Blonde Hummingbird slammed into my mind.

"I'm sorry! I never wanted to be a murderer."

Leather Jacket sneered. *"Puta, you've let us in. We've got you now. We're gonna make you snap."*

I scrambled, panting, dashing back into my tower. *I can't.* I couldn't do it.

More chains went around me, yet another layer of padlocks.

My love for Q disappeared beneath the weight of barricades, and I stumbled forward, drained to the point of exhaustion.

I wished there was some way to keep the bad locked up and let the love for Q free. But I couldn't separate the good from the wrong and I wasn't brave enough to face the worst.

Moving through the house, I didn't think to where I headed. I just needed to move.

Passing all the photos of Q's empire, I didn't stop to admire. I didn't let myself think about the future I'd had working with him before the nightmare started. The buildings no longer interested me. Property in general was no longer a passion of mine. I didn't want to sketch or help Q with new projects.

The conservatory welcomed me into its warm embrace and I breathed a small sigh. At least here no one would find me. I could hide amongst the luscious plants and fly away on wings like a sparrow.

A noise up ahead startled me; I moved forward as quietly as I could. My breathing stayed shallow and slightly wheezy, but my body moved supplely enough to let me duck around small palm trees and ferns.

Turns out I wasn't the only one seeking sanctuary inside this overgrown space.

Q stood by the huge aviary. His hands braced above his head, fingers threaded through the mesh. His head bowed and his entire body looked defeated. His black jeans and grey T-shirt were crumpled; his longer hair desperately needed a brush.

He didn't notice me as he stood there, staring with vacant eyes at the birds flittering in their cage.

I forced myself to poke at the tender memories inside. *Please let me be strong enough.* I wanted so much to stop his pain. Stop this growing deletion of my feelings.

But nothing happened. All the guilt and fear that would kill me if I let myself remember, stayed locked out of reach. So, I stood there, empty, watching the man I'd broken, unable to do anything about it.

Twenty minutes passed all too quickly. My body grew tired. I wasn't ready to stand for long periods. Song lyrics played in the background, but I paid no attention.

"She's flying free," Q whispered, freezing me. He raised his head to look at a sparrow that landed on the mesh by his hand. "She's leaving soon and I don't think I'll survive it."

The bird twittered and preened before taking wing again.

I waited paralysed, wanting to announce I was there to save overhearing his anguish. But like a lurker, I didn't move.

"Fuck," he swore, rattling the mesh. The birds squawked, flapping to the other end of the cage.

Move, Tess. Before he sees you. I didn't want to embarrass him.

Q moved suddenly, pushing off from the cage and striding toward the entrance of the aviary. He unlocked the deadbolt and entered the space. Birds chirped louder as Q stood in the centre of their world. He looked like a man robbed of his own wings. A fallen angel that had no place on earth and fought a daily battle to fit in.

I stepped forward. Should I say something? Comfort him? My heart twisted, needing to be there for him, but no longer able to. No matter how many kind words I spoke, Q would see I no longer lived inside.

My insides jangled with chains and locks, saving me but also ruining me. The longer I lived in my tower the more passion and connection faded.

I hated the numbing virus inside, spreading slowly,

deleting all memory of who Tess had been. I was replaced with a carbon replica who would float away in the wind, robbed of her convictions and thoughts. All because I wasn't strong enough to face what I'd done.

Q cursed under his breath, his chest pumping with emotion. "Why should I keep you when you don't want to be here? You're not here for me. You're here because I lock you up. You're my prisoners, my captives, my trophies."

He hung his head before waving his arms. *"Allez vous-en. Je ne veux plus de vous. Elle ne veut plus de plus alors ça sert à quoi, putain?"* Fly away. I no longer want you. She no longer wants me, so what's the fucking point?

The birds went crazy, darting left and right, spying freedom through the open door. They exploded through the exit and into the conservatory, weaving through plants and water features.

Wings rustled as I ducked from a small flock of robins.

"Get out!" Q yelled; the birds flurried harder. "Get far away from me."

I stepped backward, not wanting to see Q breakdown. I wanted it to hurt—to kill me with knowledge that I'd ripped out his heart—but all I felt was emptiness.

Q looked up and froze.

His eyes locked on mine, shining with rage and blackness. I prayed for some awakening, so I could put both of us out of our misery. I wanted to bring forth all my love for him and keep hiding from my guilt. I wanted to erase the darkness, the lostness and hate from his eyes, but I was useless.

Bowing my head, I dropped my gaze.

Q cursed, exiting the aviary, humming with anger and rage. He stalked toward me, stopping so close his body heat seared my skin.

I flinched, expecting him to lash out—to grab my hair, slap me—something to wake me up.

When he didn't touch me, I looked up. Q murmured, "So low you must think of me." He captured a curl, running it gently through his fingertips. "Fly away, *esclave*, if that is what you want. I won't stop you." His tone was bleak and derelict.

He turned away, heading toward the huge bifold doors at the end of the conservatory. With a powerful sweep of his arms, he wrenched the doors to the outside world. Instantly, birds took flight, soaring high into the open skies.

Q sighed heavily, his shoulders tight and bunched as his beloved winged creatures left without so much as a backward glance.

When the last little bluejay had flown free, he turned and stared. The lines around his eyes highlighted tiredness and grief.

I swallowed. "Q…I'm so sorry."

He shook his head as if unable to believe this was the end. "I tried, Tess. I really did. I did everything you asked of me. I did everything a man in love would do for his woman. But you don't want me and my beast no longer wants to hurt you. Whatever we had…it's lost."

I sucked in a breath as he came closer.

"Do you deny it? Will you prove to me here and now that I'm making a big fucking mistake? That you just need more time?" He slammed his hand into a palm tree, causing the fronds to tremble and shiver. "Tell me what you need! I've begged you to talk to me. What are you keeping secret?"

He snorted. "I'll tell you what you're keeping secret. The fact that you're emailing your fucking ex-lover instead of confiding in me!" He looked to the ceiling, rippling with anger. "Why, *esclave*? Why can't you cry and let it out? Why can't you let me heal you? Why do you have to shut me out and run away? *Fucking why?*"

So many questions and I had no answers. Q stood, fuming with temper. I offered the simplest response. The answer that made no sense, but it was all I could deliver. "They took my mind. There's nothing else to say."

I deserved to die under the weight of all my guilt. I killed. I tortured. I knew by locking everything deep inside it would fester like a cancer, killing me slowly. But I couldn't free myself.

It wasn't possible.

"You would kill me if told you," I whispered.

Q tensed, eyes trying to crack me open, to read my secrets. "I would never kill you. Whatever happened wasn't your fault."

Not my fault! Of course, it was my fault. I killed his precious birds. I exterminated a human life.

My skin crawled, a reminder that my tower could only protect me so far. I needed to leave before he bulldozed through my barriers.

"You have to let me go, Q. I don't want to hurt you."

He laughed, but it was laced with blackness. "*You* don't want to hurt *me*?" He moved closer, raising his palm.

Our eyes never left each other and I stood unmoving, unfeeling, waiting for him to strike.

He trembled, his hand opening and closing with rage. "How much I want to fucking hurt you, Tess. If I thought it would bring you back, I'd tie you up and not finish hitting you until you broke into tiny pieces so I could glue you back together."

The air thickened with violence and I struggled to hold onto my emptiness. Leather Jacket probed my mind, trying to find a way into my tower. A sprinkling of sweat dotted my skin as I struggled.

Q suddenly sighed, dropping his hand. He looked away, his temper dimming to surrender. *"Je ne vais pas te faire de mal parce je ne veux pas te détruire."* I won't hurt you, as I don't want to destroy you. Cupping my cheek, he ran his thumb along my bottom lip. "I can't stop you leaving, but I won't stay to see you go." His touch disappeared as he stepped back. "I don't want to see you again. Goodbye, *esclave.*"

He brushed past without another word.

Nineteen

Quincy

*You're my esclave, my soul mate, each other we own,
you're mine forever, my bird flew home...*

I'd torn one man's heart out, and now I wanted to tear
out my own. My fingers ached to pry open my ribcage and
wrench it from beating to dead. I no longer wanted to live with
this fucking agony every time I thought about Tess.

She'd successfully hurt me more than any other person in
the world. She brought me to my fucking knees and I told the
truth when I said I didn't want to see her again.

I *couldn't.*

I couldn't look her in the eye again. Suzette told me what
happened yesterday. How Tess told her ex she was leaving
without having the decency to tell me first.

The moment Suzette told me Tess was going, I lost it. I
fucking forgot I was human and ripped the kitchen apart. I
hurled the ten thousand euro coffee maker through the pantry
door, shredded packets of food, and tore the tap from the
bench-top.

Only when I'd expended my angst-riddled energy did
Suzette move closer and do something I would never have

allowed before.

She hugged me.

Her tiny arms wrapped around my waist, squeezing tight, reminding me I was human and not a monster after all.

After everything I'd done—it wasn't enough. Both the beast and man had lost.

My Tess was gone. *What the fuck did they do to her?* The passion and strength had disappeared. Looking into Tess's eyes now left me with a shiver and loneliness. All I saw was nothing. Fucking *nothing.*

She'd shutdown but I didn't have the fucking luxury of doing the same. As much as I wanted the pain to go away—how tempting the thought of freeing myself from this agony, I couldn't just leave.

People relied on me. Slaves. Staff. Countless employees.

I charged through the house, going out of my fucking mind at the thought of losing the woman I loved. A new rattle existed inside me—fresh, oozing wounds caused by Tess's betrayal. The darkness I let consume me while hunting for Tess came back with a vengeance. Gone was the urge to tend to her, make her well again.

All I wanted to do was be far, far away so she couldn't see how much she broke me. Me? The beast with no fucking feelings teetered on the edge of wrapping his arms around Tess's knees and begging with everything he had for her to remember. For her to stop this madness and man up. She let shock steal her life. She'd given in to the worst kind of disease.

Three times I'd seen this happen. Three times, I returned former slaves to their husbands, and three times the women hugged and smiled but something was missing. Something intrinsic, unique. The husbands knew straight away. They recognised the soul of the person they adored had shut down, locked tight, and sunk to the depths of their wives' being.

I'd stood by and felt sorry for the poor shmucks who lost their wives all over again. Once a mind reached its breaking point—it didn't break. It folded inward, layering like an accordion until every element of emotion was deleted. Until their horrific past, or whatever they'd endured, was gone.

All along Tess had been so strong. And now she was even stronger. Stronger in her chilliness and the sheer fact she'd learned how to block life out. Completely, perfectly, she would never feel again—neither hope nor happiness nor fear. Her life had gone from sensory overload to bleak and barren. She didn't do it deliberately, but I knew there was no hope.

After all, I'd seen proof. The three women who returned to their husbands divorced them, ruining the men all over again.

Wrenching open the door under the foyer stairs, I bolted down the steps and grabbed a pool cue from the rack. "Fuuuuck!" I yelled, throwing it at the wall. It speared like a javelin, clattering loudly off the wood panelling. The gaming room was the only place I wanted to be.

I didn't want to go back into the house. I wanted to create a den where I could pretend I never loved or lost.

I'd spent last night in the conservatory—after hearing Tess was leaving I couldn't lie beside her. I couldn't put myself through that. Instead, I fell into a fitful sleep with the sounds of birds roosting, but when I woke up, the comfort they offered me was false.

They were only there because I surrounded them in wire and locks. They weren't there for me. They were my prisoners.

I no longer looked at each sparrow and saw a woman I helped save. I no longer took satisfaction that each little creature represented the good I did. They all became a mockery—all became Tess. Bouncing around in their cage, looking for a way out.

Just like fucking Tess.

"Je ne peux pas plus faire ça putain!" I can't fucking do this anymore! I'd never been so consumed. I wanted freedom from this mania inside.

Alcohol.

That would help numb me, if not wipe away my thoughts

completely. The moment I thought about drinking myself into oblivion, I couldn't move fast enough.

I jumped over the pool cue on the floor and practically sprinted for the crystal bar. Wrenching open the large humidor, I entered the musky dark cave where ludicrously expensive bottles of liquor rested in the shadows.

Stepping back into the light, I brushed away dust on the Macallan Fine & Rare Collection of single malt whiskey. If I sold this bottle, it would probably fetch ten thousand euros from idiotic connoisseurs. Too fucking bad for them, I planned on swigging the entire thing as medicinal rather than entertainment.

I didn't bother with a glass. I didn't bother with sipping and savouring. I tore off the top and chugged.

The burn charged down my throat, splashing into my empty stomach, swilling around with flames of alcoholic fire.

I groaned as another swallow compounded the inferno until I felt sure my stomach would erode.

I took another four chugs before I had to stop to catch my breath. My fucking eyes watered like some virgin drinker, and the room already had a brownish haze.

My hope of sleeping existed in consuming this entire bottle. Maybe then I would go to sleep, and when I woke up, Tess would be gone.

Tess is leaving. Do something! Stop fucking wallowing.

She's already made the decision. Fuck if I'm going to grovel. I did everything in my fucking power and she still didn't want me. I could only take so much before I turned from tender lover who wanted to heal her, to a man who wanted to beat the shit out of her because she hurt me so much.

Throwing myself into the corner of the room, I bent my legs and rested my forearms on the top of my knees. The heavy bottle dangled from my fingers, and the only time I moved was to add more fuel to the raging fire in my stomach.

"Q? Mercer? Where the fuck are you?"

A voice pierced my drunken haze; I froze. Whoever it was, I didn't want them to find me. *Piss off. Leave me the fuck alone.*

"I can smell a shitload of alcohol, so I know you're down here," Frederick muttered as he came around the pool table to find me curled up against the wall. The wall was a fucking comfy place to be. I'd never been so warm and soft and numb.

The whiskey was my only friend. I hugged the bottle closer as Frederick's forehead furrowed. His nose wrinkled, and he sighed as if I were a mess he had to clean up.

Well luckily for him, I liked my mess and he could just fuck off.

My temper was well and truly off its leash; I snarled, *"Fous moi la paix."* Leave me the hell alone.

Frederick crossed his arms, glaring. "How much have you had to drink?"

I sneered, waving the now almost empty bottle of whiskey as if it was the most ridiculous question I'd ever heard.

He blew out a heavy breath, rolling his eyes. He hoisted the front of his slacks to squat in front of me. The urge to punch him so he fell on his ass consumed me.

His slicked-back hair was perfect, his midnight blue suit immaculate. His sapphire eyes had no strain or worry in them. He looked like a fucking poster boy for a happy and successful marriage.

Something I will never have.

Ah shit, the painful thoughts were back. I'd successfully drunk myself into a stupor before, and nothing had existed in my brain, but now the haze switched to painful tiredness. I sighed. "Just leave, Roux. I don't need you here."

He shook his head. "I'm not about to leave a friend curled up in the fucking corner reeking of whiskey without knowing what's eating him." He raised an eyebrow. "So…what's eating you?"

The terrible weight I'd been carrying in my chest for weeks exploded. "She fucking hates me! That's what's eating me." I threw my hands up and the bottle went flying.

Frederick caught it before it hit the ground. "She doesn't hate you, Mercer. You couldn't be further from the truth." He eyed the whiskey before taking a swig, wincing as it went down. "You scoured the world for her. You killed countless men to find her, and you butchered the man who took her because that's what she asked of you. You've spent every day beside her, wiping her brow, suffering through her hallucinations all without complaint. You've been there for her and she knows that. She still loves you."

I chuckled. "Oh, I complained. I've broken a lot of shit because I couldn't stand to hear her nightmares or stomach the emptiness in her soul."

Frederick smiled. "I did the same thing when Angelique got that crazy flu a few years ago. I felt so helpless. Breaking stuff was a good way of venting. That woman of mine has me by the balls—just like Tess for you."

I scowled. Frederick painted a picture of a man who'd lost his backbone to a woman. Who went berserk when he couldn't have her—who had no other purpose but nurse her back to health. That wasn't fucking me.

Was it?

That meant I cared about another more than I cared about myself. That I put their needs before my own.

Shaking my head, I argued, "You're mistaking me for a pussy. I'm a scary son of a bitch who runs an international company and saves slaves from fucked-up assholes." I snatched the bottle out of his grip and took a huge gulp.

Frederick huffed, yanking the whiskey back. "Caring for someone doesn't make you a pussy, you idiot. Yes, you run a big company—but so do I, and I manage to go home to a wonderful woman whom I adore. You can be strong and soft."

My world consisted of liquid and whiskey vapour—I only half noticed he'd stolen it and had no time to listen to his ramblings. All I could see was my old life. Working my ass off for a company that took everything I gave. I lived a lonely, ever fighting existence, but it meant I was too tired, too focused to hurt. I hadn't even known I'd been lonely until Tess fucking came into my life.

All of this would never have happened if I'd just sent her back to her moron boyfriend. Who the hell was I to keep her? Look at how screwed up both our lives were, thanks to my genius plan.

I hung my head. "I'm kidding myself, Roux. I'm not a softhearted man who can be normal."

Frederick shook his head. "You're right. You can't. So stop trying to be. I know Tess would've really appreciated you caring for her over the last few weeks, but she's on the mend. It's time you showed her the man she fell for. The master. The dominating bastard who has sadistic tendencies."

He chuckled, adding, "The last time you were drunk you'd just sent her back and told me, in very intimate detail I might add, what she let you do to her that night in your bedroom."

My mind shot back to that night. The first time I let a little part of myself free, when uninhibited with alcohol, I strung Tess up and whipped her.

I lost all control. Baring my teeth, I dropped the barrier to my demons, pounding into her. There was no rocking, or gentle lovemaking. I pistoned my hips into her, grunting, sweating, a crazed need deep inside. I needed to bruise her, mark her, claim her.

With my cock deep inside, I raked fingernails along her ass, drawing blood, thrilling at how she panted and gasped with need.

The gag barricaded her screams. She bounced in my arms, breasts jiggling with every thrust. The room erupted with the sounds of heavy breathing and slapping sweaty skin. The air temperature was too hot. Tess was too much.

I'm coming. Fuck, I'm coming.

I jumped a mile when Frederick clasped my arm. My hazy eyes struggled to leave the erotic daydream and focus. How much I wished I was balls deep in Tess right now. How much I wanted to eradicate the distance between us.

"She's your other half, Q. She lives for the sharp pleasure of pain and you live to give it to her. If there have ever been two people who belong together, it's you." He stood, hauling me to my feet. "So you're gonna do something about it."

Oh, fucking God, the room did not know how to behave. *Where the hell are my legs?* The whiskey stormed inside, looking for a way out, but I swallowed hard, managing to stay upright.

Fredrick dragged me toward the steps and shoved me up them.

I grabbed the handrail, trying to stop him from pushing me where I didn't want to go. "What the fuck are you doing?"

"I'm not doing anything. You are." His shoulder ploughed into my back, shoving me upward until I stumbled through the door and into the lobby. The rest of the house was asleep; after all, it was two in the morning.

He brushed his hands as if congratulating himself on a job well done. "Go on." He waved at the stairs. "Go fix it."

I shook my head, ignoring his stupid demands. "What the hell are you doing here this late anyway? Go home to your pretty, perfect little wife." I didn't mean to sound jealous. Angelique *was* a pretty, perfect little wife, but I made it sound like that was a bad thing.

Frederick gave me a hard look. "I won't punch you for that as you're drunk. If you really want to know, I'm here because Suzette called to let me know you freed all your birds. She was concerned you might've finally snapped." He sighed, waggling a finger in my face. "She was worried, and I think she did the right thing, so don't reprimand her."

"Damn fucking meddling maid," I muttered under my breath.

"That damn maid may turn out to be your saving grace if

you get the balls to fix whatever has gone wrong with you and Tess."

I spun, swinging wide, fully intending to deck him. If I couldn't hit Tess anymore, a surrogate was in order. "It isn't fucking fixable. I've tried."

Frederick ducked and punched me, hard, right in the gut where all that sweet, pain-stealing alcohol lived. "Before you ask, that was for being a douche. Second, it was to try and knock some sense into you. You haven't tried. You've been treating Tess with kiddie gloves. Is that why she fell in love with you?"

Rubbing my stomach, I swayed. I needed to rethink letting this man run my company. He asked the dumbest questions. "Huh?"

"Did Tess fall in love with you because you're kind and sweet and even-tempered?" He snorted, a grin spreading his lips.

"Bien sûr que non." Of course not. Even I laughed at that idiotic suggestion. Those three words had never been used to describe me, not even on my best of days.

"Did she fall in love with you because you're a dark son of a bitch who has to hit her and draw blood to be connected?"

"Merde, when you put it that way, I sound like a fucking sicko with a vampire complex." The alcohol switched from sweet to sour, and I no longer liked the thought of being drunk.

"You are. I totally agree. But you're also a man who is head over heels for a woman that wants that side of you. You told me she wanted to be your slave. She came back for you, Mercer. No woman would put herself through that unless she could see the goodness in you."

That just reminded me I let her get taken in the first place. *It's all my fau—*

Frederick slapped me. It was such a girly move, I laughed. "Resorting to a bit of palm action, Roux?"

He chuckled. "Just stopping that train of thought. I've seen it in your eyes way too often the past few weeks. It isn't your fault. Sure, your life is full of dangerous men, but you're dangerous enough to keep her safe. It was just bad luck. That's all."

"It wasn't fucking bad luck. We were both idiots about the tracker. I thought she'd removed it!"

Frederick nodded. "I agree. You're both to blame. What does that tell you?"

Anger.

Sheer, undiluted anger filtered through my veins, burning up the alcohol, making me see clearly for the first time in weeks. "Tess is to blame, too."

Frederick took a step backward, a smile tugging his lips. "Go on…"

My eyes rose to the staircase above us, already seeing Tess curled up in bed thinking she was safe. But she wasn't safe. Not from me.

"She fucked up just as much as me. She needs to apologise. She needs to thank me for all the blood on my hands. She needs to give me back what's mine."

"And that is?" Frederick goaded.

"Her fucking heart."

My legs moved on their own accord. Grabbing the banister, I hurled myself up the steps, two at a time.

I couldn't move fast enough.

Frederick followed close behind. I wanted to tell him to get lost, but I had no time. I'd wasted enough time as it was. I'd have an audience but I was past caring.

This conversation should've happened days ago. Tess owed me. Goddammit, she owed me so fucking much and she just cut me off. I was done being cut off.

The door slammed open as I heaved it with my shoulder. Tess shot upright in bed. She winced, holding her side, her bandaged finger resting on the sheet.

I licked my lips, searching her eyes for the one thing I needed to see. Fear. She should've been terrified at my entry, but her eyes were colourless in the gloom. Nothing glowed, no terror or panic. She looked as if she'd fallen asleep at a fucking church service.

"Tess," I growled, charging for the bed.

She let me come. She didn't move away or try to hide under the covers. She cocked her head. "I didn't think you'd be sleeping with me. Not after what I said."

She wore the same white T-shirt of mine to bed, and all I could think about was her undressing before I strapped her to the cross—it felt like a century ago. We'd been happy then. I'd been tormented and scared, but happy as Tess promised she'd never leave.

I pinched my brow, trying to get my thoughts under control. "I'm not coming to bed, *esclave*. You and I need to talk."

She eyed me but nodded. "Okay."

Goddammit, where was the fire? The argument that she didn't want to talk because I woke her in the dead of night. I needed to see tenacity and boldness. Nothing shone on her face, no ounce of emotion.

I squeezed my eyes, trying to understand what the fuck I was doing here.

"Q..."

Her soft voice wrapped around my heart and I struck.

I didn't mean to. I didn't give my hand permission to strike her cheek. It just happened. The force of her power over me made the monster fucking crazy. Denied for so long, it'd done what I was terrified of happening all along. It took away my control—made me hit her.

The soft sting in my palm and the resonating noise of connecting with Tess's cheek was pure heaven. I'd missed it for far too long. I opened my eyes, looking at the red handprint on her skin. My cock instantly hardened.

The first fucking erection I'd had since I found Tess so ruined and weak.

Her eyes popped wide as she touched her cheek with gentle fingertips.

I waited, licking my lips—waiting for her crystal tears that tasted so sweet, but her eyes remained dry. No salt, no amazement, or accusation.

"I know you're trying to get an emotion out of me, Q. But…it won't work." She broke eye contact. "I've tried. I hate what I'm doing to you. I loved you and can't stand to be the reason for your pain, but they made me—" She swallowed. "My thoughts aren't safe anymore. I can't be myself because everything is wrapped up in such evil." She looked up. "I'm truly sorry but you have to let me go."

The alcohol rolled in my stomach and I lost it completely. I'm not proud of what I became. I never wanted to be so out of control, but I lost all elements of the man and showed her just how much the beast fucking wanted her.

I ripped the sheets off and shoved her into the middle of the bed. The T-shirt rode up, showing her flat belly, and I had to bite her. Had to mar that slightly bruised flesh.

With a snarl, I buried my mouth against her stomach. She flinched as I bit hard. I didn't break the skin, but only because some miracle intervened.

I spread my entire weight over her, smothering her into the mattress. Eyes to eyes, mouth to mouth, hips to hips.

I thrust hard against her, groaning at how good my hard cock felt. It'd been too long. Way too long since I'd had this woman…since I'd *wanted* this woman. "Feel that, Tess. That's for you. I want you. So. Fucking. Much. Please come back to me. You *will* come back to me." I smashed my mouth against hers. Her taste intoxicated me more than any alcohol.

I forced her lips open, demanding she tongue me back. She opened, letting me kiss her, but she didn't return my affection. It was like kissing a corpse.

Please. Fucking please, come back to me.

Slowing down, I kissed her with all the unhappiness and loss inside. Showing just how much I needed the strong fiery woman who didn't take my shit but let me hurt her anyway.

I needed her so much.

I poured my heart into her…

Nothing.

My gut twisted and I pulled away, looking deep into her eyes. There were no words to describe the vacant, empty woman who stared back. No signs of lust or fear or turmoil.

Zero. Zilch. Gone.

Grabbing her shoulders, I shook her. "Wake up, *esclave*. Come out of your fucking bunker and face me. You don't have to shut down anymore."

When she didn't say anything, I yelled right in her face. "This isn't just my fault, you know. You left the tracker in. You forgot to remove it. You should've told me! You should've made sure only I had access to you."

I sat up, dragging her upright to shake her with every word. "You let me down. You ruined everything. Goddammit, Tess. Do something!"

A flicker of something sparked in her eyes before it was gone again, killed by the life-sucking void inside her.

"I'll fuck you. I'll make you come back to me. Is that what you want?" I grabbed her uninjured hand and placed it around my cock.

It leapt in her grip, hot and angry; wanting so fucking much to be inside her. "I only get hard if you fight me, Tess. So fucking fight me, because I need you so damn much." I pressed my forehead against hers, whispering, "Please tell me you won't let me touch you, all the while really begging me to. Please tell me how you'll never let me break you, all the while growing wet for me. Tell me anything, *esclave*."

I removed my hand from hers, praying she'd fist and stroke me. My heart broke as her grip went limp.

I saw red.

Grabbing her throat, I squeezed, looking so deep into her eyes I swear I saw her fucking soul. And it scared the shit out of me when I realized there was no soul to see. Nothing connected to mine—the mind link we shared was gone.

"Tess, please. I'm begging you." Pressing my lips against

hers again, I didn't move, waiting, hoping she'd kiss me back.

One breath.

Two.

An agony of waiting for her to soften, accept my protection, my willingness to give her anything she wanted, but she stiffened in my grip. Her hot skin turned chilly; she withdrew even further. The bond we shared snipped free as she sucked whatever existed between us deep inside, leaving me in the dark, all alone, once more.

"Sparrow," she whispered.

My world crunched to a halt; my heart stopped.

I didn't think anything could hurt me so bone deep. I wanted to tear out my brain and never exist. That one word. It ruined me. Smashed me with a wrecking ball, leaving me in rubble, in pieces, in dust.

I pulled back, scrambling off the bed. She'd successfully cut off my legs, tore out my heart, and left me for dead.

"Sparrow?" I repeated; my voice cracked.

She looked straight into my eyes. "Sparrow, Q. I'm so sorry." Her eyes dropped to where my shirt had come undone, zeroing in on my tattoo. She inched forward onto her knees, beckoning me to go closer.

I couldn't move, rooted to the spot. She just used the safe-word and expected me to come back to her?

The monster inside no longer lived in the realm of sanity—it tore its flesh, yanked at its head—wishing there was a way free from this nightmare.

When I didn't move, Tess climbed over the rumbled bedding and stepped toward me. Her tiny hand flashed out, tracing the sparrow over my nipple, the highest one—the one flying free.

"They made me hurt others. They made me break them. I'm not a good bird anymore. I don't know how to live with that. I'm empty. I'm lost. And time won't heal me. I can't give you what you need anymore and I wish I could." Her voice was breathy, tortured. I tried not to listen or believe. This was it.

This was the end.

"You don't mean that. You'll come back from it. Let me help you." My mind filled with images of tying her up, whipping her until she remembered who she was. I'd kill her trying if it meant she'd be mine again. "I'll do anything you ask of me. Just give me more time."

"I'm leaving in the morning, Q. I'm sorry."

"Tu ne vas aller nulle part putain!" You're not fucking going anywhere! I shoved her backward, watching detachedly as she sprawled on the bed. Why didn't she wince or show pain from her injuries? Was she so far gone she didn't feel her body either?

The beast inside roared, determined to find out. I struck with my fingers, dragging my nails down her leg.

Four lines of blood sprang and *still* nothing. Tess just lay there, breathing normally, looking so remote.

"Tess, doesn't do this to me!" I reached for her again—to do what, I didn't know. Hit her, hug her, spank her, caress her—anything would be better than nothing.

Arms bounded around me, hauling me back.

Frederick muttered in my ear, "She said no, Mercer. There's nothing you can do."

I struggled, fuck I struggled, but Frederick was strong. His arm tightened, muscles digging into my collarbone as he dragged me further from Tess.

The last image I saw was Tess sitting cross-legged on the bed with her long blonde hair drifting around her and her lifeless grey-blue eyes watching me go.

There was nothing else to say.

It was done.

Over.

Finished.

Every single door in my mind, every wall and barrier I'd ever created, slammed back into being. I compartmentalized my needs and humanity, removed myself from the equation. I shut down so efficiently, so coldly, I was left wondering if I was a psychopath.

Tess was gone.

Frederick loosened his hold on me. "I'm sorry, man."

I didn't say a word as I stalked away.

Away from the slave I fell for.

Away from my very existence.

Twenty

Tess

Tie me, tease me, let your pleasure please me. Hurt me, love me, but please don't leave me.

The moment the door shut behind Q, I started to shake. I used the safe-word.

A word that shattered Q and ruined the final connection between us. I never thought I'd have to use it, but when he kissed me, pouring all the love and need he had for me, I couldn't function. I couldn't be the cause of such agony.

Nausea sat thick and heavy in my stomach. I wished I could take it back. I wanted to run after him and promise I'd figure out a way to come back. Offer him the chance to beat it out of me, to submit completely into his control, but the longer I sat there, the more leaden I became.

The guilt and ghosts and pain roiled like a storm-whipped sea. Smashing against the walls of my tower, trying to drown me and take me straight to hell.

"Think of me. Think of me dead and rotting in the ground." Blonde Hummingbird broke my fortress, ripping my heart into pieces. *"You put a bullet in my brain. You're the reason I have so many broken bones."*

The guilt opened its eager jaws, sucking me deep.

Gritting my teeth, I fought back. I trembled as I added yet another layer of bricks to my tower. "I'm sorry. I can't!"

A memory swamped me. Something I'd suppressed— something I didn't want to see.

"Go on. Do it."

I no longer had the strength to even mentally disobey. Shuffling forward, I dragged the knife down the blonde girl's arm.

"Cut it off. Call it stocktake and we no longer need that merchandise."

The girl trembled, shaking her head, her lips working the thick rag in her mouth. The straps around her body kept her still while I grabbed her wrist and circled the barcode tattoo with the blade tip.

The drugs confused me. Why was I cutting off this tattoo? It must be important—but maybe I should cut off my own, too?

"Do it, puta. Or I'll just chop off her arm."

I pressed the tip of the knife around the outline of the tattoo, letting the sharp metal slice a border even as red blood rained.

The girl thrashed and cried and I flickered in and out of drug-consciousness.

"Nice cutting. Now peel it off." Leather Jacket appeared by my shoulder, inspecting my handiwork.

I nodded and grabbed the flesh to pull—

The stomach-churning vision fractured as I fell off the bed. Crying out, I retched and hastily reached for the bowl on the floor. My stomach emptied and my skin dewed with clammy sweat.

The sound of the door opening and closing didn't interest me as another wave of sickness rose.

The 1920s man from the night I hung in the sparrow room gently gathered my hair, waiting for me to finish retching. Once I was fairly sure I had nothing left, he took the bowl to the bathroom before coming back to help me into bed.

Once I rested under the sheets, he stood and smiled sadly. "Do you remember me?"

I nodded. "You stopped me from spinning out of control

319

when Q strung me up for a dinner meeting." For once I didn't shudder at the thought of the Russian asshole and his knife hilt. I would never know Q's reasoning behind that.

"I did. I'm also Q's work associate and closest friend." He pointed at the end of the bed, raising an eyebrow. "May I?"

I shrugged. "Sure." It wasn't often I had gentlemen sitting in their immaculate suits on the end of my bed at almost three in the morning.

"My name is Frederick, and I've known Quincy since boarding school. He's never fully come out and told me his life history, but I've put enough together to know he finds life in general incredibly hard. Even he doesn't fully understand why he is the way he is, and yet you accepted him completely. For the first time in his life, he met a woman who not only loved him for the man, but for his darkness, too."

He looked away as if too emotional to continue. "I must admit, I never thought Q would find what he needed. I envisioned him working himself into an early grave. Building an empire, dedicating his life to a cause that he believed was his redemption, and never finding what all humans want to find."

I didn't speak—just let Frederick take the stage.

"When you were taken, Q turned his back on everything he fought so hard for. He threw his company's reputation down the gutter, he walked away from the profile he'd created for himself. He even dismissed the human part of himself that he's always fought to protect."

His aquamarine eyes flashed in the darkness. "He searched everywhere for you, Tess. He killed countless men—most in barbaric, coldblooded ways, all in the name of your honour. He travelled thousands of miles, paid hundreds of men for information. He went to hell to bring you back from it, and now that you're safe, he has nothing."

Something hard lodged in my throat.

"If you truly don't think there's hope, then leave. Get as far away from Q as possible, because you'll only kill him faster by staying." He turned to face me with an angry glint in his eyes. "But if you think there might be some small chance—some miniscule hope that you can work through what they did to you—then stay. You owe him that."

Frederick stood, brushing his suit with perfect hands. "Now, if you'll excuse me. I have a wife who loves me, and I really need to go and tell her how much I care. Seeing such a perfect thing ruined between two people fucking hurts."

Without another word, he strode to the door and let himself out.

The rest of the night didn't equal sleep. I stared into the darkness, fighting a war deep inside, trying so hard to find the true me.

Frederick was right. I owed Q so much. I'd been selfish. I could be strong enough to face my guilty crimes. I needed to focus on saving the man I used to love—*still* loved.

I tried everything. Forcing myself to remember what I did, reliving all those horrible moments, even recalling the original kidnapping in Mexico, and the rape before Q found me. I put myself through every bad memory. I broke my heart with childhood memories of my parents abandoning me.

"We're taking you to the zoo today. Behave and be a good girl." My mother ducked to look me sternly in the eye.

I couldn't control my six-year-old excitement. I'd never been taken anywhere nice. Apparently I wasn't worth the admission, whatever that was. "I'll be good, I promise."

Only when we got to the zoo, my mother didn't go in with me. She waited until I'd gone through the barrier, then drove off.

I hated the zoo. Every wild animal seemed to sense my unhappiness; the monkeys laughed at me; the lions growled, tasting my fear. I spent the night huddled in the corner by the rubbish bins. No one noticed a six-year-old after hours and no mother came to pick her up.

Eventually, the cleaners found me, and much to my mother's dismay, I was sent home.

I forced myself to think of how nasty my brother had been.

"Is this scummy toy yours?" He held up my headless teddy bear. The

one I found outside a Salvation Army one day.

"Give it back." I jumped for it, but he'd always been so tall. He laughed, tore the legs off, and scooped out the stuffing before throwing it all over me.

I hardened my heart, knowing I would never find love with these people.

And yet, I found love with Q. I found an all-encompassing connection that made my childhood seem so ridiculous.

Q muttered, "Tu ne peux pas être à moi, mais je suis en train de devenir à toi."

My stomach twisted, filling with frothy bubbles. Our eyes locked and I couldn't look away. Q brushed his lips against mine ever so sweetly, repeating in English, forcing me to swallow the words. "You may not be mine, but I'm fast becoming yours."

Time froze.

His confession tied me up, stole my mind. His drunken state let me see the depth of his feelings. Time began anew, sparkling with new possibilities. My body was no longer mine, it belonged to Q. Everything belonged to Q.

How could I ever forget that I would always belong to Q?

Scrunching my face, I battered and screamed at my heavily garrisoned tower. I wanted the guilt. I wanted the nausea—for tears to spill—because it would show I was still alive in there…somewhere.

I no longer wanted to live in a void.

But no matter how I picked at old wounds, nothing worked. I'd added too many bricks, slammed closed too many locks.

I'd lost everything and I couldn't even grieve.

By the time the sun warmed the room and a new day sparkled, I'd exhausted myself into a worse empty silence than before. I could stab myself in the heart and I wouldn't feel it. I could break every bone in my body and I wouldn't care.

I was truly dead inside.

Frederick was right. I couldn't do this to Q anymore.

After showering and dressing in a pair of jeans and baby

pink blouse from the carousel room, I made my way downstairs with just my passport in my pocket. I had no idea how I'd get back to Australia. I had no money—save for the cash Q gave me. I had no plan, and I didn't care if a hitchhike turned into what happened before. Maybe some rapists would finish the job, so I could finally rest and not be so terribly cold.

Suzette stood in the foyer as I descended the stairs. Her arms crossed over her chest, a look full of sadness and disbelief on her face. "Q told us you were leaving. That Franco and I weren't to stop you. Please don't do this, Tess. Give it some time. We can wait. We can help you find your way back."

I shook my head. "That isn't fair on Q. I have nothing left and he deserves everything. It's not fair to stay and give him hope." I gave her a sad smile. "Thank you for taking such good care of me."

Without another word, I opened the front door and stepped outside. The world seemed so normal. Summer turned to autumn, and the beautiful trees in Q's gardens started the journey from green to red to gold before dropping completely.

I felt like a dried-up leaf whose only purpose was to fall to the ground and rot.

Waiting on the stoop, I tried once more, one last and final time to find some part of me alive and unwilling to go, but the numbness was my only answer.

By protecting myself, I doomed myself. I may not die from guilt, but I would never live with love or happiness again.

My first step off Q's porch should've buckled my knees and torn my heart free from my chest, but it didn't.

I'd never feel again.

Once onto the gravel, I skirted the horse fountain, heading down the long driveway. Trees loomed above, blotting out the early morning sun. I kept walking until I hit the road.

Left.

Right.

Which way to go? Should I go back to Australia? Why? There was nothing left for me there. I had no desire to go anywhere, only to leave this wondrous life that could've been.

To let Q heal without me. To let him forget and move on.

I stepped off Q's driveway.

Twenty-one
Quincy

*You're my obsession, I'm your possession, you own
the deepest part of me...*

I didn't know where I went after I left Tess. I spent the
rest of the night staring at some hideous vase, feeling nothing.

The alcohol left my system hours ago, and Frederick—the
traitorous bastard—let himself out a little while after I left Tess.

He spoke to her. I knew he did, and if I was honest, it
fucking pissed me off and made me want to kill him. But Tess
had chosen. She used the safe-word, for fuck's sake.

She couldn't hurt me any more than she already had.

I was done.

The sun slowly rose on a new day—a day where I would
have to pretend that nothing had happened. I would go back to
work and bury myself under paperwork. Someone had to deal
with the rumours going around about me. Dubois—the chief
of police—had been true to his word and banned all bad press
about *Moineau* Holdings, but that wouldn't last forever.

Franco had already prevented one attack on my home
from disgruntled traffickers. The strange thing was my shares in
other companies—the untainted by slaves or sinful underworld

investments—had grown. Turned out people liked to invest with a company that had morals and a CEO who had a saviour complex.

Tess did me a favour—she reminded me I wasn't good enough. I couldn't expect to have what others took for granted. I'd never earn the love of a woman or be stupidly happy like the rest of the human race. But I had other things to live for. I would save more slaves than ever before; I would make sure others could have a happy ending instead.

That would be my legacy.

Merde, maybe I should close the business and go on a never-ending hunting spree. Then, I might be happy.

Suzette appeared in the reading nook in the lounge where I'd hidden for the past few hours. "She just left, master." She looked out the window, no doubt seeing Tess heading down the driveway. "I did what you told me and just let her go, but Franco isn't happy. He's got the car ready to go if you want to go after her."

A sharp dagger twisted my heart, but I gritted my teeth, forcing myself to stay seated.

I wouldn't chase after her. I wouldn't. Not after the safe-word.

When I didn't move, Suzette left me to my mourning and another hour went past. Every time I wondered where Tess was I shot the thought right between its eyes. I refused to think about her. I denied the ache in my cock, the pining beast inside.

I repeated over and over that I didn't need her. I didn't need someone who didn't need me.

I don't fucking need her.

A car screeched to a halt outside, kicking gravel against the windowpane. I sat up from my slouch to see Frederick charging from his Lexus and bolting for the front door. He exploded through the foyer and into the lounge. His eyes fell on me. Tearing around the furniture, he raced forward and planted his motherfucking fist in my jaw.

"You're a dumb son of a bitch. In fact, you're as stupid as

she is." Frederick hit me again, but this time I was ready for him. I ducked and swung, connecting with his ribcage.

He sucked in a breath, yelling, "I told you if you wanted to keep her you'd have to do something drastic." He hit me again; it landed on my right shoulder.

Heat flashed through my veins and I snarled. "I *did* do something drastic. I hit her and demanded she come back to me—all while you fucking watched—and then she used the safe-word!" I grabbed the hideous vase I'd been staring at all night and hurled it across the room. It connected with another glass full of flowers, and they thundered to the floor in a chaos of breaking china. "What more can I do? I swore I'd stop if she ever used it."

Frederick poked my chest with a finger. "You can pull your head out of your ass for one." He roundhoused me, the fucker, and his foot connected with my ear. I went down, landing on one knee on the carpet.

I glared, shooting upright to deliver a thick set of knuckles to his jaw.

I forgot why we fought and laid into him. It wasn't the first time we'd beaten each other to shit, and it wouldn't be the last. Being evenly matched meant Frederick delivered as good as he got.

I landed a few fists to his upper body, while he managed to cuff me around the head, making me see stars. We huffed and groaned, circling each other like two testosterone-fuelled idiots.

Each punch he delivered gave me something I missed. It gave me a reason to get up and kick his fucking lights out. But I didn't.

Even though I lived to be violent, I kept myself tamed. I didn't let myself go killer. I would never kill someone I cared about. And even though Frederick drove me crazy, I cared enough to keep him alive.

We were both breathing hard by the time Frederick did another one of his annoying karate moves and landed me on my ass. He stood over me, offering his hand.

The peace offering broke the tension and I clasped his grip, allowing him to drag me to my feet.

I licked the interior of my lip, pleasantly surprised to find I had a cut. "You're getting vicious in your old age, Roux," I mumbled, running a finger along the slice.

He huffed, dragging his hands through his out of place hair. "You deserved it. That was for Tess. For slapping her and being an asshole. You won't get her back by forcing her further into herself."

"But that's what she always reacts to! She craves pain. She craves what I crave. She's the mirror image of me, Roux, and I miss her so fucking much." *Shit, where the hell did that come from?*

I glowered, wishing I'd kept my mouth shut.

Frederick nodded, a light slowly building in his eyes. "You said she craves what you crave." He cocked his head, pacing a few steps before spinning to face me. "Have you ever let her hit you? Whip you?"

I grabbed a drinking glass from the sideboard and threw it at his head.

What a fucking blasphemous thing to say. Let her hit me! No fucking way. Not a chance.

Frederick ducked the projectile; it smashed against the wall, adding to the pile of broken china and wilting flowers.

He held up a hand in surrender, thoughts whizzing in his gay-ass blue eyes. "Wait! Hear me out. What if you let her do the things to you that you do to her?"

My jaw locked as panic spread thick and fast. Nothing terrified me more. I gulped at the thought of Tess hurting me, tying me up, degrading me—making me beg. Having complete and utter dominance over me.

"Il n'y a pas moyen putain. Je ne peux pas faire ça." No fucking way. I can't do it. I shook my head hard. "No chance."

Frederick didn't let it go. He strode forward, talking fast. I didn't want to listen. I'd be willing to do anything to bring Tess back, but to let her rob me of everything that made me *me*? I didn't want to think about it, it hurt too much. It wasn't possible. Exactly why I hadn't dreamed up the idea myself.

It would kill me.

"Tess said last night she'd been forced to hurt others. You said yourself—she's strong enough to handle anything people do to her. But what if she wasn't strong enough to handle hurting others? What if this shutdown is to stop herself from feeling pain when she made another cry, or worse?"

I backed away, trying so hard to ignore his logic.

He cornered me by the couch, delivering his final blow. "If it were me and I loved her as much as you say you do, I would do anything."

"I *would* do anything but not that."

"What wouldn't you do? Think about it, Q. Admit it."

The temper from the fight escalated again. "You're saying I need to make her hurt me. That I need to take her back to that place and break down every fucking wall she's built. You're saying I need to sacrifice my own skin, my own pain to bring her back." I sighed, wanting to wash my mouth out. "You're telling me to do the impossible, Roux."

I clutched my skull as a roaring headache appeared out of nowhere. The monster inside tore at my brain. *No one can have that sort of power over me.*

I wasn't strong enough. I couldn't do it.

But I knew.

Even though I couldn't admit it.

Frederick was fucking right.

Images of hitting her, stringing her up, and fucking her hard, catapulted into my mind. She'd given me her trust, utterly and completely. I'd owned every part of her in that moment. Her eyes had been filled with ultimate trust, giving me the sweetest gift of thinking for her—of allowing me to own her.

She needs to own me to find her way back.

Holy fuck.

Frederick patted me on the back. "I'll let myself out. I'll check in on you in a few days. Fix this, Mercer. She's your other half, and you need to realize that before you fuck this up and end up alone. I like the man you're becoming because of her."

I blinked as Frederick gave me one last smile, and true to his word, let himself out the front door.

Thoughts ran crazy in my mind. I stood there like a fucking idiot, trying to make sense of what just happened. Where the hell had he come from? Fucking bibbity bobbity booing around like a fairy godmother. Goddammit I hated him, even though I liked that he cared enough to beat some sense into me.

The grandfather clock in the foyer struck minutes in the silence, counting down the moments I had left before Tess was too far away to find. Before I made an offer I might not survive. Before I gave Tess the biggest gift I could give anyone.

I wanted to forget about Frederick's epiphany. Surely, there was some other way to bring Tess back. I may be an asshole, but the thought of what I had to do turned me into a scared, *spineless* asshole.

You can't walk away. Not now. Not when I owed Tess everything. Not when I couldn't live without her.

"Goddammit."

The beast inside disowned me, leaving me to my ruin.

Hating myself, I raced from the house.

Twenty-two

Tess

Save me, enslave me, you will never cave me. Taunt me, flaunt me, kill whatever haunts me...

I headed toward the village where I'd first run from Q. It would take me a while to get there, but I didn't care.

Walking helped tame the cold emptiness inside. It gave me something to look at, something to think about other than memories locked tight against me.

I stopped to look at a pretty fantail darting in the late summer breeze when my legs disappeared from beneath me, and the air in my lungs escaped in a rush. I cried out as I landed over a strong, broad shoulder.

My eyes connected with the toned, sculptured ass of Q as he carried me back toward the house. I bumped and jostled and even though my ribs hurt, the protective shell my mind resided in didn't let me wince.

Q hadn't made a sound, even though the road was littered with twigs and crackly leaves. Somehow he'd tracked me down, pounced silently, and now held me captive.

I waited for the flutter of heartbeats——the knowledge and warmth that even though I hurt him so much last night, he couldn't bear to let me go.

Nothing.

Only a dark stain appeared, clouding my thoughts, reminding me I had women's blood beneath my fingernails and if I felt one emotion, I'd have to feel everything.

"Put me down," I said.

Q didn't say a word, striding purposely toward the house.

I pinched his butt, but he didn't flinch. "Let me go, Q."

"Never. You're not fucking walking out of my life like this. Not yet." His voice sounded off—fierce, angry, almost afraid.

"What are you doing?" I didn't like the energy he emitted—the uncomfortable, edgy vibe.

He growled low in his chest, muttering a curse in French. He raised his voice. "You're going to do something for me before you go."

I frowned. "What do you want me to do?"

"I'll tell you when we're back at the house. And you won't refuse, Tess. Because if you do, I'll fucking kill you to put us both out of our misery."

How much I wanted the thrill of terror at his words, the thickening of lust. I bounced on his shoulder, coaxing such feelings to manifest, but the best I could do was a pang of fear. Fear because I had no idea what Q had in store, and I hated newness. Newness always equalled terribleness. Newness meant beating up women and becoming dependant on drugs.

We didn't say another word as Q carted me back like a kill he'd just shot. I didn't whimper when my lungs ached from being squished, or complain when lightheadedness made me queasy from hanging upside down.

I didn't make a peep as we entered the house or bat an eyelash when Franco stopped short, staring at me in Q's grip.

Q took the steps two at a time, never out of breath from hauling my weight. He didn't slow as we headed down the corridor. He smelled of alcohol and strain, even a trace of blood as he kicked open a door and carried me through.

The moment he slammed the door shut with his foot, he put me down. His lip was bruised and split, a shadow bloomed under his left eye, and he looked sleep deprived and tortured. What the hell happened to him?

He gave me a hard look with unreadable eyes, prowling to the bed.

I looked around. I'd never been in this room before. Painted in golds and reds, it had an exotic feel, a bit ostentatious, but it worked all the same. Q headed to the four-poster bed and tore off the thick duvet and sheeting, leaving a bare mattress. He headed to the bathroom before returning with four towels which he placed all over the bed, covering the fabric.

I stood unmoving, watching him tear around the room. Once he'd tugged and straightened the towel for the fifth time he came to stand in front of me, breathing hard.

He stood straighter, gathering energy from the room yet all the while seeming to shrink in on himself. His eyes locked with mine, and I gasped at the torment deep in their pale depths.

"Remember. If you refuse, I'll kill you."

Twenty-three
Quincy

You crawled into the darkness, set my monster free,
so scream, bleed, call out to me, but never say stop,
never flee

I stood in front of Tess ready to do something I'd never done in my life. Something I didn't know if I could stomach. Something I didn't know if I could walk away from.

"Merde." I hung my head, running hands over my bruised face. The entire journey carrying Tess here, I tried to think of another way. A way where I could keep my fucked-up sanity and still fix her.

But I couldn't see any other logic.

There was no other way.

I had to let her take away my ownership, my very fucking life.

Tess stood there with her arms straight by her sides, her blonde curls so wild and carefree compared to her closed-off detachment.

I hated her in that moment—hated the coldness, the lack of connection. The way she left me to flounder and die of a broken heart. I wanted to throw her on the bed and make her scream. I wanted to do all sorts of things to her to get a reaction. I wanted to hurt her until she used the safe-word again but this time, ignore it. I wanted to push past her barriers and make her see the truth.

I can't. I wouldn't be responsible for destroying her mind.

Gritting my jaw, I ran hands through my hair. I couldn't stand still. I was like a fucking schoolboy about to lose his virginity all over again.

And in a way I was.

"Tu ne sauras jamais ce que ça me coûte." You'll never know the cost of this, I murmured, looking up for the first time. "The amount it's taxing me."

Tess's gaze softened. "Whatever it is, you don't have to do it. I've caused enough damage."

I growled, hating that I offered so much and she had the nerve to deny it. "It's not a negotiation, Tess. You're doing this. I'm just letting you know how much this will hurt me. How much I'm willing to put my life on the line—for you."

She froze, nostrils flaring.

The word *mistake* danced in my mouth and I swallowed it back. This wasn't a mistake. I fucking loved her, and it was time I told her that.

"I love you," I snarled, as if was a terrible thing—an abomination.

Her eyes widened and she looked away. "Don't do this, Q."

I moved closer and grabbed her chin, forcing her to look at me. I let go of everything, every barrier, every smoke and mirror. I let her see everything I was. All the fear I felt, all the love I burned with. "You could be anywhere and I would still hurt, *esclave.*"

Her eyes stayed cold, even after I showed her how much I needed her. She shook her head, trying to get free. "I can't give you what you need anymore. I've tried. I've tried so hard to unlock whatever space I'm trapped in, but it's no use."

I ran my nose along her jaw, breathing her in, imprinting

her scent of frost and orchids into my soul. When Tess did as I demanded, I doubted I'd want to be this close to her.

"It's not about what I need. It's about what *you* need." I paused, gathering my tattered courage. "I'm going to give you what you need."

Tess sucked in a little breath.

I flinched, eyes delving into hers, trying to see if she felt something, reacted to what I said.

But nothing glittered, nothing shone.

In that moment, I wanted to tear the room apart. I wanted to kill the bastards who took her all over again. Damn it to fucking hell. The fucking bastards. The fucking screwed-up world.

Tess touched my cheek, grounding me. "Are you okay?" I wished she asked me out of concern, but I knew better.

"How can you ask that? How can you honestly think I'm okay? I had everything I ever dreamed of, then had it all snatched away. I miss you so damn much, but you don't care. You don't love me anymore. You took everything from me and you have the nerve to ask if I'm okay." I laughed with the black humour of the situation. "I'm going to either ruin you or heal you. It's one or the other, Tess. Starting now. This will either fix us or leave us in fucking pieces."

"What will?"

"I want you to take me." My voice shook. What a sap. I tried again. "You're going to do whatever you want to me. You're going to take everything I have to offer by any means necessary." I pressed my mouth to her ear. "You're going to hurt me, Tess. And hurt me so fucking much."

Her mouth dropped open. She gawked, unseeing, unspeaking.

"I've fucked you. I've hit you. I've loved you in my own way, but it's not enough to fix you. I can't whip what happened out of you. You need to help yourself, and I'm offering to be the one you take all that rage and pain out on."

The air grew thick and heavy; I couldn't breathe. She

knew. She was too smart, too intelligent, not to realize what I offered.

"You don't know what you're saying."

Of course, I fucking knew what I was saying. I was going against every little cell in my body. I was going against nature. I was shooting the beast inside me with a shotgun and handing over my balls. Ignoring every instinct. Every desire I'd ever had.

"I know exactly what I'm offering, *esclave*. Take it. Before I change my mind." *Before I run away screaming like a little girl.*

Before I lose you.

Before I lose myself.

"It's not that simple. Even if I do hurt you it won't make a difference, Q. There's no point putting yourself through something you'll hate."

"There is a point if it brings you back. I'm not leaving until we get this over with. I don't make this offer lightly. I don't expect you to turn me down. You owe me."

She coughed. "I owe you?"

"Yes." I nodded hard. "And I'll tell you why. Whatever you lived through was terrible, awful and hellish, I know that, and I know you don't want to talk about it—that's why I don't push. But try and think what it was like for me. You were stolen from my office! My care and protection. You were taken away from me for seventeen fucking days. Every lead I chased was a dead-end, every hope, a fucking tease." I hit myself violently in the solar plexus, reliving that horror, the panic at not finding her. "Don't you think all of this is hard on me, too? You owe me, so hurt me. Make me suffer because I wasn't able to save you."

My chest heaved and the truth burst free. "It's all my fucking fault. All of it. The building contracts. The saving of slaves. The fact I thought I was invincible. I never thought to think of enemies and anything happening to you. I was a selfish fucking moron."

I had to stop and swallow around the lump forming in my

throat. "It's all my fault you're like this. So if I order you to make me suffer, it's the least you can do. *Libère moi de ma douleur,* Tess." Free me of my pain.

I cupped her cheek, drowning in her eyes. "I asked you once to give me your pain as my pleasure. This time take my pain as your pleasure."

It was a night of firsts and I dropped to my knees, bowing my head against her thighs. "Please, *esclave.* Don't make me keep asking. I don't have the strength." It felt awkward and horrid being in a position of submission, but at the same time, so right and perfect. The two emotions tangled, making me quiver with anxiety.

I didn't move. It was up to Tess now.

It felt like a full year before Tess shifted. Her gentle hand landed on my head. She threaded her fingers through my hair, soothing the never leaving headache, making me groan.

Was I making this worse by forcing her? Causing more damage to her already strained mind?

"I can't, Q."

I looked up, locking eyes. "You can. And you will."

She tried to untangle herself from my grip, but I tightened, not letting her go. "You're letting the bastards win, *esclave.* Do you want that? Do you want them to rule your life?" I stood, never letting go of her. "Where's the fight I'm so used to? The Tess I knew, the *esclave* I fell for, wouldn't lie down and not fight to the death."

The seconds ticked past and doubt shaded her face. She bit her lip, looking anywhere but me. I was sure she'd disagree again, and thoughts ran riot on how I could force her to hurt me. I didn't know what it would mean if this failed.

Finally, her eyes settled on mine; she whispered, "Are you sure?" Such caring, such gentleness shone from her face, that even though there was nothing else there—no soul or deep emotion—I took happiness from hope.

This would work. It had to.

I stood, bending to press one soft kiss on her lips. "I'm

sure. *Je suis à toi, tout à toi.*" I'm yours. All yours.

Her chest rose and she nodded. "Okay."

I didn't waste another moment. Grabbing her hand, I led her across the room.

She stood where I positioned her by the bed while I went to the cupboard. This room had a history. A history I would rather not think about, but it came stocked with apparatus and things required.

Opening the doors of the cupboard, I stopped short, panic running down my spine.

I was about to do something that would cripple me. I wanted to wipe this day free from my mind once it was over. I would destroy this room and everything in it so I never had to remember.

With nerves lodged in my throat, I pulled out ropes, cuffs, bondage of all types.

Tess watched remotely as I piled my arms full of things and headed back to the bed. Placing them on the towel at the foot of the four poster, I looked at Tess. "Tie me up."

I never thought I'd ever say those words. But I needed her to bind me. I wouldn't be able to go through with this if she didn't. I'd run like a fucking coward, or lash out and hurt her.

She picked up the leather cuffs, the buckles clinking. "Where?"

Trying to curb the terror and anger and so many fucking things, I forced myself to sit on the mattress and lie down.

My heart was a fucking crazy thing going a billion miles an hour; I couldn't look at Tess. I couldn't look anywhere but at the large canopy above my head. The four posters were sturdy—half a fucking tree sturdy—once she bound me, I wouldn't be able to get free.

My stomach rolled and I swore I would be sick. Shit. Oh, shit. *What the fuck am I doing?*

Tess glided closer to the bed, looking like a malnourished ghost. She eyed the cuff, then my limbs. My fists pressed against my thighs, every muscle locked tight.

I hadn't undressed. The element of having jeans and a T-shirt on was my only armament; I wanted to keep it that way.

I gritted my teeth, spreading my legs for her.

She swallowed and obediently looped the soft leather around my ankle.

Black spots appeared in my vision as she tightened the buckle around the bedpost. She fastened it and I wriggled.

"You need to do it tighter. I can get free." I hated every word. I wanted to chop out my tongue for being such a traitor, but I wasn't doing this for me. I was doing this for Tess. To somehow break the barrier she'd fortified. If it took dynamite in the form of making me shatter, then so be it.

Tess nodded, tightening the buckle until it bit into my skin. Heat travelled up my leg, causing me to shiver with helplessness.

Torturing me with fluttering touches and slowness, Tess secured my other ankle before sighing heavily. She looked at me with a thousand wishes in her eyes and no hope. Moving toward the head of the bed, she chose a length of silk rope.

Our eyes never left each other as she bent and captured my hand with hers. The moment her delicate fingers touched my trembling skin, I bucked. My cock roared to life and all I wanted to do was kiss her, fuck her, never let her fucking go again.

She bit her lip, her eyes darkening just a little.

"Embrasse moi!" Kiss me, I demanded, capturing her hand with mine.

We stared so long, so hard, I wondered if I'd die waiting for her to obey. Finally, she bent in half, lowering herself toward me. My legs might be bound, but my arms and torso weren't. The moment she was in grabbing distance, I wrapped my arms around her, dragging her hard against me.

She let out a small cry before my lips crashed onto hers. I speared my tongue into her mouth. She froze for the briefest of moments, then struggled as I held her tighter. She whimpered as I bit her bottom lip.

I groaned as her taste filled my mouth. She reminded me of happier times, of confused times, but most of all, the love I'd lost. The love I wanted to get back.

Her hands pressed against my chest, pushing me away.

Reluctantly, I let her go. She bolted upright, breathing hard. My heart lodged in my throat at the panic in her eyes.

Something had eroded, showing a little glimpse of all that emotion locked inside her.

Shaking her head, she grabbed my wrist and slammed my hand above my head. I didn't fight even though the beast inside wanted to tear her into smithereens.

Her fingers fumbled around my wrists, jerking them with every knot of the rope. She grimaced as she pulled harder, tightening the restraints to the point of pain.

I never took my eyes off her as she circled the end of the bed and climbed onto the mattress to restrain my other hand. I placed it above my head for her, drinking in her rising fear—the scent of turmoil and panic.

After weeks of nothing but coldness, the onslaught of her emotions intoxicated me better than any whiskey. Every second that ticked past, Tess lost the glassy sterile look, descending further into crazed and scared.

It's working. The curse around her fucking heart was breaking.

Tess tested the rope on my wrist one last time before scrambling off the bed and staring at me with such a soul-crumbling look in her eyes it undid me once and for all.

I fucking loved this woman. Not just for now. Not just for tomorrow. But always. Now and forever, I was hers.

I nodded, gritting my teeth. "Do it, *esclave.* Do whatever you want to me. I'll accept whatever you give. I'll live and be happy with whatever scraps you let me have." My voice was rough, laced with sorrow, but I kept going. "I give you myself, Tess. If it doesn't make you come back to me, then this is it. This is the last time I'll have you close, and I want to see passion in your eyes one last time."

I waited for a tear, a twitch, some recognition of how much I offered, but only terror greeted me. She stood stiff as a fucking board, no longer looking at me, but back there—back in the place where her nightmares brewed.

"Tess…" I wanted to tell her not to be afraid, to let them take her. That I'd be with her every step, but she shook her head, gripping her hair with desperate fingers.

She mumbled something under her breath, before exploding to the other side of the room, heading toward the open cupboard.

I strained to see what she collected and my heart bucked when she came back with whips, floggers, scissors, and vials.

She dumped it all between my splayed and bound legs.

Her eyes evolved from dove-grey to icy blizzard, glittering with hatred. She no longer looked at me from the eyes of my *esclave*—my Tess. She morphed into a complete stranger. A woman with a vendetta, a wish for death and destruction.

I nodded in response to her harsh breathing. "Wherever you are, Tess, don't hold back. Relive what happened, face your demons, inflict whatever you need to on me." I might've sounded strong, but inside I was back to being a fucking boy who buried his mother and shot his father. I felt so alone. Always alone.

Her eyes closed, and a cape of horror came over her. Her energy changed from weak and closed off to ferocious and angry, so, so angry. "You made me do so many things. And yet you think you can order me again?"

Oh, shit. She'd left me. Her mind had regressed—she'd done exactly what I told her.

She sneered, picking up a thick paddle, running it along the inside of my thigh.

I didn't mean to move. I meant to stay frozen and let her re-enact whatever she needed to, but the beast inside couldn't do it. I struggled, jerking my wrists, wincing as the rope dug deeper.

"You think you can get away? You can't. Not after what

you made me do. Not after everything." She picked up a whip in the other hand, brandishing both. "Would you prefer radiating pain or sharp pain?"

My eyes hardened, realizing I'd asked her the exact same thing when I placed her on the cross. I knew she didn't mean to sound creepy as fuck, but she looked like a little wind up doll asking me which murder weapon I preferred.

How much longer must I endure this agony?

As long as it takes for her to come back to me.

I snarled. "Anything. Fucking use anything if it means you'll use something."

She didn't flinch at my rage. Her head bowed as anger flushed her cheeks. "You always were an asshole. Telling me to hit and maim and kill. But you never let me choose the weapon before." Her eyes snapped to mine. She snarled, "Use the baton, little girl. Pull the trigger, bitch." She cocked her head as her arm flew high, holding the paddle. "Let's see how you fucking like it."

She struck.

The paddle slapped against my jean-clad thigh and I tensed, rippling with anxiety. The power behind the strike was nothing but a fucking bug bite, but the fact I willingly let her strike me made me die a little inside.

She reached out, patting where she hit me. Her smile was pure maliciousness. "Did I do it right? You were always telling me I didn't do it hard enough. Bite harder, little girl. Scratch deeper, bitch. Never satisfied."

I couldn't do this. *You can.* Staring at the dark red canopy above, I yelled, "No, you didn't do it fucking right." This was wrong. It wouldn't help her. She'd obviously lost herself too deep. I couldn't save this woman in front of me—not like this. "Tess, this was a mista—"

The sharp wallop on my thigh came from nowhere; my eyes popped wide. Tess breathed hard, pointing the paddle like a gun. "Is *that* how you like it?" She hit me again. Fire building in her gaze, nursing the hatred, the fear she'd lived with for so many weeks.

I stopped breathing. Was I seeing what I wanted to see, or was it the truth?

That spark. The flare. The ice blue smouldering to soulful grey.

"Yes," I murmured even though my answer was fucking hell no. I hated it. Hated being strung up. Every cell in my body hated it, but this was the woman I loved. This was the woman I wanted to spend the rest of my life with.

"Hit me again, *esclave.*" My hands curled into fists; I gasped as she delivered another stinging wallop. She hit me hard across my stomach and I tensed, clenching against the pain.

"Always orders with you. Do you know I wished to kill you so many times? Every second of every day I existed in a drugged stupor, I thought of ways to exterminate you."

My heart raced. Tess no longer saw me. She no longer knew where she was nor cared. Her mind had cracked, and I was both elated and petrified.

"You like it when I hurt for you? You like it when I take orders from you?" Her voice raised an octave. "You like it when I *kill* for you?"

What the fuck? She killed for them? They broke her by making her commit murder? Everything that happened in the last few weeks suddenly made sense. How she avoided all human contact. She stopped feeling. Stopped reacting.

She took a human life. That did something deep inside. It irreversibly changed a person forever.

Fuck, I would never get her back. I knew the darkness of taking a life. I could live with it—the darkness was part of who I was—but Tess... she was never meant to be such a monster.

Her arm swung, putting her entire body weight behind the strike. Her body twisted, her face scrunched as she belted me across the groin.

Holy, fucking fuck.

My cock hollered in agony; my balls disappeared into my

body. The pain ricocheted into my stomach, making me want to vomit.

"It hurts, doesn't it?" she whispered, her tone dark and sinister.

I couldn't say a fucking thing, only gasp like a dying fish. The pain. I'd never been hit so hard in such an off-limit area.

Her body language went from angry to radiating manic hatred. "You fucking made me hurt them. You made me burn them, break them." Her arm rose and she hit me across the chest. "You made me kill one of them! And I'm done. I'll kill you. I'll do what I should've done months ago."

I squeezed my eyes, no longer able to watch her come apart. To see the pain she'd bottled up inside spewing forth like a black disease.

"I hate you." She struck my knee.

"I hate you." She hit my side.

"I *hate* you!" She pummelled my chest.

My eyes flew open as she hit my cock again. I groaned with agony.

Each time she hit me, her voice rose and cracked until finally, the one thing I'd been waiting for, begging for, started to fall.

Tears.

They glossed her eyes, trembling on her bottom lashes. "You made me into one of you!" She threw away the paddle and grabbed a thick flogger. The strike landed across my face, cutting deep into my skin.

I grunted with the pain. I wanted nothing more than to dive at Tess. Pin her to the floor and turn the tables. I wanted to hit her. Inflict the same agony. I wanted to sense her submission. I wanted to be turned on and fuck her.

There was nothing sexy about this. My cock wanted no part in it. It wasn't right in my world, and every part of me screamed to end it, but she needed to kill her nightmares.

I had to give her my body because she already owned my heart.

I knew the dark place she lived in. I knew the horrors of being a killer, and I knew the moment she gave in fully, allowed herself to release all those ugly memories, she probably wouldn't stop until I was dead. But if it meant she could purge herself and move on from hell, I would do it.

I would sacrifice myself for her.

Taking a deep breath, I whispered, *"Je t'aime,* Tess." I love you. *"Nous sommes les uns des autres."* We are each other's.

Tess cocked her head, breathing hard against the tracks of tears falling endlessly from her eyes. It didn't register, and I was glad in a way. I spoke to her fractured soul, not the broken woman.

Sucking in my pride and honour and every last fucking shred of decency I had left, I growled, "You're a fucking disappointment. Did we not teach you anything? You killed—so what. You're useless. Pathetic."

Tess made a strangling noise.

"You're worthless. You can't even follow orders correctly."

Her mouth twisted. "I hate you for eternity. I hate your operation. I hate your stench. I hate your clothes. Your voice. Your lack of humanity." Her eyes glazed, turning deeper and deeper into her nightmare.

A sharp burn started in my throat at the knowledge I had truly fucking lost her.

Tess put aside the flogger and picked up the cat-o'-nine-tails. The same tool I used to break the memories of her rape.

There was no warning, no build-up—she struck.

The multiple threads whistled through the air and bit into my clothes. The tiny beads shredded my T-shirt.

The next hit landed on my thighs, burning me through the denim. Tess went feral; double fisting the whip, she struck and struck. A particularly violent hit landed across my throat—it sent shock waves echoing through my body. Tess was nothing but pure rage, gushing from a soul that had finally had enough.

Time ceased.

Tess hit and hit and hit.

She broke my skin and blood ran free, dripping and staining the towels below.

My clothes ripped with every strike until they hung in fucking tatters. The pain amplified, building and building until every part of me trembled. I wanted to scream and rage and curse. I needed an outlet. I needed to run. But I never made a sound as Tess whipped me closer and closer to death.

Through swollen eyes, I didn't recognise Tess anymore. Sweat matted her hair and tears shone on her cheeks.

My heart broke into a billion fragments for what I did to this wonderful woman. I wanted to wrap her up and never let anything happen to her again. I never wanted to lay another finger on her or cause her any pain. I just wanted her to be happy.

Her next strike caught my flayed chest, tearing deep into my skin.

I couldn't help it— I cried out. The first sign of weakness and Tess pounced on it. "You like that, you bastard."

She hit me again and again. "Die, you murderer. Just die."

The ache of tears shot up my spine, bruising my eyes.

I'd never cried.

Not once.

I always thought I was incapable. And yet, as I lay taking the brunt of everything Tess lived with, I felt myself coming apart. I'd never had the urge to give up my life to save another. I was never weak or selfless enough to put another first. But falling in love Tess took away my balls as well as my heart, and now I would pay for it.

A single tear escaped my control. The caustic pain of salt burned the cuts on my cheeks. Another tear rolled silently, motionlessly.

One tear for what I lost.

One tear for what I gained.

One tear for being helpless.

One tear for being in love.

Six tears until my body gave out, my blood ran cold, and Tess beat me into oblivion.

Cold water drenched my face.

I winced as my fiery eyes opened to a tearstained, furious Tess on top of me. An empty glass rested in her hand.

I looked down, noticing I was naked, dripping with blood, and crisscrossed with lacerations. She'd cut off my blood-soaked clothing, leaving them on the bed beside me.

"You used to wake me up like that every morning. Time to hurt another, you'd say. But now it's over. I'm done hurting you. I'm going to kill you."

She scooted off, moving to stand by the side of the bed. Her eyes no longer burned with hatred and the need to maim; now they held resolution and satisfaction.

My over-worked heart thudded with happiness. I might've been able to help her after all. My life for her life. *I'm glad.*

"This is for those women you made me ruin. For the life you made me take. I hate you and I hope you rot in hell." She raised her hands above her head, fingers wrapped around the handles of sharp silver scissors, holding them like a dagger over my heart.

"*Esclave*—" I tugged on the rope around my wrists, not ready to die. *I'm not ready to fucking die.*

My life raced before my eyes: how much I'd miss. How much I hadn't had time to do.

I couldn't do it. I wouldn't let her send me away. Not now. Not after everything.

I did the one thing I swore not to do.

I screamed.

Twenty-four

Own me, take me, you can never break me. Choose me, use me, you will never lose me.

I existed in blackness.

Nothing else entered apart from the metallic rust of blood and flashes of madness.

Q left me again.

Somehow, I transported back to the room where I shot Blonde Hummingbird, only this time, strapped down and tied up tight was White Man. He leered and cursed, telling me I wasn't good enough. That I ought to kill myself because that's all I was worth.

The vacancy inside swirled like a crazy hurricane, rattling at the walls of my tower, tearing away my chains, smashing bricks to dust.

The guilt I'd been running from sucked me deep and I was sure my heart would stop. I was a murderer, a torturer, I deserved to die paralyzing regret.

But fate had given me a chance to right the wrongs I'd done. I had the puppeteer in front of me. Hatred and fury slithered like reptiles in my blood, and all I wanted was revenge.

To make him pay.

The wash of emotions I'd been hiding from crippled me. Dumping me into a pit of grief and insanity.

White Man represented all the evil in the world and I wanted to take and take and take until there was no more. I wanted to extract every last thread of life until he existed no longer.

By killing him, I would gain redemption. I might finally be able to live with the guilt.

He didn't move as I hit him. He just sneered. My muscles ached from delivering abuse. With every strike another brick crashed free from my tower. With every lash, cracked and fissured my guilt, allowing me to breathe.

Parallel images of the past kept me company as I hit him over and over and over. I saw myself—emaciated, drugged out of my mind, scratching and breaking...delivering their wrath on innocent women.

I sobbed and hit harder as my apparition shot Blonde Hummingbird. I doubled over with agony as I watched a replay of myself swallowing the gun, pulling the trigger to end my life.

Never again. *I'm strong enough to survive. I don't need a tower to exist. I didn't do anything wrong!*

The thought was a comet, blazing with truth.

I didn't do anything wrong.

It was all them. I did the best I could to survive.

The knowledge that they'd made me doubt, that they'd filled me so full of sin, gave me a new lease of energy. I struck harder and harder until I couldn't recognise White Man from all the cuts and blood.

Every time I drew blood, I rested easier, knowing this man would never do to others what he did to me.

When he passed out, I thought I'd killed him. I wanted him dead, but I had to be sure. Checking for life, I cursed when his pulse thrummed beneath my fingertips. I knew what I had to do.

I would wake him, look straight into his eyes, then I would

stab him in the heart.

This was my duty, my honour, my destiny.

I taught him the lessons he taught me. Pain equalled power. Pain equalled pleasure.

As I stood above him with sharp scissors in my hands, ready to bury them deep into his chest, he looked up with such panic and love I paused too long.

He screamed.

It bounced around the cavern of blackness, tearing down the veil between me and the real world.

The vision disintegrated, catapulting me from dark to bright. The dungeon switched to become a decadent room with gold and red accents—it seemed familiar, but I couldn't place why.

I blinked, unable to understand. *Where the hell am I?*

My body ached, shoulders trembled with holding my arms ready to strike. My hands were cramped and slippery with blood.

Then my heart stopped.

Q lay on the bed in front of me, his naked body covered in blood, completely unrecognisable. He barely breathed, his face swollen, eyes muted, hidden by injury.

I dropped the scissors; they clattered downward, nicking the top of my bare foot before bouncing to the carpet. Air lodged deep in my lungs and I couldn't breathe.

An earthquake began in my limbs, and the angry, righteous tears I'd shed were replaced with horror. "Q—Oh, my God." I reached out with shuddering hands to touch his cooling chest. His beautiful sparrow tattoo hung in tatters with wounds and blood. His beautiful cock hung useless and bloody between his legs.

"What have I done!"

Then I was flying.

My front collided with the front of the bed before I was jerked back and pressed deep into the carpet. Someone wrenched my arms behind my back, pinning my cheek to the floor. "Don't move," a livid man's voice ordered.

The man sat on my back, holding me in place. He changed position to look toward the bed. He sucked in a rattling breath. "Fuck, Q. What the fuck."

A woman's high-pitched scream made my shaking worse. I gave up crying and turned to sobbing. I did this. I hurt Q so much he looked ready to die. How did this happen? Why did he let me go so far?

"*Merde*. Q. Oh, my god. Oh, my god," Suzette cried.

The man got off me, discarding me as if I was nothing. He jumped to his feet, rushing to the bedside.

I fumbled to sit up. I needed to know Q was still alive. That there was a way to fix this.

Franco's emerald eyes flashed back to me, glittering with ferocity. "*You* did this?" He shook his head, fingers scrambling at the bindings around Q's bleeding ankles. "How could you?"

My lungs lodged in my throat; I couldn't speak. I couldn't justify what I'd done or even remember how it happened. All I knew was I no longer existed in a lifeless void. I now lived in an eternity of self-regret and pain. I'd been given closure and revenge on White Man and what happened in Rio, but I would take that agony all over again if it meant Q wasn't lying lifeless and ruined by my hand.

"Q! Please, Q." I scrambled to my feet, wringing my hands as Franco undid Q's wrists and gently brought his hands to rest by his sides. Q winced and groaned as Suzette rushed forward with one of the discarded sheets, placing it over him.

Suzette never took her eyes off me, raining with sorrow and disbelief. "Why, Tess. Why? After everything he's done for you."

I rushed forward. I had to hold him. Tell him how sorry I was. But Franco shoved me back. "I think you've done more than enough, don't you?"

"But… I have to f—fix this. I didn't mean to. You have t—to believe me!" My body shook with wracking sobs—I'd never cried so hard. Not when I was raped or kidnapped or made to do such horrendous things. I cried as if my soul would explode from my body at any moment and leave me dead on the carpet.

Turned out I wouldn't die from guilt, but from a broken heart.

Q groaned softly, licking his broken lips. "Le—let her be."

Suzette cried harder while Franco spun to face him, ducking lower to hear. "I'll call the doctor. We'll get you help." He ordered Suzette, "Go and get Dr. Peterson in here. Now."

Suzette blanched white with shock, but she did as she was told, flying out of the room.

My heart stabbed with self-loathing and my legs wobbled as I darted past Franco to reach the bed. My eyes locked with Q's and I wailed.

The last barrier unlocked inside, letting forth all the wrongness left inside me. I awoke from the final haze of vacancy, my tower tumbled to the ground in a clatter of rubble, and my mind swarmed with everything that I'd done.

"Q!" I threw myself on the bed, wincing at his cool skin, his sticky blood. Franco wrenched me off. "Get away." Looping his arms around my chest, he hauled me backward, heading toward the exit.

"No! I need to stay. I need to fix this." But his grip never yielded. I scrambled at the doorframe.

"Wait," a thready voice demanded.

Franco froze; I trembled in his locked embrace. "Q. I'm so sorry. I don't know. I don't—"

Q sucked in a breath, hoisting himself up to rest on his elbows. Tracks of tears smudged the blood on his face. He smiled so sweetly, so full of unconditional love, I broke further in Franco's arms.

"Bring her here," Q ordered.

After a pause, Franco scooped me up and took me to Q. He placed me on the bed. I could barely see through my tears. I couldn't breathe properly from crying so hard, but Q gingerly put his arm around me, holding me weakly against his beaten body. "I forgive you. I did it for you. Don't cry."

The unequivocal acceptance set a denotation in my stomach. It mushroom-clouded until it filled my chest, my throat, until it erupted in my brain. The sobs battered me harder, granting a perfect release.

Q pressed his lips against my forehead, murmuring, *"Je t'aime, Tess. Je t'aime."* I love you.

Pain squeezed; I sucked in air, but I was suffocated by the overpowering need to purge.

I cried like I'd never cried before.

Burrowing deep into Q's side, I let go of everything.

I drenched the bed and let my soul free.

I sobbed myself into nightmares.

"You're hereby sentenced to life in prison. You almost beat a man to death. Your lover. The one you're supposed to protect and adore above all else. What do you have to say for your crimes?"

The magistrate with his big overzealous white wig glared down at me. I stood on a tiny podium with rolling waves of magma and lava licking at my ankles. It burned, and I knew I would suffer flames and incarnation for eternity.

"I have nothing to say. I did what you said. I deserve to be punished forever."

The magistrate nodded, looking down his nose. "And forever you shall suffer. You will never love, never be happy. Your smiles will always be laced with sadness, your heart always layered with grief."

I bowed my head, wanting to hurl myself into the lava. To end my misery, end my shitty life where I hurt so many. "Yes. Punish me. Make me suffer."

"A thousand years in hell. Where you will rot in fire." The gravel came down.

A black shadow swirled in like a nasty typhoon, snuffing out the waves of fire and stealing the heat of hell. "I'm the one she gave her life to. She's mine, and I say she doesn't deserve to be punished."

I daren't lift my eyes to such a kind reprieve. Instead, I hunched into a ball, pressing my forehead to my knees.

"Tu es à moi." You are mine. A firm hand landed on my shoulder. "Your life is mine, and I say I'm not ready to give you up."

I raised my eyes to meet my saviour and cried hot ugly tears. Even though I almost killed him, Q stood before me in an immaculate black suit with a soft smile on his sculpted lips. No open wounds or oozing blood. He was utterly perfect.

He crouched beside me and cupped my cheek. "It's over, Tess. It's in the past. Our future is where we live now." He kissed my lips, whispering, "Wake up, esclave. Wake up. Don't leave me. Not after everything we've been through.

"Wake up.

"Wake—"

My eyes cracked open, gritty and sore. A brief sense of confusion crushed me before I connected with a pale jade gaze.

The moment I looked into Q's wonderful dark and bright soul, I broke again. My mouth twisted in horror for what I'd done; my eyes were useless waterfalls.

I couldn't do anything but cry and shake and repair my fractured soul.

We were in bed in the carousel room. I remembered now: the doctor working on Q. Stitching the lashes too deep to heal naturally, bandaging the ones that didn't. Was it only yesterday that all of this happened?

"I'll never be able to fo—forgive myself," I stuttered between my waterworks.

Q shook his head softly; his face glistened with an array of unhealed scars and scabbed-over cuts. I did that to him. I marred his dark beauty and painted him with violence. I branded him in my rage, in my sadness, and every time I looked at him I would remember.

I would never forget hurting the man I loved more than I

loved myself.

I shut my eyes, unable to bear the agony any longer.

But Q's gentle fingertips brushed against my eyelids, coaxing them open. "Don't look away. I want you to accept me. Love me as I am."

I didn't deserve this man. I shook uncontrollably.

"Tess. Obey me." His voice hardened and I looked up, entranced by his angry eyes. "Don't you dare undo my hard work. You feel again, and you're going to get through it."

He was right. Gone was the empty void I'd existed in. I lived in a dagger-filled eternity now. The guilt lived in my lungs, tainting my every breath.

Gritting my teeth, I traced a shallow lash on his cheekbone, my touch shaky and soft. "How can you forgive me for what I did?"

He captured my hand, pressing it harder against his cheek. "How can you forgive me for what I did?" He bowed his head, kissing my neck. "I failed you. Those men should never have been able to take you from me. I failed you by not coming sooner. I failed you by keeping you. I failed you every damn time I tied you up and degraded you. I'm the one who should ask for forgiveness."

We stared at each other until my eyes burned and I swallowed gushes of salt water to stop from crying.

"I hurt birds that you save, Q. I tortured them. I broke their bones and killed a girl with a hummingbird tattoo on her hip." The confession eased some of the guilt and I kept going—spewing my crimes. "They drugged me so every day I thought you'd abandoned me. They turned me into their employee and I tried to get free. I disobeyed but it only made the punishment for the other girls worse. I don't know if I'll ever feel myself again, but you taught me I'm strong enough to live with what I've done."

I snuggled closer, wanting to crawl inside him. "I love you, Q. With everything that I am."

He sighed heavily, pressing his soft lips against mine. "I

know, Tess. I know."

From: Tess Snow
Time: 7:35p.m.
To: Brax Cliffingstone

Hi,
This is hard to write as it shows me how weak I was to contact you and make you worry. Everything has worked itself out. Q rescued me, Brax. He did something I never thought he would do. He showed me just how much he loves me.
Thank you for being there for me when I was lost.
I'll always be around if you need me, but for now, I'm going to heal with the man who brought me back to life.
All the best,
Tess.

From: Brax Cliffingstone
Time: 9:35p.m.
To: Tess Snow

Tessie,
I'm so glad to hear you're in a better place. And it gives me peace of mind to know you're with a man who adores you. As he should.
Heal and be happy. :-)
Catch you around,
Brax

Three weeks passed while I found my way back to wholeness.

Q put Frederick permanently in charge of *Moineau*

Holdings and stayed home with me. A few terse conversations with the local police and they never bothered him again about my kidnapping, or what Q did to find me.

He never talked about work or what happened behind the scenes of *Moineau* Holdings, and I wasn't ready to bring it up. I didn't want to know if I was the cause of his reputation being slandered.

We never left each other sides. Our closeness cured each other.

We fixed our maladies, became each other's healing balms. We grew to know each other in those days of soft reprieve. Chatting softly, asking questions about simpler things like our favourite ice-cream and seasons.

Suzette and Franco forgave me for everything I'd done to Q. Franco pretended to run in fear anytime I came close—until Q told him to piss off.

Suzette offered her ear anytime I needed to talk, and I might share my tale one day, but not now.

The guilt was still too sharp—the nightmares far too real. But just knowing she understood made me love her like a sister.

Q and I played cards and listened to music. We read in love-filled silence and touched each other with lingering caresses. Everything between us was sweet and healing— knitting more than just our bodies, but our minds too. We became intrinsically linked like never before.

However, Q withdrew into himself for the first two weeks. He brooded, never admitting to what ailed him. I'd catch him watching me with a turbulent look in his eyes, only for it to disappear whenever he saw me staring.

He treated me like spun glass even though something dangerous lurked within him. I knew he suffered with what I'd done. It lived in every action, every memory flitting across his face. I'd taken something fundamental from his grasp and feared he'd never be the same.

My heart healed in one moment and broke in another with the knowledge I might be the cause of his ruin.

Every day we were never far from each other's side, but we never moved past a gentle kiss or stolen touch.

We never attempted to have sex.

I think we were both too fragile, still repairing ourselves with sticky tape. After allowing myself to feel again, I'd never taken anything for granted. Even the lingering ache in my plier-snapped finger meant something—it proved I was strong enough to survive. And Q knew just how to bring me back.

Q healed fast physically. If anything, he became sexier, more alive and real to me. Once the stitches were removed from the deeper lashes on his chest, his tattoo looked darker, full of pain and misfortune, but also freedom. The puckers of scars only added to the detail.

The gunshot scar in his bicep had a horrible way of linking me back to what happened. Q earned that hunting for me, killing for me. I'd never look at it without reliving the past. Without remembering how my mind was turned against me. How I lived with history that I couldn't even recall thanks to the haze of drugs.

But it was his face that made my heart squeeze every time I looked at him.

His perfect, unmarked skin now glistened with tiny scars. Day by day, they muted from pink to silver and only added to his perfection. A constant reminder of what I did and what he gave in return.

Q looked up, smirking. "I can feel you undressing me with your eyes, *esclave*."

My tummy somersaulted and I laughed softly. "I must admit, my thoughts are heading to dirty."

Q's nostrils flared and the gentle companionship between us turned to lust-laden. For the first time in three weeks, chemistry sprang to a fever.

Leaning forward in the deck chair where we'd taken refuge on the patio outside the lounge, Q murmured, "I miss you."

The late afternoon sun was warm, but the chill in the air meant we had tartan blankets over our legs. I could imagine my life, fifty years from now, with Q as a distinguished old man and me by his side. Never again would I think about leaving. No matter how bad things got, I would never switch off or forget Q was my reason for living.

My eyes darted behind him to look into the lounge. Nobody was there. All the women from Rio, including Sephena, had been returned home to their loved ones, and for the first time in months we were truly alone. Even Mrs. Sucre, Franco, and Suzette had gone to the village, leaving us to our own devices.

The house was empty, but I knew it wouldn't stay that way for long. Q would find more survivors; he would bring them home and heal them. Just like he'd healed me against all odds.

My heart squeezed and I thanked every entity that he'd brought me back. I never wanted to live with such emptiness again.

Q's face darkened and he looked away. "I have something for you, but I'm not sure how you're going to take it." He sat straighter, dog-earing the page of the property file he was reading. "I wanted to wait a bit longer, but I don't think I can."

Curiosity and the delicious sensation of arousal made me hyper-alert. Placing my sketchpad on my knees, I scowled briefly at the jumble of buildings and how squibbly my lines were. My finger had healed, but it lost the function to bend fully and it kept getting in the way.

Q stole the sketchpad, throwing it onto the patio, along with his property reports. He stood, holding out his hand, a dominating air surrounding him.

"What is it?" I smiled. "What's so urgent?"

He shook his head, plucking the blanket off my legs, adding it to the one on the floor. "I want to show you before I lose my nerve."

Placing my hand in his, he hauled me up in one yank. I coughed and his eyes narrowed. Even after weeks of healing, my lungs still acted as if I'd been a smoker all my life. But Q didn't rush me. He took such exquisite care of me. Not once did he ask anything that I wasn't ready to give.

The one and only time I'd tried to kiss him, hoping for more, he'd pushed me away saying he needed time. Needed time to see me as the strong woman I was and not the invalid I'd been. He said he loved me, but the twisted part of himself needed me healed and capable of withstanding what he required, before he let me back into his bed.

I understood. I accepted it as part of him and didn't push, but I never stopped wanting him.

But now, with his strong fingers wrapped around mine, I hoped we'd finally be able to put the past behind us and make new memories.

Q didn't say a word as he guided me through the lounge and up the midnight blue carpeted stairs. When we got to the top, he jerked me close. I gasped as his lips pressed hard against mine. His hands dropped to my hips, pinning me in place. "I want to do something to you, *esclave*." His dark voice wrapped around me, making me eager, wet.

I kissed him back, opening, encouraging him to kiss harder. He broke the connection, dragging me down the corridor.

My heart squeezed painfully as we passed the room where I'd almost killed Q. As far as I knew the room no longer existed. A demolition crew had been in and Q had banned me from ever stepping foot in there again.

We didn't stop until we headed into the west wing, passing multiple doors.

My stomach tripped in anticipation as Q finally slowed and placed his hand on a knob.

He breathed hard, as if he'd planned this for a while but only now had the courage to go through with it. For Q to be afraid meant he wanted to do something drastic.

I tensed, waiting for the over-whelming fear of pain. The lesson White Man taught me to avoid it at all costs still had a hold on me. I lived with ghosts of what I'd done, unable to avoid the occasional spasm of regret and horror.

"I won't force you. You can say no," Q said, opening the door and pushing me through.

My mouth plopped open as he guided me inside and locked the door.

"You did this?" I whispered.

All around us was a massive, intricate birdcage. The walls were painted with silver bars, a giant silver bell dropped from the ceiling as a chandelier. Mirrors hung while oversize spray-painted branches loomed overhead. There were even real metal bars pressed deep into the carpet.

We were effectively trapped, imprisoned just like his beloved birds.

He cleared his throat, burning a hole into me with the intensity of his gaze. "I wanted a room that symbolized us. The cage is a promise." His body tensed, drawing need from me to him, building rapidly until my heart flurried. "You said you'd let me do this once. I'm hoping you won't refuse."

He captured my cheeks with harsh fingers, reminding me he might've been gentle and kind the last few weeks, but he wasn't truly that man. He'd kept the anger, the darkness away from me, carefully guarding whatever thoughts he entertained. "I told you I couldn't let you into my bed again until I was able to see past what happened. You know I need someone strong, unbroken, courageous."

I nodded, my pulse thudding thickly in my veins.

"I see the old Tess. For the first time in weeks, when you looked at me, I saw her. And I want her. So fucking much." He crashed his mouth against mine, sending my need for him spiralling out of control.

He broke the kiss, growling. "I need to be inside you, but I need to do something else first."

I breathed shallowly, trying to figure out what he wanted. "I'll give you whatever you ask."

His mouth twisted as his pale eyes glowed with darkness. "Is that the truth, *esclave*? Would you give up your life for me? Would you let me whip you? String you up and bring you completely into my world?"

I couldn't stop a conflict of emotions filling me. The old Tess, the one who got off on pain wanted everything Q offered. But this gentler Tess—the one who'd killed and hurt—wanted nothing to do with blood or screams for the rest of her life.

But it didn't matter. I knew my answer. "Yes. I would."

Q kissed me fiercely, darting his tongue into my mouth, making me drink his need and passion. Whatever he was about to ask meant a lot to him. I could taste it.

"You're mine, Tess, but you've never been a true submissive. Somehow, you give me everything you can, all the while keeping everything out of reach. You drive me fucking insane, and that's why I need to do this."

"You don't need my permission." My voice dropped to a husky whisper; my core clenched at the thought of him tying me up and fucking me. I needed to connect. I needed him inside me. "You already have it."

He opened his arms and I curled into his embrace. For a man who'd never hugged before, he held me often. He didn't hold me with just love, though. He held me with possession, aggression, obsession.

Q pulled away, his jaw tight. "This will hurt. But you've given me your word."

Fear replaced the love in my heart as Q gave me one last look before heading to the fireplace. With a click, the gas caught, and eager flames sprouted into being. Resting on the mantle were two long pokers.

Q picked one up, returning to me with it in his outstretched hands. "Take it."

I cursed my trembling, but took the pole, turning it to see the emblem at the bottom. The instant I saw it, I remembered what I'd promised. That Q could scar my skin to put his mind at rest. That he could mark me so he'd always know I was his.

I ran my fingers over the sigil. "Oh."

Q froze, bristling with black energy, restraining himself

from desires I didn't comprehend. After what happened in the gold and red room, he wore his edginess, his temper, like a cloak. I didn't know how badly I'd damaged him, but even while he was being gentle and considerate, he lurked in the shadows, living in a place I didn't know if I could find.

The emblem was a capital Q with a sparrow swooping toward the ground as the tail of the letter.

My eyes flashed to his, drowning in his gaze.

His shoulders bunched as he brushed away hair from my neck, running his thumb along the scar left from the tracker.

"I want to brand you. I need to have something of mine permanently on your skin." He bent his head to press a kiss on the scar. "I need to know you're mine."

"I am yours. You know that."

He shook his head, echoing unhappiness in his eyes. "You were going to leave me. I had to give you my life to make you stay. I need to see you're mine every time I look at you. Every time someone else looks at you, I need them to know you're taken. Call it barbaric and horrific and tell me I'm a selfish fuck-up, but, Tess, I *need* this. I can't come back to you otherwise."

I didn't wait another second. If he needed this simple thing, so be it. I wanted it, too.

Pushing the poker into his hands, I said, "Do it. It would be the highest honour to wear your mark."

His jaw worked as if he held back a huge weight of emotion. His pale eyes glittered. *"Je te remercie du fond de mon cœur."* Thank you from the bottom of my heart.

Together we walked to the fireplace. My pulse pumped faster as he placed the brand in the flames.

His fingers squeezed mine as he reached for another poker and passed it to me. I took it as tears sprang to my eyes.

This one had a capital T with a birdcage hanging from it. A pure symbol that I'd captured him completely.

I stared deep into his eyes. "Are you sure?"

He shook his head gently, stealing the pole, placing it in

the flames beside the other one. "You shouldn't have to ask me that, *esclave*."

My throat closed, and we didn't say a word as the metal went from matte black to glowing red.

Q let me go to disappear into the bathroom. He came back with salve and medical patches for afterward.

My skin flushed thinking how painful it would be, but I stopped the thought. After everything I'd endured, a burn wouldn't scare me.

Once everything was laid out, Q turned to me, pointing at the floor. "Kneel."

I did as he asked, kneeling before the man who owned my heart and soul. The master of me completely. With concentration etching his eyes and his lips pursed tight, Q lifted the hot poker, and with no hesitation, pressed it hard and fast against my neck.

The searing, scorching heat made my eyesight black out for a second, and the sickening sound of my skin hissing almost made me retch. But then it was over, and Q tossed the poker back into the fire.

Immediately, he grabbed the medical supplies and applied antiseptic cream then the bandage.

I daren't look in his eyes as he tended to me. I could taste his eagerness, his sublime joy at what he'd just done.

I wanted to see. I wanted to look in a mirror and inspect what marked me permanently as his, but Q stood and gathered the other poker. Kneeling in front of me, he offered the handle. I stood slowly upright.

Biting my lip, I shuddered with the thought of causing him yet more pain. *Can I really do this?* My own neck thundered with agony, cauterized and stinging.

With strong, sure fingers, Q unbuttoned his white shirt. Once spread wide, giving glimpses of sparrows and barbwire, he traced his fingers over his heart.

"This belongs to you, Tess. Brand me there so you'll also know."

My stomach rolled at the thought of burning him, but I tensed my muscles and angled the glowing symbol above his heart.

Q pushed his chest out, curling his fists on his thighs. "Fast and hard, *esclave.*"

I nodded and lunged. The symbol melted through his skin in a second. The smell of acrid hair singeing filled the room. A second later I withdrew, relinquishing the terrible brand back into the fire.

Q grunted as he stood and his shirt swung forward, sticking to the raw skin. I twirled around to collect the salve and bandages, before tending to Q. Pushing his shirt gently off his shoulders, I winced.

He never took his eyes off me as I massaged the cooling balm onto his wound. The design was flawless, every bar of the cage etched deep into his flesh; the T a perfect feminine cursive.

Tears fell unbidden as I covered up the mark, sticking the bandage into place.

He'd given me himself. Forever.

Q pulled me into his arms. "Already I can feel the darkness coming back to life. Knowing you're mine. That you willingly gave me your pain once again." He buried his nose in my hair, inhaling deep. "I thought I'd lost that urge. Lost that part of myself."

I didn't need to ask what part Q had lost. I always knew he lived with demons in his soul.

Q shifted, walking me backward to the bed. The mattress no longer rested on the floor—it had been designed as a miniature cage. Hanging from the ceiling with bars and chains. Swags of material cocooned the space like a perfect trap—a trap to keep us safe together.

"I want you," Q murmured, his fingers already working my blouse buttons. Everything jolted to life. I leaned into him, rubbing my nipples against his knuckles.

He sucked in a breath, pushing aside the material to cup

my bra-covered breast.

My hands went to his bare chest, inching down to his belt. He waited while I undid the buckle, pulling the leather free. His chest rose and fell as I held the leather in my hands.

His tension, awareness all sprang to high alert, and I saw the man I'd thought I'd killed when I whipped him to an inch of his life.

Q, my master, wanted to use his belt. And I wanted him to.

With a wistful plea in my eyes and love exploding in my heart, I presented the belt with outstretched hands.

Twenty-five
Quincy

I long to see your creamy skin blush, welted and marked gives me a rush, I can't contain him, you set me free...

I didn't know how long I stared at Tess.

She stood there, holding my belt, giving it to me with such trust in her eyes that the last of the horrible confusion I'd been living with unravelled.

The old me. The me I knew and thought I'd lost forever, roared back into being. After weeks of living with such crippling disorientation, I thought I'd forever be doomed to live monsterless and alone.

The dark urges inside had gone, taking with it everything I knew. It was as if the beast had left me to wallow in pitiful loneliness.

I snatched the belt from her. Shuddering, I ran the leather through my fingers. The blackness swirled into being, bringing with it growls and bestial callings. I should've been glad they'd left me alone. But I found I missed it. I missed knowing who I was. I wasn't meant to be normal. I wasn't meant to be...human.

Tess shifted, her breasts rising. I swallowed hard against thick desire.

For three weeks, I'd avoided all thoughts of sex. I couldn't stand the thought of being close to Tess when I no longer knew myself. I lost something fundamental when Tess stole my dignity, my control, my dominance.

Tess damaged me, and I spent three weeks trying to fix myself.

But not dealing with the monster's urges allowed me to grow closer to Tess than I'd ever thought possible. I was able to comfort her without needing to squeeze too hard, or let her laugh without having to throw her to the ground and fuck her.

With the absence of those needs, I grew to see myself in a different light. I saw that I could be sweet—amazing to contemplate—and I could do it without cutting off my balls.

I gave Tess space to heal, and she changed from delicate patient to strong survivor. Day by day her passion and spirit came back, and each moment that she grew stronger, my beast inched out of its cave, returning to me, slightly fearful, slightly unwilling.

My eyes fell to the bandage hiding the brand I gave her, and my gut twisted in pleasure. I'd finally figured out how to keep both the man and the monster happy, and it seemed to be working. Just knowing Tess had a clear signal that she belonged to me helped soothe the urges to cut and make her bleed. It took away the overwhelming need, letting me breathe easier, letting me be tamed.

From here on out, I would make the sole purpose of my life to acquire new memories, happy memories, bury the past, and hoard every happiness Tess and I could find.

Tess panted harder as I looped the belt in my hands, snapping the leather. I glanced at her, my cock thickening fast in my jeans. "Are you sure?"

Once upon a time, I wouldn't have given her the choice. I wouldn't have cared what her answer would've been; I would've done it anyway. But now, her permission meant more to me than taking. Her submission fed the beast more than her fight.

We broke each other, and the only way to stay whole was to entwine ourselves, gluing the jagged parts, stitching our souls into one.

She nodded.

That was all I needed. Grabbing the back of her neck, I jerked her close and kissed her. I kissed her with every fucking thing I felt. The thankfulness for letting me mark her, and the relief at finally feeling like myself again.

She clawed at my chest, bringing me closer. I pressed harder, letting her feel how much I needed her.

Moaning, she hitched her leg up, hooking it precariously on my hip. I grabbed her knee, hoisting her higher, encouraging her to wrap both legs around my hips.

The moment she held me hostage between her legs, she rode me, pressing her delicious, tempting heat against my cock.

I stopped kissing her to drop my head and bite her neck— the side I hadn't branded.

"Q. Please. I need you."

I had plans for this to be slow and intense, but the urge to connect grabbed me by surprise. *I need to be inside her. Now.*

Unlatching her legs, I tossed her on the bed and yanked on her trouser button. It popped open, and she wiggled frantically as I tugged them down her legs. Tess shrugged out of her shirt, tossing it off the bed.

I gawked at her.

She wore simple virgin white underwear. Her body was undernourished compared to her curves from before, but her survivability knocked me to my fucking knees.

Climbing onto the bed, the chains holding the mattress swung, sending us rocking and swaying. Tess looked up to the canopy, and I took her moment of distraction to bend down and latch my mouth over her pussy.

Her hips bucked the moment my hot breath connected on her flesh. Crying out, she dove fingers through my hair, imprisoning me, pressing hard, demanding.

Her command did two things to me. Before, being told what to do would've just pissed me off. Now, I wanted to obey her—to please her and do whatever she fucking asked. The beast still growled and grumbled, needing to make her apologise for bossing me around, but I was able to ignore it. For the first time in my life, I had balance.

Sitting up, I ripped her knickers off and settled below again. Her taste filled my very fucking soul as I licked her long and slow.

"Q. Goddammit, more. More!"

I chuckled as Tess cursed and moaned. Relishing in bringing her pleasure, fucking her with my tongue, dragging out every inch of wetness and need.

My cock ached with come. I hadn't touched myself since the last time I'd been in Tess. I hadn't had the urge.

But now I did. Fuck, how I did.

With one last sweeping lick, I sat up, ridding myself of my jeans and boxer-briefs in one swipe. I wanted to tie Tess up and use all sorts of toys on her. I wanted to make her come over and over again, but the urgency gripped my balls and all I could think about was diving deep inside her.

"Get up," I ordered, sitting on my knees, the belt still in my hand.

Tess instantly obeyed and I growled with pleasure. The moment she was upright, I pointed at my cock. "Sit on it."

Her lips parted and she hesitated. My hand twitched with the belt; I let the beast take control just for a second. I struck her thigh with the leather, falling in love with her all over again when she flinched then shivered with pleasure.

"Sit on me now, Tess. Or I'll hit you until you do."

She bowed her head, sending curls over her face. "I want to taste you. Like you did for me."

The thought of her lips around my cock was too much. I still hadn't forgiven her for making me come so violently before. Shaking my head, I hauled her upright, straddling her over my thighs.

"Not today."

Her eyes snapped closed as I pushed her down. Her wet folds connected with my hot cock, sinking deeper, hugging me with all that delicious fucking darkness.

I groaned as she slid lower. My cock swelled with the urge to jet into her already.

The moment she'd fully impaled herself, I flicked my wrist and struck her lower back with the belt.

She gasped as her inner muscles gripped me deep inside.

"Shit, do that again," I growled, smacking her with the leather.

The same reaction—the instant the belt connected with her skin, she clenched hard around me, milking me with strong muscles.

I thrust up once and Tess fucking detonated. Her hands wrapped deep in my hair as she pushed up and down, fucking me as she rippled, shuddered, unravelled.

Her pleasure almost made me lose it. I gritted my teeth, fighting off the urge.

The moment she stopped coming, I ripped the bandage off her neck. She winced but I muttered, "Just let me see while I make love to you. Let me know you're mine."

She nodded, twitching in aftershocks around my cock.

"I'm going to take you hard. I've missed you so fucking much." I looked deep into her eyes. "You should've waited for me to come. Now I'll have to make you release all over again."

Her lips parted; she trembled as I thrust upward.

"Goddammit, you feel good." My eyes latched onto her neck and I purred. I fucking purred in pleasure, seeing my mark seared into her skin.

Tess's fingers fumbled with the bandage over my heart and I loved the flash of possession in her eyes when she looked at the brand.

"You're mine," she whispered. Her cunt clenched harder around me and I struggled for breath.

"Les uns des autres." Each other's. Holding her hip in one hand, I struck her with the belt as I thrust upward. Not too hard, but not too soft either.

"Pain and pleasure, Tess. Remember."

Her eyes fluttered shut as I invoked a rhythm: thrust, strike, thrust, strike. She moaned with every rock, grabbing my balls, building my orgasm until it radiated in every part of me.

My heart raced and I loved the tingling aching sensation of needing to orgasm. When I couldn't keep up the rhythm anymore, I threw the belt away, and gathered Tess closer. Her breasts squashed against my chest, irritating the fresh burn over my heart. The combination of pleasure and pain undid me.

My speed increased until Tess bounced in my arms. My eyes locked on her neck. The red, angry 'Q' forever seared into her skin gave me the release I'd been looking for.

This perfect woman was all fucking mine. And now everyone would know it.

My orgasm detonated, bursting in thick waves, filling her with every stroke. My eyes rolled backward as I existed only to come deep inside her. "Fuck, *esclave*. Take it. Take all of it."

Tess cried out as I stroked her clit. Her second orgasm exploded into reality, the bands of muscles squeezed every last drop I had left, milking me until I flopped in her arms.

My thighs quivered from thrusting up and I had pins and needles in my calves, but I didn't give a rat's ass as my cock was deep in the woman I adored and my come was smeared all over her.

Tess leaned forward, kissing me ever so sweetly. "I love you, Quincy."

My back tensed. Normally, I hated my full name. It was my father's. A name I wanted to forget forever, but in that moment, I loved it. I loved that Tess loved me. I loved that Tess accepted me.

I loved her with everything I was.

"Je t'aime," I whispered, kissing her back.

Hours later, I woke to Tess whimpering in my arms. Her nightmares hadn't diminished, and every night she woke me with her screams, stabbing a dagger into my heart. I wanted to enter her dreams and slay every last bastard torturing her.

Kissing her forehead, I murmured, *"Tu es en sécurité. Avec moi."* You're safe. With me.

When she quieted, I gathered her closer. Pushing my hand beneath her pillow, I tried to grab the item I'd hidden there a few days ago. When I'd designed the poker brands, I knew if Tess let me mark her with such a permanent thing, I would go one step further to seal her to me.

Ever since I made the decision, my headaches had been miraculously absent. Almost as if the stress I'd lived with melted away, letting me know I'd made the right choice. The only choice.

No longer would I wait to merge my life with hers. There was no way I would let her go, and it was time the rest of the world knew that.

Tess mumbled, eyes opening sleepily. "What are you doing?"

The soft twilight highlighted her grey-blue eyes, glimmering gold in her blonde hair. I wished I had a camera to capture her sleep-warmed and lazy beauty. She looked so fragile and I embraced two urges: one that wanted to see just how fragile she was with the use of a whip, and one who wanted to wrap her in bubble wrap and cover her with kisses.

My hand latched around the small thing hidden under the pillow and I sat up, pulling Tess with me.

The sheet fell away from her, exposing her perfect breasts and pink nipples. My cock instantly hardened. I had to look away before I pounced and forgot what I needed to do.

Tess yawned, fluffing her hair.

Nerves attacked my stomach, making me second-guess myself. *You're doing the right thing. Man the fuck up.*

"I have another gift for you."

Her eyes dropped to the tented sheet between my legs. Licking her lips, she murmured, "A second gift would be nice."

I chuckled, shaking my head. "No, you little sex fiend, my cock is not on offer."

She pouted, reaching over to grab me.

A slight thread of temper filled me and I slapped her hand away. Goddammit, she wasn't making this easy.

I rolled the gift in my fingers, keeping it away from her sight. "I need you to wear this as much as I needed to brand you. *Compris?*" Understand?

She frowned, but nodded slowly.

It's now or never.

I unclenched my fist, shoving my hand toward her. Resting in my palm was a ring I'd painstakingly sketched and ordered the local jeweller to create.

It represented everything I was. Everything that we were. Everything that I hoped we'd become.

The same day I went to pick up the finished product, I bought a pair of lovebirds. The lucky things had the entire aviary to themselves, but I planned to add more as I returned to work, doing what I did best.

Tess shied away from the ring as if it was about to bite her. My forehead furrowed as I plucked it in my fingertips and inspected the jewellers work. He'd got it perfect: two spanning wings, bending into a circlet. Every feather hand-carved with exquisite detailing, inlaid with diamonds. The gold band was extra thick, to allow for—

"That's for me?"

Her eyes glassed with tears, and I snatched her hand before she could go running from the room. Did she not want this? How could she not accept a ring when she let me burn my mark into her neck?

Anger sat low in my gut, churning with rejection.

Tess didn't say a word as I splayed her hand, pushing the ring onto her wedding finger—the one that symbolised commitment and togetherness.

She fulfilled my humanness. I could never let her go.

A single tear dripped from her lashes as she held her hand closer to inspect the jewellery.

It'd taken a nightmare of events to bring us together. Our relationship wasn't normal, our needs and lifestyle uniquely us, but after everything we'd been through, I wanted more. I never wanted to wake up without Tess by my side. I wanted her with me when I hunted down all the cocksuckers involved in trafficking and put them into the ground. And I wanted finally to have the courage to show her just what I needed to be completely happy.

With my heart bucking wild, I asked, "*Veux-tu m'épouser?*" Will you marry me?

Tess sucked in a gasp then launched herself into my arms. Her lips crashed against mine, sending us sprawling to the mattress.

I tasted salt from her happiness and passion from her tongue.

For the first time ever, I was complete, wondrously happy and achingly content.

"You don't have to ask. My answer is already given."

I smiled, cupping her jaw. "Now that I have it on your finger, I should tell you there's a tracking device in there. I never mean to have you far from me again."

She laughed. "Consider myself warned." She kissed me again, but I pushed her back, sliding to the side of the bed.

She watched as I hoisted on jeans and held out my hand for her to take. "Get packed. We're leaving."

"Leaving?"

When she didn't move, I grabbed her ankle and dragged her to the end of the bed, trapping her between my arms.

Darkness and light and every fucking emotion bubbled inside me; I couldn't wait another minute. "We're going to get married."

Tess's eyes popped wide. "Now?"

"Now. There's no point in waiting."

I hoisted her into my arms. "I want our life to begin, Tess."

Her lips landed on mine. "It has already begun."

I kissed her back, making her swallow my words. "Your life is mine. My life is yours. I want it to be official."

"It is official. You branded me." She smiled, touching my cheek.

"It's not official until I have you in a white dress, vowing to obey and serve me for the rest of your days." I was only half joking. "I need to promise my life to you. I need you to be my wife."

Tess nodded. "I want you as my husband, now and for always, 'till death do us part."

Epilogue

Note from Author

I've sat staring at this part for weeks, and I can't wrap up Q and Tess's story in just one chapter. After everything they've been through, it's only fair to give them a Happily Ever After. Q needs to finally let go and show Tess how dark he wants to take her. Tess needs to realize Q is her monster through and through, and they need to explore their relationship now they're committed. Not to mention have an amazing wedding and saucy honeymoon.

When I started *Tears of Tess*, it was meant to be one book. But Q and Tess captured my mind and heart and kept whispering in my ear.

So, I hope you can forgive me for writing a third and final book in the *Monsters in the Dark* series.

Twisted Together will be the Happily Ever After for all those twisted individuals who found their perfect other. The ones who can't breathe without consuming the other... the ones who live slightly in the shadows.

Set for release early 2014, updates will be announced via my newsletter.

Sneak Peek into Twisted Together...

"After battling through hell, I brought my esclave back from the brink of ruin. I sacrificed everything—my heart, my mind, my very desires to bring her back to life. And for a while, I thought it broke me, that I'd never be the same. But slowly the beast is growing bolder, and it's finally time to show Tess how beautiful the dark can be."

Q gave everything to bring Tess back. In return, he expects nothing less. Tess may have leashed and tamed him, but he's still a monster inside.

The third and final instalment in the *Monsters in the Dark* series.

Prologue

"**I**'m not marrying you for the pleasure of calling you my wife, *esclave*. I'm not marrying you because it's the evolution of a relationship. I'm marrying you so I have claim on you forever. Your soul will be mine for eternity. In sickness and in health, in life and death you will belong to me. And I will belong to you."

Q brought me closer, whispering his passion into my mouth. "Don't think this is a contract between two people in love. Don't think this legal document is something flimsy and unpowerful. By marrying me you're taking all of me. Everything I am. All that I will be. You're accepting my lightness, my darkness, my fucking eternal spirit. By signing your name to mine you are no longer Tess Snow."

"What am I?" I murmured, accepting his feather-soft kiss.

"You're Tess Mercer. Now and for always. Forever and ever. It's done."

Chapter One

Yesterday, Q proposed.

Today, we'd flown by private jet to a landing strip in the Canary Islands.

Now, we were being driven by high speed boat to an island Q supposedly owned.

Tomorrow, we were getting married.

My mind hadn't stopped spinning and I needed off this crazy whirlwind ride. I needed time to think. To plan. To have a moment to breathe. But Q was possessed. The moment his ring noosed my finger, and his mark burned my neck, he'd taken complete control.

It didn't take long for the boat to pull up to a tiny jetty. As far as the eye could see turquoise ocean surrounded us.

The island we docked beside was tiny. Wild, rugged, completely unmodernized. I didn't know what I'd been expecting, but the thick palm trees and foliage reminded me of a perfect home for a beast.

My eyes darted to Q. He jumped off the bow with the rope, ready to tie us to the jetty. His beige slacks and white shirt looked perfect for this bright, sunny weather.

When he bent to tie the knot, his loose shirt gaped open, showing me the red burn of the T above his heart.

My own heart swelled to suffocate in my chest. I suddenly didn't care that this was crazy. That no planning or time had gone into it.

I twirled the ring on my finger and knew this was perfect. In every way.

While Q discussed provisions being sent to the island with the captain, and made arrangements for who knows what, I opened the well-read letter Q gave me the night he proposed.

The sharp thrill of fear and passion once again threaded around my heart, heating my blood with expectation.

Esclave…*Tess*

Once you are truly mine and I'm satisfied you'll be with me forever, I'm going to show you what I've wanted to show you for a while. I'm going to bring you into my world. I'll share everything. Treat you to every desire.

This honeymoon is going to be for us. We're going to find each other in the dark.

Until our wedding night, mon amour.

Q

About the Author

Pepper Winters wears many roles. Some of them include writer, reader, sometimes wife. She loves dark, taboo stories that twist with your head. The more tortured the hero, the better, and she constantly thinks up ways to break and fix her characters. Oh, and sex…her books have a lot of sex.

She loves to travel and has an amazing, fabulous hubby who puts up with her love affair with her book boyfriends.

Her books include:

Tears of Tess *(28 August 2013)*
Quintessentially Q *(15 December 2013)*
Twisted Together *(Coming early 2014)*
Last Shadow *(Coming early-mid 2014)*
Broken Chance *(Coming early-mid 2014)*

She loves mail of any kind: **pepperwinters@gmail.com**

Acknowledgements

I always freeze up when it comes to acknowledgements. I'm afraid I'll forget a fabulous blogger, or dear friend. My brain becomes a sieve and I don't want to leave anyone out who has been so important to my journey and success as an author. So, this time, I'm not going to name names. I'm going to thank every single reader, blogger, cover designer, tour operator, beta reader, writing partner, and amazing friend who has helped me in this process.

I love each and every one of you and thank you from the bottom of my heart. I know it's cheesy but I honestly could never have done it without the amazing support network offered by you amazing people, and I'll always appreciate you, more than you know.

xxxxxxx Thank you xxxxxxx

Songs for Quintessentially Q

My personal favourites are Demons and Monster by Imagine Dragons.

Followed by reader suggestions:
Monster by Rihanna & Dr Dre
Move like a Sinner by What Now
Deep Inside by Third Eye Blind
Everlong by Foo Fighters
My Immortal by Evanescence
Do What You Want by Lady Gaga
Pictures of You by The Cure
Closer by Nine Inch Nails
Dark Horse by Katy Perry
Cold by Crossfade
Die for You by Megan McCauley
My Last Breath by Evanescence
Hurt by Nine Inch Nails
Forever by Fireflight
Moondust by Jaymes
Skyscraper by Demi Lavato

Poems

The poem verses used at the header of each chapter came courtesy of a fantastic author named Ker Dukey. She penned the poems after reading *Tears of Tess* and I asked to use them in this book. Here are the lyrics in their entirety.

Poem for Tess
by
Ker Dukey

I relish the snap, welcome the burn, don't stop yet it's still my turn.
Tighten your grip, make me bleed, it's a hunger I need to feed.
I want it, I need it, I'll beg you to feed it.

Tie me, tease me, let your pleasure please me. Hurt me, love me, but please don't ever leave me.
Save me, enslave me, you will never cave me.
Taunt me, flaunt me, kill what haunts me.

Strip me bare, pull my hair, I don't care just take me there.
I need that high, I need that pain, it's the only thing that keeps me sane.
Don't show mercy, don't cut me loose, I need you to tighten that noose.

Tie me, tease me, let your pleasure please me. Hurt me, love me, but please
don't ever leave me.
Save me, enslave me, you will never cave me.
Taunt me, flaunt me, kill what haunts me.

Leave your mark, scar my skin, I will bow down to you my king.
Tied to a rack or down on my knees, it's you my master I long to please.
Own me, take me, you can never break me.
Choose me, use me, you will never lose me.

Poem for Q
by
Ker Dukey

I ache to see your flesh bleed, scream for me, give me what I need
Let the rivers run, the monster inside has won
Naked and restrained, this darkness cannot be contained
You, my esclave *have been claimed*

You're my obsession, I'm your possession
You own the deepest part of me
You crawled into the darkness, set my monster free
So scream, bleed, call out to me
But never say stop, never flee

I long to see your creamy skin blush
Welted and marked gives me a rush
I can't contain him, you set me free
This isn't a role I play, the monster is me
You call me Maître but I am the esclave
Slave to inflict the pain I crave

You're my obsession, I'm your possession
You own the deepest part of me
You crawled into the darkness, set my monster free
So scream, bleed, call out to me

But never say stop, never flee

Whimper and moan while I sit on my throne
We can be monsters together so we're never alone
You're my esclave, *my soul mate*
Each other we own
You're mine forever, my bird flew home

To read more of Ker Dukey's work please find her on Goodreads, and her book *The Broken* on Amazon.

"My life wasn't perfect but at least it was mine. Now, I live in hell and owned by others. I fell for a guy who promised me the world and sold me for five kilos of cocaine. I want nothing more than to end this existence of abuse and slavery. I'm not weak. I'm not giving up. I'm just done."

Owned. Possessed. Used.

Lyric is a whore. After three years as a pawn in a high class game of bastards and sex, she's had enough. Every hope and dream she's ever had is inked on her skin—a reminder of why she should stay alive. But she's lost all hope and the moment she runs out of flesh to tattoo, Lyric will find freedom. Freedom by death. As her last breath fast approaches, she needs nothing and no one...***until him.***

Kage was born to be one thing: a killer. Trained from birth, he's an expert in blood and extermination—the last shadow his victims ever see. He's the best at his profession; a ruthless, unfeeling assassin. He needs nothing and no-one...***until her.***

A man who lives to kill and a woman who wants to die. A serendipitous match...or so they thought.

A New Adult Dark Contemporary Romance, not suitable for people sensitive to slavery, cruelty, and non-consensual sex. A story about a killer with no remorse, a woman living in nightmares, and a future that binds them in servitude.

Made in the USA
Monee, IL
29 April 2021